For my nieces...

"Love must be as much a light, as it is a flame."

—Henry David Thoreau

Prologue

AMBER FLAMES FLICKERED SWIFTLY ALONG THE FADED walls of the old broken-down barn and lit up the June evening like a macabre bonfire. The heat from it seeped through Gavin's gear, making him feel as though he was wearing nothing at all. Anger and determination shimmied up his back while he and the men in his squad worked to squelch the intense blaze.

It was burning too hot.

Gavin McGuire had experienced all types of fires during his years on the job, and the ones that moved with this kind of superheated intensity usually had some help.

He'd bet his life that this was no accident.

His face mask was meant to protect him and feed him life-giving oxygen, but it practically smothered him tonight. The sound of his own heavy breathing rushed in his ears, along with the crackling and creaking of the dry wooden planks. The haunting groans of the barn as it was devoured almost sounded like a cry for help. The death wails of a structure engulfed in flames were eerily similar to the cries of a human being. Those were the shrieks and screams that tormented his sleep.

The voices of the past rarely fell silent for long.

Dark memories—the ones that simmered beneath the surface and had driven him to this profession in the first place—threatened to bubble up and consume him. But Gavin stuffed them down. Fear was a self-defeating emotion and not one he could afford, especially while leading his team. These men depended on him to make the right call every time.

There was no room for error.

Sloppy mistakes, foolish choices, or unnecessary risk got people killed.

Dirt and gravel scuffed beneath his heavy boots and he grunted with effort, directing the thick hose and its powerful stream of water onto the flames. It was a beast. Fire was a mindless, insatiable, and relentless creature that consumed anything and everything in its path.

If Gavin didn't stop it, the monster would keep on coming.

"Chief." Rick's voice came through the headset loud and clear, pulling Gavin from his thoughts. "We've got it contained, but this old barn ain't gonna make it. She's gonna come down."

"Copy that." Gavin nodded and focused on the flames that lingered along the western wall of the barn. "Have Engine Twelve's pumper keep on top of the surrounding area and continue dousing the field. It was a wet spring, but we don't want to take any chances. We've got four homes on the other side of this property that aren't empty. Stay on top of her."

"You got it," Rick said, his radio cutting out with a crackling snap.

Gavin adjusted his stance and blinked the sweat from his eyes, while steam and smoke drifted up from the almost burned-out building. He moved in closer and continued his unyielding attack on the flames that struggled for life, gasping for air but getting little.

The beast wouldn't win tonight.

Chapter 1

"PULLING THE FIRE ALARM NOT ONLY WAS FOOLISH, but also put people in danger and wasted everyone's time," said Gavin McGuire, the fire chief in Old Brookfield, as he adjusted his heavy fireproof coat, the sweat trickling down his back. "What would have happened if there had been an actual fire in town and we couldn't reach it in time because we were here dealing with your prank?"

The moment he had pulled into the parking lot, Gavin had known this would be a false alarm, and he went from concerned to angry in a blink. Mrs. Drummond, the principal, was out front with that look on her face, the one that hovered between furious and embarrassed.

The sandy-haired twin brothers shrugged and stared sheepishly at the floor. Dressed in flip-flops, baggy shorts, and graphic T-shirts, they looked like they'd stepped out of an ad for Old Brookfield's summer tourist industry. Gavin loomed over the high school juniors. They squirmed beneath his inspection, to say nothing of Mrs. Drummond's intense gaze.

His mind went to the suspicious fire call he'd been out on late last night, and anger shot through him. The arson specialist was supposed to take a look at the site today, but he was busy in a neighboring county and probably wouldn't get to Old Brookfield until later in the week. Frustration nagged at Gavin. *Damn it.* These two kids had no idea what they were screwing around with.

The darkness in Gavin—the part that drove him into burning buildings without a second thought—demanded that the pair of mischief-makers be taught a lesson. He knew that suspending them wouldn't do much good. Hell, they'd probably spend the day playing Xbox. But a couple days working around the station might make them think twice before pulling a stupid stunt like this again.

"I'm sure Mrs. Drummond has plenty of ideas about how to punish you for this incident." Gavin cleared his throat and squashed the voice of the teenage boy in his head. The one that said they were just boys being boys. *Bullshit.* He stuffed down the flicker of sympathy. Kids or not, this crap wasn't funny. "But in case she's not feeling particularly creative, I'd like to offer up a weekend of cleaning the engine and the ladder truck. And we could use help reorganizing some gear at the station house."

"Aw, man," Robert moaned. "It's gonna be gorgeous out this weekend and school's over next week. Jeez. We were gonna take out the new boat."

"I could suspend you," Mrs. Drummond said in a deceptively sweet voice. "But given that school is almost over, I'm willing to make an exception. I'm sure your parents would be less than pleased with an end-of-the-year suspension on your records, to say nothing of the colleges you'll be applying to. Although, if you were to *volunteer* to help out at the firehouse for community service hours, then I imagine they'd be quite proud. Wouldn't they?"

She folded her arms over her plump torso and smirked wickedly. Her hair, once jet-black and now streaked with white, was styled in her trademark bob haircut. The ends swung by her chin and framed her round face as she peered at the twins.

"Your choice, gentlemen."

"Okay," David said quietly. "We'll take the community service hours."

"Dude?" Robert whined and threw up his hands in defeat. "What the—"

"Shut up, Robert." David elbowed his brother. Robert slumped back in the bench and mumbled something under his breath. David turned to Gavin. "We wouldn't want anyone to get hurt. Y'know? We were just screwing around. I'm sorry."

"Me too," Robert said in a practically inaudible tone. He lifted one shoulder as his cheeks pinked with embarrassment. The kid stared at his flip-flops again. "Sorry."

After finalizing what time the boys would show up on Saturday morning, Mrs. Drummond escorted Gavin out of the main office. They started walking down the long hallway, and when they passed the brown bench outside the office, Gavin recalled sitting there more than once awaiting a lecture of his own. A funny feeling of nostalgia tugged at him. He didn't consider himself a sappy guy or nostalgic.

He found looking back on his past too painful, for more reasons than one. No, it was better to look forward and keep moving. But walking through these familiar halls made it next to impossible for him not to think back and remember. The pale yellow walls were decorated with various construction-paper concoctions, everything from fire trucks to families, and Gavin couldn't help but smile.

Even after all these years, the kindergarten-through-twelfth-grade school still felt like his second home.

"It's all still so familiar, isn't it?" Mrs. Drummond said. "Red construction-paper roses and haphazard clouds painted with pudgy little hands. You and your brothers had plenty of artwork up on this wall over the years. You McGuire boys left your mark on this school in more ways than one. Everything from football heroes to the occasional graffiti incidents."

"True." Gavin wiped sweat from his brow. "If memory serves, we *volunteered* for plenty of *community service* hours of our own."

"Yes, well. There were five of you. I only have one boy, and he's responsible for every one of my gray hairs. Five boys," she said almost reverently. "I still don't know how your mother did it."

"Neither do I. If you were to ask her, I think she'd tell you it was a combination of luck and love." Gavin nodded. "She and my dad sure do have plenty of both."

His parents had been married for almost forty years, and he still caught them kissing in the kitchen. Usually he'd tease them and tell them how grossed out he was, but truth be told, a part of him was envious. Envious that they'd found someone to love so completely.

A partner and friend to share their lives with.

Years ago, Gavin had thought he'd have that, but after getting his heart stomped on, he realized what his parents had was rare and probably not something he'd ever experience. The station was his home, and the guys on his squad were his extended family.

Brothers in arms, if not by blood.

"They have a big anniversary coming up, don't they?"

"Yes, ma'am. Forty years, and between you and me, I don't know how they did it either. They're a special couple. I haven't met many other people who have what they do."

"Your mom told me the same thing the other day at bingo—luck and love." Mrs. Drummond waved at a pair of pigtailed little girls as they quietly headed toward the lavatory. One of them clutched a giant wooden pass with *GIRLS* emblazoned on it. "That statement was quickly followed by her complaint that not one of you boys has gotten married and given her any grandchildren."

"Right." Gavin removed his helmet and swiped a hand over his sweaty head while avoiding the principal's inquisitive stare. "Well, not all of us can be as lucky in love as my parents."

"I guess you're right." Mrs. Drummond sighed heavily as an awkward silence settled between them. "They are lucky indeed. My Homer and I had twenty-five good years before he passed. Can't complain though. I have a wonderful son, to say nothing of the six hundred children in this building."

They stopped by the glass double doors that led into the vestibule at the main entrance of the school as the end-of-the-day announcements echoed through the halls on the PA system. A bake sale flyer dangled precariously from the glass window of the door, and Gavin taped it back up before it could go fluttering to the ground.

"We good to go?" Rick's voice crackled from the radio on Gavin's belt and his lieutenant sounded less than enthusiastic.

Rick leaned against the gleaming red-and-silver engine in the hurry-up-and-wait mode that all firefighters were accustomed to. They were in an all-or-nothing business but always had to stay on their toes. Gavin waved at him and snagged the radio from his own belt.

"We're all clear, Rick. You and Bill take the engine back to the station, and I'll see you in ten."

"Ten-four." Rick's voice came through loud and clear as he climbed into the engine. "Don't forget you're cooking tonight—*unfortunately*. Which of your three delights will we be graced with?"

"Keep it up and I'll make 'em all." Gavin secured the radio back on his belt but didn't miss the expression of amusement on Mrs. Drummond's face. "I guess I shouldn't have cut so many of Mrs. Beasley's home ec. classes, huh?"

"Yes, if only you could have glimpsed your future, perhaps you would have picked up four or five recipes. After all, don't you boys do a lot of cooking at the station?" she teased.

"Yes, ma'am, but lucky for me, the guys aren't too picky."

"Your mother is such a fine cook, I can't believe you didn't learn a thing or two."

"She tried to teach me, but cooking never was my thing." Gavin tapped his fingers on the helmet as he slung it under his arm. "Every time my mother comes out to my cottage, she rummages through the fridge and makes sounds of disgust. I only cook three different meals and the guys are sick of them. I'm a bachelor to the core."

"You see?" Mrs. Drummond patted his cheek quickly. "That's where you and I disagree." She winked at him and lowered her voice to conspiratorial levels. "I think if anyone was meant to be a husband and a father, it's you, Gavin. You're protective by nature and looked out for your brothers ferociously," she said through a chuckle. "And you're from one of the most close-knit families I've had the pleasure to know. Sounds like husband and father material to me."

"Me?" Clearing his throat, Gavin shook his head slowly. "Marriage and kids aren't in the cards for me. Besides, the guys at the station can be immature enough to count as kids, and I work so much that you could probably say I'm married to the job. No, ma'am. I think that ship has sailed."

"Mmm-hmm." She folded her hands in front of her "That ship wouldn't have been named Jordan Yardley, by any chance, would it? You two were caught under the bleachers by the football coach on more than one occasion."

At the mention of Jordan's name, a deep, hollow ache he'd all but forgotten bloomed in Gavin's chest. Mrs. Drummond had inadvertently unearthed more pain from his past. Gavin shifted his weight as memories of Jordan flickered through his mind. More memories that he'd worked hard to forget, to shove aside as though they'd never happened. Why think about bittersweet moments from his youth when they would have no bearing on his future?

Yet in spite of his silent denials, images of Jordan filled his mind and memories of her fresh scent—lilacs and Ivory soap—lingered in his senses like a ghost. Haunting him with her sweet beauty. Sun-kissed skin; a lean, lanky body; honey-blond hair to her shoulders; and a toothy, white smile that could blind a man.

At least, that's what she looked like the last time he saw her—fifteen years ago.

"That's ancient history." His face heated and he cleared his throat, hoping Mrs. Drummond wouldn't see right through him. "Besides, she's married to some big Wall Street fat cat now. At least that's what my mother told me," Gavin said with a dismissive wave. On the outside he was playing it cool, but his gut was twisted in knots. Mrs. Drummond had hit the nail on the damn head. "Has a couple of kids too, I think. Girls. Maddy mentioned something about it," he added.

Maddy was the only friend Jordan had stayed in touch with and consequently Gavin's only connection to her. He used to think about Jordan all the time, but as the years passed, his thoughts of her lessened in frequency if not intensity. Would Mrs. Drummond buy the act he was putting on and think that he didn't gobble up every crumb of information he could get?

One night a few years ago, after one too many beers, he'd even contemplated getting one of those stupid Facebook accounts to see if he could find her, but that seemed creepy and he'd let the idea go.

Best to leave the past in the past.

"Yes." Mrs. Drummond nodded slowly. "Two girls. Seven and five."

"Besides, I'm too set in my ways," he said quickly. "And in case you hadn't noticed, the dating scene around here isn't exactly hopping."

"Fair enough." Casting a quick glance out the windows, her grin broadened. "Looks like my next appointment is here. It's been good seeing you, Gavin, though I'm sorry about the reason. Now, you make sure those two Heffernan boys do some real work at the station this weekend."

She patted him on the arm and headed back toward her office.

"Yes, ma'am." He stood taller and adjusted his jacket. "I'll see to it."

"And, Gavin?" She stopped outside the main office door and shouted back, "Don't get too set in your ways. You never know what might be right around the corner."

Principal Drummond's round form disappeared into her office, leaving him alone in the hallway that had once seemed so much longer.

Gavin stepped out into the warm sunshine and exhaled slowly. All this talk about Jordan had him feeling tense and off his game. The flag on the massive white pole fluttered in the June breeze. The tall, white steeple of St. Joseph's Church and a few buildings from town peeked out from amid the trees, which were capped by a cloudless azure sky. Old Brookfield was a perfect New England hamlet, and Gavin had nothing but appreciation for his hometown.

Turning his face to the early summer sky, he stood on the paved walkway and allowed the warmth of the afternoon sun to wash over him. A balmy breeze wafted past, and with it came the salty ocean air. The school was a couple of miles from the shore, but even at this distance he could smell the sweet scent of freedom.

The warmer weather meant getting outdoors, and there was nothing Gavin hated more than being cooped up inside. Jordan used to say that she thought he was part dolphin because of the amount of time he spent in the water. She probably wouldn't be the least bit surprised to hear he'd moved into the cottage on his parents' property.

He had to be a glutton for punishment. The first thing he saw every damn morning was that freaking lighthouse. *Their* lighthouse.

The sound of a school bus engine rumbling as it turned into the school's long, curved driveway pulled him from his memories. He let out a sound of frustration. Would he ever be able to forget and move on? He'd dated other women and slept with his share, but none of them had ever compared to her.

But what did it matter? She was gone. She had a husband, two kids, and a life that didn't include him. Hell, his didn't include her either. His job left little time for dating, and work was a lot more straightforward than romance or matters of the heart.

Fire might be tricky and unpredictable, but at least he knew how to put it out. He couldn't say the same thing about love or a broken heart. That kind of beating stuck with you and stung like hell, and as far as he was concerned, it was not for him.

Feeling foolish for allowing himself to dwell on days gone by, Gavin rolled his shoulder and tried to shake off the uncomfortable feelings. He opened his eyes as the school bus pulled past him. He had to quit dragging his feet and get his ass back to the station.

He headed toward his four-wheel drive, the only car in the lot with red sirens on top. The town had offered to buy him a new vehicle when he was promoted to chief, but he was happy with his old Explorer from his volunteer days. He'd taken good care of it over the years and the damn thing still purred like a kitten.

Why waste taxpayer dollars on something he didn't really need?

As the tail end of the yellow behemoth went by and its puff of exhaust dissipated, Gavin came face-to-face with his past.

He stopped dead in his tracks. The years vanished. Gavin found himself staring into a pair of familiar brown eyes. Long, blond hair with golden honey-colored streaks drifted over her slim, tanned shoulders, and a yellow sundress fluttered around her legs. An ache bloomed in Gavin's chest as those full pink lips curved into that devastatingly beautiful, familiar smile.

It was like getting a punch in the gut and having the wind knocked out of him.

In that moment, he wasn't the fire chief of Old Brookfield. He was an eighteen-year-old kid looking at the girl who had stolen his heart...and broken it.

"Hello, Gavin." The musical lilt of her voice wafted over him like cool mist and willed him closer, but he held his ground. Her eyes crinkled at the corners as her smile widened slowly, almost tentatively. It still blinded him. "I—it's been a long time."

"Jordan?" He licked his suddenly dry lips and squinted. Was he really seeing what he thought he was seeing? A million questions, peppered with angry accusations, filled his head. She looked exactly the same as she had fifteen years ago, still so strikingly and effort-lessly beautiful. "When did you—?"

Before he could utter a word, a flurry of movement caught his attention and the present came crashing back with a vengeance. Two adorable little blond girls clung to Jordan's skirt, one on either side of her. They had

Jordan's fair hair and her big, brown eyes—eyes that peered at him with more than a little trepidation.

The older one on Jordan's right was casting a suspicious look Gavin's way. "Where's your truck?" she asked. "Why don't you have a truck?"

"Lily, don't be rude." Jordan gently wrapped her arm around her daughter reassuringly. "He has one right over there." She nodded toward his four-wheel drive. "See? It has the lights on top."

"That's not a fire truck, Mama. That's a regular one that regular people drive." Pursing her lips together, Lily looked over her shoulder at his truck and then back to Gavin. Squinting against the glare of the sun, she swiped a long strand of hair out of her eyes. She pointed at him. "You're a fireman, aren't you? So where's your truck?"

"Yes." Gavin found himself hopelessly charmed by the brazen questions from the curious little girl. He caught Jordan's eye, but she quickly turned her attention back to her daughter. "I'm a fireman."

Jordan and the girls stepped onto the sidewalk as she gathered their tiny hands in hers. He sensed hesitance from all three of them, but as always Jordan forged ahead. She hadn't changed a bit. Stubborn and strong willed in spite of the awkward situation.

"Lily, is it?" Gavin slowly closed the distance between them before squatting down so he was eye to eye with Jordan's girls. "Lily, you are absolutely right. I am a fireman, but I don't have the engine here. It's back at the station, which is where I have to be going. I was at home when the call came in, so I drove here in my regular truck. I don't keep the engine at my house."

He lowered his voice to a conspiratorial whisper and winked. "Wouldn't fit in my driveway."

Lily giggled and flashed him a wide, gap-toothed grin before once again clinging to her mother. Gavin tapped his fingers on the helmet he held between his hands and rose to his feet. The instant Jordan's soulful brown eyes clapped onto his, his stomach dropped to his feet. Had it really been fifteen years?

There was so much he wanted to say, but he had no damn idea where to begin, and based on her expression, neither did she. He wasn't sure if he wanted to shake her and scream at her or hug her and kiss the life out of her.

Silence hung between them for a few more uncomfortable seconds before Jordan finally took the leap.

"Girls, this is an old friend of mine, Gavin McGuire." Gentleness edged her voice. "He's the fire chief here in Old Brookfield."

Gavin stilled. She knew about his promotion to chief? What else did she know? Did she know he had spent countless nights dreaming about her and wondering why the hell she left town without a word? Why she'd left *him*.

"Nice to meet you," Lily said sweetly. She grabbed the skirt of her floral sundress and curtsied for him in an adorable old-world gesture. "I'm Lily Ann McKenna, and that's my little sister, Grace Marie McKenna, but she won't talk to you 'cause you're a stranger."

"Well, it's real nice to meet you, Lily and Grace. I'm Gavin, and now that we've been introduced, we're not strangers anymore, right?" He smiled at the smaller one who quickly hid her face in the fabric of Jordan's dress. He looked at Jordan and quietly said, "We're not strangers at all, are we, Mrs. McKenna?"

Jordan opened her mouth as if she was going to say something, but quickly shut it again and shook her head. The gesture was shockingly familiar. She used to do it all the time when they were kids, like she was silently scolding herself for whatever she was going to spit out. Then she'd decide against it and say nothing. It was a habit she'd picked up from living with her old man. He was a mean, old son of a bitch, and Gavin had gotten into it with the guy on more than one occasion.

"My father's been sick."

"Right." Gavin nodded. The guy had been sick in the head for years, and his body was finally catching up. He'd heard that the old bastard was in a bad way; couldn't happen to a nicer guy. "Maddy told me."

She nibbled her lower lip and sucked in her breath, as though debating what to say next. Just like she used to do when they were kids. The last two months of their senior year, he'd known she was holding something back, hiding it from him. She was constantly censoring what she told him until it was too late.

"Where's the rest of the family?" Gavin looked around the parking lot, apprehension crawling up his back. "I'd sure like to meet the man who kept you away from Old Brookfield all these years."

"My daddy's—"

"He's in New York," Jordan said quickly. "In the city. Working."

Gavin stilled. There was something about the way Jordan cut off her daughter that gave him pause. Maybe life with What's-his-face wasn't all it was cracked up to be. Just as well. Bumping into Jordan and her daughters was tough enough, but seeing the lucky son of a bitch who married her would be more than he could handle at the moment. He was keeping his cool so far, but meeting *Mr. McKenna* would probably push Gavin over the edge of cool and into "holy crap, this sucks" territory.

"Well, I heard he's quite a guy," Gavin said in an overly polite tone. "Big money man from Wall Street, if I'm not mistaken?"

Those dark eyes of hers grew stormy. They narrowed, and she met his challenging stare with one of her own. Fury settled over her as her jaw set and her shoulders squared, ready for a fight. In that moment, Gavin saw the feisty girl he'd fallen in love with. The one who got right back on a horse she'd been thrown from, determined to keep going at any cost. Nothing had ever stopped Jordan when she set her mind to something. Her tenacity was one of the qualities he loved most. She was as stubborn as she was beautiful, and obviously nothing had changed.

"Yes, quite a guy," she said in a barely audible tone. "Listen, it's been *nice* bumping into you like this, and I'd love to catch up, but the girls and I have to go see Principal Drummond." She took the girls by the hands and headed toward the doors of the school. "Excuse me or we're going to be late."

Gavin's gut clenched as he finally realized why Jordan was here at the school with the girls. He gripped his helmet tighter but remained calm on the surface. Hope, mixed with a healthy amount of fear, glimmered in the back of his mind.

"So you're not only here for a visit?"

"No." Jordan stopped in the open doorway, and time seemed to stretch on forever. So many unspoken words

floated between them that Gavin practically drowned in
the swell. "We're home."

The three vanished into the brick building. The sun
flashed off the glass as the doors clanked shut behind
them, and Gavin squinted to block out the light. Walking
back to his truck, he shed his heavy fireproof coat and
let the cold, hard reality of the situation settle over him
like a lead blanket. Jordan, her daughters, and by all
accounts, Jordan's husband were moving back to town.

They would be here every *single* day reminding
Gavin of what could have been…but wasn't.

Chapter 2

JORDAN PULLED TO A STOP IN FRONT OF MRS. MORGAN'S flower shop. In the rearview mirror, she glimpsed the peaceful, sleeping faces of her daughters. The girls had dozed off almost the second they pulled out of the school parking lot. Given the past couple of days, Jordan couldn't blame them. She was pretty damn tired herself.

Letting out a sigh, she stared at the lovely, little storefront without really seeing it. Who was she kidding? She hadn't really seen a damn thing since running into Gavin in front of the school two hours ago. That moment, the one she'd dreaded for fifteen years, had finally happened— and it had been like an out-of-body experience.

For a split second, she'd had the urge to run up to him and jump into his arms. To bury her face in the crook of his neck and breathe him in, to inhale the scent of soap and firewood that was so distinctly his. All these years later she could still smell it if she closed her eyes. But when she saw that hurt, hard look on his face, Jordan had known it was too late. The damage had been done and there was no undoing it. She was the one who had run off, so how could she blame him for finding solace in the arms of someone else?

A few days after she'd left all those years ago, Jordan had finally broken down and called her friend Suzanne only to find out that Gavin had already taken up with Missy Oakland. That horrid, bitchy girl had been chasing him all through high school, and apparently Gavin wasn't as uninterested as he always claimed he was. When Jordan heard that, the last thing she was going to do was come home. So she stayed in the city. Got a waitressing job and eventually a crappy apartment that was one step above the youth hostel she'd stayed in at first.

In her fantasies, the ones she let herself play out while falling asleep at night, she imagined Gavin pulling her into his arms and covering her mouth with his. Offering forgiveness without asking her for an explanation, even though he clearly deserved one. Telling her how sorry he was for betraying her and asking her if they could start over.

No. It was too late for apologies now.

The real moment—the one she'd survived and by some miracle hadn't vomited in the middle of—had been far less romantic than her fantasy. She hadn't been welcomed home by a boy who loved her, but by a man who was still painfully angry after all these years. Not even that charming, dimpled grin, the one that awakened a swarm of butterflies in her belly, could hide the hurt that edged his pale green eyes.

His thick, dark hair had been cut short and there was a whisper of gray at the temples now. That ruggedly handsome face had grown even more attractive with the years that had passed, but when his square jaw set and the smile faded, the hurt remained. And that pain she saw in his eyes, that was on her. It was one hundred percent her own damn fault.

It was no surprise that Gavin was still angry, both that she'd left town without a word to him or anyone else, and that she'd never come back. He wasn't alone.

She was pretty pissed off herself and easily recalled the pain of his betrayal. After all, she'd only been gone for a few days and apparently Gavin started screwing the first girl he could!

Nice. So much for true love, Jordan thought.

He'd obviously never really loved her, so why the hell was he so angry with her? *Jeez.*

Jordan scoffed and tapped the steering wheel with her fingers. *Right. Fine.* He could be furious with *her*, but he sure as hell hadn't cornered the market on it. She was still pretty annoyed herself.

Eyes closed, she let the cool breeze of the air-conditioning wash over her, wishing it could wash away the mistakes she'd made. There had been so many.

That was the *first* time she'd run away.

Now here she was, fifteen years later, doing the same thing. Running. Starting over. Jordan looked over her shoulder at her sleeping daughters and fought the tears that threatened to fall. It wasn't only about her anymore. They were all starting over.

Letting out a huff, she rested her forehead on knuckles wrapped in a death grip around the leather-bound steering wheel. What in the world was she doing back here anyway? Even when she was signing the rental papers for the cozy house on the beach, that voice in the back of her mind had questioned her decision. She had plenty of money from the divorce settlement; she could have gone anywhere. No matter what scenarios she ran through her head, she always came back to Old Brookfield…to Gavin.

A knock on the driver's side window pulled her from her thoughts and had her yelping out loud. Hand to her chest, she snapped her head toward the window and came face-to-face with Maddy Morgan. Maddy, her oldest and dearest friend, grinned and waved like the bubbly, beautiful woman she'd always been. The familiarity of it made Jordan's heart ache.

Putting a finger to her lips, Jordan pointed a thumb toward the backseat, praying the girls wouldn't be woken up. They might need the sleep, but Jordan needed the quiet. Without making a sound, she got out of the car and closed the door. She'd barely turned around when Maddy gathered her up in one of the giggly, bouncy hugs that Jordan loved and had missed so much. Dressed in her signature casual style—a tank top, shorts, and flip-flops—her old friend was a sight for sore eyes.

"I can't believe you're really back," Maddy said through an excited laugh. She pulled back and squeezed Jordan's arms before releasing her with a playful huff. Pushing her sunglasses onto her head, she pursed her lips. "How the hell is it possible that you still look like you did in high school?"

"Hardly." Jordan folded her arms over her breasts. "Actually, I didn't think it was possible to feel this old. My poor daughters have an old woman for a mother and a son of a bitch for a father."

"They have you and that's what matters." A warm breeze fluttered over them, making Maddy's curly, dark hair whip around her head. Her light blue eyes flicked to the girls and her smile widened. "Did you get all settled in at the house? I left something for the girls in their bedroom."

"Yes." Jordan nodded, recalling the giddy expressions on their faces when they found the two baskets full of beach toys waiting for them in the pretty pink-and-white bedroom. "You must have spent a fortune on those. Do you always blow part of your rental commission on gifts for your clients' kids?"

"You're more than a client and you know it." Maddy winked. "We've known each other for twenty years. Hell, when I moved to town in ninth grade, you were the only girl who would even talk to me."

"Some friend." Jordan's throat tightened with emotion. "You're the one who kept our friendship going."

"Hey, life happens." Maddy shrugged. "Neither of us is on Assbook or tweeting or whatever people do, so we weren't gonna find each other that way, and I was still in Europe on exchange when you split. When I got home and heard you'd left, I tried asking your mom and dad where you were, but that went down like a fart in church. Thanks to my persevering nature and the handy-dandy Internet, I found you and here we are."

"What would I do without you?" Jordan asked quietly. Her voice dropped to a whisper. "I honestly don't know if I would have had the courage to leave Ted if it weren't for you."

"Stop." Maddy grabbed both of Jordan's hands.

Those fierce blue eyes were edged with the familiar grit and fortitude Maddy had always possessed. Those qualities made her a devoted friend and a fierce businesswoman. Between the flower shop she'd inherited from her mother and her real estate company, Maddy had become one of the wealthiest women in town. And despite the time that had passed, the second Jordan had reconnected with Maddy, it was like no time had gone by at all. They picked up right where they left off.

"Jordan, you stop that crap right there. We've already been through this, girl. I love you. You're my friend and I've always got your back. You're home and that's what matters."

"I sure am," Jordan said through a nervous laugh.

"What are you doing here in town anyway? Not that I'm not thrilled to see you, but I figured you'd still be settling in at the house."

"When we spoke on the phone the other day, you mentioned that you could use some help at the shop." Jutting a thumb toward the store, Jordan sucked in a deep breath. "I could use a job, and you could use some help."

"Oh my God!" Maddy clapped her hands together and pumped her fists in the air while she hooted loudly. Jordan giggled when an older couple passing on the sidewalk looked at them sideways. "Yes! I would love it. Cookie and Veronica have been going balls to the wall since March, and we desperately need someone to help man the counter. Between weddings, communions, prom, and all that other stuff, they're going nuts. Hell, I would have asked but I figured you didn't need the dough."

Jordan hated talking about money; the subject made her incredibly uncomfortable. She never had any growing up, and then when she married Ted, she had more than she could have dreamed of. She'd quickly found that it didn't fix everything. Not by a long shot.

"I don't really. I mean, I get child support and I got half of the proceeds from the sale of the penthouse, plus a lump sum. I didn't want alimony, even though my attorney told me I was an idiot for that decision.

Anyway, the girls are going to be in camp all summer, and the last thing I need is to sit around with time on my hands." Images of Gavin wafted through her mind. "I could work weekdays and—"

"Say no more." Maddy held up one hand, stopping Jordan's babbling. "You don't have to explain yourself to me. The job is yours. How does Monday through Friday, nine to five, sound? Twelve bucks an hour? Do you need health benefits?"

"No, I have insurance for the girls and me. That's perfect, Maddy. You really are a lifesaver. It will be so great to work again and really be on my own two feet. Ted never wanted me to work." Her back straightened as she recalled his controlling nature. "Anyway, I'm on my own now and work will be good for me."

"You're free of that asshole, so I say, work all ya want. And for the record, it's a good thing I never met him because I'd probably have punched him square in the jaw. I was thrilled when you told me you were leaving him, and when you called me about renting the cottage, it was a bonus. But I'll be honest…I am sick about the reason. Ted sounds like a real SOB."

"He's something, alright," Jordan scoffed. "Between his temper, the drinking, the drugs, and the other women—"

"Being abused isn't limited to physical violence," Maddy interjected firmly.

"I know." Jordan sighed. Tears stung her eyes. She leaned back against the car and folded her arms over her chest, trying her damnedest to hold it together. "That's why I left him. Thank God I have full custody and there were no limitations on where we could move. Ted signed off on it without blinking." Her mouth set in a tight line and her voice was barely above a whisper. "Do you know he hasn't seen the girls in six months? He's barely spoken to them. Most times when I have them call him, he doesn't even pick up or he rushes them off the phone."

"What?" Maddy's jaw fell open. "But you left the city this week. I thought you said you had an apartment not far from where you used to live with him."

"I did, but it was always something with him, even when we were married. A meeting would come up or he would have some important client to tend to. Another bar to visit and another hooker to bang." Jordan nibbled her lower lip and bit back the tears. But they weren't for her; they were for her daughters who'd been robbed of a father. "I think the girls and I, the family, we were part of his image. So when I filed for divorce, that image was blown. We weren't of any more use to him."

"I'm so sorry, Jordan." Maddy's tone softened. "I didn't know it was that bad."

"How could you?" Jordan grabbed her friend's hand and squeezed. "I had cut myself off from everyone. I was determined to make it on my own and then…well, so much time had passed, it felt like it was too late. When you and I actually had time to talk on the phone over the past couple of years, the last subject I wanted to bring up was my sham of a marriage." She pressed at her eyes with the heels of her hands.

"It's ironic, isn't it? I ran away to escape my father, and I ended up marrying a man exactly like him. How pathetic. Ted may have more money than my father and look like a polished tycoon, but at the core he's a mean, controlling, and nasty drunk too." Pushing herself off the car, she sucked in a deep breath and squared her shoulders. "I stayed as long as I did because I didn't want my daughters to come from a broken home."

"What made you change your mind?" Maddy asked gently. "Why now?"

"Girl, this is a conversation that requires a bottle of wine and a couple of chairs on the beach." She squeezed Maddy's hand. "For now, let's just say that it's better to come from a broken home than live in one."

"Ain't that the truth?" Maddy murmured. "And I'm taking you up on that bottle of wine offer. You, me, and a bottle of wine on your deck. Deal?"

"Deal."

"I'll bring the wine." Maddy gathered her up in another hug and kissed her cheek. "You tell me when."

"Hey, Jordan." The gentle, hesitant tenor interrupted their conversation, and Jordan knew who it was before she even saw the man on the sidewalk. "When did you get back to town?"

Tommy Miller appeared much like he did in high school, and the sight of him was no less heartbreaking now than it was then. He was dressed in a dark gray uniform with his name stitched neatly on the front. His slightly stooped frame had filled out a bit over the years and his blond hair had thinned out to a dusty gray, but the burn scars that marred the right side of his face remained the same. They were a gruesome reminder of that fateful day from their childhood, one that haunted everyone in town, but Tommy and Gavin more than anyone else.

"Hi, Tommy. It's so good to see you again."

Jordan stepped onto the sidewalk with a wide smile. She gave him a hug and a kiss on the cheek, and the poor guy almost dropped the two grocery bags in his arms. She stepped away and tried to help him secure the bag slipping from his right arm, the side that had been weakened and scarred in the fire.

"Sorry," Jordan said quickly. "I guess I was so excited to see you that I almost knocked the bags down."

"That's okay." Tommy dipped his head and stepped back, obviously not wanting Jordan's help. "I can manage."

"Of course." Jordan gave Maddy a sidelong glance. "Sorry."

"Hey there, Tommy," Maddy said with a wave.

"You back home to see your dad?" Tommy asked. He flicked his good eye up to Jordan before looking down at the ground again. Jordan's heart broke. He was so self-conscious after all this time. "Or are ya here for good? I-I thought I saw you at the school today."

"The school?"

"Yeah." He adjusted the bags in his arms, and even though Jordan wanted to offer to take one for him, she resisted. "I'm the head custodian over there. I been workin' there since we graduated, but last year I got promoted." He stood a little taller. A hint of a smile played at his lips. "Anyway, I thought I saw you there today coming out of the principal's office."

"Of course. I think Principal Drummond mentioned that during our tour of the school. And, yes, we're back for good. The girls and I are renting the Sweeneys' old place out on Shore Road. I'd love for you to meet them, but they're sleeping at the moment."

"That's okay." Tommy lifted one shoulder and

shuffled his feet. "I don't wanna wake 'em up. I'm sure I'll see 'em in the fall once school starts again."

"Actually, if you work at the school, then you'll see them all summer. They'll be attending camp there." Jordan squeezed his shoulder briefly. "It'll make me feel better to know I have a friend there to keep an extra eye on them."

"You bet." Tommy's grin widened. "It's real good to have you back in town, Jordan."

The sudden rumbling of an engine shattered the quiet of Main Street, and Jordan's gut tightened at the sound of it. She didn't have to turn around to know it was the town's fire truck pulling around the corner and into the station on the other side of the street. Maddy inched closer and elbowed her in the ribs.

"See anyone else since you've been back?" Maddy asked, her dark brows waggling in an almost comical flurry. "Eh, Jordan?"

Gavin. Jordan swallowed the sudden lump in her throat and willed herself not to turn around. She folded her arms over her breasts while digging her fingernails into her palm so hard she'd probably draw blood.

"Well, I gotta go." Tommy dipped his head in an abrupt good-bye and hurried away and around the corner. "See ya, Jordan."

Tommy's shuffling form vanished, and the warning beeps from the backing-up fire truck filled the air. Jordan stepped off the sidewalk and leaned down to peek in the window and check on the girls. Both were still sleeping. *Thank God.* She leaned back against the hot surface of the car and kept her back to the firehouse. Gawking at Gavin might be an intriguing and tempting idea, but it certainly wasn't a smart one.

Maddy moved in next to Jordan and leaned on the top of the car, waving her arm furiously. "Hey, Gavin!"

"You are incorrigible."

Jordan swatted at her friend's waving hand and glanced at the firehouse before she could stop herself. Gavin and another man were standing by the front of the red and silver truck. Her entire body stilled and all the hairs on her arms stood on end. Even at this distance, one look from him made her belly quiver. Gavin waved back and Jordan got caught ogling him. *Damn it.* She spun around and pushed her hair off her face, wishing she could smooth her nerves as easily.

"And, yes, before you start the inquisition, I bumped into him at the school when I went to register the girls for the fall."

"What?" Maddy gave her friend the stink eye. "You mean to tell me you've been standing here talkin' to me all this time, and you failed to mention that you bumped into Gavin McGuire—the oldest of the five hottest brothers God ever put on this earth? Not to mention your first love. How did he react?"

"To say he was surprised to see me is an understatement." She fought the urge to look back at the firehouse again. "It was a surprise for both of us."

"Well, you *did* tell me not to say anything to anyone about you renting the Sweeneys' place."

"You didn't even tell Rick?" Jordan asked with genuine surprise. Rick was Maddy's longtime lover and one of the full-time firefighters in Old Brookfield. "I'm impressed."

"Not exactly." Maddy pursed her lips. "He overheard me on the phone with you, but I swore him to secrecy. If he ever wants to get laid again, he'll keep his lips zipped. I told him he couldn't say anything unless Gavin asked him about you directly. So? What happened?" Her expression twisting into a mask of anticipation. "Was it weird or awesome? Or weirdly awesome?"

"Let's just say I don't think Gavin will be asking me out for dinner anytime soon." Jordan lifted one shoulder and kept her voice light. "We dated a long time ago and we were kids, Maddy. Whatever. He has his life and I have mine."

"Yeah, well, now your life and his life are back in the same little town. Something tells me that old sparks might fly again."

"No." Jordan shook her head adamantly. "No romance. No relationships—and definitely not with Gavin. There's too much history there, and aside from all of that, I need to focus on my daughters. I want to show them that a woman can stand on her own two feet. For goodness' sake, their *father* has tossed them aside like they mean nothing to him. The last thing my girls need is for their mother to bring another man into their lives. None of us needs that kind of risk right now."

"Gavin isn't just *any* man."

"All the more reason I should steer clear."

"Mmm-hmm. Sounds to me like this also needs to be discussed over that bottle of wine…or two." Maddy made sound of disbelief and started digging around in her enormous messenger bag. Pulling a huge chunk of keys from within, she hooted with delight. "Damn if this bag isn't like a giant black hole. I am constantly losing

shit in here. Like I said, wine and girl talk soon—and
that most definitely includes chatting about Chief Hotty
Pants McGuire."

"Right." Jordan quickly changed the subject and
forced a smile. "So when should I report to work, boss?"

"Why don't you take this week to get settled with the
girls at the cottage? You can start next Monday morning."

"Great." Jordan nodded and fought the urge to turn
around and see if Gavin was still outside. "The girls start
camp then, so it's perfect timing."

Jordan kissed Maddy good-bye and slipped quietly
back into the cool air of the car. She put her sunglasses
on and waved before backing out of the space. She tried
not to look over at the firehouse as she approached it,
but the attempt failed miserably. The instant she pulled
past the fire truck, Gavin's tall, broad-shouldered form
came into view.

He was hosing off the side of the truck, free of his
gear and wearing only his summer uniform of a navy-
blue T-shirt and shorts. His tall, muscular build was on
full display. Jeez. The guy still had great legs—long,
well defined, and strong. Some men had huge torsos and
scrawny legs, but not Gavin. Oh no. He was perfectly
balanced and didn't look like he had an ounce of fat on
him anywhere.

She looked back at the road in time to see the light
turn red.

Jordan cursed under her breath. She was stopped
directly in front of the firehouse driveway—and Gavin.
Feeling him stare at her, she gripped the steering wheel
tighter with both hands. *Just keep looking straight
ahead. Don't look. Don't look. Don't do it.* But even

as the words flickered through her mind, her head was turning. A moment later she was met with those serious green eyes framed with dark lashes.

Sweet Mary, he was gorgeous. He'd filled out over the years, matured. The lanky body of a boy had been replaced with the sturdy, well-defined form of a man. There were dashes of gray in his hair. It was more than that though. Much more. Gavin's inherent sweetness, the gooey center beneath that tough exterior, had been evident when he'd met her girls earlier. That tenderness had made her fall head over heels for him all those years ago.

When Lily grilled him back at the school, the guy didn't miss a beat and squatted down, getting eye to eye with her precocious daughter. However, when he'd risen to his feet and met Jordan's gaze, his green eyes had hardened. They were shadowed from all he'd seen over the years, and wariness lingered where she'd once seen eagerness.

Gavin shifted his stance by the truck and stared at her unabashedly, as though daring her to look away. Jordan's breath caught in her throat and in that instant the world seemed to stand still. She could pull over. Jump out of the car and tell him how sorry she was for leaving the way she did. Tell him that she didn't give a damn anymore if he'd slept with Missy Oakland and that all of that was ancient history.

Hug him. Breathe him in. Love him.

A horn blared behind her rudely and ripped her from her fantasies. She didn't miss the annoyed expression on Gavin's face as he snapped his head around toward the impatient driver behind her. Jordan hit the gas, not waiting for him to look back. Fantasies would get her nowhere. Dreams about an impossible future were what got her in trouble in the first place.

No. The time for dreams and childish fantasies was over.

She smiled when Lily's sleepy face filled the rear-view mirror. She had two bundles of adorable reality in the backseat, and they were her priority.

"We'll be home in a few minutes, Lily." Jordan turned her sights back to the road in front of her, leading down toward their new home by the beach. "It's time to get settled."

Chapter 3

"To new beginnings," Jordan said quietly.

Could she have a new beginning with Gavin? *Damn it, no.* She was not going to start pining over Gavin. *Cut the crap*, she thought to herself. *Leave the past in the past and live in the present. Focus on the girls.*

"Amen to that." Maddy took a healthy sip of her wine. "Hell, if you like it enough at the shop, maybe you'll buy the place."

"Really?" Jordan's eyebrows raised. "You want to sell your mom's place?"

"To the right person, sure. I mean, my mom loved you, and I am racing around like a chicken with its head cut off trying to run both businesses." She puffed an espresso-colored curly strand of hair from her face. "Especially this time of year. It's freaking nuts."

"Own my own business?" The possibilities ran through her head before she rolled her eyes and waved off the strangely appealing idea. "I don't know the first thing about something like that. Besides, I'm not a florist."

"Neither am I," Maddy said with a snort of derision. "That's why I pay Cookie and Veronica the big bucks. Anyway, buying businesses aside, the gig is yours with no strings attached."

"Thank you."

Jordan placed her wineglass on the table and pulled her feet up into the chair, wrapping her arms around her knees. The warm summer air was filled with the scent of the sea, and two gulls fought over an old fish head along the edge of the water. The sound of the television in the family room—a cartoon the girls were enthralled by—was mixed with the comforting rush of the tide.

How many times had she dreamed of a quiet evening like this? Her daughters in their pajamas, all bathed and sweet smelling and safe in the other room, and her dear friend by her side with a glass of wine in hand.

Dark memories crept in. Jordan had never thought a day like this would come.

Silence hung between them with only the sound of the waves and passing gulls, and Jordan could feel the weight of Maddy's question coming before she even uttered it.

"So are you gonna tell me what happened?" Maddy sat back in her chair and tugged her white sweater closed. "What made you finally leave him?"

Jordan sucked in a steadying breath and dropped her bare feet to the ground. Curling her fingers around the stem of her glass, she fought the tide of fear, regret, and sadness that swelled up when she recalled that night.

"Hey." Maddy's voice dropped to almost a whisper, and she rubbed Jordan's back reassuringly. "It's okay. I don't wanna push. I mean, if you don't—"

"No." Jordan shook her head and sat up taller in her chair. "It's okay… About six months ago, after one of his drinking binges, he came home late. Three in the morning. I'd fallen asleep on the couch. I knew he'd come home sloshed, because he did it so often, and it was easier to manage him and keep him quiet if I could get to him right away. You know? I didn't want the girls woken up by such ugliness. Until that night, the strategy had worked."

Rising from her chair, Jordan went to the railing of the deck and looked out at the ocean, unable to face her friend. Shame and guilt clung to her. She couldn't bear to look Maddy in the eyes because she was too worried she'd see pity there.

Jordan knew how pathetic she'd been.

"Ted came after me. He stunk of whiskey and woke me up out of a dead sleep. He tried to pull my pajamas off. I shoved him off me." She let out a bitter laugh. "He was so wasted, he could barely stand so it wasn't hard. After my rejection, he trashed the living room and screamed about what a cold fish I was."

"It's okay, Jordan." Maddy had moved in next to her and wrapped her arm around Jordan's shoulders.

"He came after me again. Groping me. Shouting hateful, ugly things and I fought like hell to get away. I knew then that if I stayed any longer, it would only get worse." Her voice shook with a mixture of rage and disgust. "When I finally got him off me and turned around, I came face-to-face with my girls. They were crying and clinging to each other in the hallway outside their bedroom. Ted screamed something incoherent before stumbling past them to the bathroom."

"Oh my God, Jordan."

"I grabbed Gracie and Lily, went to a hotel, and filed for divorce the next day."

"Son of a—"

"Yup." Jordan swiped at her eyes and drained the last of her wine. "He sure is."

"Hey." Maddy took both glasses and placed them on the table. "You are one of the bravest women I know."

"Brave?" Jordan could barely get the word out. "I'm a coward. I ran away fifteen years ago, and here I am doing it again."

"Bullshit." Maddy grabbed Jordan's shoulders, gently forcing her to face her. To Jordan's relief, she saw no pity there. Only resolute love and acceptance. "You survived, baby. You did what you had to do. That's what you did then and that's what you are doing now. You are a survivor—and don't you forget it. Just because he didn't outright hit you doesn't mean he wasn't abusive or controlling."

Tears blurred Jordan's vision as Maddy gathered her up in a warm, lingering hug. How long had it been since anyone held her this way? Comforted her? Too many years for her to count. She'd missed her friend more than she'd realized, and the generosity of such unconditional love cracked Jordan's last line of defenses. The tears fell freely as Maddy embraced her tightly.

"Thank you," Jordan whispered. Pulling back, she kissed Maddy's cheek. "You really are the best friend I've ever had."

"True." Maddy gave Jordan a playful smack on the ass before pouring them both a bit more wine. She handed Jordan a glass and held her own up. "To good friends!"

"And surviving," Jordan murmured.

Jordan's first day of work at the flower shop reminded her of the first day of school. She was so busy learning the ropes and dealing with customers that the day went by in a flash. So fast, in fact, that she forgot to eat lunch and only caught herself from looking out the window for Gavin four or five times.

She was definitely a glutton for punishment.

With her stomach rumbling, she locked the front door of the shop and checked the time. She had a few minutes before she needed to pick the girls up from camp, and the delicious smell of fresh baked bread from the market called to her.

Checking the traffic and doing her damnedest not to even *glance* at the fire station across the street, Jordan headed over to the market and away from the station. The heat of the June afternoon had given way to a balmy early evening, making her long for sunset on the deck. She and the girls had made a habit of talking about their day while the sun went to sleep.

When Jordan tugged open the door to the market, the scent of freshly baked bread enveloped her. Forcing herself not to run to the bakery counter and gobble down an entire loaf, she snagged a small green handbasket by the register and smiled at the young woman behind the counter. Wearing a blue-and-white apron, the girl gave Jordan a brace-filled grin as she rang up an older gentleman's sale. A feeling of contentment washed over Jordan as she strolled the aisles, and she realized she didn't miss the city at all. Not the traffic. The honking horns. The rude pedestrians. The unsmiling waitstaff or the woman at her grocery store in the city with four nose rings and a chronic inability to smile.

Nope, she didn't miss it one bit.

On her way toward the back of the store, Jordan picked up a few other items she needed, cereal and milk, and a couple she didn't, like the bag of peanut M&M's

and a package of Kit Kat bars. If she wasn't having sex, then she would have chocolate.

She rounded the corner and her shoulders sagged when she saw with the line at the bakery counter, four people deep. Pressed for time and hungry as hell, Jordan grabbed two of the white paper-wrapped loaves of sourdough that had likely been made earlier in the day.

"Jordan Yardley?"

The familiar voice raked over Jordan like fingernails on a chalkboard, and while it had been years since she'd heard it, there was no mistaking who it was.

Missy Oakland.

"Hello, Missy." Jordan deposited her bread into the basket and turned to face the only woman she'd ever really disliked. Forcing a tight smile, she said, "It's been a long time."

Missy's ebony hair was tied up in a ponytail and her oval-shaped face with almost hollowed-out cheekbones was free of all wrinkles. She *had* to have had Botox, and Jordan wasn't sure if she was jealous or disgusted.

Missy's slender form was clad in a pair of white Daisy Duke shorts and a pink tank top that barely contained her chest. Basically, the woman hadn't changed an ounce since high school. She was still *va-va-voom* sexy. Big boobs. Narrow waist. Full hips. Lips like Angelina Jolie. Jordan swallowed the sudden lump in her throat and pushed her hair off her forehead. The woman was a walking sexpot, and she always had been.

No wonder Gavin had slept with her. What red-blooded heterosexual man wouldn't?

"Gosh. It has to have been like fifteen years." Missy giggled the way a young girl would and slapped Jordan on the arm playfully. "But we don't look a day older, do we? Say, I didn't know you were visiting too. If I had, I would have suggested we get together for a drink. But I'm heading home today."

A drink? Jordan had thought this girl hated her in high school. Why would she want to go out for a drink?

"Uh. Well, I'm not visiting. I moved back." She adjusted the basket because the metal handle was digging into her forearm and she was starting to sweat. "I mean, I moved back here with my girls."

"Oh! You got kids?"

"Yes." Jordan nodded. "Two girls."

"Oh, that's cool," Missy said in a tone that was agreeable but not meaningful. "I was just here for a couple days visiting my daddy. He's been after me to come home for like the past four years." She snorted with laughter. "I always fly him to LA. This time I caved, but I can't wait to get back to the West Coast."

LA. Why did that sound so perfect for Missy?

"Well, it was nice bumping into you, Missy, but I have to be going." Jordan plastered a tight smile on her face and fought the urge to back up. "I have to pick up my daughters from camp."

"Sure, sure." Missy popped a stick of gum in her mouth and pointed one well-manicured finger at Jordan. "Say, you know who I saw yesterday when I was driving through town? Gavin McGuire. The man looks as fine as he ever did. Better maybe." She let out a sigh and stretched her arms over her head in a feline-like move. "Too bad I'm not staying longer. Maybe I could actually get that guy to take me up on my offer. He's so gorgeous. I should let him know that my offer is still good."

Jordan stilled but her stomach swirled almost to the point of nausea.

"Oh shit." Missy's face fell and she grabbed Jordan's arm. "You two aren't together, are you? I mean, I wouldn't go after him if he were married."

"No, Gavin and I aren't—" Her head was swimming, and she clutched the basket almost to the point of pain. "But didn't you—I mean, I thought I heard that you and Gavin *dated* after I left town—after graduation."

"What?" Missy declared loudly. An older woman glanced at her disapprovingly in passing, but Missy didn't notice. "No way. Oh, don't get me wrong; me and every other girl in town tried to nab Gavin after you split, but the guy wasn't interested. Your buddy Suzanne tried harder than anyone, but he didn't bite. That fall when most of our class went away to college, he joined the military, I think."

"Suzanne?" Jordan asked quietly, trying to keep her voice even. "You mean my friend Suzanne? She was after Gavin?"

"You didn't know that?" Missy's voice was laced with incredulity. "I guess you aren't friends with her anymore."

"No. Well, I lost touch with most people after I moved away."

"Uh, yeah. Well, no great loss on that *friend*." Missy let out an undignified snort of laughter. "She was all over his sexy ass like the day after you left. She played nursemaid to his broken heart. Bringing him cookies and shit." Missy rolled her eyes. "Whatever. It was like a hundred years ago, right?"

The phone in Missy's back pocket started ringing. Jordan barely heard her as she said a quick good-bye, made air-kisses, and hurried out of the store to take her call.

Shocked and increasingly furious, Jordan made her way to the register.

On the drive home with the girls chattering away in the backseat, she could not stop thinking about what Missy told her.

Suzanne had lied. Gavin never slept with Missy or anyone else. Suzanne lied to keep Jordan away so she could have him for herself. Tears pricked the back of Jordan's eyes. How could she have been so stupid? How could she have believed that lie so easily and completely?

The weight of her mistakes and the choices from her past settled over her and threatened to crush her.

Jordan pulled the car into the driveway of the gray, saltbox Cape Cod cottage as the familiar and almost comforting urge to run pulled at her, called to her.

"We're home!" Gracie exclaimed. "Home again, home again, jiggety jig."

"I'm pooped." Lily unbuckled her seat belt and let Gracie out of her booster. "Camp was fun but I'm glad we're home."

Jordan shut off the engine and squeezed her eyes shut.

No more running…they were home.

Chapter 4

GAVIN STIRRED THE CHILI IN THE ENORMOUS STEEL POT on the stove and turned down the flame on the burner. He'd burned the bottom of it more than once, which of course led to endless razzing from his team. Having the fire chief burn food was ironic and more than a little sad—and happened more often than he cared to admit.

"Which of your culinary delights is it tonight?" Bill, one of his newest and best firefighters, leaned over Gavin's shoulder and lifted the lid briefly before breathing deeply. "Ah! It's the chief's famous burnt chili."

"Cut the crap," Gavin said with a laugh. He sprinkled in more salt and pepper before stirring the chili again. "I only burned it once or twice."

"Dude"—Bill scoffed and made a face—"once was enough."

"Not all of us can be awesome cooks like Rick."

"It's true," Rick said with a sigh. He grinned and laid his cards on the table in a fan shape. "Or as good at poker. A royal flush, boys. Read 'em and weep!"

Groans and a few swear words were tossed around as Rick swept up his winnings and laughed loudly. Gavin glanced over his shoulder at the guys who were playing poker at the worn, well-used butcher-block table. That old table served as the center of their world here on the second floor of the station. The common room and kitchen area were part of one large space that served as their hurry-up-and-wait room. How many days and nights had they all spent here together? Some of the guys were here more than at their own houses, and Gavin was one of them.

What did he have to go home to? An empty cottage. No wife. No kids. And that was done by design…or was it? Was that something he told himself to feel less lonely? Hell, until recently he hadn't felt lonely at all. Not really. But now that Jordan was back in town, Gavin was starting to acknowledge that there was a hole in his life. Maybe it had always been there. A tiny gap, a space that could only be filled by her. Until a couple of weeks ago it was barely noticeable.

But not anymore.

With each passing day and every time Gavin walked past that damned flower shop or looked at the little gray Cape Cod on the beach, the hardly recognizable pinprick of emptiness grew larger. Lately it was feeling like the damn Grand Canyon.

"You know, Chief," Bill said as he pulled out a chair and joined the other three guys, "for a guy who's been in this house longer than any of us, I'm kinda surprised you don't like cookin'."

"Are you kidding?" Rick chimed in. He was Gavin's best friend and the other veteran firefighter amid the youngsters and volunteers. "If he could get out of cooking, he would. But that would mean admitting defeat, and if there's one thing Gav won't do, it's admit when he's been beaten."

Gavin went to the fridge and snagged the sour cream but didn't miss the knowing look his friend gave him. Why did he get the distinct impression that Rick wasn't talking about cooking?

"On that note, you get dish duty tonight, Rick." Gavin slid the container onto the counter and tossed the dish towel to his friend. "Chili's ready and it's not burned. Next week I'm making meat loaf and potatoes."

"Will wonders never cease," Rick teased. He twirled the towel in the air. "You're a regular Julia Child."

"Ah, stick it in your hat." Gavin shook his head and chuckled while he wiped down the counter. "Not all of us can be culinary wizards like you."

"You want in on the next hand?" Bill shuffled the deck and nodded toward the empty chair. "We got room for one more."

"No thanks." Gavin glanced at the clock. It was almost closing time at the flower shop. "I have some paperwork to catch up on at my desk. You guys go ahead."

"*Chicken!*" Rick shouted after him.

Gavin waved him off and made his way down the hall to his office. He did have paperwork. Plenty of it. He should put his butt in the chair and get to it, but he didn't. Instead he slipped into his office and went to the window, the one that gave him a perfect view of the little flower shop across the street.

———

Gavin had spent the better part of the past two weeks trying like hell not to think about Jordan. Good luck to that stupid plan. What were the odds that she was going to start working across the damn street from the firehouse, so that he'd have to see her every damn day? He was starting to think that the universe was conspiring to make him crazy, torturing him for the fun of it.

"You want me to straighten out the gear, Chief?" David Heffernan asked, his squeaky voice interrupting Gavin's private pity party.

The kid had liked helping out so much last weekend during his *punishment* that he'd asked if he could stay on and volunteer from time to time. He was too young to be a volunteer firefighter, but he wasn't too young to start learning his way around the business.

"What?" Gavin snapped. He turned and went to his desk, trying not to look like he'd been caught staring out the window at the flower shop, hoping to get a glimpse of Jordan. Even though that's exactly what he'd been doing. "Sorry, kid. I was thinking about something. What did you ask me?"

"The gear." David jutted his thumb over his shoulder and shuffled his feet nervously. "It looks a little messy down there, and I figured maybe I could straighten it out. But I don't wanna mess with it if—"

"Yeah, that'd be great." Gavin gave the kid a reassuring smile when the boy bit his lip. Who could blame him? Gavin had practically taken his damn head off for no reason. "Make sure everyone's turnout gear is in the right spot and ready to go in case we get a call. You can bug out after that."

"Thanks, Chief."

"Hey, kid?" Gavin's voice stopped the boy dead in his tracks. "You really like this, don't you?"

"Yes, sir." David nodded enthusiastically. "What you guys do is about the most badass thing I've seen in real life. I mean, you see stuff like this in movies and video games, but, man, that's nothing compared to the real thing. It's a total rush. Way cool."

"What about your brother?" Gavin glanced out the window again before cursing himself for his foolishness. "I haven't seen him here since your official community service was up. He doesn't share your enthusiasm?"

"Nah." David shook his head and shrugged, an air of disappointment flickering over him. "He's more interested in taking out our boat. He's actually kinda pissed at me. We were supposed to do one of the local regattas this summer, but I bailed on him."

"Why?"

"I'd rather do this." David shrugged in the classic noncommittal teenager way and stuck his hands in the pockets of his shorts. "What you guys do is important. I dunno. He'll get over it. Our cousin is gonna do it with him instead. Thanks, Chief."

"You bet." Gavin nodded.

"And I know I said it before, but I really am sorry about pulling that alarm." He ran his hand through his hair. "I shouldn't have let Robert do it. He's always getting me into trouble one way or another. Ever since we were little. Anyway, I'm sorry."

"We all make mistakes, David." Gavin's heart went out to the kid. He knew all too well that some mistakes were worse than others and not as easily atoned for. "Let's consider it done. And if you're hungry, get on in the common room and grab yourself some chili."

"Thanks." Backing out of the office, the kid promptly bumped into and bounced off of Rick's barrel-shaped chest. Scurrying around him, David mumbled, "Sorry, sir."

"That kid makes me nervous," Rick muttered under his breath as the boy disappeared down the hall. Turning his tanned face to Gavin, he grinned wickedly. "But not as nervous as I make him."

"You're mean." Gavin laughed and shook his head. Forcing himself not to look back out the window, he went to his desk and shut down the computer. "He's been a big help this week."

"Yeah, he's okay." Rick sat in the wooden chair across from Gavin and hoisted his boot-clad feet on top of the desk. "But I'm surprised you noticed."

"What's that supposed to mean?" Gavin sat down and busied himself with organizing the reports that were strewn across his desk. Paperwork was his least favorite part about the administrative position of fire chief. "I'm the one who gave him the job."

"You know damn well what it means." Rick's voice grew serious. "Ever since *she* got back to town, you've had your head up your ass."

Gavin stilled and slowly turned his eyes to meet Rick's. They'd been friends a long time and the guy knew him about as well as his own brothers, but Gavin was still his boss.

"Is that so?" Folding his hands on the desk, he kept his voice even. "Even if it were true, I don't see how it's any of your damn business."

"Well, your love life might not be my business, but *you* having your head up your ass sure is. It's dangerous and you know it." Rick dug a piece of gum out of his pocket and unwrapped it before popping it into his mouth. He crumpled the wrapper and tossed it at the wastebasket by the window, then put both hands in the air when it landed noiselessly in the bin. "Two points."

"Duly noted." Gavin rose to his feet and struggled to keep his temper in check. He wasn't pissed at Rick for being out of line; it was exactly the opposite. "Anything else?"

"Yeah."

Rick dropped his feet from the desk and stood up. He might have been shorter by a few inches, but he was as broad and didn't back down from anyone or anything. He was a hell of a firefighter and an even better friend.

"When are you gonna stop being a stubborn dick and go over there and talk to her? Listen, I may not have been around when you two dated back in the Stone Age, but according to Maddy, you and Jordan were like peas and carrots until she split for New York." Rick frowned. "Why did she split anyway?"

"Hell if I know," Gavin said in a huff. "It was a hundred years ago."

"Yeah, well, it might've been, but based on the way you've been acting since she got back to town, I'd say you still have it bad."

"It's ancient history." Gavin lowered his voice. "Like you said, the Stone Age."

"Don't give me that shit." Rick poked Gavin in the chest. "The only woman you've dated since I've known you was that crazy Suzanne broad. At the rate you're going, you're a regular candidate for the seminary. Here's the way I see it. There are only two reasons why a single guy isn't out prowling around for a date on a Friday night. One—his equipment don't work. And two—"

"My equipment is just fine," Gavin interjected quickly.

"And two—he's hung up on a broad he thinks he can't have."

"Aw, come on, man." Gavin made a scoffing sound and waved one hand dismissively. "Damn it, Rick. She left. Fifteen years ago, the woman split without a word and *then* she married someone else. What could I possibly have to say to her? She's married. End of story."

"No wonder you didn't become a cop." Rick leaned across the desk. A slow smile cracked his weathered face, and he slapped Gavin on the cheek playfully. "She's not, genius."

"Not what?" Gavin's head spun with a hundred questions as Rick strode over to the door of the office. A painfully cruel glimmer of hope tugged at Gavin's heart. "Rick? What the hell, man? Not what?"

"If I tell you, you have to promise me that you're gonna pull your head out of your ass long enough to go over there and talk to her." Rick turned around slowly and leaned against the doorjamb. "Deal?"

"Fine," Gavin said with pure exasperation. "It's my mother's birthday tomorrow, and I have to order flowers for her anyway. Now spill it."

"Maddy told me and swore me to secrecy, but since you asked, I can tell you." Folding his arms over his burly chest, he nodded toward the window and winked. "Jordan's not married anymore."

"What?" A combination of relief, fear, and hope shot through Gavin like fire. "When?"

"Divorced. About six months ago, I think." Rick shrugged. "I dunno. Something like that. Apparently, the guy was a real piece of work."

"And you planned on telling me this when?" Gavin moved across the room, slowly closing the distance between himself and Rick. Hands on his hips, irritation edged his voice. "How long have you known?"

"Maddy told me when I overheard her on the phone with Jordan. Not long before she came back." He held up both hands. "And before you flip out, yes, I knew Jordan was moving back here, and, no, I didn't tell you because, like I said, Maddy swore me to secrecy. I wasn't allowed to tell you about Jordan's divorce unless you asked." He slapped Gavin on the shoulder. "Which you did. Kind of."

"Divorced?" Gavin walked to the window and stared at the flower shop. "Why didn't she tell me?"

"Have you given her a chance, or have you been sitting over here with your dick in your hand for the past two weeks?"

Gavin stilled as the weight of Rick's question hit him. No, he sure as hell hadn't given her a chance. All he'd done was give her a big, fat attitude along with the chip on his shoulder. *Damn it all.* Gavin turned to respond to his friend, but the doorway was empty and he was once again alone. Letting out a breath, he ran both hands over his face vigorously.

He peered out the window again and squinted against the glare of the sun that flashed off the shop's glass door. He watched it close slowly behind a customer while the latest bit of news sank in.

Jordan was divorced and back in Old Brookfield to start over.

Maybe that was something they could do together.

Jordan's first week at work had been busy, to say the least. At the moment the shop was empty, and the quiet was a welcome relief. Between weddings and graduation parties, they might have used up almost every flower in the state. Maddy had new deliveries coming in every day, and it didn't look like business was going to slow down anytime soon. Luckily Jordan wasn't there alone. The floral designer, Veronica, and her assistant, Cookie, ran the back room like the couple of pros they were. Jordan's job was to handle the customers and keep the showroom area presentable.

At first the job was merely a way to pass the days and keep her mind focused, but she was quickly finding it was more than that. She really enjoyed working with the customers and being around the flowers. The offhanded comment Maddy had made about buying the store lingered in Jordan's mind. Because they'd been so slammed, there had been more than one occasion when Veronica and Cookie were out on a job or buried in work in the back, leaving Jordan to handle any walk-in requests. It turned out she had a flair for floral design, and she enjoyed creating bouquets more than she had ever expected she would. *Who knew? Certainly not her.*

It was a good thing they'd been so busy because she barely had time to stare out the window and look for Gavin.

Barely.

When she asked for the job, she hadn't realized she'd be able to see the firehouse and all of the comings and goings.

Nope. That was a lie.

Somewhere in the back of her mind, she'd known damn well she'd be able to look over there any time she wanted. To get a glimpse of that tall, broad-shouldered frame and remember what it had been like to be held in those arms. After her marriage to Ted, Gavin's tenderness had been even more evident. In hindsight, no one had ever made her feel as special and perfect as Gavin did. Hindsight was a cruel bitch. It made you realize you'd had something beautiful but pissed it away with childish impulsiveness and pride.

Jordan dusted off the display counter and shook her head at the stubbornness of her youth. Now, here she was, a grown woman with two small daughters, pining over her high school boyfriend and fantasizing about him like a silly girl.

It was a waste of time to keep thinking about a guy who obviously had zero interest in being around her. He knew she was in town, and she'd caught enough glimpses of him at the station to know that he was totally aware she worked nearby. But the guy had made himself scarce. When she ran into him at the market, he got out of there so fast that he practically left skid marks. Any notions Jordan had about a reunion with Gavin were quickly being squashed.

"I must have a screw loose," she muttered under her breath. Satisfied the counter was clean, she squatted down and put the cleaning supplies away in the cabinet beneath the register. "Yup. There's definitely something wrong with me."

"Are you looking for confirmation on that?" Jordan's heart lurched in her chest as Gavin's familiar baritone filled the shop. "Or am I supposed to argue with you?"

She'd been so caught up in her own world that she hadn't even heard the door open. Rising slowly to her feet, she clutched the edge of the counter and prayed that she would still be capable of speech. His handsome face came into view, those pale green eyes met hers, and a slow smile spread over his face. It set that swarm of butterflies loose in her belly. He looked as strong and sexy as ever, dressed in his blue uniform. The T-shirt with the white emblem molded over his sculpted torso like a second skin.

"Something tells me you would be more likely to confirm that statement than to argue with it." Unsettled by his unexpected visit, Jordan adjusted the ceramic mug full of pens next to the register. Folding her hands on the glass counter, she forced herself to look him in the eyes again and stop being such a coward. Her voice remained surprisingly steady, but inside she was a quivering mess. "Can I help you with something?"

"Flowers," he blurted out. Gavin stuck his hands in the pockets of his blue cargo shorts and shifted his weight. His six-foot-two-inch frame filled the space in the way that only he could. "It's my mother's birthday tomorrow and I want to get her some flowers. Since this is the only florist in town, I figure that you're the only one who *can* help me."

"The grocer has flowers," Jordan said, tilting her chin and daring him to admit that perhaps he wasn't merely here for a birthday gift. "If I'm not mistaken, they have a little display right by the registers. All kinds of assortments."

"True." His voice was soft but strong, and the sound of it tickled something inside of her. He took another step so he was only inches from the counter. It was close enough for Jordan to catch a whiff of that woodsy, soapy scent of his. "But they don't have what I'm looking for."

Silence, thick and full of unfulfilled desires, hung between them, and with each passing second, her heart picked up the pace. How could the sound of the man's voice have a physical effect on her? Gavin was quiet, but an unmistakable strength lingered beneath the deep timbre. A tingling warmth simmered in her belly, a sensation she hadn't experienced in years. She'd convinced herself she was no longer capable of feeling like this. Ted had reminded her time and again that she was a cold fish and terrible in bed, a woman incapable of orgasm or pleasure. Yet here she was, standing in the middle of the store, about ready to jump over the counter and accost Gavin.

How was it possible to still be insanely attracted to someone so many years later?

Say something.

"What exactly are you looking for?"

Her hands spread out on the smooth surface of the counter, the glass cool beneath her heated, sweaty palms. She found herself almost imperceptibly leaning closer to him. Meeting his challenge. For a split second, Jordan thought he might actually lean across the counter and kiss her.

"Roses," he said abruptly, breaking the spell. Jordan blinked and immediately took a step away from the counter. "I know it's been a while, but if you'll recall, my mother loves roses. Yellow ones, if you don't mind."

The grin on Gavin's face widened. It brought out that adorable dimple in his left cheek, the one that made him look like the little devil he could be.

"Yes, I remember just fine." Jordan straightened her back and tucked a stray lock of hair behind her ear. "All of the roses we have available are right over here."

That pesky chunk of hair never stayed in any pony-tail she wore. It kept falling into her face, making her feel like a mess. As if she wasn't flustered enough by Gavin's visit, now she had to feel like a slob on top of everything else! She hurried out from behind the counter and strode directly over to the refrigerator that covered the entire right side of the store.

Jordan grabbed a pair of gloves from the hook on the wall and tugged them on without looking to see if he was following. She yanked open the large floor-to-ceiling door and shut her eyes when the cold air of the refrigerator hit her. It was a welcome relief for her overheated body. But was she all hot and bothered from embarrassment or lust?

It was probably both.

"Here you go, *Mr. McGuire*." Holding the door open with her body, the cool glass pressing against her back, Jordan gestured to the flowers. She didn't look at Gavin out of fear she'd lose her sense and jump him. "Take your pick."

"Mr. McGuire?" Gavin's deep voice drifted over her, and she didn't have to look to her left to know that he'd moved in to stand beside her. The heat and presence of his body announced his arrival with tantalizing force and whispered over her bare arms in a seductive promise.

"Jordan?" His voice was gentle and pleading. The sound of it made all the tiny hairs on her arm stand at attention—or maybe it was the cold air from the fridge. "Look at me."

Sucking in a deep breath, Jordan slowly turned her head. Nope. Definitely not because of the fridge.

She expected to find the same hard, unforgiving look she'd seen in his eyes ever since she got home. She didn't. Her belly quivered—and not from the cold air. To her surprise, she saw empathy and maybe even a flicker of forgiveness. She stilled and studied him closely, worried that perhaps she was seeing what she wanted to see instead of what was really there.

When those intense green eyes peered at her from beneath thick, dark lashes, every coherent thought was driven from her mind. His mouth set in a firm line and the muscle in his jaw flickered. She was tall for a woman at five foot ten, but Gavin still managed to make her feel delicate and tiny, as opposed to tall and gangly. Around him, she felt womanly and sexy, a feeling she'd all but forgotten.

"I think we need to start over," he rasped. "And I'm not only talking about today. We need a do-over." His lips tilted. "Just like when we played kickball when we were kids, remember? A do-over."

"That's why I came back." Jordan barely recognized the sound of her own voice. "To start over." She was shaking now and that stupid hair fell into her face again. She swiped at it quickly with quivering fingers, but it refused to budge. Nervous, turned on, and totally unsure of herself, Jordan started babbling. "Me and my girls are getting a fresh start, and besides, my father's ill, and I know my mother's going to need help. I don't think that—"

Her words were cut short when Gavin pushed the hair off her forehead and slowly tucked the wayward strand behind her ear. The sweet gesture totally disarmed her and wiped all the arguments from her head. How the hell could she ever have accused him of being like her father? Gavin was nothing like him or Ted. He was sweet, thoughtful, and protective—a far cry from her old man, to say nothing of the bastard she'd married.

Sweet Jesus, she'd screwed things up so badly. How on earth could they start over? She had no idea where or how to begin.

"Why did you leave like that, Jordan?" Gavin's voice wavered and a shadow flickered across his face. "Can you at least tell me why you never called or told me where you were?"

A hundred different answers ran through her head. *My father hit me. Suzanne said you were screwing Missy Oakland. I was angry and stubborn. I was scared.* All of those reasons and several more rose to the surface, but what was the point of rehashing the past?

"Does it matter?" she asked quietly.

"It matters to me." His dark brows furrowed and that stubble-covered jaw clenched. "I'm nothing like your father."

His words slammed into her, making her recall her terrible accusation. Regret filled Jordan in an instant and practically choked the air from her lungs.

"I know that," she whispered. "And I'm so sorry I said that to you, Gavin. I was childish and angry and hurt and—"

"And stubborn," Gavin interjected.

"Fine, and like always, I was stubborn. But, Gavin, too much time has passed." Jordan sucked in a shaky breath. She held his heated stare, every fiber of her body coming to life as the pad of his fingers rasped over her flesh. Thinking was becoming increasingly challenging, and if he kept this up, she was going to jump his bones right here in the flowers. "It's not only about me... My girls..."

"I know. I met them, and I have a feeling Lily, Grace, and I are gonna get along great. It's *you and me* that I'm talking about. Please, Jordan." The sound of her name on his lips was painfully sweet. Gavin inched closer while cradling her cheek. "Say yes," he whispered. "Give *us* a do-over. I want to get to know you again. I've missed you. I miss my friend."

She almost whimpered in agreement. God, how she'd missed him. She lay awake some nights with her eyes squeezed shut, trying to recall the feel of his hands on her, the deep lovely sound of his voice that surrounded her like a blanket, and the warm weight of his body against hers. Each year that passed made it harder to remember, but now here he stood, bringing all of those delicious memories to the surface.

He ran his thumb over her lower lip as his gaze skittered over her face. Jordan's belly tightened in anticipation. He was going to kiss her. After all this time and all these years, it was really going to happen.

And she was going to let it.

Never mind that they were practically standing in a refrigerator or that they had about a hundred unspoken and unresolved issues between them. Gavin McGuire was going to kiss her, and the consequences could be damned.

Gavin leaned in and Jordan's eyes fluttered closed as she waited for her fantasy to become reality.

"Hey, Jordan?" Cookie's voice shot through the store and brought Jordan's current reality screaming into focus. "Do you know what time the delivery is coming tomorrow morning? I think it's usually at—"

Gavin swore and dropped his hand but didn't take his eyes off Jordan's.

"Oh man." Cookie giggled from the doorway of the back room. "Sorry."

"It's fine, Cookie." Jordan smiled at her and then turned back to the fridge, avoiding Gavin's heated stare. "We were looking for some yellow roses."

"Yeah, well, you know all those flowers are gonna die if you keep that door open while you're *looking*. The way you're fogging up that glass it looks like we should be keeping hothouse flowers in there."

"Did you need Jordan for something, Cookie?" Gavin asked with thinly veiled impatience. Hands back in his pockets, he took a step away from Jordan. "Or do you merely excel at crappy timing?"

"Sorry, Chief." Cookie's short purple-and-blue hair stuck out in a hundred different directions, and she winked when she peeked out from behind the swinging door. She reminded Jordan of a fairy from the stories she read to her daughters. Her tiny delicate frame, fair skin, and mischievous grin added to the girl's fae-like appearance. "It's a gift."

"That's not what I would call it," he grumbled.

"The delivery should be here by seven or so." Jordan shot Gavin a warning glance before grabbing the bucket with the yellow roses and heading over to the counter. *Space*, she thought. *We need a little space to keep things clear.* "Maddy's been here to meet the deliveries most mornings, but I told her I can be here for the one on Sunday. The woman hasn't had a minute to rest with all the summer renters coming into town this week. The girls don't have camp on Sunday, but they can come to the store with me."

"Cool." Cookie smirked and looked from Jordan to Gavin. "Way cool."

"Bye, Cookie." Gavin waved. "See ya later."

"Right." The girl stepped behind the door so Gavin wouldn't see her and gave Jordan two thumbs up before it swung shut.

Jordan's face heated with embarrassment. Gavin strolled casually around the store while she made quick work of wrapping up a dozen roses. A smile played at her lips; she did remember that they were Mrs. McGuire's favorite flower. Gavin's mom always had them around the house in the summertime. She used to tell Jordan that sunny blooms could pretty up even the darkest places. Not that the McGuire house needed any of that. It was the happiest, brightest, and most loving home Jordan had ever been in and one she wanted to emulate with her own daughters.

Even if she wasn't a McGuire.

Gavin stared out the windows to the street, and a lump formed in Jordan's throat because she wasn't a McGuire—and she never would be. Divorced with two little girls and enough emotional baggage to sink a ship, she was not exactly a catch. She was not the kind of woman who would marry into that family. No way. Gavin deserved someone far less complicated than she was. That ship had sailed, and no matter how many do-overs they gave each other, nothing could erase the past.

"Here you go," Jordan said without looking up. She placed the paper-wrapped bouquet on the counter. "A dozen yellow roses."

Gavin strode over slowly, the sound of his rubber-soled boots on the tile announcing his approach. She saw that lopsided, dimpled grin out of the corner of her eye while she punched the sale into the register. Jordan didn't look him in the eye even though she wanted to. The swirl of emotions and physical sensations she was feeling were fogging up her head the way they had fogged up the glass of the refrigerator door.

"Her birthday is tomorrow."

"Oh, right. You needed these tomorrow. I suppose you'll want them delivered." Jordan's cheeks heated. She grabbed the bouquet but stilled when Gavin's hand swiftly covered her own. Her heart hammered in her chest as the warmth of his skin spread over hers. Licking her lower lip, she whispered, "I-I guess I forgot to ask you that."

"Things happen." Gavin's voice was tight and serious. Strong fingers curled around hers and squeezed, but Jordan slipped her hand from his. His features hardened when she took a step back. "Right. Well, maybe too many things have happened."

"Maybe," Jordan whispered. Folding her arms over her breasts, she met his challenging stare with one of her own. "Life isn't a game of kickball, Gavin. We can't yell 'do-over' and make everything go away. We're not kids anymore. I'm not a kid. For goodness' sake, I *have* kids and they have to be my top priority."

"Maybe you're right," Gavin bit out. His jaw clenched again and his brows furrowed, casting a shadow over his face. "We aren't kids anymore, but hiding behind yours won't change anything either."

Anger fired up her back, and her hands curled into fists. He could call her anything he wanted, but she would be damned if he would accuse her of using her children to avoid him. She was trying to protect them from any more upheaval in their lives, and jumping back into a romantic relationship with Gavin could be dangerous. They all needed some calm after the storm, and her feelings for Gavin were anything but calm.

"How dare you?" Jordan seethed. "I am not hiding behind my children. I am trying to do what's best for them and give them some semblance of a normal life. You have no idea the kind of turmoil we've had in our lives."

"Lots of people get divorced, Jordan." Gavin's tone softened. "It's not the end of the world."

"Maybe not." Her mouth set in a tight line. She'd figured it was only a matter of time before he found out. Even though it shouldn't, being divorced made her feel like a failure. "I've got too much going on right now and too many changes in my life to get my head all screwed up by getting involved with *this*." She gestured back and forth between the two of them. "I have to focus on helping my girls adjust to their new home, to say nothing of what's happening with my mother. It's too complicated. I can't afford the risk that would be involved."

Silence hung heavily in the air, and for a second, she thought he was going to tell her to go to hell or call her out for being the coward she knew she was being. To her great surprise, he did neither. He studied her intently while holding his ground.

"How's your dad doing?" Gavin asked in the mother of all subject changes. His cell phone beeped in his pocket, and after checking it quickly, he hit a button and turned his attention right back to her. "I heard he's in bad shape."

It took her a second to find her voice. One minute they were talking about them, and the next he was asking about her father. Jordan had been away for over a decade, but that wasn't long enough for her to forget how much Gavin loathed her father. Not that she could blame him; she wasn't too fond of her father herself.

"His body finally caught up with his spirit." Jordan stilled, feeling off-kilter from the abrupt change in subject. She leaned on the counter, hoping it would keep her from shaking. She wasn't sure if she was relieved or sad that Gavin had dropped the whole do-over conversation. "He was broken inside for years and now the outside finally matches it." She nibbled her lower lip and let out a slow breath. "Anyway, tomorrow after I see to the delivery, I promised my mom I'd come out to the house with the girls."

"You haven't seen him yet? I'm surprised. I mean you've been here for two weeks." Gavin stepped closer to the counter. "Have you seen your mom?"

"Yes. My mom's been out to the cottage the girls and I are renting—"

"The Sweeneys' old place." Gavin's lips tilted and a mischievous glint flickered in his eyes. "Out by the lighthouse on Shore Road."

"Right." Jordan's heart squeezed in her chest. "By the old lighthouse."

Their lighthouse. Her face flushed at the memory of the first and only time they'd had sex. Their lovemaking had been sweet, tentative, and driven by the eager passion of inexperienced youth. The only other lover she'd ever had was Ted, and even calling him a lover was generous. That night with Gavin was the only time she could truly say she had made love with someone.

Needing to do something other than simmer beneath his stare, Jordan cleaned up the bits of stem and paper that were littering the glass surface.

"Anyway, she's been out to my place to visit with the girls. She can only come when the nurse is at the house with my father, but no, I haven't been out to see him yet. I've been avoiding it as long as I can. Anyway, I promised her I'd come to the house tomorrow to see him."

"What time?" Gavin took a step to the left and loomed in front of her, forcing her to deal with him.

"The delivery truck usually gets here at seven." Jordan continued wiping down the counter. "But it's a Sunday, so—"

"Not that." Gavin's hand covered hers, instantly bringing her cleaning to a halt. His thumb brushed along the edge of her palm, and a slow burn crackled in her belly as his flesh slid sweetly over hers. Jordan lifted her eyes to his, and that slow burn erupted into a full-on flame. "What time are you going to your mom's place?"

As she held his stare, confusion and lust fired through her. She stood taller and reveled in the comfortable weight of Gavin's fingers curled around hers. This time she didn't pull away. It felt too good, too right, and achingly familiar.

His fingertips trailed along hers, sending shivers up her spine and making all the little hairs on her arm stand at attention. Licking her lower lip, Jordan sucked in a shuddering breath and fought to find her suddenly absent voice.

"Nine."

"So, how about if I meet you and the girls here around a quarter to?"

"You want to come with me to my parents' house?" she asked with more than a little surprise and confusion. "What? Why?"

"You haven't seen your old man in over fifteen years, and he's still a son of a bitch. I don't care how sick he is, I don't think you and the girls should go there alone."

"I'll be okay," she said through a nervous laugh, not even convincing herself. "The man is bedridden, for heaven's sake. Besides, don't you have to work?"

"I'm off tomorrow." He grinned. "One of the benefits of being the chief is having Monday through Friday hours. But I'm always on call, so I'll have the radio if a call comes in that they need me for."

"He can't hurt me anymore, Gavin." Jordan's voice wavered, and even she didn't believe that was true. "He's dying."

"I know." Bringing her hand to his mouth, he brushed his lips over her knuckles and kissed them gently. Her stomach flip-flopped from the brief contact that carried a wallop. "But he can still talk, can't he?"

"Well, yes, but…"

"I've got your back, Jordan." Gavin lowered her hand to the glass counter and squeezed her fingers before releasing them. "Regardless of what went down between us, you were my friend long before anything else. I'm not letting you and your daughters go there alone."

Jordan stood behind the counter utterly speechless and feeling like a quivering pile of jelly. A combination of surprise and relief swirled through her. As much as she hated to admit it, even to herself, she felt much better knowing that Gavin was going to be there with her.

This man, the one she hadn't seen or spoken to in over a decade, expressed more kindness and concern for Jordan and her daughters than Ted had in the ten years they'd been married. She was still shaking when Gavin put a twenty on the counter before scooping up the flowers and heading to the door.

"Gavin?" She stilled. "Why?" she asked quietly. "Why would you do this for me?"

"Why wouldn't I?" he countered.

"Are you going to answer all of my questions with a question?" Jordan tried to squelch the grin that bubbled up, but to no avail. Gavin always could make her smile, even if she was annoyed with him. It was both charming and infuriating; at the moment it was charming as all get out. "The girls—" She stopped herself and said, "We've all been through the wringer and—"

"So why don't you tell me about it?"

"It's complicated, Gavin." She let out a slow breath and her shoulders sagged, the fight going right out of her. "Far too complicated to rehash here in the store."

"You're right. There'll be plenty of time for talking later. I'll see you in the morning," he said with a wink. "And tell Lily that I'll have my regular-person truck. If she gets Gracie to talk to me, I might even let 'em turn on the lights."

Flowers in hand, Gavin strode out of the store. He jogged across the street toward the station while Jordan stood there like a stunned sheep. Her body still tingled from the feel of his lips on her flesh, and her head swam from his unexpected and certainly undeserved kindness.

She had been prepared for him to hate her. That was what she'd expected, and in many ways that would have made her homecoming easier. If he hated her, then there wouldn't be anything to talk about. He'd have his life and she'd have hers.

End of story.

Until an hour ago, she'd thought her future was clearly laid out, and there would be no escaping the mistakes of her past. It looked like she was wrong—again.

The future, unlike the past, was yet to be written.

Chapter 5

GAVIN STEPPED INTO THE MUDROOM ADJACENT TO THE bright, sunny kitchen of his childhood home and was instantly greeted by the stomach-rumbling aroma of his mother's famous chocolate chip oatmeal cookies. A Beatles tune flowed from the Bose radio that sat on the windowsill above the sink. His parents were side-by-side washing pots and pans, and singing along with Paul and the rest of the boys in the band. He couldn't help but grin at the way they still, after so many years, loved being around each other.

His smile fell when his father reached around and squeezed his mom's butt.

"You two are worse than a couple of teenagers," Gavin groaned. "If I'd come in any later, who knows what I would have walked in on?"

"Tough noogies." His mother kept her hands in the sink and didn't even turn around, but she wiggled her butt at him. "You're lucky we have clothes on."

"She's not wrong," his father sang. He glanced over his shoulder at Gavin and waggled his salt-and-pepper brows. "All kinds of fun happens around here now that we live alone."

"Aw, c'mon," Gavin groaned. "Don't gross me out. I haven't had dinner yet. It was my night to cook at the station, and you know I don't eat my own cooking." He strode up to the granite island in the middle of the sunny yellow-and-white kitchen, and his eyes widened when he spotted a massive plate of cookies. "I think I should get a cookie to help me get over seeing Dad grab your butt."

"Hold it right there, mister." Before he could snag one, his mother's hand came out of nowhere and swatted his away. "Didn't you just say you hadn't had dinner yet?"

Gavin grinned widely and held out the bouquet of yellow roses. "Will you accept a bribe?"

"Yellow roses." His mother's light green eyes widened and she flashed that million-dollar smile. "My favorite!"

Scooping his mother up in a big bear hug, he kissed her soft, plump cheek. "Happy birthday a day early, Mom."

"You're such a sweet boy." She sighed. Taking the flowers over to the counter, she waved at her husband. "Charles, you be a good man and go get me a vase from the china closet."

"Which one?"

"The tall Waterford one that your mother gave us for our first wedding anniversary."

"Sure. That was only a hundred years ago. How am I supposed to remember which one that is?" Gavin's dad rolled his eyes and shrugged. Strolling past Gavin he whispered, "You know I won't get the right one, and she's gonna make me go back ten times. I don't know why the woman doesn't get it herself."

"I can hear you," she sang as she snipped the ends of the stems. "Unlike you, I am not half-deaf. It's on the bottom of the closet on the right-hand side."

Smirking at their familiar banter, Gavin sat on one of the wooden stools at the island before grabbing a cookie and gobbling it down in two bites. A glass of milk appeared in front of him, and his mother gave him a knowing look.

"Not that I'm not thrilled to have my favorite flower for my birthday," she said, arching one brow. "But—"

"This one?"

Gavin stifled a laugh. His father stood behind him in the arched doorway to the living room holding up two crystal vases which, based on the look on his mother's face, were both wrong.

"No." She sighed with exasperation. "The bottom *right* side."

He could hear his father muttering as he left the room, which elicited an eye roll from his mother.

"What was I saying? Oh yes, the flower shop." She placed two more cookies on a plate and pushed it to Gavin before making quick work of putting away the rest. "Your choice of birthday gift wouldn't happen to be due to the recent return of a certain young lady who is working at said flower shop, would it?"

"It might," Gavin said around a mouthful of cookie before washing it down with a hearty gulp of milk. "Is that a problem?"

"Not for me," she said with a shrug. Peering at him over her glasses, she arched one brow. "How is Jordan doing? I heard she and her girls rented the Sweeneys' old place down on the beach. Her mother told me Jordan got divorced a few months ago."

"Jeez," Gavin grumbled. "Did everyone know about this except for me?"

"Probably," his mother said casually.

"Why didn't you say anything to me?"

"Why would I?" she asked innocently. "If I recall correctly, the last time I brought up her name, you bit my head off and told me it was ancient history. Or was that another one of my sons named Gavin?"

"Sorry." He let out a sigh. "Well, to answer your question, she's exactly the same." He ate the last bit of chocolate chip goodness. "She's still gorgeous and stubborn as hell."

"Yes, well, you're one to talk." Trimming off the thorns, she huffed. "If stubborn were an Olympic sport, you'd have the gold medal."

Gavin wiped his mouth with the paper napkin and avoided his mother's inspecting stare. She sure did have his number. He and his brothers never got away with much because his mom always seemed to know what was going on. It was uncanny.

"So?" Wiping the excess water off the counter, she continued her inquiry. "How was it?"

"Is this it?" His dad emerged with an ornate crystal vase that, as far as Gavin was concerned, looked exactly like the two he'd brought out before. "It was on the bottom right."

"Yes, thank you." She took it from him, and he planted a kiss on her cheek.

"No extra charge for kisses." His dad winked and smacked her on the butt again. "Or that."

"Stop being fresh," she said. "Gavin was telling me about his visit with Jordan."

"Oh yeah." His dad leaned on the counter and nodded. "I heard she was back in town; I'm not surprised. Old Brookfield is always home. Besides that, her father is on his way out."

"Couldn't happen to a nicer guy," Gavin grumbled.

"Gavin Charles McGuire," his mother huffed. "That is unkind."

"Yeah? Well, so is her old man."

"He's not wrong," murmured his father.

"Be that as it may, I don't want to hear you all say things like that." She fluffed the arrangement of roses.

His mother's intelligent greenish-gray eyes peered at him from between the yellow blooms, and he was instantly reduced to feeling like a five-year-old. He fought the urge to squirm on the stool.

"He's a dying old man, Gavin, and I think it's wonderful that Jordan came home to make peace with him. Not for him but for herself. Besides, I know her mother has been itching to have her and the girls back in town. Poor woman hasn't even been able to get to know her grandchildren. Can you imagine?"

"I can't believe Jordan wants to see the old son of a bitch again." Anger shimmied up Gavin's back. "How could she forgive him after the way he treated her?"

"I'm not talking about forgiveness for him, Gavin." Her voice softened. "It's about Jordan. You can't undo the past, but you certainly can make peace with it in order to have a happier future."

Gavin nodded slowly while holding his mother's knowing gaze. Why did he think she was talking about *more* than Jordan and her father?

"Now, Charles, please take these lovely blooms out to the table in the front hall. That way I can look at them every time I come in and out of the house."

"Yes, dear." His father scooped up the vase. "We have to get a move on, or we're gonna be late for that appointment with the caterer."

"Oh, look at the time." His mother peered at the digital clock on the stove. "We have to be there in twenty minutes."

"Caterer?" Gavin picked up his plate and glass with the intention of putting them in the dishwasher, but his mother beat him to it. "For what?"

"Our anniversary party." She shut the stainless-steel door of the machine and punched a couple of buttons. Then she untied her apron and tossed it on the counter. "As you know, Daddy and I will be married forty years this August."

"That's a long freaking time," Gavin said with genuine awe.

"Yes, it is, so we decided to throw ourselves a party." She grabbed her pink purse off the little chair in the corner and murmured, "Though how it's been that long is beyond me."

"When?"

"Saturday the twenty-eighth of August, and it's going to be right out here on the lawn overlooking the ocean. We've got a big tent rented and an eight-piece band. The whole shebang!"

"It sounds more like a wedding," Gavin said, rising to his feet.

"Well, I can't very well wait for one of you boys to get married, now can I?" She scooted around the corner of the granite island and patted his cheek. "The rate you all are going, I'm never going to have any grandchildren. My goodness, God certainly does like to take his time. I mean, for heaven's sake, it took me almost ten years to get pregnant with you. But then look at what we got. Five boys! I can only imagine how many grandchildren we'll *eventually* have. If waiting all those years to have my children taught me anything, it's to have patience and have faith. But you boys aren't getting any younger…"

"Mom," Gavin groaned.

"Oh stop it, I'm only teasing." She waved her hand in the air and swept past him toward the living room. "Anyway, save the date for the party. Speaking of the flower shop, I told Maddy what we're looking for, and she already gave a preliminary list to Veronica and Cookie. I'm sure they'll put together some lovely centerpieces. If you happen to see Jordan again, let her know I'll be in on Monday to confirm everything."

"I'm…going to see her tomorrow actually."

"Really?" She lingered in the doorway and adjusted the purse on her arm. "Getting me more flowers?"

"No." Gavin shuffled his feet and stuck his hands in his pockets, suddenly feeling self-conscious. "Like I said, she's going out to see her old man and I offered to go with her."

The smile on his mother's lips widened slightly and that knowing twinkle glinted in her eyes.

"It's not like that," Gavin insisted. "She was my friend before anything else, and I don't trust that old SOB. Hell, she hasn't seen him or spoken to him in fifteen years."

"Whatever you say, Gavin." His mother waved as she left. "Close the door on your way out."

Gavin let himself out the side door of the kitchen. Thoughts of Jordan stayed on his mind. Once he'd set eyes on her again in the shop and gotten close enough to breathe in her scent, Gavin had about lost his mind. Any anger or bitterness he'd felt vanished. Memories of their night in the lighthouse. Stolen kisses under the bleachers. The smell of her skin, the soft, velvety feel of it as it rushed beneath his fingers. Damn. What he wouldn't give to touch her like that again.

To love her.

He'd offered to go with her to her parents' place without thinking about it. He couldn't bear the idea of her and those two little girls being in the presence of such an ugly, angry man. Offering to go along had seemed like the most natural thing in the world. And that probably made him crazy or stupid, because Jordan was right.

They did have things to talk about—lots of things— and he had a bunch of unanswered questions for her. But staring into those deep, soulful eyes of hers, all he could think about was keeping her safe. Jordan's old man wasn't a danger to her physically anymore, but words could still carry a hell of a punch. His need to protect Jordan was as strong and deep-seated today as it had been fifteen years ago.

His mind drifted to their fight at the lighthouse. He'd acted like a macho, overbearing dickhead, but that was because he'd been scared—not for her, but for himself. The ironic part was that he'd said all that stuff because he didn't want to lose her. In the end, that's exactly what had happened.

As he made his way across his parents' sprawling lawn toward his cottage, the fresh ocean air filled his head. The feel of it helped him push aside those uncomfortable memories. Growing up here was a blessing and a curse; no other place on earth could hold a candle to

their family home on the bluff. He'd been stationed
around the world during his ten years in the military,
but nowhere even came close to the beauty and serenity
of Old Brookfield.

The sun started to set, the sky burning in bright hues
of orange and pink along the horizon. The lighthouse
and the little row of houses lay below along the strip of
sandy beach beneath the bluff. The Sweeneys' gray saltbox cottage was a few houses away from the lighthouse,
the one with the long gravel driveway. The house had
been empty for the past two years. But not anymore. For
the first time in a long time, it was alive inside.

Staring at the shoreline, Gavin couldn't help but
smile. At the moment, he and that damn house had a lot
in common.

Jordan double- and triple-checked the delivery list
against what had come in, while the girls colored quietly at a table in the back room. She'd checked the list
when the guys unloaded everything into the cold storage
room, but going over it again couldn't hurt. It would also
keep her mind off the fact that Gavin would be arriving
any minute.

She tapped the pencil against her chin and stared at
the steel door of the refrigerated storage room. As with
the delivery, she'd gone over yesterday's experience
with Gavin countless times; she'd had a hell of a time
falling asleep last night.

She could have refused his offer. Told him "thanks
but no thanks," and that she and the girls would be
fine. But she hadn't. Jordan had been struggling to

keep her head above water for so long that the notion of having someone help her was both a relief and completely horrifying.

Especially when that someone was Gavin McGuire.

What the hell was she doing? She'd intended to come back home and set up a stable new life for her daughters, not start mooning over her long-lost love. Frustrated and bordering on nausea from fried nerves, Jordan went to the tiny pink-and-white powder room in the back corner of the workroom. Grace was humming a tune, swinging her sandal-covered feet over the linoleum floor, and she paused to give her mother a wide grin.

"You have to go potty, Mama?" Grace asked with a giggle. "I like that bafroom 'cause it's pink."

"Nope." Jordan laughed. Grace was obsessed with bathrooms, even if she didn't have to go. Anytime they went to a restaurant, the girls would make a point of visiting the ladies' room; the fancier the bathroom, the better. "I'm going to wash my hands because we'll be going to Meemaw's house in a little while."

Jordan placed the clipboard on the table between the girls and peered at their drawings. Her chest ached when she saw Lily's. It was only the three of them. No sign of their father anywhere. For the first month or two after Jordan left Ted, the girls would ask for him. But when he stopped calling and didn't come see them, they didn't take long to get the hint.

It was heartbreaking and infuriating at the same time. She could kill Ted for being such a heartless bastard. But she wasn't just pissed at him. Not at all. Jordan was even angrier with herself for being such a poor judge of character and choosing a man like Ted as the father of her children. Oh, he had been charming at first but that didn't last long. By the time she'd figured it out, her daughters were paying the price for her bad decisions. That was something she'd never forgive herself for.

"Look, Mama." Lily pushed her picture over and grinned, pointing a yellow crayon at the paper. "That's you and me and Gracie at our new house. I like it better here than being in the city."

"It's beautiful, baby." Jordan smoothed the back of Lily's hair and fought the swell of emotion. Keeping these girls safe and assuring they didn't have a volatile childhood like hers was Jordan's top priority. "I like it better here too."

"Then how come we never came here before?" Lily picked up a blue crayon and started coloring the sky behind the house she'd drawn. "It's pretty and I love the ocean. It smells nice."

"It's complicated, Lily. The important thing is that we're here now, and I know Meemaw is so excited to have you come to her house today." Jordan looked at her watch and her gut clenched. It was quarter to nine and Gavin would be here any minute. "It's almost time to go, so clean up the crayons. Okay, girls?"

Shoving aside the cavalcade of emotions, Jordan slipped into the little powder room and shut the door. Leaning her hands on the white porcelain sink, she let out a long, slow breath. She looked at her reflection in the mirror. There was no denying the years that had passed. She was no longer the young girl with a fearless spirit, but a woman clinging to her sanity.

As if going to see her father wasn't stressful enough, now Gavin had been inserted into the mix. Jordan let out a curt laugh before turning on the water and washing her hands free of the residue from the flower boxes. The funny thing was, she was more nervous about riding in the car next to Gavin than she was about seeing her father. Nervous and excited.

The old man couldn't hurt her anymore, but Gavin was another story entirely. After their little encounter yesterday, it was obvious that she was still fiercely attracted to him. If they continued spending time together, there was a good chance they'd end up in bed. The prospect of getting involved with him again physically was intriguing, to say the least, but there was no way it could only be a physical relationship.

Not with Gavin.

In addition to wanting to strip him naked and lick him like a lollipop, she also had the urge to crawl into his arms and stay there forever. That little fantasy was a far more dangerous desire to entertain. It would mean gambling her heart, and that wasn't a risk she was willing to take. What if they did try and things didn't work out? What then? Move away? No. Her daughters needed stability.

She couldn't afford a risk like that, and neither could her girls.

Jordan dried her hands with a paper towel and tossed it into the little wicker wastebasket before giving her reflection one last look. She'd told herself she chose the light-blue eyelet sundress because it was the first thing she grabbed out of the closet, but that was a big, fat lie. Smoothing the fabric of the skirt, she let out a sound of frustration and rolled her eyes at her conflicting emotions.

Blue was Gavin's favorite color.

"You are a jackass," Jordan whispered at her own reflection. She pointed at the mirror. "Yup. A great big idiot. And now you're talking to yourself."

Shoving aside the internal argument, Jordan swung the door open and found Lily closing the Tupperware box full of crayons. Jordan scooped up the clipboard and kissed Gracie's head before tugging gently on her pigtail.

"Where's your picture, kiddo?"

"Lily took it." Gracie giggled and covered her mouth with both hands.

"She drew a picture of a bathroom." Lily held up the drawing, a swirling mass of pinks and purples, with a stick figure that was probably supposed to be Jordan. "What a weirdo."

"It's a princess bafroom," Grace proclaimed proudly. "I need glitter, but we didn't have any."

"We'll get some at the store next time we go shopping, okay?" Jordan brought the clipboard over to Maddy's desk on the far side of the room and slipped it onto the shelf. "Because what princess bathroom is complete without glitter?"

"Goody!" Gracie clapped her hands furiously and squealed with delight. "And Meemaw said we could make brownies at her house today."

"It's only nine in the morning, Gracie. It might be a little early for brownies."

"Nuh-uh." Gracie shook her head. "It's never too early for brownies."

"Mama," Lily asked innocently, "when will the fireman be here?"

The question had barely escaped her daughter's mouth when Gavin's voice boomed from the front of the store. Even though the shop was closed, Jordan had left the front door open for him.

"Anybody home?" The little bell by the register dinged three times. "Oh well," he sang in a painfully familiar way. "I guess I'll have to eat these doughnuts all by myself."

"Doughnuts?" To Jordan's surprise, Lily scrambled off the folding chair, grabbed her sister's hand, and ran to the swinging door. "Come on, Gracie."

Sucking in a deep breath as the door swung shut behind the girls, Jordan leaned both hands on the long, stainless-steel worktable.

"I'll be right behind you," Jordan called. "I have to make sure everything is secured back here."

She grabbed her purse, shut off the lights, and double-checked the back door, making sure it was locked. Satisfied everything was taken care of, and unable to think of any other reason to stall her exit, she stared at the swinging door. Sweat trickled down her back, and her quivering fingers clutched the leather strap of her bag. She could do this. It was no big deal. Like Gavin said, they were friends first. That's all that was happening now. He was being a friend. That was it.

Steeling her courage, she followed the girls out to the main showroom. The scene that greeted her stopped her dead in her tracks. Lily and Gracie were staring up at Gavin, white sugar powder on their grinning faces and half-eaten doughnuts in their hands. He was wearing a white T-shirt and plaid board shorts, and looked every bit as lickable as he had yesterday.

Drat.

He stood with his broad-shouldered back to Jordan, both arms extended toward the girls, and his hands curled into fists. A smile curved her lips as he charmed her daughters, the same way he had when Jordan had first moved to town in fourth grade. It was how he had introduced himself to her on the playground, and to Jordan's delight, the sweet disarming greeting was even more adorable today.

"Okay, take your best shot." He wiggled his wrists. "Which hand?"

"That one," Lily exclaimed, slapping his left fist.

"Nope." Gavin opened his hand to reveal an empty palm. "Wrong again!"

The girls dissolved into giggles as Gavin opened his right hand, a quarter firmly fixed at the center of it.

"Looks like I get to keep my quarter."

"I'm surprised you haven't taken that act on the road," Jordan said playfully. "If memory serves, I never did guess correctly."

"Mama," Lily said breathlessly, "did you know that Mr. McGuire can do magic tricks? He made a quarter come outta Gracie's ear and then made it disappear."

Gracie nodded and took a bite of her doughnut.

"I know." Jordan flicked her gaze from Lily to Gavin, and her stomach swirled into knots of hope and regret. "Did he tell you that he showed me that trick when we were kids?"

"You mean you learned that when you were a little kid?" Lily asked.

"Sure did." Gavin winked at Jordan before offering the quarter to Lily. "Maybe later I'll show you how it's done. But then you have to promise not to tell anyone unless it's another magician. Deal?"

"Deal." Lily nodded and wrapped her fingers around the quarter while gobbling up the rest of her doughnut. "Can I tell Gracie?"

"I dunno." Gavin made a face and bent at the knees so he was eye level with the girls. Leaning his forearms on his thighs, he folded his hands and gave them an overly serious stare. "Do you want to be a magician too, Gracie?"

Gracie nodded furiously but nuzzled closer to her sister, clearly in awe of and a little intimidated by Gavin.

"She says yes," Lily said.

"Well, I suppose that's good enough for me."

"Thanks, Mr. McGuire."

"Call me Gavin or Chief, okay, girls? 'Mr. McGuire' has me looking over my shoulder for my dad." Rising to his feet, Gavin snagged the brown paper bag off the counter and turned around, offering one to Jordan. "Doughnut?"

"Thanks." She swallowed the lump in her throat and held his gaze. "Chief."

Gavin shook the bag temptingly and cocked his head, giving her that narrow-eyed gaze he'd given so many times before. The one that screamed...*I dare you*.

"They're good," he sang. "And calorie-free. Fat-free too. Right, girls?"

Lily and Gracie laughed as Jordan peered inside the wrinkled opening, and her smile grew when she spotted her favorite kind.

"Chocolate glazed?"

"Your favorite," he said quietly, those intelligent green eyes studying her closely. "At least it used to be."

"Still is." Jordan took the doughnut and moved past him. When her bare arm inadvertently brushed his, a shiver skittered up her back and almost had her tripping over her own feet. "Thanks," she said, while trying to walk in a straight line.

"Anytime," Gavin murmured.

As she locked up the shop, all Jordan could think about was sitting in the front seat of the car next to Gavin. The warm summer sun blazed down on them, and if it weren't for a gentle breeze, the July air would be positively stifling. Or maybe it wasn't the sun. Maybe being near Gavin had Jordan overheated.

"Mama, can we ride in the chief's big truck?" Lily twirled around on the sidewalk before clasping her hands together in the traditional begging stance of a child. "Please? He said that we can even turn on the whirly lights."

Before Jordan could answer her question, the sirens at the firehouse started to blare in the clear warning of a fire in progress. It looked like fate had stepped in and saved her from what was sure to be a stomach-churning situation. Gavin swore and went to the open window of his truck, grabbing his radio. Jordan didn't have to hear him to know what was going on.

Lily and Grace covered their ears with their hands and scrunched up their faces as the sirens continued to wail. The doors of the firehouse rolled up. Opening the back door of the car, Jordan ushered the girls in and fought the wave of disappointment. *Jeez.* She was a conflicted mess.

"Lily," Jordan shouted over the siren, "help Gracie into her booster seat, okay?"

She shut the door and turned around to find Gavin right behind her. She stepped back but didn't go far, her ass hitting the side of the car with an undignified *oomph*.

"I have to go," Gavin said, his face a mask of concern. He watched the truck pull out and turn right down Main Street, and the muscle in his stubble-covered jaw flickered with unmistakable tension. "I'm sorry but—"

"Go." Jordan waved him off and folded her arms over her breasts. "It's fine and it's the thought that counts." She held his serious stare as he studied her reaction closely. She could tell he was torn about going, but she also knew he didn't really have a choice. "I mean it, Gavin…it's okay."

"Shit. I'm sorry, Jordan." Before she could respond and assure him again, Gavin slipped his hand around the nape of her neck, pulled her close, and pressed his lips to her forehead. "I'll make it up to you."

That brief, sweet, and familiar brush of his mouth against her flesh still stole her breath. She nodded absently as he shouted, *"I'll text you."*

As Gavin drove away, the red emergency lights of his Bronco flickering wildly, Jordan knew it was for the best. She also knew he wouldn't be texting her. Letting out a laugh, she leaned against the car and tossed her head back.

He didn't have her number.

Chapter 6

STANDING IN THE HALLWAY OF HER CHILDHOOD HOME, Jordan instantly felt as though she were back in high school. She stared at the faded floral wallpaper, with its pink and yellow buds dangling on green stems. Then she sucked in a steadying breath, attempting to muster up the courage to go into her parents' bedroom. Her heart raced and her palm, slick with sweat, slid over the glass doorknob as she squeezed her eyes shut. Memories of the many frightened nights she'd spent in this old house flooded her like a tsunami. If not for the laughter of her daughters downstairs, she might actually think she really had stepped back in time.

You can do this, she thought. *He can't hurt you anymore. He's a dying old man and you're a grown woman.*

"Jordan?"

The fragile, hesitant voice of her mother drifted through the hallway. Opening her eyes, Jordan looked down at the dish towel clutched tightly in her mother's hands, which had seen more dishwater than should be legal. Her mother's pale brown-and-white dress hung over a thin frame, her shoulders hunched from years of shrinking away from her husband's rage.

"The girls want to go down the street to the park. I'm happy to take 'em there, if you can see fit to stay with your father for a little while. He's already eaten, and the nurse will be here in a few minutes to give him more pain medicine. I know you don't—"

"That's fine, Mama," Jordan said quietly. "I think Lily and Gracie would love that." She looked back at the smooth, white-paneled door of the bedroom and sucked in another deep breath. "Dad and I have a lot to talk about."

"It won't do you no good, Jordan. He don't remember anything." Her mother's voice sounded thin and raspy, and the delicacy of it tugged at Jordan's heart. "Not a lick of it."

"What?" Jordan's hand fell from the doorknob as she turned to face her mother. "What do you mean he doesn't remember? How could he not remember? Is it the medication?"

"No." Her mother's haunted, hollow-looking eyes met Jordan's, and she squared her shoulders, as though mustering up some long-forgotten courage. "It's dementia. Doc said it was brought on by the cancer. But whatever the reason, he don't remember and it won't do no good to have you bring anything up to him." Her mother's mouth set in a tight line before she took a deep breath and whispered, "He probably won't even know who you are. Besides, the man can't hardly speak anymore."

"Mama." Jordan folded her arms over her breasts, hugging herself in an effort to still her shaking body, anger and sadness swirling through her like a storm. "But you said—"

"I *know* what I said." Her teary eyes stared down at the dish towel in her hands as she let out a slow breath. "It's been so long since you came home, and I, well, I suppose

I was worried that if you thought you couldn't say your piece, then maybe you wouldn't come home at all."

A shroud of guilt hung heavily over Jordan as tears spilled down her mother's cheeks, tears that were because of her, because she'd been a coward and stayed away for so long. Jordan couldn't blame the old man for the pain on her mother's face right now. Nope. This was entirely on her.

"Oh, Mama," Jordan whispered as she closed the distance between them and gathered her mother in her arms.

In that moment, with her mother's face cradled against her shoulder, Jordan realized how much she'd missed this. How much she'd longed for her mama's hugs and the faint scent of jasmine that was so distinctly hers. With that familiar flowery smell came memories from Jordan's early childhood in Oklahoma, her life before they came to Old Brookfield. She remembered sitting on the porch with her mother. A white rocking chair and her father nearby, singing and laughing.

Like a wisp of smoke, hazy and unclear, the image hovered in her mind, teasing her before vanishing almost as swiftly as it had come.

"I'm so sorry I stayed away for so many years, Mama. But it had been so long, and so many things had gone unsaid. I guess that I thought it was too late."

That was true. When she was younger, Jordan had never thought her mother would want to see her again. After having her own children, she'd realized how silly that was. Nothing would keep her from being with her girls.

She'd spoken with her mother from time to time on the phone after Lily was born, whenever Jordan's father wasn't around, but communication had been spotty at

best. In the past couple of years, her mother had managed a few day trips to New York under the guise of
volunteer work for the church, but any more than that
was out of the question. Jordan had tried to get her to
leave, to come and live with them in New York, but she
had always refused.

Just as well, Jordan thought. It's not like her life
with Ted had been happy or stable. The irony of her life
was not lost on her. She had run away from an unhappy
home as a girl, only to end up in the same situation as a
woman. Jordan kissed the top of her mother's head and
squeezed her tightly before pulling back.

"That's why you've been able to call more in the past
few months, isn't it?" Jordan squeezed her arms gently.
"He couldn't keep an eye on you anymore."

"Yes." Her mother nodded and sniffled before swiping at her teary eyes with the dish towel. "The man don't
even know me most days, and the crazy thing is that the
dementia might be the best thing that ever happened to
him. It's like he forgot how to be ornery." She let out
a curt laugh. "Do you know he even thanked me the
other day? I about fainted. That man ain't thanked me
for nothin' in almost forty years…"

The sound of little feet pounding up the stairs echoed
through the old Colonial house, and a moment later, two
adorable blond heads peeked around the corner.

"Meemaw," Lily whined, "you said you would only
be a minute and it's been a hundred minutes."

"A hundred minutes," Grace said through a giggle.
"A hundred billion minutes."

"Well then." Her mother smiled brightly and the
beauty of it made Jordan's heart skip a beat. When she

looked at her granddaughters, that weary woman faded away and she emanated joy, a joy Jordan had rarely seen growing up. "That's a long darn time, isn't it? What do you say we go down to the playground? I heard that Laurie's grandchildren were visiting this summer too, and if I'm not mistaken, I think they're right around your age."

"Boys or girls?" Lily asked skeptically.

"Girls, I think."

"Good." Lily grabbed Gracie's hand and headed back downstairs. "Boys are smelly."

"Not the chief," Gracie said with a giggle. "He smells like doughnuts and he can do magic."

"Go on down, girls." Her mother raised her salt-and-pepper eyebrows as she cast a sidelong glance in Jordan's direction. "I'll be right behind you. Why don't you wait for me on the porch?"

"Thank you, girls."

"The chief, hmm?" Jordan's mother said a moment later, folding the dish towel into a neat square.

"Yes." Jordan straightened her back and shrugged as though it was no big deal that the girls had met Gavin. Of course, if it hadn't been a big deal, then she might have mentioned it to her mother instead of intentionally omitting it. "He came by the flower shop this morning and gave the girls doughnuts," she said, not mentioning what his original intentions were. "Don't make a thing out of it."

"Uh-huh." Her mother nodded slowly and tucked the dish towel in the pocket of her dress. "Well, I guess it ain't a problem. You aren't married no more, are you?"

Jordan fought a surge of frustration because even though her mother never said it, she could hear the disappointment in her voice. It wasn't a surprise to Jordan though, after everything she'd put up with over the past forty years. Divorce was a big old sin in Claire's world.

"No, I'm not. The divorce has been in place for months now. But I'm not dating him or anyone else, okay? Gavin is a friend. That's all. We have no plans to be anything other than that."

"Well, I'm surprised the man will still speak to you after you left the way you did." Her mother held up both hands before Jordan could say a word. "I'm your mama and there ain't nothin' in the world you could do that would make me stop lovin' you, but he ain't your family. I'm just surprised, is all. I mean, you weren't here when he came lookin' for you that day. The boy was angrier than a snake when I told him you were gone. He didn't believe me."

"Gavin came here?" Jordan's voice wavered and a lump formed in her throat. "After I left?"

"He surely did. The boy was convinced your daddy was hidin' you and keepin' you from him."

"I had no idea," she whispered. "Why didn't you tell me?"

"Didn't think it mattered." Her mother sniffed. "But maybe I was wrong and shoulda told ya."

What difference would it have made? Her mother was right. It didn't matter anymore. What's done was done, and while she couldn't change the past, she sure as hell could face it. But would he ever forgive her for leaving the way she did? For believing Suzanne's lie so easily? Why should he?

"You're right." Jordan's shoulders sagged a bit and weariness started to creep in. "It was a long time ago, Mama. Gavin and I are just friends. It's fine."

"Maybe." Her mother slipped her hands in her pockets and shrugged. "But that don't mean all that happened between you two is gonna go away just 'cause y'all want it to. Upset feelings like that have a way of bubblin' up to the surface."

"We're both grown-ups, and the past is in the past."

"That so?" Her mother grabbed the mahogany banister and nodded toward the closed door of the bedroom. "Then what are you doin' here?"

Jordan opened her mouth to respond but thought better of it.

"*Meemaw!*" Lily shouted. "Can we go now?"

"I'm comin', darlin'." Jordan's mother started down the stairs but stopped halfway before letting out a slow breath and looking back up at Jordan. "You can't change what you did to Gavin any more than your daddy can change what he did to you."

Jordan stood at the top of the stairs and listened while the girls' chatter faded as they headed off to the park with their grandmother. A smile played over Jordan's lips. She'd wondered so many times if this day would ever come—her daughters playing at the park with their meemaw. This wasn't the way she would have chosen, but at least it was happening.

Squaring her shoulders, Jordan turned around and strode across the hall to the bedroom door. Lingering outside, she reminded herself why she was here. She wanted closure with her father. No, not only wanted it but needed it, and no matter what Gavin said, he needed it too. The two of them couldn't move into the future as friends, or anything else, until they'd dealt with the past.

But first things first.

Wrapping her hand around the knob, she sucked in a shuddering breath. With all the courage she possessed, Jordan opened the door to face her past. As the hinges squeaked, she fought a sudden wave of nausea and slowly pushed the door open, preparing herself for whatever was waiting for her on the other side.

Would he look the same? Would he seem as intimidating as when she was young? Would that voice, the deep rumbling of it, still cut her to the core and stop her in her tracks?

No. She stood taller and shook her head while giving herself a good old-fashioned talking-to. She would not shrink from him or this opportunity. Dementia or no dementia, she was finally going to tell him exactly what his words did to her. She would finally, after so many years, stand up to her father and let him know that he didn't break her. She wasn't trash. She wasn't a whore.

And she sure as hell wasn't beaten by him.

With her gaze pinned to the worn wooden floorboards, Jordan settled her shaking hand on the doorjamb and forced herself to face her father. When she finally mustered the courage to confront her past and the man who'd made life remarkably unbearable, Jordan was rendered speechless.

Withered and small.

A ghost.

The old man in the bed was a shadow of who he had once been and a clear reminder that fifteen years had passed. Her father was no longer the towering, scary

figure who could shout her into submission but a frail
shell of human being. A thin blue blanket and a white
sheet were pulled up to his chin, which was covered by
a scruffy gray beard. His body, ravaged by illness and
years of drinking, lay motionless and nearly skeletal on
the bed, outlined by the covers in an almost macabre
way. His face—which had been round, ruddy, and often
twisted in anger—was gaunt and pale. The thick, blond
hair was gone. What remained was thin and white, and
reminded Jordan of cobwebs.

She stood in the doorway for what felt like hours but
was probably only a minute or two as the old man in
the bed slept. Closing the door quietly behind her, she
made her way over to the small wooden chair by his
bedside. The shade was drawn, but the sunlight stream-
ing in around the edges kept the room light enough. The
only sound in the room, aside from her father's rattled
breathing, was that of the shade bumping the windowsill
from the occasional breeze that drifted in through the
open window.

She sat there for a while in silence and stared at the
husk of a man who lay before her. Jordan had known
she'd feel anger and some fear, but the one emotion
she didn't expect to feel, the one that swelled and rose
above the rest, was sadness. Her mother had been right.
No good would come of telling him off or unloading
her anger on him. The man who'd been such a bastard,
who'd frightened her into silence and submission, no
longer existed.

That man was gone.

Much like the memories of her early childhood
in Oklahoma.

Jordan had convinced herself that those memories of him singing and laughing with her and her mother had been a dream, because the notion that he had been that way and then changed… That was almost too much to bear.

The father she'd known most of her life was now also a memory—albeit a much more vivid and unpleasant one.

Letting out a hitching breath, Jordan leaned back in the chair and folded her hands in her lap, a sense of defeat filling her.

"You were a son of a bitch," she whispered shakily.

His lips twitched at the sound of her voice and Jordan froze. Her body went numb with apprehension as his eyes fluttered open. He turned his head toward her, a soft swishing sound filling the room as his flesh rushed over the pillow. Those bushy gray eyebrows furrowed as his watery gaze settled on her, and Jordan held her breath, waiting for some sense of recognition.

An admonishment. Disapproval. Disgust.

None came.

He licked his dry lips and continued staring at her as though he had no idea who she was. Her mother had been completely right. Based on the vacant expression on his face, her father had absolutely no idea who Jordan was, let alone any recollection of what their lives had been like.

"When's the train leavin'?" he asked in a brittle, raspy voice. "Don't wanna miss it."

Jordan almost laughed out loud, but not out of humor. The ridiculousness of the question caught her completely off guard and while she knew, logically, that getting involved in any kind of conversation with a person in his condition was ridiculous, she answered his question.

"There's no train, Dad." Sitting up taller, Jordan leaned a little closer and kept her voice quiet. "You're at home."

"Can't miss that train," he croaked. "You gonna take me to the train? Where's Claire? You're not Claire."

Claire…her mother.

"No." Jordan's hands curled into fists, her fingernails dug into her palms as she fought the rising surge of anger. "I'm not Claire. I'm your daughter, Jordan. Don't you recognize me?"

"I don't have no kids." He coughed and licked his lips again. "I gotta get to the train."

Clearly he didn't know who she was, and that infuriated her. How could he forget her? She was his daughter. His only child, and he had no clue who she was.

"Yes, you do have a daughter." She let out a bitter laugh, the irony of the situation not lost on her. "Not that you ever really acted like you wanted me, at least not very often. But I *am* your daughter. I'd say that you're my father, but the truth is…you aren't…not really. I don't suppose it matters though, does it? Would it matter to you if I told you how much you hurt me? Would you care if I let you know that for years I thought I was worthless because you made sure to tell me that almost every day? Would your heart break if I said that I never really believed I was worthy of love?"

Jordan rose from her chair, her voice growing stronger with each passing word, with each layer of her confession.

"I didn't believe I was capable of truly loving anyone else until I had my daughters. Not even Gavin could get through to me, but then again, how could I believe that he really loved me? I wasn't worth it? Was I, Dad? All you ever did was tell me how worthless I was." Her voice dropped to a whisper. The mattress sagged as she settled both hands on the edge and leaned close, staring into his confused expression. "Would any of that matter to you?"

Recognition flickered across his face briefly, and for a split second, Jordan thought her words had gotten through, that somehow he'd heard her and understood. His thin, pale lips quivered and Jordan held her breath, waiting and hoping that finally, after all this time, she might get some kind of satisfaction.

But none came.

"Miss?" he rasped. "When's Claire takin' me to the train?"

Chapter 7

GAVIN STOOD OUTSIDE THE SMOLDERING WRECKAGE OF the abandoned house. Sweat trickled down his back as he stared at the charred remains. Wisps of smoke rose slowly from the structure, and the pungent chemical scent of burned plastic filled his nostrils. A sense of dread nagged at him. This house was on the outskirts of Old Brookfield and had been abandoned for the past two years. The place had gone into foreclosure and the bank still hadn't been able to unload it, but someone sure as hell had been there recently.

At least long enough to set the fire. Just like the barn blaze the other night.

"You thinkin' what I'm thinkin'?" Rick asked.

"Possibly." Dread crawled up Gavin's back and he rolled his shoulder. The scarred, puckered flesh always tingled more at a fire scene. "Let's have it."

"That Heffernan kid has been hanging around the station a whole damn lot, and now he's here at the scene of a suspicious fire. If you ask me, that's sketchy. He's too damn interested, Gav."

Rick had moved in silently next to Gavin and kept his voice quiet, obviously not wanting the Heffernan kid to overhear them. The boy had been at the station when the call came in, and since regulations prevented him from riding in the engine, he'd followed in his own car. At the moment he was sitting on the hood of his black

Honda Civic and staring in awe at the charred remains of the house.

The expression on the kid's face was nothing short of excited.

"Let's not go jumping to any conclusions. Besides, he wasn't at the barn fire the other night." Gavin adjusted his helmet. "The most intense heat came from the back left corner of the house, and I spotted a V pattern along one of the walls."

"Could have been an accident," Rick said as he glanced over his shoulder at their latest volunteer. "Maybe David and a few of the high school kids have been using the house to party. It's isolated out here, and the next house is a quarter mile down the road."

"True." Gavin nodded but he couldn't shake the feeling that it wasn't. Not by a long shot. "But I didn't see any kind of debris like that. Did you? No furniture or any kind of makeshift party pad. The place is empty and abandoned."

"Yup. Just like the barn." Rick coughed and spit a hunk of gray phlegm onto the grass. "By the time we busted out the windows and ventilated the place, it was a hot mess in there. But no, it doesn't look like a party pad gone wrong. You and I both know this was deliberate."

"Shit." Gavin rolled his left shoulder again. Keeping his gaze on the charred house, he kept his voice low. "Call the police chief and let him know we have another possible arson. I'm sure the bank will have their insurance people out here in a hot minute."

"You're gonna leave this to them?" Rick asked with more than a little skepticism.

"Hell no." Gavin started toward the house. "I'm going to have another look at the point of origin."

"All clear, Chief." Bill trotted down the front steps of the house. The newest firefighter on the team was young and eager, tall and wiry. He reminded Gavin of himself when he first started—charged up and ready to take on the world. "We'll get the hoses back on the engine."

"Nice work today." Gavin slapped him on the arm. "Rick and I need to have another look inside. Why don't you and the guys show the Heffernan kid how to get the hoses put away properly? He may as well learn something while he's sitting here."

"Roger that." Standing a bit taller, Bill strode away toward the street and waved the boy over. "Come here, kid. Let me show you a couple things."

"Now he'll be totally unbearable," Rick grumbled as they climbed the steps.

"Which one?"

"Both."

Gavin stepped through the open doorway. The smell of burnt plastic and insulation assaulted his senses, making his gut clench. Even after all these years and countless fires, it still turned his stomach.

Debris crunched beneath their boots, and the sound of water trickling filled the air as they made their way carefully through the damaged house. Most of the fire had been contained to the back of the house, but broken glass, water, and other debris littered the floor. Putting out fires was not only dangerous but messy as hell.

"There." Stepping into what used to be the kitchen, Gavin pointed to the far wall by the back door. A scorched black pattern in the clear shape of a V was seared into the wall to the left of the half-open door. "We have a clear point of origin. There's no outlet there, and even if there were, it wouldn't matter. This place hasn't had electricity since the Davidsons moved out."

"Yup." Rick moved closer and squatted down before pointing to a dark streak along the walls on what was left of the wooden floors. "Whoever did it used an accelerant too. There's a clear path away from our point of origin, and it seems to fade out just past the door."

"Son of a bitch," Gavin seethed. "We need Brian to tape off the property. Nobody else comes in here. We need to keep the area around the house secure too. Damn, this is gonna be a long day."

"I guess this puts a damper on your plans today?" Rick asked as they headed back to the front of the house. Gavin hadn't told Rick about his offer to Jordan, but Rick had obviously seen the two of them outside as he drove out of the station. "It is supposed to be your day off, you know."

"Not anymore."

—⁓—

The police chief and two of his officers showed up at the scene, and Gavin gave them the lowdown on their suspicions but refrained from mentioning the Heffernan kid. No point in throwing the kid under the bus based only on Rick's hunch. By the time the insurance adjustor and arson investigator arrived, it was well after six at night. Some guys were territorial and would have a bug up their ass if someone else came onto their turf, but not Gavin. All that mattered to him was finding out who did it and putting their crazy ass in jail.

They used up the rest of daylight taking pictures and collecting evidence from all around the property. Gavin could have left. Hell, he probably should have. But the possibility that a firebug had come to Old Brookfield kept him there. He loved this town and the people in it, and he'd be damned if someone was going to go around lighting fires and risking the lives of people he cared about.

He stayed out of the way but kept his eyes and ears open.

"Oh, it's arson, alright." Rogers was the arson investigator for the county and had been in town looking at the other site earlier in the day. He had a rough, gravelly voice, and his face was mottled by age, sun exposure, and a serious smoking habit. "This was definitely set intentionally. So was the old barn. Looks like your man forced open the back door here and squirted an accelerant of some kind before torching the place. We took samples and should be able to confirm that, but based on the visual evidence it looks like a classic torch job. I found a similar MO at the other site."

He pulled out a cigarette and made quick work of lighting it before taking a long drag. His wrinkled face scrunched up as he stared at the house, and wispy white hair flew around his balding head.

"Too sloppy to be a pro. Too soon to say for sure, but I'd say you boys have a firebug on your hands."

"We've never had any kind of arson in town." Gavin glanced at the police captain who looked as unsettled as Gavin felt. "Maybe it was someone passing through. A transient or something. The highway isn't far from here."

"Maybe, but I'm not taking any chances." The police chief took a handkerchief out of his pocket and wiped the back of his neck. "I've got two of my guys out now interviewing the neighbors. Hopefully we'll get lucky and somebody saw something."

"Could be someone passing through…or not." Rogers nodded and blew out a stream of smoke. "I'll keep you posted on what we find, but you'll know soon enough if it's a transient or someone here in your town."

"How's that?" Gavin asked warily.

"Firebugs can't stop, you see? They love it. They're obsessed with watching the flames and they get off on it. The crazies love to watch stuff burn, and once they do it, they don't stop. Hell, they can't stop." He dropped the cigarette onto the gravel along the side of the road and crushed it with the tip of his black boot. "My point is… he'll do it again. So, you'll know if you have a firebug in town because—"

"We'll have another fire," Gavin murmured.

"Yes, sir." Rogers nodded solemnly and handed Gavin his card. "Call me if you have any more trouble. I'll be in touch when the lab gets back to me."

———

Jordan tucked the girls into bed after their bath, and then, after about five minutes of squeals and begging, she caved in and gave them an extra half hour of reading time. She kissed their smooth little foreheads before leaving them to their picture books and shutting the door most of the way. She padded quietly down the hallway to her bedroom and resisted the urge to crawl right in bed and go to sleep because she was exhausted after the visit with her father.

"Exhausted" didn't cover it. Jordan was bone tired.

There was a mess in the kitchen from dinner, a lavish spread of Kraft macaroni and cheese, and she should probably go straight downstairs and clean it up, but she was desperate to change her clothes. A shower would have been optimal, but that would have to wait until later when the girls were definitely asleep. There was no point in trying to take a long, leisurely shower when it had the potential of being interrupted.

She slipped into her bedroom and quickly changed into her favorite blue tank top and black yoga capris, seeking comfort over style. Besides, she thought as she tossed her dirty clothes in the hamper, it wasn't like she'd be seeing anyone tonight.

She and the girls had stopped at the market in town on the way home, and the clerks had been buzzing about the fire. Supposedly it was arson. When Jordan heard that, she knew she wouldn't be seeing Gavin tonight. No matter how badly she might want to.

She rolled her eyes at the fantasies she'd played out in her head most of the day. The ones where Gavin rolls down the driveway in his truck and pays her a surprise visit. A visit that ends with him in her arms. Her bed. Her life.

"Get a grip, Jordan," she muttered under her breath. "The guy has been fighting a fire all day and dealing with God knows what. He's *not* going to come babysit you or your drama."

She sat on the edge of her bed and tried to pull open her nightstand drawer in search of a hair clip, but the drawer, swollen from the heat, was stuck. Jordan growled with frustration and yanked on it harder, the stubborn wood finally giving way. She grabbed the black hair clip in the back corner, but when she pulled it out, her gaze skittered over the papers and the faded red leather journal.

It was her diary from high school. That night when she ran away, she had neglected to grab it from under her mattress. After all these years, she'd forgotten about it until her mother gave it back to her the other day. At first, she couldn't quite believe her eyes, and Claire, in her typically nervous fashion, had started apologizing about how she would have given it back sooner, but...

Jordan hadn't had the nerve to read it yet. She'd stuck it in that drawer and pretended the damn thing wasn't there. Too many memories. Good. Bad. Too much regret and too many countless reminders of what could have been.

The red cover was worn and faded along the spine and around the gold lock, which wasn't really a lock, but more of a clasp. Anyone could have opened it and read it, though Claire assured her she hadn't. She was a better woman than most. How many people would find a diary and not read it?

Especially the diary of a daughter who ran away.

Jordan nibbled her lower lip and quickly swept her hair into the clip. She was being a coward. If she really was going to start over, then she had to suck it up and face her bad decisions. Acknowledge them so she could move on, and then maybe the admonishing voice of regret would vanish for good.

After another minute of staring, she finally snagged the diary out of the drawer. With shaking fingers, she pinched the clasp before it popped open with a tiny click. She cracked open the old book, its spine creaking in protest after years of solitary confinement.

What she found inside made her heart skip a beat.

It was an old Polaroid photo of her and Gavin. The captured moment in time was faded by the years, but that day they took the picture was clear as a bell in Jordan's memory.

It had been Memorial Day weekend, only a few weeks before she left. She, Gavin, Ronan, and some of their friends had been enjoying the beginning of summer on the shores of Old Brookfield. His brother had taken the picture. She was riding on Gavin's back, her arms around his neck and her cheek nuzzled against his. Their smiling faces glowed with the openness of youth and their love for each other. Tears blurred her vision as she ran one finger over the image from so long ago.

Much had changed since that day on the beach, but not everything.

Gavin was still carrying her...or trying to.

He may not be giving her piggyback rides down the beach anymore, but today he'd offered his support to her. Again. And he always would because that's who he was—who he *always had been*. He may not have been able to follow through on his offer and come with her to see her father, but he *would* have.

And wasn't that the point?

The sun was starting to set by the time all the others had left. Gavin closed up the back of his truck, after securing his spare gear. He'd learned a long time ago that his job as chief wasn't the kind of gig he could leave when he went home. He was never really off duty, at least not in his own mind.

Groaning, his body sore and tired, he got behind the wheel and snagged his cell phone off the dash. He looked at the screen with the irrational hope that there would be a missed call or text from Jordan, but there wasn't. Not that there could be; he didn't have her number and she didn't have his. That hadn't dawned on him until after he said he'd text her.

Dumb ass.

Gavin swore under his breath and put the phone in the cup holder. Even with everything that had happened today, Jordan had never been far from his thoughts. He'd felt like crap leaving her there and bailing out on what he'd offered to do, but he couldn't let the guys go out on that call without him. Rick was experienced, but the other guys were green and fresh out of training and their volunteer force rarely saw real action. Oh, they'd all been trained, but more often than not when they showed up, it was a false alarm or something minor.

How had things gone with her old man? Was she at home crying herself to sleep or did she pack her stuff and leave again?

Damn it.

Starting the engine, he pulled a U-turn and headed back toward town, all the while going over all the different reasons he shouldn't go over to her house unannounced. It was getting dark, and the girls were probably going to bed. She might not even be there. Even if she was at home, why the hell would she want him stopping over unannounced?

When he reached Shore Road though, Gavin idled at the stop sign and tapped his fingers on the steering wheel. He stared out at the tall grasses along the edge of the road and listened to the seagulls overhead as the sun finished its slow descent. He was tired, sweaty, and probably stunk to high heaven. He should take a left toward his place up on the bluff, go home, take a shower, and see her tomorrow at the flower shop.

As that rational thought went through his head, Gavin hit the blinker and took a right. The old Sweeney place was only a few houses from the end of street, and for a moment, Gavin thought Jordan wasn't home. But once he took the left into the long gravel driveway, her shiny silver wagon came into view. The sky burned orange and pink along the horizon as the indigo hue of the night sky began to emerge.

He put the truck in park and stared at the large picture window, with the soft glow of a lamp burning from within. Gavin gripped the gearshift. This was stupid. Totally freaking stupid. He should leave right now, he should—

Every thought went out of his head when Jordan's tall, lithe form appeared in the window. He held his breath for a second. When he thought that he had indeed done something beyond stupid, Jordan waved. And he was pretty sure he saw a smile on those gorgeous lips.

"Too late to back out now," he said to no one but himself.

Shutting off the engine, Gavin got out of the truck and stuck the keys in the pocket of his shorts. When he got a good look at his hands, still smudged with soot and grime, he groaned and cursed at himself.

"Nice job, showing up looking like a grimy pigpen," he muttered, with only the seagulls to hear him.

He climbed the wooden steps to the front door and

threw a prayer to the universe that this gamble would
pay off…and that she'd let him use her sink.

Chapter 8

WHEN JORDAN HEARD A CAR PULL IN THE DRIVEWAY, every irrational fear she had came roaring to mind. Was Ted here, drunk and furious? Had her father died? Did Gavin get hurt today on the job? Those thoughts, and more, shot through her mind one after the other.

After returning from her parents' house, she'd turned on her cell phone only to discover three voice mails from Ted, each one angrier than the last. He was demanding to see the girls and furious that she'd moved out of the city. Based on the slurred speech and aggressive, angry messages, he was getting worse and his drinking was escalating.

She thought for sure that when she looked out the window, she'd be met with his hateful drunken glare. Already exhausted both physically and emotionally from the time with her father, she almost burst into tears at the prospect of having to face Ted.

She'd never been so happy to be wrong.

Instead of her drunken ex-husband, Jordan was met with the fierce green-eyed gaze of Gavin McGuire. Still dressed in his T-shirt and board shorts from this morning, he looked war-weary from the fire he'd been dealing with out on the edge of town. She'd overheard the two cashiers gossiping about it when she'd stopped at the market. Once she'd heard the word "arson," she'd figured Gavin would have his hands full. After a day like that, the man should be on his way home to get some rest.

But here he was, standing in her driveway.

The poor guy looked dog-tired as he strode toward the house, and she couldn't fathom why on earth he'd be here and not at home falling into bed. That thought instantly led to images of Gavin in bed, and Jordan's cheeks heated at the idea.

Flustered and uncertain of what exactly was happening with Gavin, she waved at him through the window before going to the front door. The girls were still looking at books in their bedroom before lights out, and with any luck, they wouldn't hear his arrival. She had a sinking suspicion that getting them back in bed after that would be a true battle. Gracie hadn't stopped talking about Gavin or his magic trick all day.

Checking her reflection quickly in the little oval mirror next to the front door, Jordan grimaced. She took her hair out of the clip and ran her fingers through it quickly. Tucking a few stray hairs behind her ears, she wiped at the smudges of leftover mascara under her eyes. Not exactly a hot look. There wasn't time to do much about it, however, and when he knocked, Jordan froze. Her feet wouldn't cooperate. She stared at the door for a second before rolling her eyes and shaking her head with a growl of frustration.

What was she so nervous about?

Everything.

Jordan flipped the lock and tugged the heavy mahogany door open. Even though she knew Gavin was standing on the other side of it, the instant their eyes locked, she stilled. The wide, easy grin on his handsome face was both heartbreakingly familiar and strangely foreign. It gave her a glimpse of that boy she had loved so long ago behind the man who was something of a stranger. Or was he?

They stood there for a moment, eyes locked and neither one sure of what to say or do—until finally they both burst out laughing.

"Sorry," Jordan said as their laughter faded. "Come on in."

"Thanks." Gavin nodded and stepped past her across the threshold. The lingering aroma of the fire he'd been dealing with clung to him in an invisible cloud. "Sorry I didn't call first but—"

"You don't have my number." Jordan smiled and shut the door tightly. "It's okay, Gavin. I realized that after you pulled away this morning."

He surveyed the space casually, hands at his sides, before turning to face her. The entry hall, which had never seemed small before, suddenly felt like a sardine box as Gavin's tall frame loomed large in front of her. What was it about him that filled every room and surrounded her so completely?

"The girls are in bed," she said quietly. Jordan pointed to the staircase behind him. "If we're quiet, we might luck out and it will stay that way."

"Gotcha." Keeping his voice low, Gavin glanced casually in that direction before taking a step closer. "I guess it's a good thing I got here before you went to bed too."

His eyes twinkled with mischief and that lopsided grin curved his lips, bringing out the dimple in his left cheek. Jordan nodded her agreement and tried not to notice the way the heat from his body wafted enticingly over hers. Gritting her teeth against the pulse of desire and the urge to touch him, she fought to find her voice and prayed she wouldn't sound like the sex-starved woman she was. The funny thing was, until she saw Gavin again, she hadn't given sex much thought for more years than she cared to admit.

"Why don't we go into the living room?" Jordan swallowed the thick lump in her throat and quickly slipped past him. "It's more comfortable in there."

"I was pretty comfortable right where we were," he murmured.

"Can I get you something to drink?" Jordan asked as she tried to ignore the suggestive tone in his voice. "Have you eaten yet? I was cleaning up from dinner. It's Kraft macaroni and cheese. Not very fancy, I'm afraid."

"Actually…" he said, holding out both hands, which were smudged with what looked like soot. He gestured to the open, airy space of the family room. "I don't want to sit down or touch anything in here. All of the blue and white will get dirtied up. I'd love to use your sink and some soap, if you have it."

"I have two children," she said with a smile. "I have plenty of soap and a sink or two. Come on."

She went into the kitchen with Gavin close behind. Just as it had been in the foyer, her kitchen seemed to shrink the instant he stepped into it. Gesturing to the faucet, she stepped aside and went to the fridge.

"How about a beer?" She glanced over her shoulder at him, her gaze skimming over his broad shoulders as he washed his hands. The T-shirt clung to him, revealing every muscle and the subtle movement of each of them

as he shut off the water and dried his hands. "Or wine…
I think I have wine somewhere."

Jordan stilled, her hands gripping the edge of the
stainless-steel refrigerator door, as she realized how
right it felt to have Gavin standing in her house. She
stared into the fridge without really seeing anything
and nibbled her lower lip. After all of these years, with
so much still unsaid between them, it felt completely
normal to have him in her home. Why did it feel like he
belonged here with her? Was she imagining it? Was it
simply wishful thinking, or did Gavin fit perfectly in this
picture? He sure as hell did.

The revelation was wonderful and terrifying.

"Jordan?" Gavin's deep voice pulled her from
her thoughts.

"Did you say a beer?" She was starting to babble and
she knew it but still couldn't stop herself. "I have some
Amstel Lights in here or milk or juice boxes."

"An Amstel is perfect, and if it's cold, that's even
better."

"A cold beer coming right up." Jordan grabbed two
beers from the fridge, and when she shut the door, she
found Gavin standing to her right. She immediately
stepped back and handed him a bottle. "Here you go."

"Thanks." A smile slowly spread across his face as he
opened the beer and took a long sip. He made a sound of
appreciation and tipped the bottle in her direction. "That
was exactly what I needed."

"Really?" Jordan tossed her bottle cap in the sink
and leaned against the doorway that led into the casual
dining room, wanting and needing to keep some kind of
space between them. She rubbed her thumb along the

wet glass bottle and met his inquisitive stare with one of her own. "Came all the way out here to drink my beer, did you?"

"No." Gavin's smile faltered. "I—ah hell, Jordan. I was worried about you."

"I know." Her heart squeezed in her chest. "I'm sorry, Gavin. I didn't mean for that to sound bitchy. But I am wondering why you came here after the day you had. I overheard the girls at the market talking about the fire. They said that you guys suspect arson."

Keep him talking about regular everyday stuff, she thought. Anything except the two of them because that conversation, the one she'd been avoiding for fifteen years, seemed frighteningly close. Then she'd have to admit to everything, and she wasn't sure if she had the strength tonight.

Bullshit. She wasn't sure if she'd ever have the nerve.

"Yes. That's where the evidence points at the moment." Gavin nodded and put the beer bottle on the counter behind him before leaning both hands on the edge. "But I wasn't the only one putting out a fire today, and I definitely didn't come all the way over here to bore you with stories from work." The tone of his voice softened. "How'd it go with your dad?"

"It was…not what I expected." Jordan lifted one shoulder and wrestled to maintain her composure. "The man didn't even know who I was, Gavin. He's got full-on dementia. Honestly, I could have been the Queen of England and he would have reacted the same way."

"Right." Gavin narrowed his gaze. "So you couldn't tell him off like you'd planned?"

Jordan clenched the bottle tighter. It was remarkably unsettling to have another human being see her so clearly. How long had it been since anyone had seen through her calm, cool facade? She'd gotten so good at pretending everything was okay, she'd almost forgotten how it felt like to truly share herself with another human being.

"How did you know that's what I wanted to do?" Jordan whispered. "I never told you that's why I was finally going back there. I mean, I never told anyone that's what I planned to do."

"I know you, Jordan." He dropped his arms to his side and moved toward her. His voice was low and gruff. "Even after all this time, I know what drives you. Facing your old man and telling him what a son of a bitch he was, that was something you always wanted to do, even when we were kids. You came back here to rebuild your life, and I figured part of that plan involved telling your father that he couldn't hurt you anymore."

Gavin inched closer, his body wavering dangerously close to hers. The pungent smell of smoke, still clinging to him from the fire today, filled her head in seductive waves. His voice dropped to a gravelly whisper. "But there is something I still don't understand, and I'm hoping like hell you can help me figure it out."

"Wh-what?" Jordan shifted her body as he invaded her space, so that her back was pressed against the wall and the only thing between them was the bottle of beer clenched in her hand. "What is it?"

"It's one question, really." Gavin placed both hands on the wall, one on either side of her, caging her in. He leaned closer so that his face was a breath away from hers, and those intense, gorgeous green eyes zeroed in on her with laser-sharp focus. "Why did you leave me?"

Silence pulsed with each rapid beat of her heart, and Jordan swallowed the sudden lump in her throat. This was it. The moment of truth—and with it came the familiar urge to run. Duck under his arm and get the hell out of there. She could have. He would have let her leave, but she would only be prolonging the inevitable.

She had to tell him the truth. She owed him that much.

"I-I wasn't leaving you," she whispered shakily.

"You could've fooled me," Gavin growled.

"That night at the lighthouse, when you laughed at me, at my dreams of being an actress, of building a new life away from here, I was so hurt, Gavin. For most of my life growing up, my father did nothing but tell me how stupid my dreams were and how foolish I was. And then when I *finally* told *you*—the one person I thought had my back—what I wanted to do, you shot me down and told me I couldn't do it. You said it was a stupid idea and…I snapped."

"I was only a kid, Jordan." Anger edged his voice and a shadow passed over his face as he pushed himself off the wall, increasing the distance between them. "I mean, come on. I know I acted like a stupid, overbearing dickhead that night. I get it. But why did you leave town and then completely cut me off? I had no idea where you were. I was worried as hell! Do you have any idea what that did to me? You vanished into thin air."

"I wasn't leaving you," she whispered. "I left because of my father."

Jordan tilted her chin defiantly, her own anger and frustration bubbling to the surface. Straightening her back, she held his furious stare and finally told him the truth.

"After I got back from the lighthouse, my father came after me. He'd always been a bully, but that night he took it to a whole other level. I knew, deep in my gut... I always knew that his bullying, menacing, and screaming jags would eventually lead to violence. And that night they did."

She slammed her beer on the counter and stepped closer to him, finally telling him the story she'd never told anyone. She unloaded her shame and spilled the dirty secret she carried around, the one that made her feel useless, weak, and defeated. "He punched me. Square in the face."

"What?" Gavin paled visibly and his hands curled into fists as his entire body tensed. "He hit you. I knew it."

"Let me finish." She held up one hand and moved closer as she continued, her self-loathing bubbling to the surface. "Then, when I fell on the ground in a pathetic weeping heap, he kept telling me what a whore I was. That I was trash. He kicked me in the stomach a few times, until I thought I'd vomit or pass out. He might have actually killed me if he'd been a little less drunk. My mother finally pulled him off me and distracted him long enough for me to drag my bleeding ass up to my room."

"Son of a bitch," Gavin seethed between clenched teeth. "I knew that bastard did something to you. If the cops hadn't shown up when they did, I could've gotten him to tell me what happened and where the hell you went."

The frustration that laced his voice was matched by her own.

"They didn't know where I ran off to, Gavin," Jordan said wearily. "No one did. No matter what you did or said that night…they couldn't have told you anything."

Gavin winced and folded his arms over his broad chest. The look of hurt etched into his features was almost more than Jordan could bear. After she'd run away, part of her believed that Gavin wouldn't care or that he'd get over it quickly enough in the arms of Missy Oakland. But now, seeing the wounded expression on his face, his pain from that day bubbling back to the surface, fresh and raw, Jordan knew how wrong she had been.

There was no longer any doubt that she had hurt him more deeply than she'd ever realized.

"After my parents fell asleep, I threw what I could into a bag and I left. As for why I didn't get in touch with you? I was hurt, Gavin, angry and humiliated." Her voice wavered but she fought for control, refusing to collapse into the pathetic weeping mess she'd once been. "You were the only person I trusted, and you had told me what an idiot I was for having dreams of a different life. It felt like a slap in the face."

"Damn it, Jordan." Hands on his hips, Gavin swore under his breath and his mouth set in a tight line. "When you talked about going to the city and being an actress, that scared the ever-loving shit out of me. Can you understand that?"

"Now I can, yes. But—"

"No." Gavin held up one hand, stopping any further protests on her part. "You had your say. Now it's my turn."

"Alright," Jordan said quietly. "I'm listening."

"When you told me what you wanted to do, all I could think was that I would lose you. And that terrified me. I know now that I should've told you that. But back then I was a stupid eighteen-year-old kid and I got angry instead of being honest with you or myself about how damn scared I was."

"I'm sorry, Gavin," Jordan whispered in a barely audible voice. "I don't know how many times I can say it until you'll believe it. I can't undo the past any more than you can."

"Fair enough," he said tightly. "But I'm not finished."

"Go on…"

"Okay. I can understand now, after hearing all of this, why you left that night—but why didn't you come back, Jordan?"

"I was—"

"Scared?" Gavin scoffed. "Don't give me that, Jordan. I would never do anything to intentionally hurt you."

"I know that," she whispered.

"Granted, I may have reacted badly that night, but after everything calmed down, why didn't you call me then? A month later. A year? Damn it all. I know this was before everyone had a cell phone or was posting their every waking thought on Facebook, but you still could have called or written me a letter. A card or something? I can get my head around why you went away." His voice dropped to a whisper. "But why the hell did you *stay* away?"

"Because of Suzanne." Her cheeks heated with embarrassment, recalling how easily she'd believed the lie. "And Missy."

"Suzanne and Missy?" he asked with genuine confusion. "Huh? What the hell do the two of them have to do with anything?"

"About a week after I left, when I'd finally cooled off, I called Suzanne to feel things out. I knew I wouldn't be able go home but I thought maybe you…" Her voice trailed off as she struggled to keep her emotions in check. Even after all this time, the memory of hearing that lie still stung. Bitterness and frustration edged her voice, which hovered above a whisper. "She told me you were too busy screwing Missy Oakland to even notice I was gone."

"What? That's bull," he seethed. "How could you think that I would hook up with her? Come on. Missy Oakland? Hell, Jordan, I didn't want anyone except *you*."

Jordan put a finger to her lips and pointed upstairs, referencing the girls. The last complication she needed was to have them hear her fighting with another man. Gavin's mouth set in a tight line, and his shoulders squared as he wrestled with his own set of frustrations.

"*Shit*." He hissed the word on one long, slow breath and ran a hand over his face. Jordan knew exactly how weary he felt, and the gruff, raw sound of his voice tugged at her soul. "Listen, the morning after our fight, I went out to your parents' place to apologize to you. I almost got my ass arrested when I got into it with your father because I thought he was keeping you from me. I-I thought he'd hurt you. Aside from all of that, I would *never* have touched Missy Oakland with a ten-foot pole back then—or anyone else for that matter."

"I know that now but at the time I didn't," Jordan said quietly. "I thought Suzanne was my friend, so it never occurred to me that she'd make up something like that. But obviously I was wrong…I was wrong about a lot of things. I guess I should've known she was lying. She always did have a thing for you."

"I should tell you… I did date Suzanne a couple of years ago," Gavin said flatly. He shifted his weight, as though uncomfortable with his admission. "It was right after I moved back to town, but it didn't last long because she's as crazy as I thought she was in high school."

"It's fine." Jordan held up both hands, preventing him from telling her any gory details. "Really. It's okay. I already know. Maddy told me about that."

"Right." Gavin cleared his throat and stuck his hands in his pockets. "But nothing happened with anyone after you left, Jordan. Hell, I had to join the damn army and leave town to try to get you out of my head." His voice dropped to a gravelly whisper, and his glittering gaze slid over her face. "Hell of a lot good that did me."

"Like I said," she murmured gently, "I know *now* that it was a lie."

"But how could you think that I—"

"Really?" she responded quickly. "And how could *you* think that my wanting to be an actress in New York would mean leaving you?"

He opened his mouth to respond, but shut it and simply nodded his understanding.

"Okay." She sucked in a deep breath as some of the tension eased from the room. "With all of these facts in mind, what on earth did I have waiting for me here? As far as I knew, you had moved on with Missy, and Maddy was still overseas. Going back home wasn't an option. What did I have to come back to?

Nothing. So I stayed in the city and got a waitressing gig. A couple years later, I met Ted, which is a whole other conversation. And I'd say marrying him was a complete mistake, but it wasn't because it gave me my girls. They are the best thing that ever happened to me."

Jordan held out both hands, daring him to tell her she was an idiot for doing what she had, but he said nothing. Struggling to keep her voice even, she poked him in the chest.

"So there you go, Gavin. That's why I left, and I'm sorry that I hurt you. I'm sorry I was a stupid, impulsive, weak, little girl who was so humiliated, she couldn't even speak to her own mother for years. Now do you understand?" Tears filled her eyes and her voice sounded strangled as she fought the tide of pent-up emotion. "I did what I had to do to survive."

Jordan waited what felt like forever for Gavin to say something. The sounds of the waves crashing and the dripping from the faucet echoed through the kitchen, marking the silent seconds that passed. What was he waiting for? Why in the hell wasn't he saying anything?

Damn it. Do something. Tell me I was weak. Agree that I was a coward. Anything.

Gavin stared at her silently and so intently, she thought that perhaps he could see right inside of her. Maybe he could. Shaking with adrenaline and a tsunami of emotions that were so overwhelming she couldn't separate one from the other, Jordan tried to blink away the tears, but to no avail.

Gavin's image blurred as his strong, warm hands cradled her cheeks.

Jordan shut her eyes, and in spite of all the time that had passed, or the litany of reasons she shouldn't, she let herself sink into his touch. The warmth of his hands, coarse from years of hard work, rushed over her face, and that simple expression of tenderness sent the tears falling. Exhausted and spent from finally letting it all out, she felt a shuddering sigh shake her shoulders as Gavin gently brushed the remaining tears away with his thumbs.

"I'm so sorry, Jordan." He rested his forehead against hers. She gripped the damp material of his T-shirt, pulling him closer. If it were possible, she would have crawled inside his chest and stayed there, surrounded by the rock that was Gavin McGuire. "I'm so damn sorry I wasn't there to protect you from your father. If I hadn't acted like such a dick that night, you wouldn't have run off like that."

"I guess the old man was right after all, wasn't he? Failed actress. Failed marriage." Jordan fought the surge of self-loathing and swiped at her teary eyes. "And here I am, right back where I started, except now I have two little girls in tow."

"You *are not* a failure." Gavin tilted her face, forcing her to look him in the eyes. "Neither of us are kids anymore and we both made mistakes, but the past is in the past. And we can still have a do-over. How about it?"

Jordan wanted nothing more than to say yes, to wrap herself in his arms and remain sheltered there forever. But now, more than ever, it was important for her to stand on her own. As much as she wanted to run, literally and figuratively, into Gavin's arms, she resisted. The idea of making yet another mistake that could impact her daughters was more terrifying than the notion of going back to Ted.

"I can't, Gavin." She pushed gently at his chest and slipped out of his embrace. His expression hardened briefly, his arms falling to his side. She took another step back, increasing the distance between them in more ways than one. "I have a life to rebuild and two little girls to raise. The ink is barely dry on my divorce papers—and please, don't get me wrong, this isn't about Ted. I don't love him anymore and the truth is, I probably never did. Not really."

"Then what's the problem?"

"Getting involved in a relationship, sex, and all that goes with it isn't a smart idea. At least, not right now. I have to show my daughters that I can stand on my own."

"Who said anything about sex?" he asked all too innocently.

Jordan said nothing but gave him a narrow-eyed look as she squelched the giggle that threatened to bubble up. He always could get her to laugh at the most inopportune moments.

"Okay, okay. I *might* have thought about it, but to be fair, I didn't *say* it." Gavin nodded slowly and slipped his hands in the pockets of his shorts. As he studied her intently, that lopsided grin bloomed again, bringing out that mischievous-looking dimple. "Then we'll be friends. That's how we started, so that's how we'll finish."

In a flash, he reached out and tucked a strand of hair behind her ear before holding up a quarter between two fingers.

"Just friends. Deal?"

Part of her wanted to scream *yes* and the other wanted to yell *hell no*.

God help her, she was a conflicted hot mess. She wanted Gavin every way that a woman could want a man, and a huge portion of it was dripping with lust. The needy, moan-inducing, curl-your-toes kind of lust. But giving in to that base animal instinct would not be smart. It would only be confusing for her and him, and *that* wouldn't be good for her girls.

Jordan resolved to shove aside the gnawing physical attraction and take the friendship he offered. Even if the affection-starved woman inside of her begged her not to make such a stupid damn deal.

Without a word, and remaining calm—like a duck on the pond, she thought, gliding along with her feet moving furiously under the surface, while trying to keep her head above water—Jordan held out her hand to accept his offer. Gavin inched closer and placed the quarter in her palm. He drew his hand away slowly, and the pad of his finger trailed over hers in one tantalizing pass.

Friends? Yeah, right. She didn't have any other friends who made her want to strip them naked and climb them like the Himalayas. She was opening her mouth to answer him when Lily's voice called from upstairs.

"Mama, will you read us one more story before bed?"

Saved by an adorable little bell.

"I'll be right up," Jordan called without taking her eyes off Gavin. Closing her fingers around the quarter, she murmured, "Deal."

"Good." Gavin stepped back abruptly and wagged one finger at her. "And don't try to get me into one of those friends-with-benefits deals. I'm not having sex with you, no matter how much you ask. We're only going to be friends. That's it."

"Oh really?" Jordan laughed and shook her head as she followed him to the front door. Standing in the foyer, she held the door open for him and delighted in the sweet, silly side of him that he rarely showed the rest of the world. "Well, I'm glad we got that cleared up."

"Me too." Gavin slipped out the door and trotted down the steps. "It's such a relief to know that we won't be sleeping together. That will make having lunch with you tomorrow so much easier. You know? No strings attached—an *only friends* kind of lunch."

"Lunch, huh?" Jordan leaned on the edge of the doorway as he strode toward his car. "At the shop?"

"Okay, it's a date."

"Gavin"—she laughed—"what are you talking about?"

"See you around noon," he said as he climbed into his truck. "I'll bring sandwiches and you get some drinks."

His headlight beams bobbed through the early evening twilight as he backed out of the driveway, illuminating the tall grasses along the edge. Jordan let out a sigh of relief. Closing the door, she flipped the lock before leaning back against the smooth, cool wooden surface. Looking around the open, airy house, with the comforting scent of the ocean air filling her head, Jordan felt safe for the first time in years.

Chapter 9

"ARE YOU GONNA STARE AT THAT SANDWICH OR EAT it?" Gavin asked, finishing off the last of his turkey on rye. Jordan sat ramrod straight on the bench next to him with her gaze pinned to her half-eaten ham sandwich. "Jordan?"

"My father still doesn't know who I am," she said quietly. Long strands of blond hair blew around her with the rush of the warm summer breeze. "I've been going over there every day after work, you know. The girls stay downstairs with my mother while I sit with him, and I keep waiting for something. For some kind of awareness or a flicker of recognition. *Something* that would tell me he remembers how awful he was, how terrible he was to my mother and me." Her voice was quiet but shook with frustration. "To tell me he's sorry... I want to hate him," she whispered. "But I can't."

"Okay," Gavin said slowly. He shoved aside the urge to pull her into his arms. Apart from the fact they were in the middle of the park, he didn't think he could stop with a simple hug. "So why keep going over there? Let it go."

"You know what the craziest part is?" She squinted against the sun. "In spite of everything...I still love him. Believe it or not, he wasn't always such a bastard."

She let out a shuddering sigh as a breeze whisked over them, lifting her hair off her neck. He fought the desire to tangle his fingers in the long, silky strands, but if they were going to be friends, then he had to keep his hands to himself. *Jesus. Let's be friends. What a stupid idea.* He rested his forearms on his knees and watched the heavy summer traffic as it rolled by on Main Street.

"Really?" He cleared his throat. "I don't remember you ever talking about him like that. I know I never saw that side of the guy."

"His heavy drinking started a couple of years before we moved here from Oklahoma. I was pretty young then, not much older than Lily. Even though I mostly remember the bad times with him, there were some good ones too, at least in the beginning." A wistful smile curved her lips. "He used to sing to me at night before I went to sleep. He'd sing 'Twinkle, Twinkle, Little Star.'"

Swiping at her eyes, she let out a short laugh. "Silly, isn't it? You know, I'd practically forgotten all about it until I had children of my own. When Lily was born, I sang it to her, and that's when I remembered my father singing it to me. I've... I mean I'm thinking about letting the girls see him."

"Okay," Gavin said slowly.

"Lily asks about him." Jordan sniffled and swiped at her eyes. "She's curious and I can't suppose I blame her...but...I haven't made up my mind."

Honking horns from cars on Main Street interrupted their conversation, and for a minute Gavin thought she was going to clam up. Jordan fiddled with the paper around her uneaten sandwich, and he could feel how conflicted she was. The woman was in pain and he wanted to fix it, to make it better, to put out the fire that raged inside of her. He wanted to say something but didn't have the first clue what it should be, so he opted for staying quiet. Better to let her get it all out.

"Anyway," she said firmly, as though steeling her strength, "from what my mother tells me, his friend and business partner screwed him over. The bottom line was that he and my mother lost everything—his business, their savings, all of it. They moved here because of a sales job my father had to take, and he absolutely hated it. That's when the drinking started. The unhappier he got, the more he drank.

"He absolutely loathed being beholden to someone else and then, as you know, he was constantly getting fired. He'd bounce from one job to the next, and every time he got laid off, it was a longer dry spell between jobs. No work meant more drinking, and that meant more screaming." Her voice wavered with emotion as she brushed crumbs off her floral print sundress. "In some ways, I guess it's easier to remember the rotten stuff."

"Why?" Gavin nudged her knee with his, needing some kind of contact, no matter how brief. "I'd rather *forget* the bad stuff." He might have uttered those words in a teasing tone, but he meant them. He wished like hell he could forget some of his own dark memories. The scarred flesh on his shoulder tingled, threating to pull him into memories better left undisturbed. Gavin cleared his throat and focused on Jordan. "Why on earth do you want to shut out the good times?"

"I guess it hurts less to think about the bad stuff," she whispered.

Turning her large brown eyes to his, Jordan got that look on her face, the one that told him she was contemplating whether or not to say what was on her mind.

Damn. That look tore at his heart just as much now as it did back then. Probably more.

"Because every now and then, when I remember what it was like to have my father hug me, sing softly, and kiss the top of my head, the ache in my chest gets so big, I think it might swallow me whole." Straightening her back, Jordan stared out at the street. "I go back to that house every day now, not because I want to tell him off, but because I want him to tell me he still loves me. It's crazy, isn't it?"

"It's not that crazy, Jordan." Crumpling up the brown paper bag, he tossed it into the garbage can by the bench, then turned his attention back to her. "He's your father."

"And I married a man just like him." Jordan wrapped up her sandwich with more force than necessary and slapped it on the bench between them. "I think that's what's bothering me more than anything else. I went and married a son of a bitch, and gave my daughters a bastard for a father. Is this their future, Gavin? Are they going to be sitting around one day wishing that their absentee father would love them?"

"I don't know the answer to that. But I do know that you are a much different woman than your mother." He held up both hands and quickly added, "Don't get me wrong. I think Claire is a sweetheart, and I give her a hell of a lot of credit for sticking it out with your father all of these years, but—"

"It's okay, Gavin." Her hand drifted over and settled on his knee in a familiar, reassuring gesture. He stilled beneath her touch and she must have felt it, because she pulled her hand away quickly. "I mean, I know what you're saying. My mother stayed and I didn't. I left Ted because I didn't want my daughters growing up in a love-less household with a drunk. It's a terrible way to live." She settled her hands on the edge of the bench on either side of her thighs, her shoulders hunched. "Ted barely paid any attention to the girls one way or the other. After I had the children, he barely even noticed *I* was there."

They'd been having lunch every day for the past two weeks, and this was the first time she'd really opened up to him. Prior to this, she would steer the conversation toward him or his parents' upcoming anniversary party, his brothers or his job, anything but herself. The fact that she was talking to him about this stuff gave him hope. He wasn't a big one for talking out his feelings, but he was all for the idea of Jordan opening up. The more she shared with him, the better the odds that he could convince her to give him, to give *them*, a second chance.

"He sounds like a real prince." The bench creaked in protest as Gavin leaned back. "This Ted guy must have been nice at the beginning. You never did tell me how you met him."

"It's not that exciting a story." She lifted one shoulder and rolled her eyes. "I was on my home from an audition, and I literally bumped into him at the bank. He was handsome and charming...at least at the beginning. We had a whirlwind courtship and got married at City Hall about three months after we met. At first, I thought I'd hit the jackpot, you know? He was rich and handsome, and he seemed wonderful. But it didn't take long for me to figure out that he wasn't the guy I thought he was.

"He blamed the pressures at work for why he drank so much—that or entertaining clients. Ted always had one excuse or another. Anyway, a little over a year into our marriage, I was going to leave him. But by then I'd found out I was pregnant with Lily, and Gracie came along a couple years after that." She sighed heavily and whispered, "I didn't want to get a divorce, Gavin."

"I imagine most people don't." Jealousy reared its head like the ugly monster it was. "You loved him. I get it."

He fought the surge of envy as she spoke about her ex-husband, the man who'd been given the gift of having Jordan as his wife and squandered it. Gavin felt like a jackass. Hadn't he asked her to tell him about this? He had officially become a masochist.

"No, I didn't," she said quietly as she stared at her interlocked fingers. "Maybe I did at first. I mean it wasn't like it was with—" Jordan stopped abruptly.

Gavin's gut clenched. Was she going to say, "What it was like with you"? Hope glimmered cruelly and silence hung between them as he waited for her to finish the thought and put him out of his self-imposed misery.

"It wasn't like I thought it would be. And even though I wanted to leave, the idea of being on my own with two little girls scared the hell out of me. The really pathetic part is that I probably would have kept staying. Honestly, if he hadn't come after me in front of the girls that night, I probably would have stayed…just like my mother did."

"He hit you?" Gavin's entire body tensed, and his hands curled into fists as rage simmered brightly beneath the surface. "In front of Gracie and Lily?"

This Ted asshole hit Jordan? Fury bubbled and rolled, threatening to erupt, but he stuffed it back down.

Flipping out wouldn't do anyone any good. It was bad enough to think that this Ted bastard had laid hands on Jordan, but that he would get violent in front of those two little girls made Gavin's blood boil.

"No." Jordan shook her head and tears glimmered in her eyes but none fell. "But if I'd stayed…"

"Right. Well then, I won't have to rip his head off if I ever meet him." Gavin nodded curtly and some of the fury eased from him—but not much. "He may not have hit you, Jordan, but it sounds like he was an abusive son of a bitch. Leaving him was the right thing to do for you and the girls."

"Anyway, after that, staying with him was a far more frightening prospect than going it on my own. We all have our demons, I guess. But do you want to know what really kills me? Thanks to me, my daughters already have theirs."

"You're not the one who was abusive," Gavin said tightly. "Sounds to me like Ted is the one who's responsible for any demons. You've done a great job, Jordan. Your girls are terrific, and if you ask me, it's better they have no father than to be around a guy like that."

Before he could stop himself, he reached out and rubbed her lower back reassuringly. She stiffened briefly beneath his touch, but only for a moment before she relaxed. That infinitesimal shift toward acceptance was what he'd been looking for.

"True," she murmured. "But unfortunately, he *is* their father and he'll never really go away. Ted will always hang around just enough to make our lives miserable. Case in point, he left me a few unpleasant voice mails this week and even threatened to come here and take the girls."

"I don't think that would be good for his health," Gavin murmured. "Does he know where you live?"

"He was hammered when he called, and I doubt he remembers leaving half the messages. Besides, I have full custody, and thanks to his substance abuse problem, all of his visits have to be supervised. He doesn't love me or the girls, Gavin. He's pissed that I left him and he didn't win. It's a power play. That's it. There's no love there. I don't know if he's really capable of loving anyone other than himself."

Jordan glanced over her shoulder at him, and when her brown eyes met his, it was like a punch in the gut. The sadness that lingered there almost did him in, and it took Herculean strength not to drag her into his arms.

"I-I should be getting back," she said, gathering her bag. "Cookie and Veronica are really busy getting things ready for the Posman wedding tomorrow, and I shouldn't leave them alone in the shop too long."

"Right." Gavin dropped his hand, his fingers trailing briefly over the curve of her hip as she rose from the bench. "I should get back too."

"You've been pretty busy yourself these days." Jordan slung her bag over her shoulder. They walked side by side toward the intersection, and Gavin stuck his hands in his pockets to keep from touching her. "It seems like you guys are out on at least three or four calls a day."

"We have been. It's always busier in the summer." Gavin stopped at the corner and pushed the button on the crosswalk pole. "Most of them are false alarms or the usual stove-top mishap, but we've had two more suspicious fires. Both were on the edge of town and in empty buildings, luckily. One was the abandoned gas station on Route 2, and the other was an old toolshed on the Thompsons' property. Whoever is doing it seems to be getting bolder. They're choosing locations closer and closer to town."

"You really think someone in town is setting fires deliberately?" Jordan asked as they crossed the street toward the shop. "That seems crazy, Gavin. Who would do that?"

"A crazy person, but I can't believe it would be anyone who lives here," Gavin shot back. He stepped onto the sidewalk and instinctively rolled his left shoulder, the scarred skin feeling tighter than usual. "You'd have to be insane to *intentionally* start a fire and invite that monster into the world. Make no mistake about it, Jordan. Fire is a living, breathing monster that eats everything in its path. It doesn't discriminate or feel pity or remorse. All it does is burn."

His jaw clenched as he fought the surge of fury mixed with shame that bubbled up as sinister memories from that day in the barn reared their ugly heads. He stared at the firehouse, his voice gruff and strained as he recalled the worst moment of his life.

"If you're not crazy, then you're a stupid kid who doesn't know any damn better. But stupidity is what gets people killed, and no matter how many times you want to go back and fix it…you can't. Some mistakes can't ever be atoned for."

Wrapped up in the dark tangle of memories, Gavin squeezed his eyes shut as faint echoes of Jimmy's screams filled his head. He'd tried to get to him, to pull him from the flames like he had with Ronan and

Tommy, but he couldn't. The flames had been too hot and the smoke so thick he couldn't breathe. Even all these years later, Gavin could still hear the boy screaming for his brother.

The only sound worse than Jimmy's screams had been the deafening silence that followed.

Gavin gritted his teeth against the stomach-churning memory, but the fury dissipated slowly when soft, warm fingers curled around his clenched fist. He stilled and opened his hand as Jordan tangled her fingers with his and inched her lithe body closer, pressing it gently against him. Flicking his eyes open, Gavin immediately caught Jordan's empathetic stare. Bit by bit, the tension seeped from his body like smoke.

"You were children, Gavin. Babies really. And it was an accident. A horrible, tragic accident," Jordan whispered, her other arm linking through his, pulling him closer still. "Gavin, that fire wasn't your fault. You have to know that. Especially after doing what you do for a living."

Looking into her compassionate face, he wished more than anything that what she said was true. Just as that thought rippled through Gavin's mind, his attention was captured by a flicker of movement behind Jordan. Tommy Miller came shuffling toward them with his familiar, off-kilter gait. His scars, unlike Gavin's, were visible and covered almost the entire right side of his body. Gavin caught his eye only for a moment before Tommy acknowledged him with a shy nod and climbed quickly into the van with the school's emblem emblazoned on the side. The engine roared to life, and the muffler sputtered and coughed as he backed out of the space.

Tommy was always cordial to Gavin. Even back then, he never came right out and blamed him for Jimmy's death. No one did. Tommy and Ronan never ratted him out, but they didn't have to. Gavin knew the truth. He was the one who had stolen the cigarettes and matches from his father's nightstand. If Gavin hadn't done that, there never would have been a fire in the first place.

It had been his fault. Plain and simple.

Jordan must have sensed the shift in his demeanor because she held him tighter, her breast pressing against his bicep, taunting him with what he couldn't have. Maybe he didn't deserve to be happy. Maybe being this close to Jordan and not being able to have her was the universe's way of punishing him.

Tommy drove away down Main Street, and a pall of guilt bloomed around Gavin like a plume of black smoke so thick and heavy that he practically choked on it.

"Like I said," she murmured. "We all have our demons, Gavin."

"Maybe," he said tightly in a barely audible tone. "But you didn't kill anyone."

"No." She tilted her chin, daring him to defy her. "And neither did you."

"Tell that to Tommy Miller," he said flatly.

Jordan blanched at his tone, which sent a pang of guilt flickering through him. What the hell was he doing? She didn't need to deal with his baggage. The woman had plenty of her own crap to wade through, and here he was dumping his nonsense on her like some sappy dope on a talk show. Feeling stupid for allowing himself to get sucked into the darkness, he shrugged.

"Whatever, Jordan. Forget it. It's not the same thing, okay?"

"You're a piece of work, you know that?" She dropped his hand and slipped away from him as swiftly as she'd come, a flash fire going from hot to cold in a split second. "I see how it is. So it's okay if I sit there and spill my guts to you, but the instant *you* have to talk about anything real, the conversation is over? You know, for a guy who claims he wants to be friends, you have a funny way of showing it. Last time I checked, friendship was a two-way street."

"I don't know what you're getting your panties in a bunch about," he groused. An older couple walking past them raised their eyebrows. Gavin lowered his voice and ran one hand over his face, fighting to keep his emotions in check. "You might want to rehash shit with your old man, but not all of us want to keep bringing up the past. What's done is done. Okay? Drop it."

"Fine. Consider it dropped. Thanks for lunch," she seethed. "I have to get back to work. Good-bye, Gavin."

Her dark eyes glittered with anger, and the harsh edge in her voice left no mistaking how pissed she was. He knew enough about women to know that saying "fine" was about the same as telling a guy to screw off. Before he could say a word, she stormed away and disappeared into the shop. He swore under his breath. He could go inside and try to explain himself, but based on the state he was in at the moment, he'd only mess things up more. She was right. Everyone had demons, and at the moment, his were fighting to break free.

—⁓—

Jordan had been twisted up in knots ever since her spat
with Gavin, and as the clock ticked closer to closing
time, she continued debating whether or not she should
go to the firehouse to see him. Part of her was still pissed
that he had shut her out, but the other part, the more
dominant part, was heartbroken for him. She'd assumed,
foolishly, that Gavin no longer blamed himself for the
death of Jimmy Miller.

Gavin was strong, solid, and an immovable force,
so the idea that this hulking man who ran into burning
buildings for a living was still blaming himself for an
accident decades ago seemed impossible. She'd stupidly
thought that he'd conquered that demon, especially since
he seemed hell-bent on helping her battle hers. Based on
his curt reaction earlier, it was all too clear he remained
a man haunted by his past.

The more she thought about her reaction, the worse
she felt. It was the first time she had seen darkness
bubble up beneath the surface of his typically even-
keeled demeanor. Even when they were kids, Gavin
seemed to hold it together. The man was the calm in the
storm. When his brothers got in trouble, he was the one
who came to their rescue or their defense, depending on
what the situation called for. But that was typical with
the oldest child in the family, wasn't it? She remembered reading somewhere that the eldest was usually the
caretaker, and that was a perfect word to describe Gavin.

He took care of everyone except himself.

Glancing out the window for the fifteenth time in as
many minutes, she realized that his cool manner had
wavered one other time today. When Jordan told him
about Ted's temper and the way he'd behaved in front

of the girls, the shadow that passed over Gavin's face had sent a shudder down her spine. For all his sweetness and thoughtfulness, something dark and dangerous simmered beneath the surface. She suspected that was the part of himself he called upon every time he ran into a burning building—and the same darkness he'd been stewing in out on the sidewalk.

This incident between them was a glaring reminder that nothing with the two of them would ever be easy or simple. Being friends with Gavin, let alone getting involved further, was a really bad idea. Individually, they had enough baggage to pack up the entire town. Twice.

The familiar lilt of Cookie's voice pulled Jordan from her thoughts. She quickly pretended to be inspecting the flowers in the case instead of staring at the firehouse.

"So you and your boyfriend have been having lunch every day for like, two weeks. When do you two kids graduate to dinner and a real date?" Cookie asked with her typically perky energy. Arms full of flowers, she leaned both elbows on the glass counter as the door to the workroom swung shut behind her. "Veronica and I are taking bets. In fact, before she left tonight, she made me promise to text her if the chief showed up again."

"He's not my boyfriend," Jordan said in an unconvincing tone as she straightened up the tower in the center of the room. She adjusted the position of the various knickknacks for purchase and shrugged. "We're friends."

"Yeah, right." Cookie snorted with laughter. Tugging open the refrigerator, she restocked the roses. Her tattoo-covered arms moved with the ease of experience. "I've seen more of that dude the past two weeks than I have in the past two years. A hot man like that was made for more than friendship. And from what I hear, the two of you used to be…y'know."

"Cookie, it's complicated." Jordan looked at the clock again before taking the remaining bunch of flowers from Cookie's hands. She jutted her thumb toward the door. "Go on, girl. Beat it. I can finish restocking the case. Why don't you go home? You and Veronica got here when the sun came up to get everything ready. Tomorrow you have to be up at the crack of dawn to set the flowers up at the church and the country club, and Veronica will be here at the shop all day. Not to mention that Mrs. Posman will pop a gasket if you're late. Really, I've got it. My mom picked the girls up from camp today and took them back to her place for a little while."

"Really? Thanks." Cookie's pierced eyebrow arched and her tone softened. "I've been meaning to ask you. How's your dad doing?"

"Not good," Jordan said flatly. "But the hospice nurse will be there tonight until about eight and it's good for my mother to get a breather from all of it. The only time I see her smile is when she's with the girls, and if anyone deserves a smile or two, it's my mother."

"Hey, Jordan…um…can I ask you something?" She bit her lip nervously. "It's kinda personal."

"Sure."

"How'd the girls do when they met him?" Cookie shrugged and stuck her hands in the pockets of her ripped jeans. "I mean, he's really sick. I remember when my grandpa was dying. It kinda freaked me out."

"The girls stay downstairs," Jordan said quickly. "They've never met him. But Lily has been asking about him." She growled with frustration. "I just don't want to make the wrong decision, and lately, it seems like that's all I've been doing."

"Gotcha." Cookie nodded slowly and hesitated as though she wanted to say something.

"What is it?" Jordan prodded. She could tell that the well-meaning young woman had something on her mind, and even though they'd only known each other for a month or so, she'd already become something of a kid sister. Cookie's outward appearance was rough and edgy, but underneath it all she was a sweet kid with a big heart. "It's okay, Cookie. Tell me."

"Your dad is dying, right?" Cookie asked, her light blue eyes studying Jordan's. "I mean, like, soon probably."

"Yes," she responded quietly. "He is... It's only a matter of time."

"And he's never met his granddaughters?"

"No, but it's—"

"Complicated?" Cookie interjected. "I guess it is. Look, I know we don't really know each other well, but if Lily is asking about it, why not let her meet the guy? He can't do anything to hurt her, right?"

"Not really, but...I don't know..."

"Sorry." Cookie held up both hands and added quickly, "I mean, you told me some and I'm sorry if I'm outta line, it's just that family is family, you know?" She made a scoffing sound and waved her hands quickly. "Ah, never mind. I'm punchy from lack of sleep and listening to that Posman broad yammer on about her freaking purple roses. Sorry, Jordan."

"Hey." Cookie started to leave, but Jordan grabbed her hand before she could get away and gave it a quick squeeze. "Thank you."

"For what?" Cookie laughed. "Being nosy?"

"No." Jordan smiled and held the young woman's wide-eyed stare. "For being a good friend. When I was married to Ted—" She snapped her mouth shut and shook her head. "Never mind. I'll leave it at thank you."

"You're welcome." Cookie placed a quick kiss on Jordan's cheek. She hurried to the door and pushed it open, but before she slipped into the back room, Cookie gave Jordan what could only be described as a wicked grin. "Then as your friend, I'll say one more thing."

"What?" Jordan adjusted the thorny stems carefully and yanked open the door to the case. "I'm all ears."

"My lack-of-sex radar goes haywire around you and the chief." She pointed at Jordan and laughed as the door swung shut. "You both need to get laid."

"Cookie!" Jordan's face heated, and in spite of the outrageousness of Cookie's comment, she found herself looking out the window at the firehouse. "You're crazy."

Still laughing at Cookie's brazen suggestion, Jordan finished stocking the case and closed it tightly. She leaned against it. If Cookie only knew how much Jordan wanted nothing more than to crawl into Gavin's arms and stay there. But they'd both agreed—friendship was all there would be between them. Today, when he'd gently stroked her back to comfort her, it had taken every ounce of self-control to stop herself from falling into his arms. She wanted him. There was no denying that.

But like she'd told the girls so many times, some-times what we want and what's smart are two different things. Spending all this time with Gavin was what she wanted…but it sure as hell wasn't smart.

Eyes closed, she pressed her back against the cool glass doors. A moment later she heard Cookie shout her good-byes. The familiar sound of the back door slamming shut shot through the room, and then there was silence. For the first time in ages, Jordan was alone.

Alone and with a head full of thoughts about sleeping with Gavin.

"Awesome," Jordan muttered.

Rolling her eyes, she shoved herself away from the door and saw that it was after five thirty. Traffic on the street had slowed. As with most Friday nights this summer, people were strolling the sidewalks, but buying flowers wasn't on their schedule. The lilies and hydrangea needed to be restocked as well, and given her current state of mind, work was the only cure. Jordan changed the sign on the door to *Closed* and flipped the locks, dutifully avoiding so much as a glance toward the firehouse. They were only going to be friends.

After their little spat today, maybe not even that.

Jordan tied her hair back with a spare elastic from a drawer behind the counter. Maybe their little tiff was for the best. She bumped the swinging door open with her hip and flipped on the little radio that sat on the desk. Perhaps music would help her keep her mind off Gavin. The sounds of Bon Jovi filled the workroom and immediately brought a smile to her lips. There was something about that band and their music that always reminded her of summer fun.

She yanked open the enormous metal door that led to the refrigerated storeroom and stood at the center for a moment or two before finding the lilies. Goose bumps erupted on her bare arms from the damp, cold air and she shivered, hastening her search. Jordan carefully pulled out a bunch of lilies, hurried out, and slammed the door shut with an undignified grunt. She puffed a stray lock of hair off her forehead, and when she turned around, she found herself staring into a pair of familiar green eyes.

Gavin.

Chapter 10

"GAVIN." HIS NAME RUSHED FROM HER LIPS, AND HER hand curled around the long, cool metal handle of the storeroom door as she instinctively took a step back. With nowhere else to go though, all she did was press herself against the handle, which was now digging into the flesh of her ass. Swallowing hard, Jordan held the cluster of flowers against her chest, the only barrier standing between her body and his. She flicked her gaze to the door that led to the alley and then back to his fierce, hungry stare. "I guess Cookie left the door unlocked," she murmured.

Gavin's tall, broad-shouldered frame loomed in front of her. He didn't make a move to come closer; the man simply stood there. His hands were curled into fists, arms at his sides, and he looked like a tiger ready to pounce. His dark brows knit together as he kept her pinned to the door with a look that practically devoured her. He wasn't exactly blocking her exit. He caged her in with his presence more than his body. It wasn't threatening or menacing the way it had been with Ted.

It was predatory and hungry.

Jordan knew she could have walked around him—that is, if her legs would cooperate. At the moment, doing more than standing there was above her pay grade.

"I saw Cookie leave a few minutes ago." Gavin's voice was tight, bordering on a growl. His jaw clenched and the muscle beneath his stubble-covered flesh flickered. "I wanted to speak to you without the peanut gallery chiming in."

"Fine."

Jordan eased away from the door handle and forced her body to move, quickly stepping around Gavin. She walked to the other side of the long, metal worktable and spread out the lilies. The ends didn't really need to be cut again, but she had to do something other than stand there and simmer beneath his gaze. It was bad enough that her stomach swirled with a tornado of butterflies and her face felt like it was on fire. Grabbing the shears from the toolbox on the counter behind her, she started snipping the ends with more ferocity than necessary.

She could still feel his eyes on her.

"Aren't you supposed to be at work, Gavin?"

"Rick and Jeff have it covered for a few minutes." He sidled nearer, his deep voice drifting over her seductively. "Rick knows how important it was for me to come here tonight, and I'll be able to hear if we get a call."

"Great. I'm so glad you can confide in him." She snipped another green stem forcefully. "What did you want to talk about? Because you sure weren't chatty earlier."

"Us." Gavin moved slowly around the table, and even though she wasn't looking at him, she could feel him getting closer. "I made a mistake and I need to fix it."

"Look, Gavin. Like you said earlier, let's forget it."

Jordan tossed the shears back into the box, scooped up the bits of stem scattered around the stainless-steel surface, and dumped them in the garbage underneath the table. She gathered the lilies into one big bunch and walked away from him around the other end of the long table, but he clocked her every move.

"It's complicated, Gavin, and too messy. I knew this would happen, okay? We have too much unresolved stuff of our own, let alone between us, for us to be friends. If this keeps up, one or both of us will get hurt."

Before she could get to the door of the showroom, Gavin stepped in front of her, blocking her exit. Puffing her hair off her forehead, Jordan forced herself to look him in the face. The moment she did, she knew it had been a bad move. Her gaze skittered over the sharp angles of his jaw. The baby fat of youth had given way to hard edges and shadows, but those glittering green eyes remained the same. They still made her stomach flutter and bored through her with his trademark intensity.

"We can't be friends," he said quietly. The line between his brows deepened. "I was fooling myself."

"Fine." Her heart thundered in her chest and blood rushed in her ears, the sound blocking out everything else. "We're done. Move, please. I have to finish this and go pick up my girls."

Good, she thought. He was being the brave one and saying what she didn't have the courage to say. Tears pricked the back of her eyes, and her breath stuck in her throat as she struggled to find her voice again. Clutching the flowers to her chest with both hands, she licked her suddenly dry lips, her eyes searching his. He remained resolute and unmoving. *Damn him.* What was his problem? Would he not be satisfied until she was a weeping heap on the floor?

"Please move," she whispered.

"No." His mouth set in tight line and a deadly, feral look flashed in his eyes. "We are far from done."

"What do you want from me, Gavin?" she asked shakily as her vision blurred with tears. "Tell me what you want."

"This," he growled.

In a blur, he cupped his hand around the back of her neck and pulled her to him, covering her mouth with his. The kiss was hot, firm, demanding, and laced with desperation. Jordan moaned and opened to him as his tongue slid along the seam of her lips, seeking access. The flowers fell to the floor as she linked her arms around his neck and clung to him with fifteen years of pent-up need. His taste was foreign and familiar at the same time, and Jordan hadn't felt desire like this in years—maybe ever.

His hands cradled her face, tilting her head to get a better angle as he kissed her and walked with her, backing her up against the wall. She tangled her fingers in his hair and met the hard demand of his kiss with equal urgency as they bumped into the unyielding surface of the wall. With anyone else, being pinned with nowhere else to go would be terrifying, but not with Gavin.

Jordan didn't feel trapped. Far from it. She felt free. Unencumbered. Desired.

She had been such a fool.

This was what she needed, what they both needed. The taste of him and the pressure of his strong, hard body against hers sent the surge of desire boiling over with every delicious sweep of his tongue.

Breaking the kiss, Gavin trailed his lips down her throat. One hand cradled her head and the other swept down her side and over the curve of her hip, tugging her against the hard evidence of his desire. Jordan let out a gasp of pleasure as she pulled his shirt from the waist of his pants and slipped her hands beneath the fabric, damp with his sweat. The hot flesh of his lower back seared her fingers, and she clung to him as his mouth once again sought hers. Jordan whimpered when Gavin's lips slanted over hers hungrily. Her tongue swept along his, meeting every hard, passionate stroke with equal fervor.

This was nothing like the kisses they'd shared in their youth. There was no awkward fumbling or tentative grappling. Instead the kiss was swift, sure, and all consuming, and Jordan could stay here forever. He tasted like cinnamon, and she fleetingly wondered if he'd been eating oatmeal cookies. That's what the taste reminded her of. Cookies fresh out of the oven. Sweet, hot, and addictive. Those three words summed it all up, and as his mouth seared hers, she knew she'd never, ever get enough.

Gavin groaned as he grasped her wrists and pinned her arms over her head, kissing her deeply. The movement made her back arch and pressed her breasts against the hard planes of his chest. She shook with lust, need, and anticipation; she slid her leg up and hooked it over his hip, pulling him closer.

He suckled her lower lip before settling his forehead on hers. He held Jordan there, her body deliciously pinned between him and the wall. Gavin's thigh had slipped between her legs and he put pressure on exactly the right spot. If he moved, even a fraction of an inch, she might come right then and there. Her sex pulsed with need and every nerve ending was on fire.

"I can't only be friends with you, Jordan," he whispered harshly.

Gavin tilted his hips against hers, and she whimpered as licks of pleasure flickered from her clit to her core. His fingers curled tighter around her wrists, and he brushed his thumb along her sweaty palms. Their breath mingled and their bodies shuddered against each other with every word that rushed from his lips.

"I thought I could do it, but there's no way I can be around you and not touch you. Today, when you told me what your bastard ex-husband did, I could have killed someone. And then when we saw Tommy, I lost it. I'm sorry I snapped at you, but ever since you came home, I've had my head up my ass. I thought I could do it—just be your friend—but I was wrong."

He kept her pinned to the wall and struggled to catch his breath, his chest pressing against hers with as it expanded and contracted. "Do you know how many times I've thought about this? About tasting you and seeing this look in your eyes? I'm feeling lots of things toward you, Jordan, and *friendly* is an understatement."

"Gavin?" Jordan murmured as a grin curved her lips and she rocked her hips against his thigh. "Shut up."

Before he could say another word, she popped up on her toes and covered his mouth with hers. Tangling her hands in his thick, dark hair, this time she took control of the kiss and pressed herself against him. In one swift motion, Gavin grabbed her ass with both hands and picked her up. Kissing her deeply, he carried Jordan to the table in one effortless stride. She hooked her ankles behind his back as he deposited her onto the cool stainless-steel surface and trailed kisses down her throat.

He nuzzled her breast and wrapped one strong arm around her waist, his fingers pressing against her, anchoring her to him. Desire erupted inside her as Gavin's hot mouth covered her breast. She moaned when his teeth grazed her nipple through the fabric of her dress. Threading her fingers through his hair, Jordan held him to her. She gasped when Gavin slipped his hands beneath the hem of her dress and those long, warm fingers clutched her thigh just as the shrill sound of her cell phone chirped from the showroom.

"Don't answer that." Gavin stilled and lifted his head, that fierce, hungry stare boring right through her. His fingers clung to her tighter and he growled, "I'm begging you not to answer that."

Through the fog of lust and the enticing sensation of Gavin's rough, heated hands on her bare legs, Jordan needed a minute to recognize the ringtone newly assigned to her mother.

"It's my mother," she said in husky voice she barely recognized. "The girls are with her. I have to get it."

Gavin's grip tightened briefly. His mouth set in a firm line, and he nodded his reluctant understanding. Jordan mourned the loss of his touch as his hands slipped from her thighs and he stepped back, allowing her to hop off the table. Her legs felt positively rubbery when her feet hit the floor, and she didn't miss the knowing smirk on Gavin's face. Adjusting her dress so that her lace bra was no longer peeking out, Jordan hurried to the showroom and grabbed her ringing phone from the bag under the counter.

"Hey, Mom." She pressed the phone to her ear as Gavin's tall frame slipped in behind her. His muscular arms snaked around her waist while he nuzzled the ponytail off her neck and planted butterfly kisses on the sensitive flesh. She giggled and elbowed him, but he kept it up. "I'm sorry; I'm running a little late tonight." Slipping out of his embrace, Jordan spun around and stepped back, wagging her finger at him. "I had an unexpected *event* at work." Gavin waggled his eyebrows back at her, and she fought the laugh that threatened to bubble up. "Are the girls okay?"

Silence hung on the other end of the line, and all humor dissipated when she heard an unmistakable sniffle.

"Mom?" Panic laced Jordan's voice as every awful scenario ripped through her mind. Did Ted show up at the house? Had the girls gotten hurt? "Mom, what's wrong?"

"It's your father, Jordan." Her mother's voice was barely above a whisper, and it sounded as though she'd been crying. "The nurse said it won't be long... Come home."

"Okay." Jordan's throat tightened with a swell of conflicting emotion. Gavin moved in next to her and slipped his arm around her waist, pulling her close. Jordan's eyes fluttered closed as he kissed the top of her head. "I'll be right there."

Jordan hung up, and without having to say a word, Gavin gathered her in his arms and held her. Tears stung her eyes and she buried her face against the warm expanse of his chest as he gently rocked her.

"I have to go." Jordan was dizzy with a flurry of conflicting emotions. "My father—"

"I'll drive," he said without missing a beat. "Come on. We'll take my truck. That way if we get a call, I can meet them there."

"Are you sure?" Jordan swiped at her eyes and grabbed her bag. "What if—"

"Hey, it's fine." Gavin's voice was gentle but firm. He tilted her chin with one finger, forcing her to look him in the face. "There's more than one kind of fire. Right now, you need help with yours."

Jordan didn't utter a word during the entire ride to her parents' place, and her silence was more painful than Gavin expected. He called Rick and let him know what was happening, in case they needed him. Glancing into the rearview mirror of his truck, Gavin caught a glimpse of his gear. It was reassuring to remember that if a call came in, he could get there in a hot minute.

As chief, he had what were considered administrative hours, but that didn't matter too much. Gavin felt an overwhelming responsibility to his team and the town, and his job wasn't limited to certain hours. Not as far as he was concerned. They had plenty of backup with the volunteer firefighters, and given the unusual amount of activity lately, all of the guys were on their toes even more than in the past—and that was saying something.

Pulling into the cracked paved driveway of the old Colonial house, Gavin threw a prayer to the universe that whatever went down tonight would give Jordan a certain amount of peace. She hopped out of the truck before he even put it into park. She ran up the porch steps to greet her mother, who was standing in the doorway, a grim expression on her face. Wasting no time, Gavin hightailed it out of the truck and was a few steps behind Jordan as she followed her mother into the front hall.

"Gavin." Claire nodded at him before turning her weary gaze to her daughter. "It's been a while."

"What's going on, Mom?" Jordan asked breathlessly before Gavin could respond. "Is he—"

"He's been goin' on and on, but I can't make much sense of it most of the time. Although, I think he actually knew who I was...for a moment." Claire kept her voice low. Lily and Gracie were sitting on the braided rug in the living room watching television, but Gavin could tell they were both more interested in what was happening out here. "You should go on up and say your piece, Jordan. Your daddy ain't gonna last much longer. His breathing is gettin' real ragged, and the nurse said he probably ain't gonna make it through the night."

Jordan nodded but remained quiet as she settled her sights on the girls. She put her purse down on the little table by the front door. Gavin curled one hand over her shoulder and moved in behind her, gently kissing the top of her head. Jordan leaned into him, instinctively seeking comfort.

"Are you alright?" Gavin asked quietly. "Do you want me to take the girls outside or down to the park for a little while?"

"No." Jordan shook her head and squared her shoulders, as though bracing herself for a challenge. "I'm not the only one who should have a chance to say good-bye."

"Do you really think the girls should see him like this?" Claire asked, shuffling her feet. She flicked her wide eyes to Gavin briefly, as though asking him for help. "They ain't never met him, Jordan. Well, Lily's been awful curious and peekin' round the corners of the stairs sometimes when I go up to check on him, but I don't know if you should have 'em go up there."

"I know, Mama. But the more I think about it, the more I think keeping the girls away from him was a mistake. Just one of many that I've made." Taking her mother's hand in hers, Jordan pulled her in for a quick hug and kissed her on the cheek. "But this is one mistake I can fix right now."

"Girls? I need to speak to you about something important." Slipping from her mother's embrace, she crossed into the sparsely decorated living room and shut off the television. Taking both the girls by the hands, she pulled them to their feet before giving each of them a huge hug. "You know that my daddy is sick. Right?"

"Yes." Lily nodded as Gracie inched closer to her. "Meemaw said he's going to heaven soon."

"That's true." Jordan dropped to her knees and gathered their little hands in hers. "I'm going to go upstairs and sit with him for a little while so that I can say good-bye. Now, I know you girls haven't met him, but I wanted to give you the chance to see him before…"

Her voice wavered and the pained sound of it hit Gavin like a ton of bricks, making him want to pull her into his arms. But he didn't. Stuffing his hands in his pockets, he shifted his weight and stayed in the archway, not taking his eyes off Jordan or the girls.

Lily seemed more curious than afraid, but little Gracie was another story.

"I don't wanna," Gracie said quickly. Shaking her head, she ran over to Claire and clung to her skirt before burying her face in it. "Can we make cookies, Meemaw?"

"It's okay, baby." Claire stroked the child's head with quivering fingers and took her by the hand. Her raspy, almost paper-thin voice echoed through the entry hall as she forced a smile for her granddaughter. "How about if we eat some of those cookies we already made this afternoon? You ate all of your dinner, so it seems to me that you get to have your dessert. How about that?"

Gracie nodded furiously and bit her lower lip.

"That's a fine idea, Gracie." Jordan rose to her feet, Lily's hand clutched tightly in hers. "You go with Meemaw, but be sure to save us some of those yummy cookies."

Gracie smiled at her mother and nodded before throwing a shy glance in Gavin's direction.

"We'll be in the kitchen if you need us," Claire whispered. "Come on, baby."

Giving Gavin a quick pat on the arm, Claire led Gracie away through the dining room before disappearing into the kitchen at the back of the house.

"Lily?" Jordan walked into the hallway with her daughter. Lily was the spitting image of her mother, so much so that they could have been twins. In fact, Gavin thought, she looked just like Jordan had when her family first moved to town. Stopping at the foot of the staircase, Jordan white-knuckled the banister. "Do you want to come with me to see your grandfather, or would you rather go have cookies with Gracie? Either way is fine with me."

Lily swiped a strand of long blond hair from her eyes and looked from her mother to Gavin. Grabbing Jordan's hand with both of hers, she fiddled with the silver ring on her mother's pinky finger and stared at it intently before turning her large brown eyes upward.

"Mama?" Lily leaned against Jordan's legs while peering up at Gavin. "Can the chief come too?"

"I don't know, Lily," Jordan said hesitantly.

"Of course I'll come." Gavin smiled at Lily and winked. "I am paid to protect the people of Old Brookfield, aren't I?"

"Uh-huh." Lily nodded before giving her mother a wide-gapped grin. "He's gonna come with us, Mama, 'cause he's the chief and he'll keep us safe."

How was it possible for one little girl to make Gavin feel like a big pile of mush? Something inside his chest ached, and as he looked from Lily to Jordan, he knew in that moment his life was forever altered. Not only was he still in love with Jordan—that was now more apparent to him than ever—but he was falling head over heels for her little girls too.

His goose was officially cooked.

Jordan, her eyes rimmed with tears, simply nodded her agreement. She held her daughter's hand and ascended the narrow, creaking staircase to the second floor. Gavin stayed close behind and his heart did a somersault when Lily peered over her shoulder, as though making sure he was still there. Giving her a thumbs-up, he followed them up the steps.

When they reached the landing, Jordan stopped outside the bedroom door and squatted down to speak with Lily face-to-face. Gavin knew Jordan was a good mother, but seeing the way she was with her daughters drove it home. The woman was smart and loving, and had a steely strong core that would put most men to shame.

"If you get scared or feel like you want to leave, then

let me know." She took Lily's face in her hands and kissed her gently on the cheek. "Okay? You ready?"

Lily nodded but said nothing. Gavin gave her a reassuring wink when she once again checked to see if he was still there.

"I'm right here, kid." Reaching out, he pretended to pull a quarter from her ear. "Me *and* my bag of tricks."

Lily's smile widened as she took the quarter from Gavin's fingers and Jordan opened the door.

Chapter 11

ANY DOUBTS JORDAN HAD ABOUT BRINGING LILY TO see her grandfather dissipated almost as soon as they stepped into the room. It wasn't scary or dark, and her father didn't look like the boogeyman but simply an old man with little life left in him. As it did every afternoon, the sun shone brightly through the windows and there was a vase of colorful wildflowers on the nightstand.

In spite of the situation, the room looked positively cheerful, and Jordan wondered why she'd never seen it that way before. Perhaps she'd been too caught up in her own anger or frustration to see anything else.

The hospice nurse was a lovely Jamaican woman named Bitsy. She smiled broadly when they arrived, instantly putting Jordan at ease. Her braided hair was piled high on her head, giving her an almost regal look. The pink scrubs she wore covered a soft, round body, but her finest feature had to be her bright, beautiful smile.

"Well, now," Bitsy said, rising from the chair by Jordan's father's bed. As usual, he was staring at the wall, openmouthed and with a vacant expression; this time his breathing was more labored. "Look here, my friend. You have some visitors—and a pretty little one at that." She fixed his blanket so that he was well covered and adjusted the pillow behind his head. "You're a lucky man to have so many fine people here to see you. He's been askin' for you, Miss Jordan."

"He has?" Hopeful and hesitant, Jordan inched farther into the room and kept her voice low. "Really? When I visited before, he didn't know who I was."

"That's the dementia, miss. It comes and it goes, but today he's been coming more than going." Hands on her ample hips, she nodded and gave Gavin the once-over. "Where you been hiding this handsome fella? And a fireman, no less?" She pointed at the emblem on his shirt and shook her head. "The firemen by my house don't look nothin' like you."

"Oh, sorry. This is Gavin." Jordan's face heated as she made the introductions. "He's an old friend."

"I bet he is." Bitsy leaned back and looked him up and down. "Nice to meet you, Mr. Gavin. Now then, I'll go outside and give you some privacy so you can have a nice visit."

"Thank you, Bitsy." Lily nestled back against Jordan, who settled her hands on Lily's shoulders. "Lily wanted to come see her grandfather before…but…"

"Of course she did." Bitsy tapped Lily's nose with one finger and flashed that million-dollar smile. She pointed to the colorful drawings on the wall by his bed. "It's about time she came up here. She made these lovely pictures, and now he can see the pretty girl who made them. Yes, sir."

The faded, blue-painted wall had been bare days before, but now three drawings with familiar-looking sparkles were taped to it. Lily's nervousness seemed to ease when she saw her handiwork on display, her little body relaxing against Jordan's legs.

"You made those for your grandfather?" Jordan asked quietly. "You and Gracie?"

"Uh-huh." Lily smiled and pointed at them, the quarter Gavin had given her still clutched in one hand. "Gracie's has the sparkles but I made the other two. We made them at camp, and Meemaw hung 'em up for us today."

"I gave him something for the pain, sweetie." Stepping away from the bed, Bitsy leaned in and whispered to Jordan. "I'll be right outside if you need me."

Gavin hung back as Jordan settled into the chair by her father's bedside and pulled Lily into her lap. She could have wept with relief when Gavin automatically agreed to come up here with them and—more so—did it without hesitation. Driving her out to the house was one thing, but coming up here as moral support was quite another. He was no fan of her father's, but he was obviously becoming a fan of Lily and Grace. She suspected that the man would literally and figuratively run through fire for them—for all of them.

"Dad?" Jordan's voice was quiet but strong. She wrapped her hand over his frail, wrinkled one lying against the cream-colored blanket. "It's me, Jordan. And I brought someone special for you to meet."

The old man blinked, as though finally realizing he was not alone in the room. His body, worn and weak, twitched as he turned his head. He seemed to catch sight of them, but his watery brown eyes didn't focus on Jordan, as she'd hoped they might. The instant he spotted Lily, however, his gaze widened and a smile bloomed on his gaunt face, his bushy gray eyebrows flying up in wonder.

"Jordan," he rasped. Lifting his hand, he waved weakly and a brittle laugh rattled in his chest. "Where you been, girl? I been waitin' on ya."

"Dad?" Jordan glanced over her shoulder at Gavin, who looked as confused as she felt. Turning back to her father, she scooted to the edge of the chair and hung tightly on to Lily. "I'm Jordan and this is Lily, your granddaughter."

"You're gettin' so big, baby girl," he said, as though he hadn't heard Jordan at all. He sucked in a shuddering, labored breath and kept his gaze pinned to Lily. "I love the pictures you made me. Your mama brought 'em to me and hung 'em right there," he wheezed. "I like lookin' at 'em, and they sure do make me happy."

Jordan's heart ached and tears stung her eyes at the realization. Her father thought that Lily was actually *her*. She kissed the back of Lily's head and smiled through her tears, hugging her daughter firmly.

"I'm glad you like them," Lily said, her legs swinging as she sat perched in Jordan's lap. "I made the one with the stars, and Gracie made the sparkly one 'cause she said sparkles make her feel better when she's sick."

"You're such a good girl." A brittle cough racked his body. Without Jordan having to say a word, Gavin swooped around the other side of the bed. He tried to help her father, adjusting the pillow so he could sit up, but the coughing soon stopped and devolved into rattled breathing. Between gasping breaths, her father said, "I'm sorry if I've been ornery lately, but you know that I love you. Don't you? Even if I'm ornery," he wheezed, "I still love you."

Her throat tight with emotion and with tears blurring her vision, Jordan swiped at her eyes with the back of her hand. Unable to say a word, too worried that she'd erupt into a weepy mess and frighten Lily, she simply nodded and allowed his words to sink in.

Words she'd waited decades to hear.

In the most unexpected way, her father had given her the one thing she'd wanted. In that instant she knew that everything would be okay—that she'd be okay. Seeing her father weakened by illness and beaten by life, Jordan had a new understanding about him. Like her, he'd made his share of mistakes. Somewhere along the way, he'd lost himself and allowed his regrets to poison him *and* his life. He'd let errors from the past stain his future, and Jordan knew that was not a mistake she wanted to make. He'd used booze to drown his failures, and while it certainly wasn't an excuse, was it any different from Jordan running away to drown her own?

A moment later, Gavin's strong hand stroked the back of her head. It took Jordan a minute to realize he'd come back to her side of the room. Glancing up to her left, she felt the tension ease from her when Gavin gave her a reassuring nod, his fingers drifting along the back of her neck.

A rock. The man was an immovable force. Strong, steadfast, and solid. In that moment Jordan knew, beyond a shadow of a doubt, that she wanted Gavin in her life. Not only for today but every day. He was right. They did deserve a do-over.

Everyone deserved a second chance at happiness. Perhaps that was something her father never figured out. He'd never looked for or recognized his chance for a do-over in his life. Maybe he didn't even think it was possible.

"Do you want to sing a song with me?" Lily asked with the innocence that only a child could have. "My mommy sings it with me sometimes, and Meemaw said that you sang it to Mommy when she was a little girl."

As Lily started singing "Twinkle, Twinkle, Little Star," the smile on Jordan's father's face widened. Too weak to sing, he simply grinned and wagged his fingers as Lily sang the slightly off-tune melody. The tears fell freely down Jordan's cheeks.

With her daughter in her arms and Gavin by her side, Jordan vowed she would no longer be defined by the sins of the past.

Jordan didn't want to leave her mom alone, and Gavin would be damned if he was gonna drive away with her old man on the verge of dying.

It was a good thing he'd stayed, in the end, because the guy clocked out not long after midnight, with both his wife and daughter by his side. Gavin felt kind of guilty for thinking it, but it was a better send-off than the man deserved. He kept his feelings to himself though, especially after seeing how peaceful Jordan seemed.

As the sun peeked over the horizon and the coroner's van disappeared around the corner, Gavin stood on the porch and drank his fourth cup of coffee. Leaning against the railing, he pulled out his cell phone and sent a quick text to Rick, letting him know what was going on. He got an immediate response saying that Bill would cover Gavin's shifts for the wake and funeral.

Good men, good friends, and a damn good team.

Gavin was a lucky man professionally, and for the first time in years, he thought his good fortune might actually be spilling over into his personal life.

Jordan had told him ten different times that he could leave, and each time he'd simply shaken his head before pouring another cup of coffee. The girls had fallen asleep on the couch and he'd helped her carry them upstairs, Jordan taking Gracie, and Lily draped over him like a rag doll. As he carried Lily up the stairs, a warm ache seeped through his chest.

How in the world could their father have let them go?

Hell, Jordan and her daughters weren't even his family, and he already blanched at the notion of losing them.

The sound of the screen door creaking open caught his attention, and a moment later Jordan was standing next to him on the porch. Her long, lovely body, the one that always seemed so effortlessly graceful, looked weary and bone tired. Her big, brown eyes were puffy and red from crying, and the light that usually burned from the inside seemed to have dimmed.

"My mother's finally asleep," Jordan murmured. "You know, I think she's almost relieved that he's gone, and I can't say that I blame her. Maybe 'relieved' isn't the right word," she added quickly. "She loved him, in spite of everything. She loved him, but there's no denying her life with him was more than difficult."

"She'll be okay, Jordan."

"What's she going to do now? Her whole world revolved around him. Making sure he wasn't too upset, always walking on eggshells to keep him happy." Letting out a sigh, she leaned against the post. "I'm worried about her, Gavin."

Jordan stared out at the horizon, and as her eyes fluttered closed, she folded her arms over her breasts and her body wavered, like flame in a draft. One rush of wind would knock her right over. The woman was

exhausted, and for a second, Gavin thought she was
going to fall asleep standing up.

"That's it." Gavin put the coffee cup on the little
wicker table by the window and, before she could protest, scooped Jordan off her feet and into his arms. "You
can worry about her, and I'll worry about you."

"What are you doing?" Jordan asked through a big
yawn. She settled her head on his shoulder and melted
against his chest. Gavin tried not to think about how
perfectly she fit there, her curves settling into his, like a
lock slipping into place. "I'd fight you on it, but I'm too
tired, and as we've established, I think you like fighting
with me."

"I'm taking you to bed." He smirked and flicked the
screen door open with the toe of his boot. "And believe
me, this is not the way I pictured getting you there."

"You're a regular scoundrel." She linked her arms
around his neck and snuggled deeper into his embrace.
"But there's too much to do. I have to call the funeral
home and—"

"It's six in the morning, Jordan." Gavin shook his
head and let out a gruff laugh. "Most people are asleep,
and you can take care of all that stuff later on with your
mom. Right now, you have to get some rest."

"But what if the girls wake up?" Her voice was
sleepier by the second and she fought to keep her eyes
open. "They won't know where I am, and they've never
slept here before."

"That bed that they're in is plenty big enough for all
of you."

Gavin climbed the stairs with ease, keeping his voice
to a whisper. He took each step carefully, trying to keep

the old boards from creaking. Turning the corner at the top of the landing, he carried her down the hall and gently bumped open the door to the spare bedroom.

"See?" he whispered as he silently brought her into the room. Standing by the edge of the bed, they both looked down at the girls. They were sleeping peacefully, tucked up together like a couple of kittens. "They left you half of the bed as if they were waiting for you to join them."

It took him a moment to realize Jordan was staring at him. His gut clenched when he shifted his gaze down to hers. He held her soft, warm body firmly against his. Awareness throbbed between them as her fingers drifted along the nape of his neck and his hands tightened their grip on her. The look in her eyes shifted to one of unmistakable desire, and Gavin swallowed hard.

"You can put me down now," she murmured, her fingers easing up his neck and tangling in his hair. "Not that I'm not enjoying the royal treatment."

Without a word, Gavin gently placed Jordan on her feet. But he didn't release her. His hands moved down her back and settled along the top of her ass, his fingers lightly cupping the soft curves of her bottom. Letting his gaze float over her flawlessly beautiful face, Gavin took in every delicate inch. The woman looked as lovely today as she had fifteen years ago. Maybe more.

"There's nothing I'd like more than to pick up where we left off," he said in a raspy whisper. Gavin's fingers trailed up her sides, and he let his thumbs graze the underside of her breasts. Jordan's eyes widened and her fingers fluttered over his chest seductively. "But…you need sleep."

"True." Jordan glanced over her shoulder at the girls. Grasping the front of his shirt, she tugged him gently against her. She opened her mouth to say something, then shook her head. He knew she was mulling over exactly what she wanted to say. She stared at his chest and ran her forefinger over the emblem on the right side of his shirt. "Thank you, Gavin. I think Lily said it best... You keep people safe."

"Always." He pressed his lips to Jordan's forehead and murmured, "Now get in that bed before I lose my sense and forget I'm a gentleman."

Jordan let out a soft, almost musical laugh before slipping from his embrace and crawling beneath the covers, careful not to wake the girls. She adjusted the blankets over them before casting one last smile his way. Gavin stood in the doorway, his fingers lingering on the smooth glass knob for a moment before he quietly closed the door and walked away.

Making his way out of the house, he shut the door tightly behind him. Once he got in his truck though, he sat looking at the old Colonial for a long time. His thoughts drifted to the last time he'd been here. It was the day after Jordan ran away, and Gavin had been so mad he couldn't see straight. The shouting match with her old man had quickly turned into a shoving match. It wasn't much of a fight because her father was older and drunk as a skunk. Gavin had gotten off one good shot right before the cops showed up and hauled his ass out of there.

That day, he'd felt like his life was over. Jordan was gone. He'd been dragged into the police station, and the only reason he didn't get arrested was because Claire had talked her husband out of filing charges. Gavin had never really believed he'd get a second chance with Jordan. Like the fires he fought, life seemed to be full of surprises.

Chapter 12

"IT WAS A LOVELY SERVICE." THE WOMAN'S VOICE WAS steeped with empathy, and she sounded like the handful of others who had attended the funeral and reception at the house. And as with the rest, Jordan didn't really know her. Truth be told, most of them barely knew her father but had come to pay their respects to Jordan's mom. In spite of all the years of her husband's bad behavior, Claire had still managed to invest herself in the community.

"I'm so sorry for your loss, dear."

"Thank you." Jordan nodded and shook the woman's hand "Thank you for coming."

The old lady left, carefully making her way down the porch steps.

Smoothing the fabric of her black linen dress, Jordan peered through the porch window. Most of the guests had gone. Claire was sitting on the sofa with two of her friends from church, looking through her old wedding album. The caterers were cleaning up the last of the mess in the dining room, and Jordan could hear the girls' playful shrieks as they ran around the backyard with Maddy and some other neighborhood children.

"Hey." Gavin's deep voice rolled over her, and his strong arms curled around her waist. Pulling her against him, he kissed her ear, then took her by the hand and led her to the white wicker porch swing. "Take a load off.

You've been going nonstop for the past three days, and this might be the longest I've seen you standing still in the past twenty-four hours."

It was true. From the moment her father died, she'd had to make a series of phone calls for the funeral arrangements, not to mention sifting through her father's paperwork with her mother. Wakes. Caterers. Life insurance. One task immediately begat another, and through it all, Gavin had been there—in the background, ready and waiting. He draped his arm over her shoulders when she sat next to him on the swing, and she let out a sigh of contentment. The joyful sound of Lily's laughter filled the air and brought a smile to Jordan's lips.

"Is Maddy still playing hide-and-seek with all the kids?" Jordan asked with a giggle. "I think she likes it more than they do."

"Yeah, she is, and if Rick were here, he'd be right back there with her." His fingertips made lazy circles on her upper arm. "He's actually an enormous, hairy toddler pretending to be a grown-up most of the time. He sends his sympathies and was sorry he couldn't make the funeral, but he's on shift."

"I know. Maddy told me. I'm surprised they've never married. I mean, they've been together for years and both of them would be great parents." Jordan leaned further into his embrace. "But it's not for everyone, I guess."

"It's the job," Gavin said quietly. "Rick's father was killed when he was about six or seven, and he doesn't want to risk doing that, you know? Work is his baby and always will be. I've even heard Maddy refer to herself as Rick's mistress because he's married to the job."

Jordan nodded her understanding but said nothing. Part of her wanted to know if Gavin felt the same way. Did he want a family, or was he married to his job like Rick? She opened her mouth to ask but snapped it shut and thought better of it.

Given the way their relationship was evolving, she didn't want him to misunderstand the question or feel pressured. They had only begun exploring this *thing* between them, so it seemed too early to be asking about his thoughts on marriage and children. Besides, he'd stayed single and childless so far. What would make her think he'd want to change any of that because of her?

"It was nice of your parents to come," she said, wanting desperately to change the subject. "Honestly, other than them, Cookie, Veronica, and Maddy, I didn't really know anyone here. A few have come into the shop, but I don't *really* know them." She let out a slow breath. "Funny thing is, I don't think most people who came knew my father well at all."

"They came for Claire," Gavin said evenly. "All the church ladies were here, and even Mrs. Drummond paid her respects at the service. All in all, I'd say your father had a good turnout at his funeral because of your mom. She's a doll and everyone loves her. Present company included."

"You've been wonderful." Leaning her head on his shoulder, Jordan closed her eyes. He rocked the swing gently. "Thank you again…for everything."

"I didn't do much."

"Yes, you did." Sitting up, she turned her body so she could look him in the eyes. Cradling his face with one hand, she stroked his beard-scruffy cheek with her thumb. "Do you have any idea how much it meant to me to have you here? Whether you were showing the girls magic tricks or helping my mom move furniture around for this little gathering, or simply *being here*."

"Ah, that's no big deal, Jordan." He played with the ends of her hair and lifted one shoulder. "It's what people do."

"No." Jordan shook her head and let out a curt laugh. "No, it's not what most people do, Gavin. It's not what Ted would do. It certainly wasn't what my father did for most of my life, and living in New York City will quickly make you believe that *everyone* is only out for themselves. I know that you McGuires don't think stuff like that is a big deal, because you're used to it. Your family is unique, Gavin. You would do anything for the people you care about. But not everyone is like that."

"Maybe not." He gathered her hand in his and kissed her palm before lowering it to his lap. "But you're like that, and you're raising two little girls who will be too."

"I hope so," Jordan whispered. Tears stung her eyes but she squeezed them shut, hoping to will them away. "I'm trying to make it right, Gavin. Staying away for as long as I did was cowardly. It was the cowardly thing to do, and I wish like hell I'd come back sooner. Maybe if I had…"

She trailed off, unable to finish her sentence for fear she'd dissolve into a puddle. She hadn't cried other than that day when her father had first passed away, and not because she didn't care. In fact, in many ways, she felt more love for her father now than she ever had. She hadn't let herself cry because she couldn't afford to fall apart. She had to hold it together for her mother and her girls.

At least that's what she told herself. The truth was, she didn't want to break down because that would mean really feeling it—giving in to the pain and succumbing to the grief. That scared her more than anything else. Allowing herself to sink into it would mean acknowledging all she'd lost. There would be no second chances with her dad.

"Hey." Gavin pulled her to him. He wrapped those big, strong arms around her, murmuring against her hair. "You're here now and that's what counts."

Snuggled up against Gavin's chest with the warm summer breeze drifting over them, Jordan felt the dam finally break. She let out the flood of tears that she'd been holding back. His embrace tightened and she buried her face against the comforting, unyielding expanse of his body, one heavy, quiet sob coming after another. She wept for all of it: her father's wasted life, her mother's uncertain future, Ted's disinterest in his children, all the time she couldn't get back, and all the mistakes she couldn't undo.

Sniffling and struggling to stem the flow of tears, Jordan sucked in a few shuddering breaths. Gavin stroked her back reassuringly. She lifted her head only to find a wet stain on Gavin's pale green button-down shirt, the cotton also streaked with black smudges of mascara. Mascara she could only assume was now under her eyes, making her look like a raccoon.

Gavin gave her a small smile and swiped at the tears and presumably the eye makeup. Jordan giggled and sat up, quickly wiping away what was left in a feeble attempt at making herself presentable.

"Jeez. I ruined your shirt." She shook her head and rolled her eyes at her unusual display of emotion. "I'm a mess."

"I have plenty of shirts. And believe me, a few tears aren't the worst I've gotten on my clothes. Remember the food fights I had with my brothers? My poor mother said she should have bought stock in laundry detergent." Gavin's hand cradled her cheek and he tilted her chin, forcing her to look him in the eyes. When those intelligent green eyes latched onto hers, the storm inside of her stilled. The swirl of emotions and tsunami of guilt settled as Gavin cupped her face, the rough skin of his palm rasping deliciously along her cheek. "And you," he murmured, "are beautiful."

Caught up in the feel of his touch and the gentleness in his voice, Jordan didn't hear the car pull in the driveway. If she had, she would have been more prepared for what came next.

"Well, no moss grows here, I see," said an unwelcome and all-too-familiar voice. "Looks like you didn't waste any time moving on, Jordan."

Jordan's heart clenched in her chest as Gavin's hand fell away. Ted slowly climbed the steps of the porch, staring at them with nothing short of contempt. Dressed in a blue jacket, a white button-down shirt, and rumpled khaki pants, he was a disheveled mess. He'd gotten worse. Jordan hadn't thought it was possible for Ted, the man who was always perfectly coiffed, to look like such a disaster. His brown hair was longer than the last time she'd seen him, but those dark eyes—the ones filled with thinly veiled disgust—peered at her with stomach-churning familiarity.

She could smell the booze, and based on the look of him, he hadn't showered or slept in days. He'd obviously been on a bender of epic proportions, and the sway in his step confirmed his drunken state. Fear glimmered as she thought of the girls and prayed they would stay in the backyard until she could get Ted back in his limo.

Rising to her feet with Gavin firmly by her side, Jordan folded her arms over her breasts and bit back the surge of fear and fury. Yesterday, she'd finally responded to Ted's texts to tell him her father had died, but she never thought her ex-husband would show up. Tucking her hair behind her ears, Jordan squared her shoulders and braced herself for whatever would come next.

"What are you doing here, Ted?" Jordan asked in a stronger voice than she expected. There was a black stretch limo in the driveway, and as she caught another whiff of booze, she was grateful that at least he wasn't driving. "You really should have called first."

"I did." He flicked his woozy, heavy-lidded eyes to Gavin, smirked, and tried to tuck his Ray-Ban sunglasses into the inside pocket of his jacket. He missed the pocket on the first try but got it on the second. "I talked to Claire. Told her I wanted to surprise you."

"More like ambush," Gavin murmured. He kept his hands at his side, but Jordan could sense the tension in his body and hear it in his voice. "Surprises are usually more fun."

"I don't believe we've had the plea-ssure," Ted said, slurring his words. He flashed that charming smile and stuck his hand out to Gavin. He stared at it for a moment before briefly shaking it, only to drop it like a hot potato. "Ted McKenna. Jordan's husband."

"Ex-husband," Jordan corrected.

"Right. How could I forget? She left me." Ted's smile fell. "Who the hell are you?"

"Gavin McGuire." He seemed to stand even taller than before, his six-foot-two frame easily dwarfing Ted's slimmer, shorter stature. "Fire chief in Old Brookfield and an old friend of the family."

"Can't be much of an old friend," Ted scoffed. "I didn't even know she had *parents* until two years after we were married, and she never mentioned *you*."

"That's funny," Gavin said evenly, taking one step forward. "I've heard plenty about *you*. Or more to the point, your behavior."

Ignoring Gavin's last comment, Ted stumbled to his right and looked around the porch of the old Colonial as though it were the biggest dump on the planet.

"So this is where you grew up. I guess it explains a lot." As he turned around to face them, all humor left his voice. "Where are the girls?"

"They're in the backyard, but I really wish you'd let me know you were going to be here," Jordan said quickly. Anxiety rippled up her back as she moved toward him, Gavin right behind her. "They haven't seen you in six months, and you haven't even taken their calls for the past two. I really don't think surprising them at their grandfather's funeral is the best way to see them for the first time in months. Besides, you're drunk, Ted."

"Are you trying to keep me from my children?" Ted's eyes narrowed and he moved toward Jordan. He stopped dead in his tracks when Gavin took one more step in his direction. "I have a right to see my kids. You can't keep me from them. You may have moved them out here to this beach-town shithole, but you can't stop me from seeing them."

Gavin took another step closer but Jordan put her hand on his arm, preventing him from going any further.

"Actually, Ted," Jordan said in a cool, calm tone, "due to your series of failed drug tests, the judge ruled that you can't have unsupervised visits with them until you submit a *clean* drug test and complete a ninety-day rehab. Until you do that, all of your visits have to supervised by a court-appointed psychologist." Her tone softened. "*Please* get some help and go to rehab. If you love Gracie and Lily, and really want what's best for them, then you'll leave now and go straight there."

"This is bullshit," Ted spat out. "You want me to be *watched* with my own kids? Have some headshrinker spying on me? I don't need to go to some stupid rehab, Jordan. I'm fine."

"Yeah," Gavin scoffed. "You're in great shape."

"Fuck you." Ted wavered on his feet and would have fallen over but grabbed the railing and remained upright. "This is none of your business."

"It's not *only* my request," Jordan said calmly. "The judge made that ruling, and maybe if you hadn't been hungover in court all the time, you'd have remembered that part. Your attorney wanted to argue the point, but you were so hell-bent on getting rid of us that you told him to shut up."

"No way." Ted's face was beet red and the vein in his forehead bulged more with each passing second. His hands curled into fists and Jordan took an involuntary step back. "You think I'm going to let you raise my daughters to be white-trash whores like you?"

In his alcohol-fueled rage, he lunged toward Jordan. Eyes squeezed shut, she braced for the impact but none came.

"That's it," Gavin grunted. "You're outta here."

Instead of getting ahold of her, Ted was met with the immovable force that was Gavin McGuire. In a flash, Gavin grabbed him by the back of the neck and the belt of his pants, easily dragging the smaller man off the porch. Ted kicked and screamed profanity as Gavin escorted him to the waiting limo. The driver, who'd obviously seen them coming, was already out and holding open the door for his unruly boss.

At this point, Jordan's mother, the caterers, and the last few guests were spilling out onto the porch to see what was happening.

If Jordan hadn't been so furious, she'd have been completely mortified.

Shaking with a sure shot of adrenaline, Jordan turned in time to spot Maddy and the girls coming around the side of the house. Maddy quickly realized was going on and immediately shooed the girls to the backyard, keeping them from witnessing their father's outburst.

Letting out a whimper of relief, Jordan turned her attention back to the driveway and her blood ran cold at the sight before her.

Gavin's fists were curled around Ted's lapels, and he had Ted pinned against the side of the limo. Gavin loomed over her ex-husband with a ferocious, deadly look that she'd never seen before. His face was inches from Ted's and she could tell he was saying something, but they were too far away for her to hear.

And there was a better-than-average chance that Gavin's seemingly endless stream of patience had run out.

------※------

"I'll sue you and this whole crappy town if you don't take your hands off me," Ted spat out. Spittle clung to his chin and the distinct scent of whiskey wafted over Gavin with every word. "Do you have any idea how much I'm worth? A lot more than some loser fireman."

Gavin kept him pinned against the limo, rage bubbling up and damn well about to boil over. When Ted made the stupid mistake of lunging at Jordan, Gavin had almost lost it. But once he got his hands on the guy, he knew it wouldn't be a fair fight. Memories of tangling with Jordan's old man came roaring to the surface as he dragged Ted to the limo, but that wasn't what stopped him. It was the knowledge that Lily and Gracie might come into the front yard at any moment and see him pummeling their father.

"I'll have your job for this," Ted seethed. "I have witnesses."

"So do I," Gavin growled. His fists were firmly fixed around the guy's jacket, and he pressed him harder against the limo. "And they live in this, what did you call it? *Beach-town shithole*? Yeah, I think that was it. Unlike you, they care about Jordan and her mother, and I don't think they like seeing her threatened by her drunken ex-husband."

Gavin pushed his knuckles harder into the dirtbag's chest, making the guy wince.

"So here's what you're gonna do, *Ted*. You are going to put your whiskey-soaked ass in this shiny limo and go somewhere to dry out. If and when you sober up, *then* maybe you can contact Jordan about visiting her daughters. But in the meantime, I'll be taking Jordan down to the police station to file a formal complaint so she can seek a restraining order.

"You won't come within fifty feet of her or those girls. And if you do…" Gavin leaned closer so that his face was inches from Ted's. The man's eyes widened with the unmistakable flare of fear. "If you do, then you will deal with me. And I don't care if you own all of Manhattan. If you so much as breathe the wrong way near Jordan, Lily, or Gracie, I will personally kick your sorry ass so hard that not even your own mother will recognize you."

Gavin dropped his hands and stepped back as Ted's driver held the door open.

"This isn't over." Ted's dark, beady eyes narrowed, and he smoothed the wrinkled linen jacket before slipping into the limo. It did little good. The guy was a mess. "Not even close."

"Bye, Ted." Gavin stepped back as the car door slammed shut, and the limo backed up and sped away down the street. "Go to hell," he murmured.

Gavin suspected that wouldn't be the last he saw of good old Ted. It was a better than fair chance that the asshole would try to pay Jordan a visit at her house. Striding up the driveway, Gavin scanned the area to make sure the girls weren't anywhere in sight. While he didn't see them, there was an audience of wide-eyed women on the porch. Letting out a sigh of relief that at least Lily and

Gracie probably didn't see that exchange, some of the tension in his shoulders eased and he trotted up the steps.

"I'm sorry," Jordan said quietly.

"What are you apologizing for?" Gavin took her hand and gave it a squeeze. She was almost exactly his height while he was standing on the step below her, and the pained expression on her face about did him in. "You didn't do anything wrong. In fact, you handled him like a pro. You kept to the facts and cited the custody agreement."

"It's my fault," Claire said in a shaky whisper.

Wringing her hands together, with a church lady friend on either side of her, she looked every bit the beaten woman she'd been for most of her life. It was no surprise to Gavin that she hadn't stood up to Ted, given the guy she'd been married to. If a man told her to do something, she did it.

"He said he was comin', and I told him it might not be a good idea. But he kept insistin' that he wanted to see his girls and make it a surprise. I'm so sorry, Jordan. I didn't know he'd show up and act like that."

"Mama, stop." She gathered Claire in a hug, the two older women giving way for her. Gavin didn't miss the knowing look they exchanged as Jordan cradled her mother. "How could you know? You haven't spent any time with him, and I haven't exactly been a fountain of information about my life for the past few years. It's okay, Mama." Pulling back, Jordan gestured to the church ladies. "The caterer is about done cleaning up. Why don't you go on inside and relax?"

Claire nodded and started to go in the house, but she stopped in the doorway. Her frail hand lingered on the screen door for a moment before she set her weary sights on Gavin.

"I'm glad you were here, Gavin." Claire's salt-and-pepper hair fluttered as a late summer breeze drifted over them again. Tears filled her eyes and her voice came out in a strangled croak. "I-I don't want to think about what might have happened if you hadn't been."

As the screen door clacked shut behind her mother, Jordan immediately wrapped her arms around Gavin's waist, hugging him tightly. Claire's words haunted him. He'd made the restraining-order comment to Ted on a whim, but it actually made a hell of a lot of sense.

"I think you should consider getting a restraining order."

"A restraining order." Jordan stilled before lifting her head slowly. Her hands lingered along his waist and, staring into that gorgeous face, he could see the wheels turning. "I don't know, Gavin. I mean, that's taking it to a whole other level, and what's a piece of paper gonna do?"

"He cares about his reputation, right? If you file one against him, I doubt he'd do anything to violate it and get his sorry ass arrested. Those fancy clients of his wouldn't like that, would they? I think a restraining order would keep a coward like him at bay."

"Great idea!" Maddy's typically perky voice piped in. She strode around the side of the house and climbed the steps, a big grin on her face and her dark, curly hair bouncing around her head. "See? I knew you were more than a pretty face, Gavin."

"Where are the girls?" Jordan tensed and looked around for her daughters. "Did they see—"

"Not a thing." Maddy held up both hands and made the sign of an X over her heart. "I swear! When I saw Gavin with a squirrelly little man by a limo, I figured it could only be one person. The girls are in the kitchen having cookies with the kids from down the street. Listen, if anyone can pull a fast one and use the old distract-and-confuse trick, it's a Realtor," she said with a wink. Her smile faded and she leaned back against the railing, her long skirt fluttering in a gust of wind. "But I think Gavin is right about the restraining order, Jordan. Seriously? Your ex isn't wrapped right."

"Do me a favor." Tangling Jordan's fingers with his, Gavin pulled her to him and pressed a kiss to her forehead. "At least think about it."

"Right now…" Jordan sighed and spun around so her back was nestled against Gavin's chest. She pulled his arms around her waist, her body molded to his, and it felt so right that he never wanted her to move. "I'm so tired, I can't make any decisions. It's been an emotionally exhausting day."

"You said it!" Maddy hopped off the railing and glanced at her watch. "Listen, kids, I have to head out. I promised Rick I'd bring dinner by the station so the two of us can actually have a conversation while we're both awake." Giving Jordan and Gavin each a quick kiss on the cheek, she yanked open the screen door and waggled her eyebrows. "And maybe more than a conversation," she said before disappearing into the house.

"She's too much." Jordan laughed. "I'm going to check on the girls and have them gather up their things. I offered to stay here with my mom for a couple more days, but she wouldn't hear of it. Then I asked her to come stay with me, but she didn't want to do that either."

Sadness edged Jordan's voice as she looked through the screen at Claire. "I'm worried about her."

"This is her home, Jordan. She lived here with your dad, for better or worse, for over twenty years." Gavin let her hand slip from his as she went to the door. "But I have to be honest, with Ted lurking around, I wish like hell you weren't staying out at the beach alone."

"I'll be fine, Gavin." She tossed him that breathtaking smile, the one that lit up her entire face, and his heart did a somersault. "Ted won't come out there. He's probably halfway to the city by now."

"Really?" Gavin folded his arms over his chest and tilted his head. "You mean kind of like he wouldn't come to your father's funeral reception and make a scene? Like that?"

"What do you want me to do?" The tone of her voice ratcheted up, her fear and frustration—the things he knew she was trying to hide from him—roaring to the surface. "Crawl into a hole and hide? Deep down under all that booze, Ted is a coward. You said it yourself. I will not live in fear. That's one of the reasons I left him. And there's no way I'll let my daughters live that way."

Her face was etched with determination as she tilted her chin, daring him to argue with her, and in that moment, Gavin realized how much he loved her. She was scared, but in spite of that, the woman would do anything, suffer through anything, to give her daughters a safe, stable home.

"Fine." He nodded slowly. "You have a spare bedroom at your place? If I remember correctly, the Sweeneys' house had three bedrooms. Right?"

"Uh, yes." Jordan blinked and released the screen door's handle, letting the door close quietly. Gavin took another step nearer, hands in his pockets. He smiled when her nostrils flared ever so slightly upon his approach, and she leaned toward him almost imperceptibly. "There are three bedrooms," she said quietly. "The girls share one and I'm in the master. There's a small guest bedroom down the hall from mine. Why?"

Gavin smirked as a wide-eyed expression of understanding bloomed on Jordan's face.

"Oh, no you don't. I don't need a bodyguard, Gavin." Holding up both hands, she continued. "Besides, you have enough going on with all the fires lately and things being so crazy with your job. The last complication you need is feeling like you have to babysit me and my daughters."

"Well, actually, you'd be doing me a favor," he murmured.

"Oh really?" Jordan arched one eyebrow. "How's that?"

"I've been meaning to have my place painted." He tried to keep the smile from sliding across his face, but it was no use. "And those fumes gimme a headache."

"Oh really?"

"Sure." He tilted his head to the side. "Remember that summer before senior year when I painted houses with Nate and Vince? I had headaches the whole damn summer."

"Mmm-hmm." Jordan poked him in the chest. "Or were they from the cases of beer you guys drank?"

"Beer? Fumes? Who can say?" He put both hands over his heart in an overly dramatic gesture. "You wouldn't want me to take a chance like that, would you?

Of course not. So I'm gonna need somewhere to crash until the job is done and the fumes are clear."

"Is that so? Well, your parents' house is enormous, Gavin." Hands on her hips, she narrowed her eyes. "They have seven bedrooms in that place and are only using *one* at the moment. Why don't you stay there?"

"Naked time," he said flatly.

"What?" Jordan laughed.

"Don't ask." Making a face of derision, he shook his head. "Let's just say that if you make me stay with my parents, I might see things that would scar me for life."

"Gavin," she said, sighing. "What about your job? You can't *not* go to work. Come on. You can't be watching out for us every second."

"Let me worry about that." Taking her hands in his, he brought her fingers to his lips. "Besides, if Ted gets wind of the fact that I'm around, it might discourage him from causing more trouble. So whaddya say?" Tugging her close, he whispered, "Think you can handle a houseguest for a few days? Until we're sure Ted isn't a threat."

"Cool!" Maddy's smiling face appeared on the other side of the screen. They stepped back and she pushed the door open, staring at them with a wide grin. The door swung shut behind her. "You guys are moving in together?"

"Maddy," Jordan said in a warning tone. "We are *not* moving in together. Gavin is going to stay in the spare bedroom, *only* until we know that Ted is no longer in the area. That's it. He's being a good friend."

"Yeah, right," Maddy snorted. Giving them each a quick kiss, she trotted down the steps toward her car.

"Well, you two *friends* take care. I'm going to be more than friendly with my man, and we are going to make good use of Gavin's office."

"Great," Gavin groaned. "Not only is Rick getting laid, but he's doing it in my office."

"Jealous?" Jordan teased, elbowing him gently.

"Well, I *am* a guy."

"True." She nodded but stared straight ahead while Maddy got in her car. The setting sun cast golden light over Jordan's perfectly carved profile, giving her an almost ethereal glow. "But you're certainly not a regular guy…at least not like the ones I'm used to."

Side by side, they watched Maddy's car disappear around the corner, neither of them saying a word. The silence hung between them thick with the unspoken possibilities. Spare bedroom or not, the taste of Jordan's lips still lingered on his tongue, and their encounter at the shop flickered along the edges of his mind like the tease that it was.

"Okay," she said quietly.

"Okay, what?"

"You can stay at the house. But under one condition."

"Alright," he said slowly, bracing for the chance that she was going to throw the let's-be-friends card back at him. "Shoot."

"We share the kitchen duties." She arched one eyebrow, and a playful lilt edged her words. "Whoever cooks doesn't have to clean up. Deal?"

"Deal. But I'm a rotten cook." Gavin's lips tilted and he stuck his hand out to her. Jordan's lip quivered as her palm settled against his, the soft feel of it making him yearn for more. "Anything else?" he asked, pulling her so that her skirt fluttered over his legs. "Roomie?"

"Yes." Jordan nodded and her tongue flicked out, moistening her lower lip. Dropping his hand, she backed away to the door, her cheeks pinkening as the words tumbled from her lips in a rush. "I do appreciate you doing this, but I don't want to confuse the girls. They've had so many changes in the past few months, and I'd hate to give them the wrong idea or make them think that we're… So…when we're around each other, we should be…"

"Friends." He gave her a tight smile and nodded slowly. "I get it. I didn't suggest this so I could sleep with you."

"I know," she said quickly, her hand reaching out to touch him before quickly dropping it back to her side. She glanced through the screen door and lowered her voice. "I know that's not why you're doing it."

"Good. I'm glad we cleared that up." Gavin studied her closely before leaning in and whispering into her ear. "But make no mistake about it, Jordan. When the time is right and you're ready"—he trailed his forefinger along the edge of her palm and stilled when she shivered in response—"I have every intention of getting you into bed. And *sleeping* will have little to do with it."

Before she could respond, Gavin opened the door and slipped past her into the house. Claire caught his eye when he stepped into the foyer and tilted her head, as though acknowledging exactly what was going on with him and Jordan. To her credit, she didn't say a word. She simply smiled before turning her attention back to the photo album on the coffee table.

Strolling through the dining room toward the kitchen, Gavin pushed the swinging door open. His heart melted at the two grinning faces on the other side.

The neighborhood kids had left, and Lily and Gracie were sitting at the small, round table with crumb-filled plates in front of them, both of them sporting milk mustaches. Their sandal-clad feet swung from the chairs as though the girls didn't have a care in the world. These two sweet-faced children were blissfully unaware of the recent ugliness with their father, and if Gavin had anything to say about it, things were going to stay that way.

Chapter 13

IT WAS WELL PAST ELEVEN O'CLOCK AT NIGHT AND THE girls had been asleep for hours, but Jordan had done nothing but toss and turn and occasionally watch TV. With a growl of frustration, she snagged the remote from her nightstand and shut off the television. She'd hoped that maybe watching some old movies would help lull her to sleep—or at least keep her mind off the fact that Gavin was sleeping in the spare bedroom down the hall.

Nope. Fat chance. All she did was think about him. This was only the second night he was staying there, but it was also the second night she was going to go without sleep. What was her problem?

Lust and sexual frustration, she thought with a roll of her eyes.

With a huff, she flopped back on her pillow and stared at the ceiling while fiddling with the sheets. The light of the full moon spilled in the windows, and not even the familiar comforting sound of the waves helped soothe her restlessness.

Maybe a glass of warm milk would help. Jordan had never tried that old wives' trick. She'd always thought it sounded stupid, but if she didn't get some sleep soon, she was going to go nuts.

Shoving the sheets aside, Jordan swung her legs over the edge of the bed and tiptoed to the doorway of her bedroom. Clad only in her short white nightie, she opened the door a crack and peered into the hallway to find it empty. The narrow hall was illuminated only by the light that flowed from beneath the closed bathroom door. She'd asked Gavin to leave it on in case the girls woke up in the middle of the night. Jordan smiled as she stepped into the hall, the floral runner rough and warm beneath her feet. It was a lovely surprise to have a man actually listen to her.

She tiptoed quietly down the hallway, but before she got to the stairs, the bathroom door swung open and a puff of hot steam swept over her. Like a scene out of a movie, Gavin stepped out of the steamy cloud, dripping wet and wearing only a small, white towel around his waist.

With her hand curled around the top of the banister and her mouth wide open, Jordan stood there wordlessly, taking in every delicious inch of him.

Wet and gorgeous, his dark hair slicked off his forehead, the man looked like sin and sex rolled into one. Standing stone still with those ropy, muscular arms at his sides, Gavin studied her with piercing green eyes. The only flicker of movement was the flutter of muscle in his chest as rivulets of water trickled over the dips and curves of that perfectly sculpted torso.

The temptation to touch him was almost more than she could bear.

She couldn't breathe. Or move. Or speak.

All Jordan could do at the moment was stand there and soak in the tall, enticing sight of him. She allowed her eyes to drift over him from head to toe and back again in one long, slow pass. It was bold, brazen, and practically an invitation for sex. Hell, why didn't she drop her panties right there in the hallway?

"Sleep tight," he murmured.

To Gavin's credit, he simply gave her that cheeky grin before winking, striding down the hall to his room, and disappearing inside. The back view, even with the scar on his shoulder, was as moan-inducing as the front. The expression "a feast for the eyes" finally held real meaning.

Shuddering with a rush of lust and adrenaline, Jordan hurried back to her room and closed the door tightly behind her. With her hand practically melded to the doorknob, she leaned her forehead against the cool wooden surface and fought to catch her breath. Round one of the sexual tension games definitely went to Gavin. *Jeez.* Letting out a huff of frustration, Jordan shoved herself away from the door and flopped onto her bed facedown.

It was gonna be a long night.

—◦◦◦—

Almost a week had passed since her father's funeral and Ted's unexpected visit, but since then life had been surprisingly quiet. There hadn't even been any fires, and Gavin had been home every night. But after that awkward, albeit sexy midnight hallway run-in, Jordan had paid better attention to his showering schedule so as to avoid any further embarrassing moments.

She had also done as Gavin requested and filed a formal complaint about Ted with the police, but she'd resisted going for the restraining order. She wanted life to be as normal as possible, and doing *that* would be the polar opposite of normal. As she'd expected, Ted hadn't made a peep since he left. She hadn't received as much as an angry text message or a phone call from her lawyer. Life in Old Brookfield had gone back to the status quo after her father's death. Wasn't that always the way of things?

Life goes on.

The shrill ring of the telephone cut through the kitchen and almost made Jordan yelp with surprise. Shaking her head at her foolishness, she snagged the cordless phone from the counter and put it to her ear.

"Hello?" She leaned one hip against the counter.

"Jordan?" The familiar voice of her attorney, Richard Montvale, filled the line. "It's Richard."

"Oh, hello, Richard." Nervousness shimmied up her back and she bit her lower lip. "What's going on? Did I forget to sign a paper or something?" she asked with a shaky laugh.

"No." Richard cleared his throat, and his deep, somewhat bland voice came through staid and steady. "I'm calling about Ted. Or rather, about a call I received from Ted's attorney."

"Alright." She held the cordless phone and leaned the other hand on the counter, bracing herself for whatever was coming. "What is it? Is he fighting for custody and contesting our agreement? Because if that's the case, he can forget it. He showed up at my father's funeral drunk and started a fight with—"

"Ted was arrested."

"Arrested?" Jordan clutched the phone tighter and whispered, "When?"

"Over the weekend. He was upstate at the country house and got busted for drunk driving and resisting arrest. He was released on bail today and admitted himself to a rehab facility outside the city. It's a three-month resident program, and after that he'll have a court date for the charges. I'm sure his attorney will get it postponed for as long as possible. Matthews is a sharp lawyer and deals with guys like Ted all the time. Rich troublemakers. At any rate, Matthews wanted me to let you know and give you the contact information for the facility. The girls can call him there but only during certain times."

Unsurprised by the news, Jordan took down the phone number and address of the rehab facility and, after a few pleasantries, hung up the phone. It had finally happened. Ted's bad behavior had caught up to him and he'd checked into rehab, but Jordan knew that only time would tell whether or not this was a temporary recovery.

The sound of Lily and Gracie's laughter mixed with the crashing waves captured Jordan's attention, and the joyfulness of it made her heart ache. She wanted nothing more than to shield her girls from the ugliness of addiction and abusive behavior. Thank God she'd moved back to Old Brookfield, but more than anything she was grateful for Gavin.

He was doing exactly what he'd promised. He was being a friend to her *and* her girls. Life was as peaceful, normal, and blissfully quiet as she had ever dared hope for.

Gavin had made them all spaghetti and meatballs for dinner and, as agreed, she was on dish duty. They'd alternated cooking nights and slipped into a comfortable routine with almost frightening speed. Turning back to the sink, she rinsed the last pot and realized that she and the girls had laughed more in the past week with Gavin than they had in the last two years with Ted.

Shutting off the faucet, she placed the pot in the drying rack before wiping her hands on the dish towel. She leaned one hip against the counter and spotted the back of Gavin's head, the deep amber glow of sunset spilling over him. He was standing on the deck, with Lily and Gracie sitting in rapt attention, while he showed them yet another card trick. She tossed the dish towel on the counter, enjoying the sweet and perfectly natural scene outside.

It felt so absolutely right to have Gavin here in her home with her and the girls. Closing her eyes, she leaned against the doorway into the dining room and sucked in a deep breath of clean ocean air. The combination of their chatter mixed with the inherently relaxing scent of the salt spray had Jordan feeling more at home and safer than she ever had.

A smile curved her lips as she pondered the simplicity and normalcy of the past week. During the day, the girls went to camp, while she and Gavin went to their respective jobs. At night, after dinner, they all retreated to their own rooms. That last part? Well, that was the only piece of the puzzle she wasn't thrilled about. Her brow furrowed, and she let out a sigh.

This past week had also been a lesson in self-control—or self-torture, she wasn't sure which. Having Gavin sleep down the hall from her night after night was more temptation than she'd prepared herself for. Memories of him emerging from the steamy bathroom came roaring back with a vengeance, and with them all kinds of ideas about what she'd wanted to do—but didn't. Or wouldn't. Or couldn't.

Damn it.

Silently scolding herself for entertaining thoughts of the same behavior she'd told Gavin they couldn't do, Jordan resolved that she would take a cold shower after the girls were tucked safely in bed. Resigning herself to yet another night of hot fantasies starring Gavin, Jordan flicked her eyes open and found herself face-to-face with the star of the show.

"You okay?" He moved past her into the kitchen and deposited his beer bottle in the sink. "You're all flushed."

"I'm fine," she said a little too quickly. "It's hot in here, that's all." Oh sure. It was a little hot anywhere he was. The kitchen…the living room…the polar ice caps…

"You should come out on the deck with us. It's cooled off a lot and the sunset is gorgeous tonight. There's a storm coming, so the waves are crazy big. The girls asked if we could go boogie boarding, but I figured it was too close to their bedtime and it's gonna be dark soon. Tomorrow, maybe. It's Saturday and we're both off, so boogie boarding could be a killer way to spend the day after the storm breaks."

Jordan tried not to stare at his fine backside as he grabbed a beer from the fridge, but that was an effort in futility. She looked away about a second too late, and Gavin caught her staring at his butt. A wide grin lit up his face and that one dimple appeared in his cheek, making him look more desirable than ever.

Closing the door to the fridge, he hooked his thumb in the front pocket of his board shorts and tilted the beer bottle at her, his muscles flexing beneath the white T-shirt. "You sure it's hot in here? Feels fine to me."

"My attorney called," she said abruptly, needing to

change the subject. "Ted was arrested for drunk driving and resisting arrest. He checked into a three-month rehab program right after he got out on bail."

"I see." Gavin frowned briefly as he rubbed his thumb over the label that was peeling off the bottle. "That means I can go home. I mean you don't need me here anymore… Do you?"

Need? Want? Desire? *Yes, please. All of that and more.*

But before Jordan could answer him and say she didn't only need him but wanted him so much she could barely breathe, Lily and Gracie came running into the kitchen.

"Mama, can we have extra book time tonight?" Lily asked, clinging to Jordan's legs and staring up at her with big, moony eyes. "Please?"

"Sure," Jordan said. She pushed Lily's blond hair out of her eyes. Gracie was, as usual, standing right behind her big sister. "Why the burning desire for more book time? Not that I'm complaining."

"Look." Gracie held up a book with a shiny black cover. Taking it in her hands, Jordan turned it over and grinned when she saw the top hat and rabbit. It was an older book and had clearly seen some use, but it was still in good shape. Jordan recognized it immediately. "The chief gave it to me and Lily. He said it will help us be 'gicians."

"*Mr. Magic's Twenty Best Tricks for Kids*." Glancing at Gavin, she teased, "Did you write this? You are, after all, Mr. Magic."

"That's what I asked him," declared Lily. "But he said no."

"He said no," Gracie repeated.

"This was yours," Jordan murmured. "I remember it."

"Yeah, it's no big deal." Gavin shrugged and waved it off. "It was sitting around my parents' house collecting dust, and since Lily and Gracie are so keen on learning new magic tricks, I figured…what the heck? May as well put it to good use. Right, girls?"

"Right," they said in unison.

"Right," Jordan whispered. Her throat thickened with emotion as the purity and genuine sweetness of his gift sank in. Clearing her throat, she forced herself to speak up. "Okay, girls. Go on up and get ready for your bath. You can have an extra half hour of book time tonight, but then it's lights out. I'll be up in a minute."

Shrieks of glee filled the kitchen as the girls jumped up and down before grabbing the book and heading for their bedroom. About two seconds after vanishing, Gracie reappeared in the kitchen, ran up to Gavin, and wrapped her little arms around his legs, giving him a hug.

"Fank you, Chief." Tilting her head back, her messy dark-blond hair spilling down her back, she said, "I hope your house stays stinky wif paint for always and you haf to stay here wif me and Mommy and Lily forever!"

Leaning back on the edge of the counter with both hands, Jordan looked at the man across from her and swallowed the sudden swell of emotion. Silence hung between them, with the sound of the waves and Gracie's giggles as she ran from the kitchen.

Giving the girls that book—a book from his childhood that she knew meant something to him—was more than merely a sweet gesture. It was stirringly heartfelt and personal, and that was what scared her. Actually, if she was going to start being honest with herself, that was only *part* of what frightened her. Having Gavin in the house had been difficult, but now she realized that the really big challenge, the toughest part, would be when he left.

This past week hadn't only been about lots of laughs for the girls and sexual tension-filled moments for her. Not even close. When she got right down to it, these past few days were the first time Jordan had really felt like they were a family.

A loving, happy, joyful, and safe *family*.

But now that Ted wasn't an imminent threat, Gavin could leave and would take all of that with him. How on earth could she let that go? Would she have a choice? Was Gavin even interested in getting permanently mixed up with her, essentially signing on to be a father to her girls?

That was a hell of a bigger commitment than he'd likely bargained for, and it was about time she started figuring things out. The girls were quickly growing attached to Gavin, and she couldn't blame them. Jordan was too. But she was a grown-up and they were children. They'd already been abandoned by their own father, so losing another man could be catastrophic. She had to get an idea of where he was really coming from and what he might be looking for—or not.

"Thank you for giving that to them," she said quietly. She watched him carefully, wondering how he would react to the mere mention of something more meaningful. "I know you, Gavin, and I know that's not just any book. You had that memorized when we were kids, and you probably still do."

"Don't make a thing out of it, Jordan." His mouth set in a tight line and he took a sip of his beer. He lifted one shoulder in an annoyingly nonchalant gesture. "It's only a book. No big deal."

"Right." Jordan nodded and her heart sank. "I should go up and give them their bath before it gets too late."

What had she expected? He was being her friend, and yes, he was as attracted to her as she was to him, but wanting sex was a far cry from wanting an instant family. *Damn it all.* Tearing her gaze from his, she pushed herself off the counter and headed for the living room.

"I'm doing what you wanted. This is what we agreed on, isn't it?" Gavin's words stopped Jordan cold. She stood in the doorway but didn't turn around. "You and me. Just friends so we don't confuse the girls. But I gotta be honest, Jordan. I'm feeling pretty confused, and I don't know which end is up."

Jordan spun around, but before she could respond, he slammed his half-finished beer bottle on the counter.

"No point in wasting those waves. I could use the opportunity to burn off some extra *energy*." Yanking his shirt off over his head, once again putting that gorgeous chest on display, Gavin held up both hands and backed out of the kitchen toward the deck. "Tell the girls I said good night. I'm going for a swim."

As he slipped through the dining room and out the sliding doors to the deck, Jordan's heart slammed in her rib cage. He was right. He had been doing *exactly* what she asked him to do. Then why did it feel so shitty? It looked like she wasn't the only one feeling confused. After the girls went to bed, she was going to make sure she and Gavin got a few things straight.

Gavin hadn't been swimming in surf that rough for far too long, and the coming storm provided exactly the stress relief he needed. He dove and tumbled through wave after wave. The sand and shells scraped against his belly and legs, but he barely felt the pain. If he stayed out there long enough, the surf would beat the stupid out of him. Right now, that was the only excuse for the way he was acting.

He never should have given the girls that book, and not because he didn't want them to have it. In fact, handing it over to Lily and Gracie had felt like the most natural thing in the world for him to do. But he should have known that Jordan might freak out. His own mother had raised her eyebrows when he'd gone to the house to find it. Oh, she hadn't said anything, but she'd given him *that look*.

That "Are you sure you should be doing that, Gavin?" look.

Shoving his wet hair off his face, Gavin strode out of the surf and swore under his breath. What the hell was he doing? These weren't his kids, and Jordan wasn't his wife. But he'd been here playing house all week long, and the worst part was that he'd loved every damned minute of it. He'd almost lost it when Gracie had hugged him tonight, but the terrified look on Jordan's face had been like cold water on a fire.

Based on that look, he could only assume she didn't agree with Gracie's sentiment.

In that instant, Gavin had known it was time for him to leave. Ted was safely tucked away in rehab and wouldn't be trouble for anyone for a while. Besides, Jordan said he wasn't even picking up the phone when the girls made their weekly call to him, and there was a good chance she wouldn't hear from that dirtbag again for a long time. She had been right about Ted. That guy didn't give a shit about her or his own daughters. He was just pissed that he'd lost the perceived battle. Like many successful men, he didn't like to lose. The jerk had probably only checked into rehab to look good in front of the judge.

Gavin spotted his towel and bent to pick it up. The cool wind whipped around him, the sand stinging his flesh. He shivered in the unseasonably cold air as he wiped the water from his eyes and turned his face to the starless indigo sky. The sun had finished setting, but there was enough light to see the thick cloud banks as they rolled in the atmosphere. There was definitely going to be a big storm tonight. And as if on cue, thunder rumbled in the distance and lightning streaked across the night sky.

He towel-dried his head, and when he pulled the towel down to dry the rest of his dripping wet body, he found Jordan standing in front of him. The girls' bedroom light was out; he must have been out here a lot longer than he thought.

The temperature had dropped significantly and the woman had to be freezing, wearing only her long, blue sundress. If it were lighter out, he'd probably see her skin covered in goose bumps. He was about to ask her what the hell she was doing out there with a storm about to break, but she shoved at his chest and swore loudly.

"Why did you give them that book?" Jordan shouted over the crashing waves, the wind whipping her hair around her face. Tugging a strand from her eyes, she shoved him again. "Tell me, Gavin. Why?"

"I told you…" He squared his shoulders and kept his voice even. She was angry with him and he didn't blame her. He'd pushed it and she wasn't ready. "It's no big deal. It's only a book."

"Bull!" Hands on her hips, she glared up at him, her eyes flashing. The storm in the sky was matched only by the fierce look on her face. "You and I both know that book was like your bible as a kid. Your brothers used to tease you and say that you probably slept with it under your pillow. For God's sake," she shouted, "you saved it for over twenty years like a damned heirloom. So *do not* tell me it's only a book. That book means something to you, Gavin." Her voice softened and broke with emotion. "And you gave it to my girls."

"What do you want from me, Jordan?" He threw the towel to the sand and stepped closer, looming over her and intentionally invading her space. "Tell me. Huh? Because I am too tired to try and figure it out. Okay? You wanted to *just be friends* around your girls, so that's what I've been doing."

He inched closer and she backed away, but Gavin grabbed her wrists and tugged her against him. His voice dropped to a gravelly whisper, and her face, shadowed in the dim moonlight, had an unreadable expression. Her breasts pressed against his chest and her legs tangled between his, making him want to peel that dress off her and dive deep.

"All I can do is think about you, Jordan. About touching and tasting you." He dropped her arms abruptly and backed up. Holding his hands out in surrender, he yelled, "But I don't. Even though it's torture, I don't."

Swearing under his breath, he let out a sigh of defeat and settled his hands on his hips. She was standing there staring at him like he'd lost his mind. Maybe he had. But there was one fact he was certain of: his state of mind was still up for debate but his heart was long gone. He'd lost it to Jordan and her daughters.

"I'm sorry if you're angry with me for giving them the book," he said firmly. "No. You know what? Screw that. I'm not sorry. It was mine to give, and I know Gracie and Lily love it."

Lightning flashed, closer now, and illuminated Jordan's face long enough for him to see she was crying. His gut clenched and something inside him crumbled. Those tears were because of him—not her shithead ex-husband—*him*.

"Damn it, Jordan." His voice lowered to a restrained growl. "I thought I could be here with you and the girls, and keep my distance. But I was wrong. I was only supposed to be here long enough to make sure he didn't bother you, and now that he's in rehab, you don't need me to stay anymore. I'll get my stuff and be out before the girls wake up in the morning."

As he brushed past her toward the house, her hand snagged his, stopping him from taking another step. Anticipation, desire, hope, and a harsh glimmer of fear curled inside his gut, begging to bust free. Gavin's mouth set in a tight line as her delicate fingers tangled with his. He slowly looked to his left, his eyes fixed on hers. He expected to see pity, sadness, or maybe even regret, but those pools of brown glittered at him with something else. Lust? Anger? Need?

"I'm not angry with you." The low, husky sound of her voice rushed around him in the wind. Moving to stand directly in front of him, she peered up at him through wide, teary eyes. "And I don't want you to leave. Not now, and definitely not like this."

"Then what is it?" Standing tall, his body taut, Gavin waited for the next punch in the gut. "Spit it out. No more games. You and I are too old for this crap, Jordan. Tell me why you're so upset that I gave them that book."

"I don't want to do this anymore," she whispered.

And there it was.

"Fine." Hands still at his side, Gavin fought the driving need to touch her. "Like I said, I'll get my stuff."

"Hold it." Jordan pressed her hand to his chest but Gavin didn't retreat. Instead he leaned into it. "Let me finish."

She was right. They had to finish this. It was time to cut the crap and tell her exactly how he felt. No more beating around the bush and acting like this thing between them wasn't a big deal. It was. It was the biggest deal of his life, and he'd be damned if he was going to let her go without a fight.

"No," Gavin growled, leaning in further still and bracing for the rest of her rejection, her fingertips digging into his flesh. "You know why? Because I'm not finished. I still have something else to say to you," he shouted, frustration edging every gritty syllable. "You wanna know why I gave them my book? I gave Lily and Gracie that book because I am hopelessly in love with their mother and I always have been. There. I said it. I love you, Jordan. I've loved you since the fourth grade, and I'll love you until the day I die.

"That guy, Ted? Your ex-husband? He's a stupid son of a bitch. That man had you and those two girls for his family, and he pissed it away. For the past week, I've been living in a damn fairyland, pretending like you're *my* family, and tonight, when you looked at me in the kitchen, after Gracie asked me to stay? It was clear to me that you don't feel the same way."

Breathing like he'd run a race and emotionally spent from spilling his guts, Gavin stood, his hands curled to fists at his sides, waiting for the rejection. He could take it, he told himself. She'd left before and he'd survived. He could do it again. It would hurt like hell and he'd probably have to leave town again to get over it, but right now he would stand here and take it like a man.

She opened her mouth to say something, but snapped it shut. For a split second, Gavin thought she was going run away. But she didn't, and then she did something even more unexpected.

Cursing, Jordan grabbed his face with both hands, popped up on her toes, and captured his mouth with hers. The second those sweet lips touched his, the dam broke. Gavin groaned and opened to her, his tongue immediately seeking entrance. He kissed her deeply, tangling his hands in her long, windblown hair as they both dropped to their knees on the soft sand. She tasted sweet, spicy, and hot, and fed his desire but not enough to satisfy. He wanted more.

He gathered her hair in his hands, his fingertips grazing her scalp before he pulled back and reluctantly broke the kiss. Jordan whimpered, fingers digging into the flesh of his waist as she leaned in, seeking more. Gavin held her there, his mouth inches from hers. The wind howled around them as they both fought to catch their breath.

"I want more from you, Jordan," Gavin rasped, his shoulders heaving.

He tightened his hold on her and, in one teasing stroke, brushed his lips over hers without giving in to another kiss. Her taut, toned body wiggled eagerly against him and a needy whimper escaped her lips.

"Do you understand me? I want all of you, Jordan, and tonight I won't be satisfied with one kiss. If we keep going, right here and right now, then it is *on*. No more games. No more back and forth. It's you and me. Get it?"

"I get it." Jordan nodded and tried to kiss him, but once again he pulled back. She let out an unmistakable growl of discontent as her fingers dug into the flesh of his waist and she tugged his hips against hers.

"I don't know," Gavin murmured. "I'm not sure you really understand what I'm asking you."

"I think I'm pretty clear on it," she murmured. Her pink tongue flicked out and swept over her lower lip in one sexy stroke. "I only have one question for you."

"What?" He stilled, worried that perhaps this moment, the one he'd waited for and dreamed about, would vanish in a blink. "Well?"

Silence lingered and the waves crashed wildly, the spray of the ocean wafting over them as the weight of her unknown question lingered like a giant dead end. Frustration swirled, and if she didn't ask him soon, Gavin's head might explode.

"Are you gonna kiss me or not?"

Relief and lust shot through him, and he linked one arm around her waist, tugging her to him. Jordan gasped, her hands settled over his biceps, and those full lips parted in a clear and unmistakable invitation.

Taut with need, Gavin cupped the nape of her neck. His thumb trailed along the edge of her jaw in one slow stroke.

"The better question is…" he growled, lowering his face so it was scant inches from hers, "once I start, am I ever gonna stop?"

Before she could respond, he slid his thigh between her legs and in one swift movement laid her out beneath him on the sand. He pinned her body under his, dragging her hands above her head and holding them there. Gavin had never seen anyone so beautiful in all his life. With her eyes glazed with desire, her hair spilling around her like a halo in the dim moonlight, and her body laid out for him, she was all of his fantasies come to life.

Perched over her, need clawing at him from the inside out, Gavin tilted his hips and rubbed himself against her in one slow pass. He wanted her to know what she did to him, to be certain of how desperate and needy she'd made him. Jordan gasped and arched her back, the movement highlighting her full breasts. The sight made his dick twitch.

Gavin dipped his head and slanted his mouth over hers as a strangled cry escaped her parted lips. Soft and pliant, weak with lust, Jordan opened to him as he slowly and languidly slid his tongue along hers. With each passing second the intensity of the kiss grew, as though fifteen years of waiting and wishing were bubbling to the surface all at once. He fleetingly thought about the most dangerous fires. The ones that burned really slowly, right under the radar and out of sight, until finally, at a certain point, that red ember erupted into a full-blown blaze.

That's what this was, this *thing* between him and Jordan, the one he couldn't escape or shake off. No matter where he went or what he did, his feelings for Jordan were always there, right beneath the surface, waiting to erupt. It was the slow burn before the inferno, and right now, the flames burned hot.

Breaking the kiss, he trailed his lips along her throat, then inched lower to the valley between her breasts. Releasing one arm, he dragged his fingertips down to the thin strap of her dress and tugged it off her shoulder. Jordan yanked her arm free, and Gavin let out a groan of appreciation as the fabric slipped away, revealing her full, round breasts. Leaning on his elbow, he shifted his weight, lowered his head, and drew one rosy pink bud into his mouth. Taking his time, he lavished attention on one and then the other, not sure which one tasted sweeter but eager to take the time to find out.

Jordan cried out when he grazed his teeth over her nipples. She threaded her fingers through his hair, holding him to her as he licked and suckled. Need and desire surged through him, and his erection throbbed harder with every passing second. As if knowing exactly what he was thinking, Jordan let her hand drift down and curl over his heavy length. He swore and nuzzled her breast as she stroked him through the thin, wet fabric of his swimsuit.

"Let me touch you, Gavin," she whispered, slipping her hand beneath the waistband of his suit. "I need to feel you. I've thought about this for so long."

Her warm fingers curled around the length of him, and he almost came right then and there. He squeezed his eyes shut, fighting for control as she worked him in her hand. Gavin pushed himself up on his elbow and flicked his eyes open, immediately latching on to her heavy-lidded stare. It was intimate and erotic to look Jordan in the eye as she pumped the length of him with slow, sure strokes. Still, he needed and wanted more.

"No reason you should have all the fun," he rasped. His fingertips trailed over her breasts, along her rib cage, and over the curve of her hip before tugging the fabric up. Gavin's hand rushed up the smooth flesh of Jordan's bare thigh, his thumb trailing along the inside until he bumped up against the lacy fabric of her panties. Hooking his finger under the edge, he pushed them aside and the tangle of need in his gut swelled. "You are so wet for me, Jordan."

Gavin slanted his mouth over hers at the same instant he ran his thumb over her clit. He slipped his thumb between her slick folds. She pumped him faster as he slid two fingers in and out of her sex, alternating with swift passes over her clit. Each time he pressed the tiny nub, slick with her desire, Jordan moaned into his mouth and tilted her hips toward him, begging for more. Her tempo increased and Gavin's own orgasm started to crest. It was too soon.

Damn it. He didn't want it to end.

A huge crack of thunder and a shot of lightning seared overhead, making them realize they had to move this little party inside.

Kissing her deeply, Gavin grabbed her wrist and gently pulled her hand away. He settled, once again, in between her wide-spread legs. Resting his forearms on either side of her head, he brushed sand off her cheek. Her hands played over his back and down to his ass.

Thunder rumbled again and the wind howled over them, and he started to feel the first droplets of rain.

"The storm is about to unleash on us," he murmured, kissing the tip of her nose. "Why don't we go inside and continue what we started?"

"Afraid of a little rain?" she teased. Hooking her ankles over his legs, she tugged him against her. "Wait until the guys at the station hear that one, Chief."

"It's not the rain I'm afraid of," Gavin said quietly. Even in the dim moonlight he could see that her hair was a mess, her lips were swollen from his kisses, and she looked absolutely perfect. His heart ached with the perfection of her. She was made for him. He knew that now more than ever. "I want tonight to last. Come on."

Gavin pushed himself to his knees, and as Jordan sat up, he helped her put the top of her sundress back in place. Giggling, she brushed the sand off and held out both hands before Gavin yanked her to her feet. She kissed him firmly, linking her arms around his neck, and then hugged him. Her face nestled against his throat, and the warmth of her breath fanned his skin like a caress. He laced his hands in her hair and breathed her in as the scent of the beach and a hint of her shampoo filled his head. She smelled like *home*. That's what scared him and thrilled him. For the first time in his life he wanted to build a home, a real home, and it would be with her.

Hand in hand they walked toward the house. Just before they hit the steps to the deck, Gavin heard the distinct and familiar sound of sirens in the distance.

"So much for making tonight last," he murmured.

"I'm sorry, but I have to go. I'm not on duty, but I'm always on call."

"It's okay. If you and I are going to be…*you and I*, then this is part of the deal." Jordan wrapped her arms around his waist. "Promise me you'll be careful, and we can finish this when you get back," she purred.

Giving her a quick kiss, he reluctantly left the warmth of her embrace. He threw on dry clothes and grabbed the keys to his truck, the whole time wishing like hell he didn't have to leave. As he backed out of the driveway, Gavin saw Jordan's tall, lovely form standing in the window, watching him go. The danger of his job was never lost on him. But this was the first time in his career that he actually had something to lose.

Chapter 14

GAVIN PULLED UP TO THE SCHOOL. ORANGE FLAMES were shooting out of the first-floor windows along the south side of the building, lighting up the night with a macabre glow. Not only had his squad shown up but Rick had called in Engines 11 and 13 from neighboring towns. Fires in buildings like this could go from bad to worse in record time, and having backup on hand was protocol.

Hauling his gear, Gavin ran over to Bill, who was manning their pumper engine.

"Rick's inside?" he asked, pulling on his air tank.

"Yup. He's with Jeff, Mark, Owen, and four other guys, two from each engine. They're ventilating the first floor by busting out the windows. We're trying to take it horizontal to see if we can keep it from taking out the second floor," Bill said, referring to the fire. Gavin nodded his understanding. Fire was a hungry beast and it ate oxygen, so it went where the air was. The trick was to try and make the flames go where you wanted them.

"We've got the volunteer guys on the hose and the kid wanted to help," Bill added, referring to David, "but I have to keep reminding him he's too freaking young."

"David's here?" Gavin glanced over to the crowd of onlookers, and sure enough, his eager future firefighter was in the mix with that same expression of awe and excitement. Dread clawed at him but he shoved it aside. "Keep that crowd back. Including the kid."

"Rick said it's creeping along the south side." Bill's face was a mask of concern as he kept his serious stare on the water gauges. "We have to get this one under control quick or we're gonna lose the entire building."

"Understood." The other two pump engines were attacking the blaze from both sides of the school, and it looked like the flames were starting to shrink back. "I know it's late on a Friday, but did they find anyone in there on the sweep? Is the building clear?"

"Yup. All clear." He nodded to the small crowd of people that had gathered by the police cars. "The principal showed up right before you did and she's freaked out, but she said the building should be empty. All of the campers cleared out by four o'clock and the building was supposed to be locked down by six. Damn good thing this didn't happen during the school year. We'd definitely have people in there."

"Right." As Gavin secured his mask, he studied the crowd. In addition to the Heffernan kid, it consisted of the usual EMS personnel, some of the other volunteers, and police, but Gavin did a double take when he spotted the school's van. The cold finger of dread ticked up his spine as he scanned the crowd, not finding the person he was looking for. "Where's Tommy?"

Before Bill could answer him, Gavin ran over to the group standing a safe distance from the building. Mrs. Drummond was crying and let out a sound of relief when she saw Gavin.

"What happened, Gavin?" She grabbed his coat and uttered strangled cry. "My God. I was here a few hours ago and everything was fine. Tommy locks up at six every night. I don't understand how this could have happened."

"Where is Tommy, Mrs. D.?" Gavin had a pretty good hunch that this fire was no accident, and right now he had to find Tommy. "The van is still here. Doesn't he take that home with him?"

"What?" she asked absently before looking around. "The van? Well, yes. He does take that home. Why do you…" She stopped speaking when her teary eyes fell on the vehicle in question. "Oh my God, Gavin. Tommy could be in there. He's not out here. Have any of you seen Tommy?" she shouted, looking frantically around the crowd.

The others all confirmed what Gavin feared. Tommy was nowhere to be found, and in all likelihood he was still somewhere inside the school.

"Okay." Gavin kept his voice calm and commanding even though under the surface he was panicked. He settled his hands on Mrs. Drummond's slim shoulders and looked her square in the eye. "I need you to think and tell me where he might be. If he's in there and he's not calling for help, then he's probably passed out from the smoke." His gut clenched as he recalled that day so long ago and the fire that had changed both of their lives forever. "Given what Tommy's been through in the past, he might even be hiding."

"The basement," she sputtered. "He has a room down there that he uses as an office. Oh my God. It's under the gym in the back left corner of the school, on the south side of the building. If he was here after his usual hours, then that's where he would be. I know sometimes he stays later during the week, but it's Friday and I didn't think…"

"It's okay." Gavin pulled his mask on and immediately

radioed to Rick as he headed toward the building. "Rick. It's Gavin. You copy?"

"Ten-four." Rick's voice came through loud and clear, but he was breathing heavily. "We've ventilated the first floor and the smoke is still thick as hell in here. So far we're keeping it from climbing, and those pumpers are starting to stamp it out. The game's gonna change if these flames hit the boilers in the basement, but it looks like we have most of it contained to the back right side of the building."

Gavin moved faster, forcing the voices of panic away as he tried not to notice the tingling in his shoulder. He had to find Tommy.

"This was definitely our firebug's handiwork, Gav. It went too hot too fast. The sprinkler system went off, but this baby just laughed at it and kept on coming. There had to be an accelerant used—and a hell of a lot of it. My bet is that when that arson investigator gets in here, he's gonna find a clear V pattern and an accelerant trail as dark as the devil."

"Copy that, but we have another problem." Ax in hand, Gavin strode through the smoky hallways of the school, the familiar sound of his breathing echoing through his mask. Visibility was low in the hall, and as he moved farther down, the heat increased tenfold. "Tommy's van is parked outside and he's nowhere to be found. There's a good chance he's in his office. Drummond says it's in the basement. Back left corner under the gym."

"Ten-four." Rick's breathing picked up, a sign he was moving fast. "I'll meet you on the lower level. I'm comin' down the back center stairs. Mark and the others are heading out now."

"Roger that. Mark, do you copy?" Gavin confirmed.

"We copy, Chief." Mark's voice crackled through loud and clear. "Clearing out."

"Ten-four." Gavin made his way down the side stairwell. The smoke grew even thicker as he went—not what should have been happening, based on where the fire was situated. "You said the fire's contained? I'm getting heavy smoke down here. I think we have another hot spot somewhere—a slow burn—in the walls maybe."

Every warning bell went off in his head as he turned the corner. The heat was undeniably stronger. Senses alert, sweat dripping down his back, Gavin made his way down the basement's dark hall. The emergency lights had come on, but even that did little to help illuminate the underground level of the building.

"Rick, after we find Tommy, we need to make another full sweep of the lower level. There's something else going on down here, man. I have a bad feeling about this." Gavin moved down the hall, stopping at the first door on his left. "If he's not in there, we gotta sweep any rooms leading to the south side of the building." He knew he sounded slightly panicked, but as he did a sweep of two storage closets and two larger storage spaces, hope dwindled. "I hope like hell he's in that office."

The minutes ticked by, and with every passing second, Gavin's level of panic rose. The smoke was dense and toxic, thanks to the materials in the building that were being burned, and if they didn't find Tommy soon…

Shit.

Gavin shoved the awful thoughts aside and kept

moving. The scar on his left shoulder tingled, but he pushed through with one thought on his mind. He had to find Tommy and get him the hell out of this building.

"Found him," Rick grunted. Relief bloomed in Gavin's chest and he picked up the pace, barely feeling the heat anymore. "Gavin, come straight back. Drummond was right. He's in the office past the south stairwell, directly below the gym. He's passed out behind his desk and his breathing is shallow. Getting the RIT mask on him now," Rick said, referring to the lifesaving tool they each carried. "Hang in there, man."

"I'm almost there."

Gavin ran down and turned the corner at the four-way intersection, relying on his years of experience of attending the school within these walls. It was a labyrinth of hallways, especially down here, but he and his brothers had spent more than their share of time exploring places where they weren't supposed to be.

As he rounded the corner, he spotted Rick emerging from the doorway, Tommy's body thrown over his shoulder.

"This little guy hardly weighs a thing," Rick said, his voice a welcome relief in a tense situation. "Let's get out of here, Gavin. I've got a gorgeous woman waiting for me back in my bed."

Gavin and Rick, with Tommy slung over his shoulder, headed to the back stairwell. The moment before they hit the first step, a massive explosion erupted to their right, rocking the building. Debris rained down. Concrete. Drywall. Pieces of the building, the school he'd loved for so many years, slammed into Gavin. His breath rushed from his lungs as he was pummeled to the ground.

The last sight Gavin witnessed was Rick pulling Tommy down and in front of him, in an effort to shield the injured man.

———∿∿∿———

The shock of the explosion knocked Gavin's face mask askew. Stunned from the blow and with toxic smoke leaking in through his mask, Gavin gasped and struggled to fix it. Sucking in a few deep breaths, he coughed and hacked in a desperate attempt to clear his lungs. His eyes stung and his chest burned as he fought to regain his bearings. As the smoke cleared, his first thoughts were of Rick and Tommy.

As Gavin blinked the sweat from his eyes, his heart thundered in his chest. He spotted them. Both men were facedown on the stairs and covered in debris, Rick's body protectively covering Tommy's. Gavin scrambled to his feet and ran to the two men, pulling various sections of debris off them. Neither of them moved.

"Chief!" Bill's frantic voice came through the speaker. "Chief? Do you copy?"

"I copy," Gavin ground out. "I'm okay, but Rick is down."

"We're comin' in."

"Negative," Gavin shouted, pulling pieces of the ceiling off Rick's legs, along with what had to be parts of the wall. Black smoke curled around them like a snake, and visibility was getting worse by the second. "No one else comes in. That felt like a damn bomb going off. For all we know, that's exactly what it was."

"I'll radio the bomb squad from the county," Bill responded.

"Son of a bitch," Gavin growled as he pulled a heavy section of stone off Rick's back. He went to turn his friend over, but let out a strangled cry and dropped his hands. A jagged piece of metal pierced Rick's jacket and protruded from his back, directly between his shoulder blades. "Oh my God."

Tearing off his glove, Gavin pressed his fingers to Rick's throat, frantically searching for a pulse. Something. *Please, God.* Letting out a strangled shout of rage, Gavin checked again but was met with nothing. The vacant, wide-eyed gaze staring back at him answered the question he didn't want the answer to.

Fury and grief flooded Gavin. Tears stung his eyes and a knot of unbridled rage coiled in his chest as the truth settled over him. Kneeling on the step, with Rick on one side and Tommy on the other, only the sound of debris falling nearby and the heat of the flames pulled him from his personal loss.

If Gavin didn't move fast, Rick wouldn't be the only casualty. He had given his life to save Tommy. Gavin would be damned if he'd allow his friend's death to be in vain.

He checked Tommy's pulse. It was weak and thready, but it was there. He adjusted the RIT mask, securing it back in place and ensuring that Tommy was getting clean air. Gavin felt for any other injuries that he might make worse by picking him up, but didn't find any. Grabbing Tommy's arm and leg, he leveraged his body weight and, with a grunt, hoisted him over his shoulder.

"I'm coming out the south side exit by the gym," Gavin seethed. His body strained with effort, and guilt tugged at him as he moved up the stairs toward the doorway. "I've got Tommy. Have EMS standing ready with a stretcher and keep everyone else back."

Climbing over various hunks of debris, Gavin reached the landing and shoved the door open with a grunt. He burst into the night air, Tommy passed out over his shoulder. Gavin ran to the EMS personnel who were waiting at a safe distance. He put Tommy on the stretcher and immediately turned to go back, but Bill grabbed him by the arm, stopping him.

"Where's Rick?" Bill's worried brown eyes studied Gavin's. "Chief?"

Unable to say the truth out loud, Gavin simply shook his head. He yanked his arm away and ran toward the building. Flames continued to shoot out the windows, dark smoke billowing toward the night sky. "I'm going back in for him."

He hadn't gone a few yards before another explosion erupted, sending glass and debris flying through air. Gavin and Bill were thrown back by the blast, and when he scrambled back to his feet, it was painfully obvious he wouldn't be retrieving his friend's body anytime soon.

The reality of the situation hung over Gavin like a shroud. Suffocating him.

Rick was dead.

He had been Gavin's coworker and his friend, but above all, he had been Gavin's responsibility.

One thought kept going through Gavin's mind like a broken record.

He had failed Rick.

Stoic and sitting ramrod straight, Gavin kept his serious gaze pinned on the casket. He had said barely two words since the fire—to Jordan or anyone else. She had assumed that he would come back to her house afterward, but he had insisted on being at the station. He had even gone straight there after leaving the hospital and stayed.

He didn't have to say a word for Jordan to know the kind of pain he was in. It was evident in every averted gaze and every unspoken word. He was blaming himself for Rick's death.

She kept her arm around Maddy, who was weeping quietly and dabbing at her eyes. She still hadn't looked away from Rick's picture. The colorful image perched on an easel behind the flower-covered casket—of Rick in his dress uniform and with that cocky glint in his eyes—was a painful reminder of the heroic, loving man they had lost.

The ceremony had ended almost thirty minutes before, and several people were already gathering at the church community room for a reception, but Maddy didn't want to go anywhere quite yet. Jordan couldn't blame her. Those post-funeral receptions were emotionally draining. If Maddy didn't want to be put through that, Jordan sure as hell wasn't going to force the issue.

"I should go to the reception, and then I have to get back to the station," Gavin said, abruptly rising from his seat. "Rogers said he has more information about the arson at the school."

He looked as handsome as ever, wearing his dress uniform, but the haunted look in his eyes made Jordan's heart hurt. She squinted against the sun to look him in the eye, but he artfully avoided both her gaze and Maddy's. Placing his white uniform hat under his left arm, he stood at attention. Grief was etched into his features, and the lines in his face seemed to have deepened over the past few days.

Bowing his head, he whispered, "I'm so sorry, Maddy. I want you to know that if I could trade places with Rick, I would."

Jordan's eyes welled as a fresh wave of grief flowed through. Gavin secured his hat and saluted them stoically as a flock of geese flew overhead. His square jaw clenched and his green eyes welled with tears, but before they could fall, he turned on his heel and headed to his truck.

He wasn't merely saying something he thought he should say. Jordan was certain, with every ounce of her soul, that if Gavin could have died instead of Rick, he would have. That knowledge was frightening and heartbreaking at the same time. She could just as easily be sitting in Maddy's place. If she stayed with Gavin, that was a risk she and her girls would be taking. But that paled in comparison to the risks he took on every day when he left for work.

She loved him, and that far outweighed any risk.

Gavin's self-loathing and guilt dragged behind him almost visibly as he strode away. Jordan hugged Maddy tighter as her friend's body finally shook with heavy sobs. A moment later, Veronica and Cookie appeared in the empty chairs on the other side of Maddy. The two women, so much more than mere employees, had stayed behind to make sure she was okay. Maddy didn't have any family left, and neither did Rick.

The two of them always said that at least they had each other.

Until now.

Veronica whispered words of encouragement and wrapped her arm around Maddy, kissing her cheek. Cookie looked on through red-rimmed eyes, and a nod of understanding passing between her and Jordan.

"Gavin, wait," Maddy cried, suddenly rising to her feet. Gavin stopped but didn't turn around. His back straightened and he squared his shoulders as though bracing for impact. "Don't go yet."

Maddy ran over to him, her long, black skirt flapping in the breeze and her dark curls blowing around her wildly. Jordan, Cookie, and Veronica rose from their seats and followed at a respectful distance. Gavin turned when Maddy laid her hand on his arm, urging him to face her. He stared over her head, unable or unwilling to look her in the eyes, and the pain on his face made Jordan's heart ache. She pressed her handkerchief to her mouth, Cookie and Veronica standing on either side of her, as the touching scene played out before them.

"I have something to say to you." Maddy swiped at her eyes before grabbing Gavin's jaw and forcing him to look down at her. Her voice wavered, but her steely strength shone through. "And I want you to look me in the face when I say it. Got it?"

Gavin gave her a curt nod but said nothing.

"Good." Maddy dropped her hand. "Rick loved his job, maybe even more than he loved me, and there wasn't a damned thing anyone could do to stop him if he had his mind set on something. He knew this was a risk. He went to work every day knowing that he could buy it in a fire like his father did, but that didn't stop him. He knew the dangers of the job and so did I." She grabbed Gavin's arms with both hands, and her normally lighthearted tone was edged with stone-cold seriousness.

"Don't you *dare* blame yourself for what happened. You didn't kill him, Gavin." Her voice wavered. "You aren't responsible for his death. Whoever set that fire and planted those pipe bombs is the person we should be angry at. It's gonna be hard enough for me to get through this, and you blaming yourself isn't going to help me or anyone else."

"I may not be responsible for the fire," Gavin ground out, "but I am responsible for Rick and every other man on my team. I'm sorry." He glanced at Jordan briefly, and the detached look in his eyes gave her pause. "I have to go."

Veronica and Cookie ran directly to Maddy, but Jordan made a beeline for Gavin. She reached him before he got in his truck. Placing a hand on his shoulder, she felt him stiffen beneath her touch. He was slipping further and further away from her with each passing second. She'd never felt more helpless in her life.

"Hey, Gavin, wait a minute." She folded her arms over her breasts, trying to squelch the horrible feeling that she was losing him. Ever since that night, it seemed as though he was worlds away. It scared the hell out of her. "Please, wait."

"What is it, Jordan?" He leaned one hand on the door and other on the roof as he glanced over his shoulder at her. Taking his hat off, he tossed it onto the passenger seat before finally turning to face her. "I have to get back to the station."

"Okay," she said slowly. "Why don't you come by the house tonight? The girls and I were going to make burgers, and Lily has been eager to show you a magic trick she taught herself with the book you gave her."

"I can't," he said curtly. Gavin unbuttoned his uniform jacket and loosened the collar of his shirt before getting in the driver's seat and shutting the door tightly. "I'll be at the station late, and then I have to get some shut-eye. Rogers and I are going back out to the scene tomorrow."

"Alright," she said softly. Stepping off the curb, Jordan curled her hands over the edge of the open window and held on, as if that could actually stop him from pulling away. Her throat thickened with fear and desperation as she studied his profile. She was losing him. He white-knuckled the steering wheel and stared straight ahead.

"Okay, then. How about tomorrow?"

"No." He shook his head as his hands tightened further and his entire body tensed, the muscle in his jaw flickering. "I can't."

"Can't what, Gavin?" Dread curled in her belly as he seemed to slip further away by the second. "Please," she whispered. "Don't shut me out."

"I won't do this to you, or to them."

"Do what?" Her vision blurred, and she had a horrible hunch about what he was going to say. Her hands slipped from the car. "Gavin…"

"I won't put you and the girls through something like this." Turning his fierce gaze to hers, he slammed the steering wheel and shouted, "Rick was my responsibility and I failed him. Don't you get it, Jordan? I *failed* him. He's dead, Maddy's alone, and I won't put you and the girls in that position. I failed Jimmy, and now Rick, and I refuse to fail you too."

Before she could respond, Gavin peeled away, the squealing truck tires breaking the silence of the cemetery with ear-shattering volume. Jordan shouted after him, but he kept driving. Tears fell from her eyes as she watched his taillights disappear around the corner. As he vanished from her view, she couldn't help but fear that he was about to exit her life as quickly as he'd returned.

Chapter 15

In the two weeks since Rick's funeral, Jordan only saw Gavin through the windows of the shop. She'd texted and called a few times in an attempt to rouse him from his self-imposed isolation. He never picked up the phone however, only responding with one-word texts. As much as she wanted to be patient, Jordan's feelings were beyond hurt. The girls had been asking for him, and Jordan was running out of excuses for why the chief had suddenly disappeared from their lives, almost as quickly as he'd entered.

Luckily their summer camp had been relocated to the community center, so Lily and Gracie were still busy during the week. Jordan was grateful for her job. It kept her mind off Gavin's cruel rejection of her and the possibility of a life together. She knew he was grieving, but he wasn't the only one. And her patience was starting to run out.

The door to the workroom opened, the noise pulling her from her thoughts.

"Hey, Jordan?" Cookie held the swinging door open and jutted a gloved hand at the little table in the corner. "What's with the duffel bag? This thing has been here for days. Can I put it somewhere else? We're busting at the seams back here, getting ready for the two parties this weekend."

"Right." Jordan's face heated. That was Gavin's bag, and it was filled with everything he'd left at the house that night. "Sorry. I've been meaning to drop that off to Gavin."

She could have brought it to the station, but she kept coming up with excuses not to. Most of her believed that Gavin would come around; she kept telling herself that he just needed some space. But her confidence dwindled with each passing day, and a future with Gavin seemed less and less likely.

"Oh, jeez, sorry." Cookie scrunched up her face and came all the way into the showroom. "Is everything okay with you guys?"

"That's a good question." Jordan let out a heavy breath and pushed her hair off her face, leaning back on the edge of the counter. "I don't know, Cookie. He's grieving and angry, and he's totally shut me out. I mean, Maddy is bouncing back better than Gavin is."

"Yeah, I guess," Cookie said quietly. "I saw her the other day. She was sitting at her desk in the real estate office, staring out the window. I waved, and she waved back, but it was out of habit, y'know? She just looks so sad, and there's nothing we can do to help her." She let out a growl of frustration and tugged her gloves off. "God, it sucks. I hope they catch the son of a bitch who set that fire."

"Me too," Jordan whispered. "I know Gavin's working with the arson investigator, but I haven't heard anything else about it."

"Right." Cookie nodded, her attention captured by something outside. "Looks like we've got a customer," she said, a smile playing over her lips. "I'll be in the back if you need me."

Jordan's heart leaped in her chest at the familiar sound of the front door swinging open. In that fleeting moment, she hoped against hope that it was Gavin. Cookie disappeared into the back room, and Jordan turned around and found herself face-to-face with a McGuire—but not the one she was expecting.

"Oh… Hello, Mrs. McGuire," she said, trying not to sound as disappointed as she felt. "How can I help you?"

"Now, Jordan." Gavin's mother wagged a finger at Jordan as she strode toward the counter. Placing her pink purse on the glass surface, she smiled and winked. "How many times have I told you to call me Carolyn? It's silly for us to be so formal after all these years."

A knot of nerves curled in Jordan's belly, and she could feel Carolyn's eyes on her. During their conversations over the past month about the flowers for the anniversary party, Carolyn had never said a word about Jordan and Gavin's relationship. She'd never pried or inquired, but there was a distinctly different air surrounding this particular visit. Dressed in khaki shorts and a simple, sleeveless white button-down shirt, Carolyn looked both perfectly coiffed and totally casual at the same time. The McGuires were wealthy, but they were the most down-to-earth family Jordan had ever known.

"Of course." Jordan pulled the order book from under the counter and placed it next to Carolyn's purse. Snagging a pen from behind her ear, she flipped to the pages with the McGuires' anniversary party information. "I assume you want to go over the final details? The big day is only a couple of weeks away, and I know you must be getting excited."

"Absolutely." Carolyn's voice was light and edged with her typically warm tone. "The band we've hired is wonderful. But I'm mostly excited about the rest of my boys coming home for a visit. It wouldn't be much of a celebration if our children weren't with us, after all! Not that I'll be able to get those boys to dance." She rolled her eyes and waved her hand dismissively. "Well, maybe Ronan. He's a bit more willing to be silly. The rest of them will probably avoid dancing at all costs."

"If memory serves, Gavin isn't much of a dancer." Jordan was met with Carolyn's warm smile. Her green eyes, so similar to Gavin's, peered back at Jordan with that same mischievous glint. "I know that I would want my girls with me at a party, but unlike your boys, they would be at the center of the dance floor."

"Well, I bet they would," Gavin's mother said brightly. "I hope they'll show us some of those dance moves at the party."

"My girls?" Jordan stumbled over her words. "Oh. Well, I don't think that we're going to be there. I mean, Gavin mentioned the party to me a few weeks ago, but he didn't actually invite us. To be really honest, I'm not sure what's going on with us right now." She squeezed her eyes shut and shook her head, feeling more embarrassed by the second. After a moment, she forced herself to look Carolyn in the face again. "I'm sorry. I know I'm babbling. You didn't come here to hear about this. You came about the flowers, and I can assure you everything is all set."

"Hang on, now." Carolyn covered Jordan's hand, stopping her nervous tapping of her pen on the open book. "I didn't come here to talk about the party, at least not about the flowers. I'm confident you, Cookie, and Veronica will have it all done beautifully, and I know Maddy appreciates that you're here. I can't even *imagine* how much harder these past few weeks would have been without you girls."

"Oh." Flustered and completely uncertain, Jordan quietly closed the book and slipped it back to its spot beneath the counter. "I see. Then what can I help you with, Mrs. M—I mean, Carolyn."

"That's better," she said gently. "I came here to talk to you about my son."

"Gavin?"

"Of course." She leaned in and dropped her voice to a conspiratorial whisper. "Unless you think one of my other boys is in love with you?" All Jordan could manage was to shake her head. "That's what I thought."

"I didn't realize that you…"

"I'm sure you know that Gavin is a mess over what happened to Rick."

"Yes." Jordan nodded. "I've tried reaching out to him, Carolyn, but he's completely shut me out."

"Mmm-hmm." Carolyn's mouth set in a firm line. Letting out a sigh, she wandered over to the refrigerated case, studying the colorful selection behind the glass. "I don't doubt it. He's a stubborn son of a gun like his father. And in addition to being stubborn, the boy gets blinded by duty and doing what's right. It's served him well most of his life, but sometimes, like now, it can take a dark turn.

"After that fire that killed little Jimmy Miller, Gavin didn't speak for almost three months." She turned around, bringing her attention back to Jordan. "Did you know that? Actually, that's when he started learning magic. The therapist we sent him to suggested it. She said it would help him feel more in control, and I suppose it did."

"No. I didn't know that." Jordan shook her head, a fresh surge of grief welling up. "The accident happened the year before I moved here. I've asked him about it in the past, but he hasn't really wanted to talk about it. I never really understood how he could blame himself. Gavin and the others were merely children."

"True, but Gavin has always seen himself as the caretaker." Carolyn shrugged. "I suppose it comes with being the oldest in a big family. He's always felt responsible for his brothers, and now for his squad. And, yes. We all know, rationally, that Gavin isn't to blame for Jimmy or for Rick, but *he's* the one who has to understand that. The way I see it, you might be the only one who can get through to him."

"Me?" Jordan swallowed and hugged her arms around herself. "He's made it clear he doesn't want to speak to me."

"Of course," Carolyn said, laughing curtly. "He's a man. Men hate talking about their feelings. For the love of all that's holy, do you know how long it took me to get Charles to start opening up?"

"Really?" Jordan nibbled her lower lip. "Mr. McGuire seems so…"

"Honey, please." Carolyn let out a loud laugh and grabbed her purse off the counter, slinging it over her shoulder. "You don't think he came that way, do you? That's forty years of work you're seeing in that man. It's a good thing we were married for so long before all the boys came along. It gave me time to work on him.

"Anyway…" She sighed. "I know my boy loves you. And I also know that he's been shutting everyone out, me and his father included. He's on a dangerous spiral, and if his brothers were here, I might be able to get one of them to get through to him, but he's not taking their phone calls. Ronan is about ready to spit nails, he's so mad."

"They're coming for the party though, right?"

"Yes, but that's not for a couple weeks. We don't have that kind of time." Hands folded in front of her, she moved directly in front of the counter. "I have one question for you. Are you in love with Gavin?"

Jordan licked her lower lip, her heart fluttering like a rabbit. She did love him, but she hadn't admitted it out loud. Not to him, nor anyone else—not even to herself. But staring into the determined, loving face of his mother, Jordan could no longer deny the truth.

"Yes," she whispered. "I love him very much. He's the best friend I've ever had."

Carolyn leaned across the counter and grabbed Jordan's hands in hers. Pulling them onto the glass surface, she squeezed them tightly. Tears welled in her eyes, and for the first time, her voice wavered. "Like Gavin always says, you were his friend first. You *are* his friend, and right now, that's exactly what he needs."

Before Jordan could respond, Carolyn patted her hands and swept out of the shop. As she disappeared down the sidewalk, Jordan's gaze drifted to the station across the street in time to see Gavin's truck pull out of the station parking lot. Without wasting one more minute thinking about it—because she could easily talk herself out of what she was about to do—Jordan picked up the phone and called her mother.

After what felt like forever, Claire finally picked up.

"Hello?" Her mother sounded lighter and unencumbered since the death of Jordan's father. As painful as it was for her to lose her husband, and as frightened as she was to be on her own, his death had freed her. She'd never admit it, but Jordan knew that was true. "Claire Yardley speaking."

"Mom?" Jordan bit back the urge to chicken out. "Hi. It's Jordan."

"Hello, baby." A smile lit up her mother's voice. "I was thinking about you and the girls. I was hoping you might come over for supper one night this week."

"Actually, that's kind of why I was calling. Would it be okay if the girls had a sleepover at your house tonight? There's something I need to take care of and it might take a while."

"Why, yes!" she exclaimed. "I would love it! You tell Gracie we'll make her favorite brownies again too."

"Great." Jordan let out a sigh of relief. "I'll bring them over after work. Mom, thank you so much."

"No, baby," she whispered. "Thank *you*."

After finalizing the details, Jordan hung up and went over to the glass case, pulling out one of the premade bouquets. She set it aside and quickly paid for her purchase. If she was going to get through to Gavin, she had to make one other stop first.

—◦◦◦—

Gavin stood outside what remained of Old Brookfield School. Rage fired up his back as Rogers confirmed what they'd all suspected.

Arson.

The police chief stood with them in front of the wrecked building, going over the report. Contractors were about to start construction on the school, and Gavin needed to have one final look before the town started repairing the place.

"It was definitely arson. The firebug had four pipe bombs set to go off." Rogers hitched up his pants and referred to the report in his hands before passing a copy to Gavin. "The son of a bitch had one rigged with a timer, and at least two of 'em had remote triggers."

"Timers and remotes?" A finger of dread rushed over him. "Do you mean that this asshole *wanted* people to get hurt? He was waiting for us to go in there?"

"Probably."

"Son of a bitch," Gavin spat out.

"It's way too sloppy to be a professional job. With enough research online, any asshole can find the plans to make something like this. We have a beginner on our hands, but a smart beginner."

"I still can't believe that someone in our town did this," Gavin murmured. The image of the Heffernan kid sitting on the hood of his car watching the school burn came rushing back to mind. "Any leads on who it could be?"

"We're following up on some eyewitness accounts about a car seen in the area," the police chief said. "It matches the description of one spotted near the Thompson place, not long before their shed was torched, and by the old gas station."

"Yeah, but that's one vague-ass description," Rogers groused.

"Yup." The police chief flipped open his notepad. "A dark-colored, two-door hatchback, possibly black or blue, with local plates. Maybe a Honda, but could be a Ford."

"Well, shit." Gavin folded up the report, fighting his burgeoning frustration. Like the Heffernan kid's car. *No way.* "You described about a third of the town's vehicles. We need more than that."

"We'll find him," Rogers growled. "These guys get caught eventually. The car is a good lead, but I'm more curious about checking out the crowds that showed up at the fires."

"Why?" Gavin's brow furrowed. "You think that our firebug would come watch his handiwork?"

"Probably." Rogers pulled out a cigarette and lit it before taking a long drag. "Like I said, they love to watch shit burn. Anyone come to mind?"

Gavin stared at the burned-out building and swore under his breath.

"What?" Rogers flicked ash onto the ground. "You got an idea?"

"Not one that's gonna make me feel any better." Gavin folded his arms over his chest and crumpled the paper in his hand. "We have a kid, local high school student, who's been working for us around the station. I think he's just an eager future firefighter but... well...shit. I can't believe the kid would be involved, but he's shown up at every scene like it's freaking Christmas morning."

"Name?" Rogers clicked his pen.

"David Heffernan."

"The Heffernan kid?" The police chief made a face of disbelief. "Hell, I could see you pointing the finger at his twin. I mean, Robert has been causing trouble since he could walk, but David? That's crazy."

"So is a firebug," Rogers said, the cigarette dangling between his lips.

"Well, I say that kid's not good for it, but we'll check out his whereabouts during the time of the fires. I'll reach out to the local news station too." The police chief pulled out his cell phone and started poking at the screen. "They were here the night of the school fire, and I'm sure they got shots of the crowd."

"Good," Gavin seethed. "And when you figure out who did it, you better find him before I do."

"Hey, Gavin?" Rogers sucked down another drag. "You look like shit, man."

"Thanks." Gavin shot an irritated look at him. "I haven't exactly slept well since all of this crap started."

"You aren't gonna be any good to anyone if you fall asleep standing up. Why don't you go home?" The police chief slipped his notebook in the pocket of his jacket and jutted his chin toward Rogers. "We've got the investigation under control. Do the town a favor: go home and get some sleep."

"He's right." Rogers started toward his car. He flicked his cigarette into the driveway of the school before tugging open the driver's side door of his car. "And if you don't get rid of that big albatross around your neck, it's gonna be *you* next time. Get some sleep. I'll call you after we get the test results back on the materials. That might help us narrow things down."

Gavin stayed for a few minutes after the other men left. They were right; he was dog-ass tired. But stopping to sleep felt like a betrayal.

While sleep might not be on his agenda, a cold shower and a big pot of coffee sounded like a good alternative. Gavin wouldn't be able to rest until they found the fire-bug and stomped him out.

Jordan stood on the porch of Tommy's small ramshackle cottage, flowers and a pizza in hand. She rang the bell for a second time before peeking in the little arched window at the top of the door. Tommy had been released from the hospital a couple days after the fire. She knew that much, and that his injuries were limited to some scrapes and bruises. He'd been at Rick's funeral, but as usual, he'd stayed along the fringe of the crowd, doing his best to disappear and emerging only long enough to pay his respects to Maddy.

She was about to give up when she spotted a famil-iar silhouette shuffling toward the front door. Jordan stepped back and adjusted the flowers in her hand before putting on a big smile. As the door swung open, she hoped like hell she wasn't overstepping her bounds.

"Hey, Tommy." Jordan held up the pizza box and smiled. "I thought you might be hungry, and I figured you probably weren't up for making yourself dinner. I know the ladies at the church made you a bunch of meals to freeze, but I thought you might be looking for something other than a casserole. Can I come in?"

"Oh…uh…I don't know." Tommy smoothed

the tuft of gray hair on the scarred side of his head before opening the door a little more. "The place is kinda messy."

"No worries," Jordan said with a wide smile. "I have two kids. Believe me, I don't even see messes anymore."

He glanced over his shoulder as though weighing his options. "Can we eat out on the porch?" Tommy asked, gesturing to the little café-style table and chairs to the left. "I wasn't expecting company," he said quietly.

"Of course." Jordan quickly brought the pizza to the table and placed it on the chipped wooden surface. "I'm sorry, Tommy. I guess I should have called first, but I didn't have your phone number. I was worried about you."

"It's okay." His soft-spoken tone brightened a bit as he closed the door behind himself. "It's just that I don't get visitors often, and I'd be embarrassed for you to see my place the way it is. I'm not much of a housekeeper. I guess cleaning up after the kids at the school all day is enough."

"I really don't mind. It's a nice night, so eating alfresco sounds good to me." Jordan opened the box and sat on the little wooden folding chair. She hung her purse on the back and handed Tommy the flowers. "These are for you too."

"Really?" His face reddened as he took the paper-wrapped bouquet. "Nobody never gave me flowers before. Especially not a pretty lady like you, Miss Jordan. You should be the one getting flowers. Not me."

"Flowers are for everyone." She took a slice of pizza and held it out to Tommy. He sat down across from her and laid the bouquet in his lap. "And so is pizza!"

—₥—

They ate and chatted for close to an hour, and to Jordan's surprise, Tommy was actually quite the conversationalist. In addition to being passionate about the town, he was a big fan of car racing, ultimate fighting, and online gaming. It was nice to know that he might be shy, but he was hardly the sad figure that everyone painted him as. He was introverted, to be sure, but based on his gaming exploits, he had a large online community that he considered an extended family. And among them was a lady friend he hoped to meet in person someday.

Eventually, as the light began to dwindle, it was time to ask the one question she'd been holding back.

"Tommy, can I ask you a personal question?" She closed up the pizza box and caught his eye. "It's about you and Gavin."

"Okay." He lifted one shoulder and looked down at the bouquet of flowers still in his lap. He picked them up and smelled them. "What do you want to know?"

"Well, it's about the fire when you were children…"

"That was a long time ago," he said quickly.

"I know. And I know that Gavin tried to save you and your brother."

"Jimmy didn't listen," Tommy said quietly, his face getting a faraway look. "Gavin told him not to mess with the matches, but he took some when we weren't lookin' and went up to the loft. Dumb kid." Anger and pain etched his features and his voice wavered. "He shoulda stayed down there with us. We were only smokin' a few stupid cigarettes, but Jimmy kept wantin' to light the matches and Gavin kept tellin' him no."

"So Jimmy is the one who actually started the fire?" Jordan asked gently.

"Yeah." Tommy shifted in his seat and kept his eyes on the flowers. "I went up to the loft to get him, but the fire spread so fast and he was trapped behind the hay bales. I got real scared and kinda froze. The flames got so big and they were so hot, and it was like my feet wouldn't cooperate. But Gavin came up that ladder and got me. I was too afraid to move, but not him. He brought me down himself, and he wanted to go back up for Jimmy, but…it burned too fast and everything started to come down."

"That's when he got hurt?" She squeezed Tommy's arm and whispered, "When both of you were injured?"

"Yeah." Tommy nodded and swiped at his eyes before turning a harsh glare in her direction. "Why don't you ask him about it?" Tommy asked in a surprisingly curt tone. He turned his good eye to her briefly. "Aren't you and him goin' together again?"

"Sort of," she said quietly. "But he's in a lot of pain right now after what happened to Rick. To be honest, I don't think it's only because of Rick's death. I think he's carrying around a lot of guilt about what happened in that barn when you were children. I guess I was hoping you could help me shed some light on it so that I could understand him better." Jordan reached over and laid her hand on Tommy's forearm, hoping he would look her in the eye again. "So that I can help him," she added softly. "Both of you."

"You should go now," Tommy said, abruptly rising to his feet. "It's getting late and it's almost time for the next game with my guild."

"I'm sorry." Jordan stood up as guilt swamped her. *Damn it!* She'd pushed it too far. "I didn't mean to upset you. I only wanted to help."

"It's fine." He shuffled to the door and didn't look back, but the pitch of his voice rose. "I-I don't want to talk about this anymore. Thanks for the pizza and the flowers. Good-bye, Jordan."

Without waiting for a response, Tommy disappeared inside and slammed the door. Jordan let out a huff of frustration before getting her purse and going to her car. She started the engine and backed slowly out of the gravel driveway before making the turn toward the McGuires' house. She'd succeeded in finding out more about what happened during that fire so many years ago, but all it did was make her heart ache further. There was a good chance that Gavin would be about as receptive to her meddling as Tommy.

But then, there was one big difference between the two broken men.

Gavin McGuire was in love with her.

It was a good bet that when she got to his house, he was going to push her away and pretend he didn't need her. He would probably say hurtful things to get her to leave, and it was going to sting like hell.

No more running.

Chapter 16

GAVIN LEANED ON THE DECK RAILING OUTSIDE HIS COT-
tage and stared out over the crashing waves below. He
was finishing off his fourth cup of coffee. The cold
shower had peeled away some of the fog and the pot
of coffee was finally kicking in, but nothing could help
him shake the overwhelming shroud of grief and guilt.

The sky burned orange and pink along the horizon as
the sun made its leisurely descent over the edge of the
world. When he was a kid, he'd squeeze his eyes shut
and try to hear the sound the sun made when it finally
disappeared. Sometimes, he'd sworn he could actually
detect a subtle *thunk* as the brilliant orb vanished.

His gut clenched when his gaze settled on Jordan's
gray-shingled cottage below. Swearing under his
breath, Gavin drained the rest of his coffee and
slammed the mug onto the table behind him. He slipped
his hands into the pockets of his jeans. He was doing
what was best for her and the girls. They had all been
through enough.

Jordan and her daughters should have someone in
their lives who wasn't at daily risk of buying it on the
job. Rick had been right about that. It would be selfish of
Gavin to pursue his relationship with Jordan any further
than he already had. She and her daughters deserved
better than what he could give them, and the way he
was feeling lately, Gavin had little left to give.

A knock at his front door pulled him from his thoughts and had him checking his watch. *Who the hell was here?* It wasn't his mother, he thought, rolling his eyes. She never knocked. Gavin grabbed his T-shirt off the back of the chair and pulled it on as he made his way back into the house. Closing the slider behind him, he strode through the living room, his uninvited visitor pounding on the door like the place was on fire.

"Keep your pants on," he shouted. "I'm coming! What the hell is…?"

Gavin tugged the door open and was about to rip his intruder a new one when he saw who it was. Dressed in a simple white sundress with a blue cardigan, Jordan looked absolutely gorgeous. Her long hair hung loose over her shoulders, and her face was, as usual, free of makeup. He soaked in the sight of her from head to toe, but his reverie came to a halt when he saw his duffel bag in her hands.

He'd been meaning to go get his things from her place but kept coming up with excuses not to…even though he knew it was inevitable. Lucky for him, Jordan was stronger than he was. She had done what he was too afraid to do.

"No wonder you hardly have any visitors here," she said before slipping past him and letting herself in. "If you answer the door like that all the time, I'd be surprised if the mailman ever delivers any mail to you."

"Come on in," he said with more than a little sarcasm as he shut the door. He bit back the urge to pull her into his arms, reminding himself again that this was all for the best. "I assume you came by to drop off my stuff. I'm sorry I didn't come get it sooner. You can leave the bag on the kitchen table." Jordan ignored him and went into the living room. "Or you can put it on the couch."

"This is nice," she said, her back to him. She strolled around the room before depositing the bag on the coffee table. She pointed to the kitchen and smiled. "That's the kitchen?"

Without waiting for a response, she headed into the small white-and-red kitchen and started rummaging through his refrigerator. Gavin leaned both hands on the breakfast bar that also served as a divider between the kitchen and the living room and wondered what exactly she planned on doing.

Within about three minutes, his question was answered. She'd found everything she needed to make eggs and bacon, probably because that's about all he had in there. The woman even put the last two pieces of stale bread in the toaster. The entire situation rendered Gavin momentarily speechless.

"What the hell are you doing?" he finally asked, more harshly than he intended. "It's almost eight o'clock at night. Why are you making breakfast?"

"You look like shit, Gavin." Jordan turned over a few pieces of bacon on the griddle, not looking at him while she spoke. "I'm betting you've hardly eaten or drank anything except coffee and doughnuts in the past three weeks." Glancing at him over her shoulder, she smirked and looked him up and down before turning back to the stove. "Actually, I take that back. Just coffee."

Gavin wrestled with how perfect it was having her in his kitchen. *Son of a bitch.* He didn't *want* to want her—to want *this. Damn it all to hell!* Frustration and anger shimmied up his back as he fought his conflicting emotions.

He stormed around the island and into the kitchen.

"I'm fine." Looming next to her, he growled, "I didn't ask you to come here and take care of me. I'm not a child."

"Nope," she said brightly. "Well, you're part right. You may not be a child, but you certainly are acting like one."

Jordan transferred the bacon to a plate covered with paper towels and turned off the burner. She continued her impromptu cooking escapade without missing a beat, pouring the egg mixture into a heated pan that sizzled with butter.

In spite of how uncomfortable Gavin felt, he couldn't stop his stomach from rumbling as the delicious aroma filled the room.

"Now, Chief, why don't you stop glowering at me and get us a couple of plates?"

"Stop it," he whispered. Gavin's hands curled into fists as he fought the urge to touch her, to tangle his fingers in her long hair and lose himself in the feel of her. To forget how shitty he felt—but that would be selfish. He didn't deserve it, and he sure as shit didn't deserve her. "I mean it, Jordan. You should go. I thought I made myself clear at the cemetery. I can't do this."

"Do what?" she asked, scraping the scrambled eggs onto another large plate next to the bacon. The pan clattered on the stove top. Jordan wiped her hands on a dish towel before tossing it onto the counter. "Eat? Take care of yourself? Stop blaming yourself for Rick's death or for Jimmy's? Love me?" Her eyebrows flew up and she poked him in the chest with one finger. "Which is it, Gavin? All of the above?"

"No," he seethed. "Damn it, Jordan." He stepped back but she kept coming, meeting his glare with her own. "I can't do *this*. You and the girls. Us. All of it," he shouted. "I was wrong and I shouldn't have started any of this back up again. Okay?"

"No, Gavin, it's not okay," Jordan said in a surprisingly calm tone. She got right in his face, hands on her hips, but he held his ground. "You can't come storming back into my life like some kind of hurricane and then slink away because you get scared." He flinched and narrowed his gaze. "Yeah, that's right. I see right through your bullshit, and so does everyone else."

"It's not bullshit, Jordan." Gavin's voice was rough and edgy, barely above a whisper. "I don't have anything left to give. Even if I did, I'd be of little use to you, Gracie, and Lily. You said it yourself—you came home to start over. The last complication the three of you need is to have me in your life." His jaw clenched and his mouth set in a firm line as he fought to get the words out. "I'm trying to protect you."

Jordan inched closer and her clean, flowery scent cut through the pall of smoke that clung to him in a seemingly ever-present cloud. With it came hope. Need. Yearning. All he'd smelled for weeks was smoke and burnt plastic but not now. Soap. A hint of suntan lotion and a whisper of flowers wafted off her in a deliciously sexy way. His body and mind were waging an all-out war, and the conflict was going to drive him mad.

"No, you're not," Jordan countered. Her breasts brushed against his chest. The edge of the counter dug into his ass as she trailed one finger up his arm. Her voice, soft and seductive, drifted over him like a caress. It threatened his resolve as did the trail her finger blazed along his flesh. "The only person you're trying to protect is yourself."

Gavin stilled when her empathy-filled, intelligent brown eyes met his. Fear, guilt, regret, lust, and overwhelming need flooded him as her delicate hands drifted over his chest and down his stomach before finally settling at his waist.

She pressed her body against him and lowered her voice to a whisper. "You didn't kill them."

"That's not what this is about." Gavin grabbed her arms and gently but firmly pushed her away before striding out to the living room. "Stop. This is done. I'm sorry, but that's the way it is."

He stood at the glass sliding door and stared out over the ocean. Hands on his hips, he kept his back to her. Maybe, just maybe, if he pushed hard enough, she would leave.

"Jimmy was playing with those matches up in the loft," she continued, all of her natural strength and determination shining through as she persisted. Jordan kept coming at him like the relentless waves in the ocean below. One after the other, she persisted. "Before you tell me that I don't know what the hell I'm talking about, I'll let you know that I spoke to Tommy. He told me what happened, and, yes, you brought the matches and cigarettes, but you tried to keep Jimmy from touching them. Tommy said that his brother stole them when you weren't looking and took them up to the loft. *Jimmy* lit the fire that killed him and wounded you and Tommy."

She moved closer but Gavin held firm.

"Tommy tried to get to his brother first, but he got scared by the fire and you saved him. He said you tried to save Jimmy too, but fire and debris started to rain down on you. What else could you have done? And Rick? Rick did what he had to do, Gavin. He did what you and all of the men in your squad have done countless times. He put his life on the line to keep someone else safe, and this time…this time he lost."

Her voice wavered, her hand settling on his shoulder where the scarred and puckered flesh lived. A grim daily reminder of his failure. "The scars you carry aren't only on the outside, Gavin. But you have to stop torturing yourself. You didn't kill Jimmy." The warmth of her palm seeped into his shoulder, soothing the wound and bringing the numb flesh to life at the same time. She sniffled, her voice cracking with emotion. "And you didn't kill Rick."

A swell of grief swamped Gavin, making him squeeze his eyes shut against the surge of emotion, but the gentle sound of Jordan's voice tugged at him. It called to him, preventing him from falling over the edge like the sun and vanishing into the abyss.

Jordan's hand dropped from his shoulder, and he could feel her moving away from him. She was right. He was scared. Scared shitless both of losing and of loving her. The sound of his front door clicking open forced his hand.

He couldn't let her leave. Not now. Not ever.

He was a selfish bastard.

"I don't want to hurt you," Gavin ground out.

When he spun around, Jordan was standing in the open doorway with her back to him. A warm ocean breeze blew through the house and lifted her hair from her shoulders like wings. The lights from his parents' house glimmered in the distance, making it even more evident that his home was right here with her.

"You're right. I'm scared, Jordan. I am absolutely *terrified* that I'll die on the job and leave you, Lily, and Gracie alone. I don't want that for you. Can you understand that? I want you and the girls to have a big life, a life full of magic tricks and bodysurfing. Not nights of wondering whether or not I'm gonna die in a fire and leave you all alone. You deserve better than that."

"I don't need you making my decisions for me," she said, her voice rising with impatience.

"Damn it, Jordan." He ran one hand over his face and shouted, "*I don't want to fail you!*"

There it was. He'd finally spit it out. His worst fear was out in the open and exposed like a wound that wouldn't heal. Failing Jordan was the one tragedy he simply had not been willing to risk.

Gripping the doorknob tighter, Jordan turned around slowly. She closed the door before leaning back against it. A smile curved her lips and she tilted her head, keeping her hands clasped behind her. She studied him with a knowing expression for what seemed like an eternity before finally pushing herself away from the door and striding slowly toward him.

"I love you, Gavin, and in spite of how you're acting, I know that you love me." She stopped a few feet away from him with that steely, determined expression on her face. "But I am not your responsibility, and *you* don't get to choose who *I* love. Okay? And as fate would have it, I love you, you big idiot. And it's not just me. My girls love you. You've been more of a father to them over this summer than their own father ever was. I know you're scared and so am I, but that's part of the deal, isn't it?

"Love is scary. It's terrifying. Whether it's the love we feel for our child when we first look into their face on the day that they're born or the love we have for a parent who's frighteningly imperfect, or if it's the love I have for a man who's hell-bent on not letting me love him. Love is scary and wonderful, and it's what makes us human." Arms wide and with a smile brightening her face, she whispered, "I love you, Gavin, and I need you. You didn't kill Jimmy or Rick."

Her hands dropped to her sides as she closed the distance between them, stopping only about a foot away.

"But if you cut me out of your life…" Tears filled her eyes and her voice wavered. "Then you just might kill *me*."

––––⁓––––

Gavin glowered at her from beneath his furrowed brow, and his green eyes glittered with something she couldn't quite identify. Passion? Desperation? Fury? Perhaps all of those things? With the moments hanging heavy and silent between them, Jordan feared she was too late and that she really had lost him.

And then, in a flash, he was on her.

Gavin's mouth slanted over hers, hard and fast. His strong hands tangled in her hair and tilted her head, taking immediate control of the kiss. Jordan opened to him as his tongue demanded entrance and speared hers with swift, wicked strokes. Desperate to get closer, she grabbed his shirt and tugged it up, exposing the warm expanse of his back. She groaned into his mouth, his muscles moving beneath her hands.

Breaking the kiss and breathing heavily, Gavin reached behind and quickly yanked the shirt off over his head, tossing it hastily aside before capturing her lips once again.

As she clung to him desperately, Jordan's fingers grazed the puckered flesh that marred part of Gavin's back, and a swell of love filled her. This man would give every bit of himself to protect others. If she'd let him, he would have sacrificed his own happiness, thinking he was securing hers. How wrong he was.

The only one, the only man who could ever bring Jordan true happiness…was him.

Kissing her deeply, Gavin walked her backward, his hands exploring her body with urgent, almost desperate speed. Jordan gasped as her back bumped the door and Gavin dragged his mouth from hers. He grabbed the fabric of her skirt and yanked it up, reaching between her legs and cupping her sex with one hand. Gripping his shoulders, Jordan gasped again. His other hand tugged her top down, exposing her breasts to his hungry stare.

Her fingers dug into his muscular shoulders and she cried out, his hot, wet mouth covering her breast. He flicked her nipple with his tongue, while sliding two fingers beneath the edge of her panties. His rough touch rasped over her clit in one wicked pass. Pleasure swamped her, and Jordan moaned as Gavin brought her to the edge. He massaged the tiny nub with his thumb before sliding two fingers deep inside her, putting pressure on that spot she wasn't even sure existed. *G-spot? Yes, please.*

"I want you to come for me, Jordan," Gavin murmured against her breast. He lifted his head, lust stamped on his handsome features, his fingers continuing their merciless assault. Crying out, she hooked her leg over his hip, giving him better access to, her hot, wet center. His fingers moved faster, sliding in and out of her sex as her orgasm started to crest. "That's it, baby. Open up and give me everything."

Shaking and on the edge of no return, Jordan whimpered when Gavin removed his hand and dropped to his knees. Gasping for breath, her body clinging to that exquisite cliff of impending climax, she leaned against the door for support.

Kneeling between her legs, Gavin peered up at her with that wicked, mischievous grin, the dimple appearing in his cheek. Reaching up, he grabbed the front of her dress with both hands and yanked it open.

"Too many buttons," he growled as tiny disks went flying around the room, clattering one by one somewhere in the distance.

Jordan didn't care; all she could see or feel was *him*. She clung to his shoulders, his fingers trailing over her breasts, flicking her sensitized nipples, then settling on her hips. Jordan's entire body hummed with unfulfilled desire, the orgasm exquisitely close.

Gavin hooked his thumb beneath the edge of the lacy fabric of her panties and pulled them down her legs, flicking them aside.

"You're so beautiful, Jordan," he murmured, sliding his hand along her thigh. He lifted her leg and hooked it over his shoulder, grasping her knee. He peered up at her. "I have to taste you."

Biting her lower lip, Jordan nodded, unable to utter a word. One sound might shatter her taut, overheated body into a million pieces.

On a curse, Gavin clutched her by the hips and dove deep. Jordan cried out as his hot mouth covered her sex, licking and suckling her already swollen clit with total abandon. The orgasm started to bloom with lightning speed. Only one thing would make it complete—make it perfect.

"Wait," she said through heavy breaths. Threading her hands through his hair, she tugged gently, urging him to stop. "I have to have you inside me, Gavin. Right now."

Gavin rose to his feet. Jordan's leg slipped from his shoulder, and she grabbed the waist of his jeans eagerly. Muscles straining, Gavin braced both hands on the door on either side of her as she made quick work of releasing him from the confining, unyielding fabric. Looming over her, caging her in, Gavin swore as Jordan's fingers curled around the steely length of his thick shaft. He moaned with pleasure as she ran her hand up and down the rigid stalk of flesh. He shuddered when she slid her thumb over the swollen head, slick with moisture.

He captured her mouth with his, kissing her deeply as she massaged him. The pace was swift and sure and pushing him to the edge. Unable to wait any longer, Jordan released him and shoved his jeans down his hips. Knowing what she wanted, what they both wanted, Gavin grabbed her ass and lifted her up, momentarily breaking the kiss. With her body pinned firmly against the wooden surface, her mouth hovering near his, and her legs wrapped around his waist, Gavin lifted her higher and tilted his hips, deftly positioning the tip of his shaft against her swollen entrance.

"Don't stop," Jordan gasped. She tangled her hands

in his hair and rested her forehead against his. "Are you trying to kill me?"

"I'm trying to love you," he whispered. "You're mine, Jordan." As her name hissed from his lips, Gavin slipped inside her with one slow, deliberate stroke. Inch by inch, he claimed her. "Forever. I'm never letting you go, ever again."

Jordan cried out as he thrust into her, filling her more completely than anyone. Physically. Emotionally. Gavin McGuire filled Jordan in every way possible. As his body moved inside hers, she knew, with every ounce of her soul, that this *was* forever.

This loving, passionate, sensitive, devoted man was her past, her present, and her future.

Jordan held her to him as he pumped into her time and time again. He buried his face in the crook of her neck, and the orgasm erupted brightly, lighting her body up in one merciless wave after another. She shouted his name as the powerful climax ripped through them both. He thrust into her with one final pass, leaving them shaking, sweating, and bone-meltingly satisfied.

Tiny aftershocks rocked their tangled bodies, and Gavin swept his mouth up her throat before kissing her deeply once again. His lips suckled hers in slow gentle passes as he carefully disengaged from her body. Jordan's feet found the floor but her legs felt like jelly, while Gavin gently peeled the scraps of her dress from damp flesh, allowing them to fall noiselessly to the ground. He kissed her again and quickly adjusted his jeans before scooping her up in his arms and pressing his lips to her forehead.

"That was…incredible," Jordan whispered. She linked

her arms around his neck and flicked his earlobe with her tongue. "You've learned a few things over the years."

"What are you saying? You mean that was better than the lighthouse?" He arched one eyebrow as he carried her through the living room to the hallway off the kitchen. Pushing the bedroom door open with his shoulder, he brought her to the foot of the king-size bed. The spacious bedroom was sparsely furnished and had all the markings of a bachelor's sleeping space. "We were kids then. Fumbling around in the dark. Nervous, turned on, and not sure what went where."

"True." Jordan giggled. Now, with her naked body curled up in his arms, she knew what it was to be truly cherished. To be loved. She brushed a lock of hair off his forehead before cradling his scruffy cheek in her hand. "That was a special night but, oh my God... Do you remember how you fumbled with the condom and—" Jordan's eyes widened as she realized what they'd forgotten. "Oh shit."

"What?" Gavin stopped by the bed. "The lighthouse was better?"

"No." Jordan squeezed him tighter and pressed a kiss to his lips. Nuzzling her face against his neck, feeling awkward even bringing it up, she said, "We didn't use anything...you know."

"Oh...right." Gavin's grip on her tightened and his voice grew gruff. "Shit. I didn't even think about that." His thumb rasped over her arm, sending a fresh surge of lust through her. "You know what that means, don't you?"

Jordan shook her head but couldn't still her quaking body.

"We have to do it again. I wanna make sure I get it right." He waggled his eyebrows at her and kissed her firmly. "And I can promise you that there will be no fumbling tonight or any other night." He strode around to the side of the bed and laid her out gently, almost reverently. "I love you, Jordan, and if you'll let me, I'll spend the rest of my life proving it."

Chapter 17

THE DELECTABLE SMELL OF BURGERS COOKING ON THE grill drifted past Jordan and Maddy as they sat in their beach chairs while the girls played in the lapping waves. Between the sounds of their laughter, the stomach-rumbling aroma of the grill, and the gorgeous August weather, Jordan couldn't help but think it was a perfect summer day. In fact, ever since that night at Gavin's cottage, life had been better than ever. The only thing that would make it truly perfect would be if she could heal Maddy's grieving heart.

"Burgers will be ready in a few minutes," Gavin shouted from the deck.

Jordan smiled at him over her shoulder but when he grinned at her, spatula in hand, she lost it and started giggling.

"I'm really happy for you, Jordan," Maddy said quietly. She was wearing large, dark sunglasses and had her curly brown hair swept up in a clip, and sadness clung to her like heavy blanket. "You deserve to be happy, and so does Gavin. I have to tell you, he's like a different person ever since you came home." A wistful smile curved her lips as she drew lazy circles in the sand with one of her feet. "Rick knew this was where you two were headed. In fact, he said you'd probably be married by Christmas."

"Married?" Jordan adjusted the straps of her red one-piece bathing suit and laughed nervously. She and Gavin hadn't discussed marriage at all, but Jordan would be lying if she said she never thought about it. Because she did. A lot. "Oh, that's kind of rushing it. I mean, we just got back together. Marrying me is way more than just marrying *me*." She gestured to the girls. "If that happened, he'd get an instant family."

"Girl, please." Maddy sat up in her chair and jutted a thumb at Gavin. "Look at what's happening here. He loves you and your girls. Hell, he's cooking on your grill on your deck and drinking a beer like you two have been married for twenty years." She pushed her sunglasses onto her head and grabbed Jordan's hand. "Go with it, Jordan. I don't regret one single second of my life with Rick, but if he were here, I'd tell him to cut the shit and marry me already. You have something special with Gavin, and I hope you hang on to it with everything you've got."

Before Jordan could respond, assuring her she had no intention of letting Gavin go, Maddy's phone started chirping. Letting out a creative curse, Maddy started rummaging through the big colorful bag that was sitting on the sand between their chairs until she found it.

"It's my assistant at the real estate office." She let out a big sigh and pushed herself from the chair. "I have to take it, sorry."

"Go. It's fine." Jordan gave her a reassuring smile. As Maddy strolled away to take the call, Jordan noticed Lily and Gracie on their backs making sand angels. "You two are gonna have sand in every single crevice," she shouted playfully. "You better rinse off. Dinner will be ready soon."

"Burgers are done and ready when you are."

Gavin swooped in and planted a firm kiss on her lips. He dropped to sit on the sand next to her, pulled his knees up, and rested his forearms on them. Beer in hand and clad in only his blue plaid bathing suit, he looked effortlessly gorgeous. He took a sip of his beer, then gestured toward Maddy, wading in the water while taking her call.

"How's she doing?"

"She's okay, I guess." Jordan brushed sand off her hands before pulling her feet up on the chair. "I mean, as okay as she can be. I wish I could do more to help her, you know?"

"Well, it's a good sign that she's here and not at home alone. In fact, I think the best thing for her is to be around people. Do you think you can convince her to come to my parents' anniversary party next weekend? My brothers would love to see her, especially Ronan."

"Interesting." Jordan squinted against the sun. "If memory serves, he had the hots for Maddy all through high school."

"Ronan has the hots for *all* women," Gavin countered, his smile faltering. "I spoke to him the other day. I finally called all four of my brothers back. I was threatened with a good old-fashioned beating if I didn't. Anyway, if she goes, he'll make sure she has fun at the party. I think it could be good for her."

"I'll see what I can do." Jordan settled her hand on his arm and gave it a quick squeeze. "You're pretty terrific, you know that?"

Those gorgeous eyes crinkled at the corners, and he winked. "Yup."

"And modest too," she said, shoving him away from her playfully.

"Are you lookin' for a fight, missy?" Gavin shifted to a crouching position while placing his empty beer bottle on the sand. "Let's see what you've got."

With lightning-fast reflexes, he whipped his hands out and linked them around Jordan's biceps, pulling her easily from the chair. Letting out a shriek mixed with laughter, Jordan barely had time to catch her breath before Gavin threw her over his shoulder and started toward the water.

"What do you think, girls?" Gavin stopped next to Lily and Gracie, both wet and covered in sand. The two of them giggled and clapped as he pulled Jordan off his shoulder and into his arms. Cradling her against his chest, he said, "Should I throw her in?"

Gavin strode into the waves amid their shrieks of agreement, Jordan clinging to him tightly. She sucked in a sharp breath when the chilly water splashed over her.

"Are you ready?" he shouted, shooting a sidelong look at Jordan. Turning toward the girls, he started swinging Jordan back and forth. "One for the money."

"Gavin, you can't be serious," she shrieked.

"Two for the show," he shouted, swinging her higher this time.

"Oh my God." Jordan plugged her nose with one hand.

"Three to get ready." He swung her higher still. "And four to go!"

With one final swing Gavin tossed Jordan into the ocean. She flew through the air before landing in the cool water, a big smile on her face. She didn't even have time to swim to the surface, because Gavin's strong arm linked around her waist the moment her feet touched the sandy bottom. She broke through the surface of the water as he dragged her against his chest, planting a warm kiss on her lips.

Linking her arms around his neck, Jordan hugged him tightly. She wiped the salty water from her eyes and waved to the girls, who were cheering from shore with Maddy. Amid the squeals, they were begging to be thrown into the ocean as well.

Though the cool water lapped over her and Gavin, Jordan barely felt it anymore. Studying his strong profile—the square jaw, strong brow, and firm lips that had explored almost every inch of her body with heart-breaking tenderness and insatiable need—she felt her heart swell with love.

Gavin finally turned his attention back to Jordan, but his smile faltered. "What?" His eyebrows flew up and a glimmer of panic covered his face. "Shit. You're not mad, are you?"

"No," she whispered, licking the salty water from her lips. "But I am madly in love with you."

Gavin's mouth, warm and firm, found hers and a low groan rumbled in his chest. She sank into the sensation, her fingers threaded through his hair. They stood in the ocean enjoying one long, languid kiss. She'd never get tired of the feel or the taste of him, and she knew that there was nowhere else on earth she wanted to be. Ever. Old Brookfield was her home. Perhaps it always had been, but wrapped in Gavin's arms in the waters of the Atlantic, Jordan was more convinced than ever that this was where she belonged.

Breaking the kiss, she cradled his face in her hands, wiping beads of water from beneath his cheek with her thumbs. His tanned skin made those beautiful eyes of his seem even greener, and they were currently peering at her with heightened curiosity.

"What's going on in that head of yours?" he asked, his hands slipping down to the curve of her waist. "I see the wheels turning."

"I want to stay here."

His eyebrows flew up. "In the ocean?"

"No." She giggled and tugged him against her. "In Old Brookfield. I want to stay for good."

"I didn't realize you'd planned on leaving," he murmured. Concern edged his voice and his fingers clung to her that much tighter. "I thought…"

"I don't plan on leaving," she added quickly. "I mean, not anymore." She rolled her eyes and made a growl of frustration. "Sorry. What I mean is that I only *rented* this house because I wasn't sure if I was going to stay more than a year or so. But now I *know* I want to."

"Okay," he said slowly. "So…"

"So, I'm going to buy the flower shop from Maddy." She kissed him and slipped out of his embrace. "Come on, Chief. Those burgers are getting cold."

"Are you serious?" Gavin caught up to her easily and gathered her hand in his, stopping her before they reached the shoreline. As the water lapped over their calves, he took both her hands, urging her to face him. His thumb rasped over her knuckles and his brow knit with concern. "You're sure that's what you want?"

"Yup." She kissed him quickly and murmured, "And you, Chief. I'll always want you."

"Mama, I'm hungry bungry," Lily shouted from the beach. Both girls were wrapped in towels and heading to the deck.

"Me too," Gracie chimed in. "Hungry bungry."

"Okay. We'll be right there, girls." Jordan squinted against the sun and studied Gavin carefully. His reaction was not what she'd expected. Not that she'd thought he'd do backflips but she'd expected a little more excitement, and the lack of it gave her pause. "What do you think?"

"I think it's great." The line between his eyes deepened as they walked hand in hand toward their towels. "What do you plan on doing when your lease is up? I thought you wanted to buy this house eventually."

"The money I got in the divorce settlement will be more than enough to buy the business, but I won't be able to buy this place right away. The lease was for the summer, and after that it goes month to month. The Sweeneys really want to sell it." She snagged her towel from the chair and wiped herself off quickly before pulling on her white cotton cover-up.

"I was thinking about moving in with my mother for a little while. I could stay here on a month-to-month basis, but I don't feel like dealing with potential buyers coming in and out. It's too disruptive. Besides, I know my mom would love it, and the girls would too."

"Right." Gavin nodded, his mouth in a firm line. "That sounds like a good plan."

"Hey, you two." Maddy strolled over, cell phone still in hand. "I'm starving, and those burgers smelled great."

"I'll go get the girls their food," Gavin said absently. "You two have a lot to talk about."

As Gavin jogged up to the house, Jordan's gut clenched. Something in Gavin's reaction made her nervous, but she couldn't put her finger on why. She knew he loved her and that he wanted her to stay in town, but his seemingly unenthusiastic and almost distracted reaction gave her pause.

"What's going on?" Maddy picked up her bag and slung it over her shoulder. "What do we have to talk about?"

Shaking off her silly overreaction, Jordan grabbed the beach chairs and started dragging them to the stairs. She was reading too much into Gavin's response and had to stop doubting herself. She'd spent so many years walking on eggshells with Ted that she was probably seeing something that wasn't there. Gavin wasn't Ted, and she had to stop overanalyzing everything.

"Business," Jordan said firmly. "More specifically, me buying your business."

"Hang on." Maddy ran to catch up with her, and they both stopped at the foot of the stairs. "You want to buy the flower shop?" A smile bloomed across her face and the beauty of it made Jordan's heart ache. It seemed like forever since she'd seen it. "Are you sure?"

"Completely." Nodding and settling her hand on her hips, Jordan glanced at the trio on the deck. Gavin was doling out Gracie's burger like he'd been doing it since the day she was born. "How about you and I sitting down after I give the girls their bath, and we can talk turkey?"

"Well, it's good timing, I guess." Maddy linked her arm through Jordan's and tugged her close, keeping her voice low. "That call I got?"

"Yeah?" Jordan said with growing apprehension.

"The Sweeneys got an offer on this place earlier this week. I didn't want to say anything until it was definite…but they accepted it." Letting out a slow breath, Maddy pursed her lips. "Sorry, girl. I know you were thinking about buying it."

"It's okay," Jordan said, trying to convince herself more than Maddy. "You're right. It is for the best. If I'm going to be buying a business, then the last thing I need to worry about is carrying a mortgage." She kissed Maddy on the cheek and grabbed the railing. "Come on, let's eat."

As Jordan climbed the steps, Gavin winked at her before taking a hearty, man-sized bite out of his cheeseburger. It amazed her how such a small gesture instantly put her feelings of apprehension at ease. She would miss this little house and the fond memories they had begun to create there, but everything was going to be okay. A house was only a house; it was a home because of the people in it. She knew that now more than ever.

Sitting on the bench next to Gavin, and with her girls' joyful chatter drifting through the air, she knew. *They* were her home. Wherever they were, that was where Jordan wanted to be.

─⁓─

Gavin was so nervous, he was worried that he might puke if the kid didn't get here soon. Pacing around his office, he checked his watch for the tenth time in as many minutes. Sweating, his stomach churning, he went to the window. Some of his nervousness eased when he saw the *Open* sign clearly hanging in the door across the street. If Jordan got wind of this, it would blow the whole plan.

"Hey, Chief." David rapped on the door of Gavin's office before stepping inside. "My dad asked me to bring you the keys to the lighthouse, and he told me to tell you good luck."

"Kid, you're the best." Gavin let out a sound of relief as David placed the silver keys in his palm. He clutched them tightly in his fist, his excitement about tonight growing by the second. "Tell your dad that I owe him one. If he ever needs someone to take over for him as the lighthouse keeper, I'm happy to cover. I'll get the keys back to him tomorrow."

"No problem." David shuffled his feet. "My dad thinks it's the coolest place in the world, but I think it stinks like low tide. He used to make me and Robert help him clean up around there when we were little. I didn't mind it all that much, but Robert really hated it."

"I'm on your dad's side, kid."

"Why do you want the keys to the old lighthouse, Chief?"

"It's part of a surprise for someone."

Gavin stuck the keys in his pocket and wiped the sweat off his forehead before shutting down his computer and gathering up the arson file, which included pictures from the school fire. He'd carried the file to and from work every day since the fire and had spent hours upon hours staring at it, but so far that hadn't done any good. The only good news was that their firebug hadn't made any more trouble since Rick died.

Gavin slapped the file closed and checked his watch. Rogers was supposed to get back to him today with progress on the case but so far nothing. He and the police were looking into the Heffernan kid, but Gavin could not believe that this young man was responsible.

No way. He was only a kid.

"But remember, David." He cleared his throat and turned his attention back to his partner in crime. "You don't breathe a word about this to anyone. Got it?"

"Sure." David nodded. He started to leave but lingered in the doorway. "Um, Chief?"

"Yeah?"

"I never really got to tell you how sorry I am about Lieutenant Rick." Hands in the pockets of his baggy shorts, he kept his eyes on his flip-flops. "I mean, I know he kinda thought I was a pain, but he was nice to me and real patient with all of my dumb questions." He finally turned his mournful expression to Gavin. "I...I'm real sorry about what happened to him. He didn't deserve that."

"Thank you." Gavin's throat thickened with emotion, and he fought the fresh swell of grief that the boy's remarks had evoked. Squaring his shoulders, Gavin gripped the folder tightly in his hands and met the boy's somber stare. *Damn.* If this kid *was* involved, then Gavin would never forgive himself for letting the boy be around the station in the first place.

"You were lucky to see a guy like Rick on the job. He was one of the best, and losing him was...tragic...but Rick would be the first one to tell you that what we do is risky as hell. He knew this was a possibility."

"Yes, sir." David stood a little taller, his mouth setting in a grim line. "I understand."

"Thanks again, David." Striding around the desk, Gavin extended his hand to the young man, who took it and shook it eagerly. "I know Rick would appreciate what you said, and I sure as hell do. And if you keep up the focus and drive you have, you're going to make one hell of a firefighter."

"Wow," David said, his smile growing. "Thanks."

"You'll be eighteen soon, right?"

"Yes, sir." He dropped Gavin's hand, excitement edging his voice. "Our birthday is in October. Me and Robert."

"You'll be old enough to volunteer. Do you plan on joining the volunteer force?"

"You bet I do. Like I said, you guys are badass." David waved as he backed out of the office. "Good luck at the lighthouse tonight, Chief."

When David spun around to leave, he ran right into Tommy Miller and almost knocked the poor guy to the ground. David grabbed him by the arm to help him, but Tommy steadied himself on the doorjamb.

"I'm so sorry, Mr. Miller," David sputtered. He pushed his hair off his face and looked skittishly back and forth between Gavin and Tommy. "I'm real sorry."

"It's okay," Tommy said through a soft laugh. He turned his good eye to Gavin and then to the kid. "I'm usually better at dodging teenagers in a hurry, but I guess I'm a little outta practice. You kids are always in such a rush. I better brush up on my skills before I get back to work. School will be starting before you know it."

"Yeah, my brother and I were wondering where we're gonna go to school. I mean, are they gonna be able to fix it in time for us? Robert is hoping we don't have to go back."

"No such luck, kid." Gavin shook his head curtly and tightened his grip on the folder in his hands. "All of the students from Old Brookfield will have to attend classes in Stonington, at least until Christmas. Hopefully the construction will be done by then."

"Oh, cool." David nodded and looked between Gavin and Tommy, an awkward silence falling over the three of them. "Well, I guess I better go."

"Thanks again, David," Gavin said. "I'll see you on Monday."

The boy disappeared down the hall, and Tommy made his way into the office. Gavin gestured toward the chair by his desk in invitation. Holding a Red Sox baseball cap in his hands, Tommy seemed even more nervous than usual. It was a feeling Gavin was becoming familiar with.

"Do ya have a minute?" Tommy asked quietly as he looked around the office, fiddling with his hat. "They have any idea who set the fires?"

"No." Gavin shook his head. "But Rogers has some leads he's checking out, so hopefully we'll know more soon."

"Oh, okay." Tommy shuffled his feet. "There's somethin' else I need to say."

"Sure." Gavin placed the closed folder on his desk and gestured to the chair again. "Have a seat."

Apprehension shimmied up his back, and the scar on his shoulder felt more present than ever. What could Tommy possibly have to say to him? Whatever it was, he would take it all in.

"Oh no." Tommy smoothed the gray tuft of hair over his scarred forehead and shifted his weight nervously. "It won't take long. I know you have that big party tonight at your parents' place."

"Alright." Gavin stood by the desk and folded his hands in front of him. He was ready. Swallowing his nerves, he nodded. "What is it?"

Silence hung between them thick as smoke, and Gavin thought he might actually choke on it. Sweat beaded on his brow while Tommy clearly struggled to speak.

"You were lucky," Tommy murmured, barely audibly. "That day in the barn. It coulda been Ronan who died." He shot a sideways glance at Gavin who blanched at the notion. "Yeah, coulda been anyone. Fire don't discriminate."

"True."

"I should probably thank you."

"You don't owe me any thanks, Tommy," Gavin said quietly.

"Let me say it." Tommy held up one hand. His voice grew stronger and had a deeper timbre than Gavin had ever heard from the usually soft-spoken man. "I know ya think that Jimmy dyin' was your fault, but it wasn't. If it weren't for you, I'd be dead too, instead of just scarred up." He smirked. "Twice. I'd be dead twice if it weren't for you."

"I-I was doing my job," Gavin murmured, shame and guilt tugging at him. Two people were dead; being thanked was inappropriate. "And it was Rick who saved your life…not me."

"Yeah, I know. But you did too. If you hadn't a'been there, I woulda died…but I'm still here." He sniffled and shuffled his feet awkwardly. "And so are you."

Uncertain of exactly how to respond, Gavin simply extended his hand to him. After what felt like forever, Tommy grabbed it and shook it briefly, then put his Red Sox hat on.

"Thank you, Tommy," Gavin said gruffly, afraid his emotions might get the better of him.

"Right." Tommy nodded. But he lingered in the doorway. "Tell your parents I said happy anniversary."

"I sure will." Gavin picked the folder up again and whistled. "Forty years is a long damn time."

"Yeah…it is. You're lucky to have such a nice big family." Tommy frowned slightly, a look of confusion flickering across his face. "I thought the party was at your parents' place up on the bluff. I saw 'em settin' up a big, white tent yesterday."

"It is."

"So what are ya doin' at the old lighthouse?" He jutted a thumb over his shoulder. "The Heffernan kid wished ya good luck at the lighthouse tonight."

"Oh, that." Gavin's face heated. He instinctively slipped his hand in his pocket and touched the keys. "It's a surprise for Jordan after the party tonight."

"She's a special lady, Miss Jordan. So I guess that makes you extra lucky." Tommy smiled and tipped his hat to Gavin. "Good luck with it. But then, a guy like you don't need luck."

The man disappeared around the corner and Gavin's cell phone buzzed. He snagged it from his pocket and read the text from Jordan that scrolled across the screen.

I'm ready to go when you are.

A smile cracked Gavin's face. He was more than ready.

Chapter 18

JORDAN SIPPED HER CHAMPAGNE AS THE INSTRUMENTAL music from the band drifted through the air and the two hundred or so guests mixed and mingled during the cocktail hour. It was a breezy evening, and she was glad she'd opted to wear her hair up. She'd hemmed and hawed for days over what to wear before finally settling on a classic black strapless gown. The fitted body-conscious dress was understated and elegant, perfect for the McGuires' party.

Now if only she could stop sweating from overactive nerves.

Coming to this event with Gavin shouldn't have felt like such a big deal, but in spite of that rational thought, Jordan was a mess. All of his brothers were here, and the McGuires' extended family was massive. Most of the guests were cousins from both Carolyn's and Charles's sides of the family. Until she'd had her daughters, Jordan's only family had been her parents. While she loved the notion of a big family, tonight was proving to be a little overwhelming.

Everything was moving so fast. As wonderful as it was, it was also a little scary…but love *was* scary. Isn't that what she'd told Gavin? Now if only she could talk *herself* off the proverbial ledge the way she had with him.

The tent was filled with dozens of beautifully decorated tables. The white linens practically shone in the dwindling light, and the floral arrangements that Cookie and Veronica had put together were simply stunning. A mixture of hydrangeas, violets, ivy, and sterling roses adorned the centers of the tables, and each of the tent poles was wrapped with a similar floral combination. Tiny white lights were interwoven up the poles, and at least a hundred strands of twinkling lights were delicately draped from the massive tent ceiling, which had three glittering chandeliers dangling around the top of each main tent pole.

To the left of the tent was the McGuires' enormous Victorian house, on the right was an expansive view of the Atlantic, and at the edge of the property sat Gavin's cottage. The entire scene looked like something out of a movie.

Lily and Gracie thought they'd died and gone to heaven. Aside from loving the gauzy pink-and-white dresses they'd picked up especially for the party, Gracie thought that the lights looked like glitter. She'd announced to everyone she met that she was a princess, and the tent was her castle.

A smile broke out on Jordan's face as the girls danced in front of the band, twirling over and over again so that their dresses would puff out. Claire was there too, fussing over her granddaughters and happier than Jordan had ever seen her. She hadn't planned on coming to the party, even though Carolyn made a point to call and invite her personally, but after Gracie and Lily begged her, she finally gave in. But only if she could serve as the girls' babysitter.

"Boys, do your old mother a favor and smile for the photographer," Mrs. McGuire said, her patience waning.

"Honestly, I would have thought that getting a picture of you five would have gotten easier over the years."

The expression "Boys will be boys" instantly came to mind.

"Thank you," Mrs. McGuire said in an overly sweet tone as the five men settled down. "Try to act like grown-ups for five minutes." She leaned closer to Jordan. "I swear, individually they act their age, but get them together and they instantly slip into silliness."

"It's kind of sweet." Jordan sipped champagne, the cool, crisp beverage doing little to quell her nerves. "I never had any siblings growing up and I was alone a lot, which is why I'm so glad Gracie and Lily have each other. I always envied the bond you all have." She lowered her voice and fought to keep her burgeoning emotions under control. "No matter where they live or what happens, those five men will always have each other. You should be proud of them, Carolyn. You and Charles have raised five great guys who would go to the ends of the earth for each other and the people they love."

Carolyn sighed and smiled at her handsome brood. Dressed in a floor-length ivory gown with some beaded detailing, Gavin's mother looked every bit the elegant, classy lady she was. Charles stood by her side and gave his five sons a pleading look. Dressed in black tie and tails, he was as dashing as ever. Jordan had a hunch Gavin would look a lot like him when he got older. Charles was over six feet tall and had a head full of thick, white hair that had once been almost as dark as Gavin's. Arm in arm and champagne flutes in hand, the couple looked like royalty, but without the pomp and circumstance.

"True," Carolyn said. "We did alright, didn't we?"

"Damn right," Charles chimed in. "Now all they need are some women to make 'em civilized." He leaned forward and raised a glass to Jordan. "Well, one down and four to go."

Jordan met his warm, brown-eyed stare and smiled, raising her glass in return. She could have responded, or should have, but she was afraid she might burst into tears if she tried. Their acceptance of her had been swift, complete, and genuine. Sucking in a deep breath, she took another sip of champagne and squelched the sudden onset of emotions.

"You know, Jordan"—Carolyn sighed—"sometimes I wonder if men ever really do grow up."

Standing behind the photographer, Gavin caught Jordan's eye and waggled his eyebrows at her.

"You see?" Carolyn said with a wide grin.

"What a goofball." Jordan giggled.

The five McGuire brothers stood in a row for the photographer. All of them had donned classic black tuxedos, and every one looked like he could model for one of those beefcake calendars. While they were all undeniably handsome, Jordan only had her eyes on one. Gavin was the tallest of his brothers, though not by much, and as far as Jordan was concerned he was the best-looking man on the planet.

"Mom!" Ronan called. Standing next to Gavin, he tugged at the black bow tie and made a face. "Are we done yet? This thing is choking the life outta me."

"Ronan Michael McGuire," Carolyn huffed. "*I'm* gonna choke the life outta you if you don't give it a rest. For Pete's sake, it's only a tie."

"He's right, Ma." Tristan, the middle one of the five, winked at Jordan and cast her a wide smile. "Oh, *hey*, Jordan. You sure do look pretty tonight. In fact, you look as pretty as you did in high school, and I think you would make the picture much nicer. Come on over here next to me."

"Hey." Gavin reached behind Ronan and smacked Tristan on the back of his dark blond head. "Don't get fresh with my girl."

"Jeez." Tristan rubbed the back of his head and grinned. "See? He knows I'm the better-looking brother, and he's worried you'll run off with me."

"Ha!" Finn and Dillon said in unison. The fraternal twins, the youngest of the five brothers, stood on the end of the line, casting doubtful looks in Tristan's direction. "Fat chance."

Carolyn and Charles handed their champagne flutes to a passing waitress and went over to join the photo. Jordan stood next to the photographer while he checked the pictures on his camera.

"Alright now," he said, trying to assert some kind of authority over the rowdy bunch. "How about if we put Mom and Dad in the middle so we can get a nice family shot." Putting the camera to his eye, he started snapping away. "That's great. Just a few more."

Looking at Gavin with his brothers and parents, Jordan felt a fresh swell of love and admiration, bringing tears to her eyes. The love the McGuires had for one another was genuine, honest, unwavering, and pure. This was what she wanted for her girls. For the first time she was certain she'd be able to give that to them. Gavin wasn't their father, but he was a good, strong, loving man who had certainly become a father figure. And she couldn't think of anyone better to help her raise her daughters.

She deposited her crystal flute on the bar along the edge of the tent before making her way over to the girls and her mother.

"Are you all having a nice time?" Jordan asked.

Claire was seated at the table along the edge of the dance floor, wearing a brand-new navy-blue dress and looking as pretty as Jordan had ever seen her. Lily and Gracie were the only ones dancing at the moment—and having a grand time doing it.

"Can I get you anything, Mom?"

"Oh no, darlin'. I have my soda right here and that lovely young man over there keeps comin' by with the pigs in a blanket. I love those." Her smiling face didn't leave the girls as she clapped along to the tune. "I can't tell you the last time I had such a nice time. I hope I get a chance to say a proper thank-you to Carolyn for invitin' me along."

"Of course." Jordan nodded. "Mom, I'll be right back. I'm going to use the ladies' room."

Gathering her long dress in her hands so it wouldn't drag in the dew-covered grass, Jordan slipped through the crowd of guests and quickly made her way toward the house. It had been years since Jordan had been inside the McGuire home, but when they'd arrived for the party, Carolyn made it clear that Jordan should use the bathroom in the house, not the port-o-johns that they had for the party.

Climbing the steps to the side entrance, Jordan opened the glass-paned door leading into the spacious white-and-yellow kitchen. The house was quiet and the kitchen was completely empty; the catering staff had their own separate tent for cooking. Letting out a sigh of relief, Jordan made her way through into the enormous family room. It had been redecorated over the years but the warm, welcoming feeling remained the same. Leaving the family room, she found herself in the large entry hall, and a flood of memories came roaring back. How many times had she and Gavin stood in this hall together when they were kids?

As she made her way toward the small powder room off the foyer, Jordan's heart squeezed in her chest. She wasn't only in love with Gavin. She was in love with his whole family, and probably always had been.

Jordan slipped into the bathroom and quietly closed the door before settling her black clutch on the granite counter. Sucking in a deep breath, she made quick work of touching up her makeup and ensuring there wasn't anything in her teeth, but more than anything she'd needed a minute to get her spinning heart under control.

A soft rap at the door made her jump, and she knocked her purse onto the floor along with all of its contents. Making quick work of putting the bag back together, she called, "I'll be right out."

"Jordan?" Gavin's voice, gentle and edged with concern, drifted through the door. "Are you alright?"

"I'm fine, aside from making a mess of the bathroom." She squatted down and scooped up her lipstick, which had rolled along on the tiled floor. "Come on in."

The door swung slowly open and Gavin leaned on the doorjamb. With his hands in his pockets, he looked as effortlessly handsome as ever. His tie was undone and hanging around his neck, framing the unbuttoned collar. The crisp, white tuxedo shirt lying open against his tanned skin made those stunning green eyes stand out even more than usual. Rising to her feet, lipstick in hand, Jordan couldn't take her gaze off him.

"You okay?" His dark brows flew up as he studied her with obvious concern. "I saw you leave and…I don't know…it seemed like something was wrong." The line between his eyes deepened as he stood tall in the doorway, jutting a thumb over his shoulder. "Did my brothers' razzing bother you? Because I'll go kick some butt if it will make you feel better. Tristan may be broader than me *and* built like a tank, but I have the psychological advantage of being the older one." He tapped his temple and moved into the bathroom, invading her space in the most enticing way. "The head games will beat 'em every time."

Staring into his loving and playful expression, Jordan swallowed hard and placed her bag on the counter. Inching closer to him, she moved in so their bodies were barely touching.

"Do you have any idea how much I love you?" Jordan curled her hands around the lapel of his jacket and tugged him closer. In her heels, she was almost his height, and when she pressed her body against his, her mouth was a scant inch away. Jordan flicked her tongue over his lower lip and whispered, "It might even border on obsession."

"Is that so?" Gavin's hands wandered over her hips before sliding down and palming her ass. "And what do you suppose we do about that? Because I have lots of ideas, and most of them involve you being naked. But there's a party full of people out on the lawn, and if you get naked, it might cause a scene." He kissed the corner of her mouth, and in between kisses down her throat, he murmured, "What do you say we close that door?"

Jordan's smile grew as Gavin's mouth came crashing down on hers. She sighed, savoring the sweet taste of him as his tongue slid along hers. Champagne with a tinge of mint. Jordan groaned. She could lose herself in him. All of him.

His talented fingers gathered the fabric of her dress up, and he kicked the door closed. She moaned with pleasure as his heated hands slipped under her skirt, and when his fingers drifted over her ass, Gavin stilled and broke the kiss.

"No underwear?" He growled against her lips. "You saucy little minx. I knew you were the perfect woman for me, but this has clinched it."

"I thought it might be a nice surprise for later," she said before nipping his lower lip.

"Or now," Gavin rasped, slipping his hand over her bare sex.

Jordan moaned and lifted her leg to give him better access, but a loud knock at the door brought their stolen moment to a halt. A dark expression flickered over Gavin's face, and Jordan let out a whimper of frustration.

"What are you guys doin' in there?" Ronan's muffled voice came through clearly enough, and the teasing lilt only made Gavin's expression darken further. "I'm tellin' Mom."

Jordan pressed her mouth against the warmth of his throat as she dissolved into giggles.

"I'm gonna kick his ass," Gavin grumbled as he reluctantly let her dress fall back into place. He kissed the tip of her nose before shouting through the closed door, "You better run, Ronan! If I catch you, you're gonna wish you brought Bowser with you for protection."

Ronan's laughter faded slowly as he obviously left for safer territory.

"Who's Bowser?" Jordan asked, tugging her dress back into place.

Gavin opened the door, looking for his younger brother, but the hallway was empty.

"It's his partner." Standing in the open doorway, he held his hand out to her. "Ronan is a K-9 cop in New York. He usually brings Bowser everywhere, but he had to have some kind of medical procedure and is on the mend at the vet. Ronan doesn't seem to know what to do with himself without that dog around."

Hand in hand, Gavin and Jordan strolled through the house. When they reached the kitchen, they found Ronan eating cookies out of the jar.

"Dude?" Gavin draped his arm over Jordan's shoulder. "What are you doing? Mom has the best caterer in the state outside with all kinds of great food, and you're stuffing your face with cookies?"

"Yeah." Ronan swallowed the last bite and put the lid back on the green ceramic jar before wiping his mouth with the back of his hand. "But they're *Mom's* cookies. No caterer, I don't care how fancy they are, can make *her* chocolate chip oatmeal cookies."

"Good point." Gavin nodded and kissed the top of Jordan's head.

"Oh wait." Ronan reached in his pocket and tossed a set of keys to Gavin. He looked flustered, but in spite of that caught them midair. "I almost forgot to give these back to you, big brother."

"Right." Gavin cleared his throat and stuck the keys in his pants pocket. "Did you get everything settled alright?"

"Yup." Ronan grinned broadly at Jordan. Mischief. That word always came to mind with Ronan. He always looked like the cat who ate the canary. "Sure did."

"What's up with you two?" Jordan narrowed her eyes and looked back and forth between the brothers. "Ronan looks like he's up to something."

"Nope." He brushed crumbs off his hands. "Gavin offered to let me crash at his cottage. Mom's highly allergic to dogs and Bowser's dog hair is all over my stuff, so I'm staying out there so it won't make her allergies go crazy."

"Yup." Gavin shifted his weight and pulled her closer. "Uh…can I stay at your place tonight, babe?"

"Sure," she said through a confused laugh. "But…"

She was about to ask him why he was acting so weird when a ruckus outside caught their attention. The distinct sound of male laughter grew louder as Tristan, Dillon, and Finn burst through the side door and piled into the kitchen. All of them had ditched the bow tie one way or another. Except for Finn. He still looked well pressed and put together.

Dillon's smile faded when he saw the cookie jar out and brown crumbs strewn across the granite countertop. Finn and Tristan bumped into him when he stopped short, and now all three of them were glaring at Ronan.

"Did you eat all the cookies?" Dillon leaned over and grabbed the cookie jar before yanking off the top. His irritation faded as he reached in and pulled out two. "Ha! Two left."

The lid clattered back on, and before his brothers could react, Dillon strolled out to the family room with both cookies in hand. By the time Finn and Tristan got to him, he'd already eaten the cookies and his brothers were loudly voicing their dissent.

"Aha!" Maddy's voice cut through the chaos. She sidled in next to Jordan, the door closing behind her and muffling the music from the party outside. "I should have known we'd find you with your hand in the cookie jar, Ronan McGuire."

"Well, you know me, Maddy." His grin widened and he leaned both hands on the counter. "I just can't help myself. Resisting temptation has never been one of my strengths."

"Is that so?" Maddy arched one eyebrow and slipped her small evening bag under her arm before folding her hands in front of her. "Run into a lot of temptation in the kitchen, do you?"

"I've got a wicked sweet tooth." He winked. "And the kitchen is my second favorite room in the house."

"Oh Lord." Maddy rolled her eyes, but in spite of her feigned annoyance, Jordan thought she saw a spark of attraction. Maddy's cheeks pinkened and she quickly turned her attention to Jordan. "I'd love to stay and play with the *children*." Shooting a sidelong glance at Ronan, she continued, "And Gracie and Lily too…but I'm really beat. I don't want to distract your parents, Gavin. They don't need the grieving girlfriend bumming them out on their special night. Would you tell them I said good-bye?"

"Sure." Gavin nodded. "You gonna be okay getting home?"

"I'd be happy to provide you with a police escort," Ronan interjected.

"No, thanks." Maddy held up one hand before pulling Jordan into a hug. "I love you, girl, but I can't stay." Her voice wavered. "This is all a little too much for me right now. I guess I'm not ready for a party like this."

"Well, let me at least walk you out and make sure the valets can find your car." Ronan jutted a thumb toward the front door. "Come on. I promise I'll keep my hands out of the cookie jar and be on my best behavior."

Jordan's heart ached as Maddy followed Ronan out, and she heard the good-byes from the other men. She curled her arms around Gavin's waist and hugged him tightly.

Her life seemed charmed at the moment. So painfully perfect that part of her felt guilty in light of the loss Maddy had suffered.

All of this could vanish in a blink.

Love was precious, and taking it for granted was so easy. All those years ago, that's what she had done with Gavin. As a young girl, she hadn't been savvy enough or worldly enough to realize what an amazing man she had in Gavin. If she had, she wouldn't have been so quick to turn away from him—and not believe in him or them.

It was a mistake she vowed never to make again.

"I love you, Gavin," she said, her cheek buried against his shoulder. Pulling back, she looked in him the face. "I love you and your entire crazy, male-dominated family." Her lips quivered as she struggled to get the words out without crying. "I was alone for so long and now…now it

seems like I have more love around me than I know what
to do with. I want you to know how much I appreciate
you. Thank you," she whispered. "Thank you for making
me and my girls part of your family."

"You have no idea, do you?" He cradled her face with
one hand, gently rasping his thumb along her cheek.
"None at all," he murmured.

"What?"

"*You're* my family," he whispered gruffly.

Tears blurred Jordan's vision as she stared into his
ruggedly handsome face. Laughing through her tears,
she pressed her mouth to his and threw a prayer of gratitude to the universe or God or the fates, or whatever,
for bringing him back to her. For bringing them back to
each other.

"Now, what do you say we get out there and hit that
dance floor?" He winked. "Gracie and Lily are hogging it."

Their sweet moment was broken when Tristan, Finn,
and Dillon came barreling out of the family room, running past them to the door.

"What's going on?" Gavin asked, pulling Jordan out
of the path of the stampede.

"It's Mom." Dillon held the door open as Finn and
Tristan disappeared outside. "She spotted us through the
window and gave us *the look*," he said through a laugh.
"Gavin, you better get your butt outside or you're gonna
be in deep shit. You too, Jordan. After all, you're practically part of the family now. But then again, you kinda
always were."

"Good-bye, Dillon," Gavin said in a warning tone.

As Dillon closed the door behind him and disappeared outside, Jordan laughed and rested her head

against Gavin's shoulder. A moment later, she heard Dillon loudly blaming Ronan and the others for the cookie kitchen invasion.

"He's right, you know." Gavin dragged her hand to his mouth and brushed his lips over her knuckles as he opened the door. "May I have this dance? Scratch that. Not only this dance. I call dibs on every dance with you for the rest of your life."

Her hand linked firmly in Gavin's, Jordan followed him outside with a huge smile on her face and a heart full of love. In that instant, she felt like Cinderella at the ball. Everything was perfect. The right man. The right time. All of it.

Happiness was a choice, and it had taken her a long time to figure that out.

With effortless strength, Gavin pulled her through the crowd and twirled her onto the dance floor, pulling her against his tall, muscular frame. She sighed as the heat of his body seeped through his tux and surrounded her. They'd only been out there a few minutes when Gracie ran up to Gavin and tugged on the back of his jacket.

"I wanna dance wif you too." Gracie's gap-toothed grin widened. "You and Mama."

Before Jordan could say a word, Gavin gathered her daughter up in one fell swoop and placed her on his hip.

"You bet, Princess Grace." His other arm was wrapped firmly around Jordan's waist as he swayed them both gently to the music. "I'll dance with you ladies any day of the week."

Gracie's giggles peppered the air as Gavin swung them around the dance floor but it didn't stop there. He spent the rest of the party showing off his goofy dance moves with Jordan, Lily, and Gracie, and he even coaxed Claire into one twirl around the floor.

It seemed that Gavin's magic wasn't limited to cards and quarters.

Chapter 19

"GAVIN, ARE YOU EVER GOING TO TELL ME WHERE we're going?" Jordan sat next to him in the passenger seat of his truck wearing his bow tie as a makeshift blindfold. "It's late, my poor mother is probably exhausted, and if I know my girls, they're bouncing off the walls with a sugar high from all that cake they ate at the party. To say nothing of the cookies your mother sent home with them."

"Claire is fine." He made the turn into the parking lot of Lighthouse Park and drove through the deserted area with a big, stupid grin on his face. "She and the girls are settled in at her house, and I'm sure they're all fast asleep by now."

"At her house?" Jordan fidgeted in her seat, her long, delicate fingers immediately going to the tie currently tied around her head. "What's going on? I thought she was staying at my place until we got back. Gavin, where are we? For goodness' sake, I'm still wearing this ridiculous dress."

"Nope. No more questions. I made all the arrangements for a sleepover with their Meemaw, who is so excited about it she can barely see straight. Now, stop being such a nudge."

He shut off the ignition and opened his door, but stopped and looked at her before he got out. Her hands were curled in her lap, and she was fidgeting with the gold bracelet on her wrist. He sensed her excitement and a hint of nervousness, and even though he wanted to shout from the rooftops what he was up to, Gavin held on to his surprise a little longer.

"Are you this much of a pill at Christmas, trying to sneak a peek at your presents?"

"Gavin!"

"Oh, fine. Stay right there—and don't you dare take that blindfold off."

Jordan grumbled her discontent as he shut the door and went around the front of the truck to let her out. So far everything had gone as planned. Claire had the girls sleeping over at her house, and Ronan had assured him that he'd set everything up on the watch deck of the lighthouse.

Tonight was going to be perfect.

Gavin opened the passenger door and took Jordan by the hand, gently helping her from the truck. When her feet hit the gravel, she reached out for his other hand and clutched him tightly. Tilting her face to the air, she breathed deeply and a smile curved those lovely lips. Lips he couldn't wait to kiss again and again for the rest of his life.

"We're by the ocean, and I'd say we're at the beach. But if we were going to the beach, you would have taken me home."

"True." Closing the door, he linked her arm through his and led her around the truck toward the base of the lighthouse. Sucking in a deep breath, he took Jordan by the shoulders and turned her body so she was facing the tall white-and-red structure. "Are you ready?"

"Are you kidding?" She clapped her hands together and shivered as a gust of wind came off the water. "I'm more than ready and I'm freezing, so I hope this little surprise is somewhere warm."

Reaching behind her, he breathed in her perfume, a mix of lilacs and Ivory soap, as he lifted the blindfold off. He stepped aside, finally revealing their location. Her expression shifted from surprised to confused, then her openmouthed smile grew wider by the second.

"We're at the lighthouse," she stated, as though confirming that fact for herself. Standing by his side, her fingers swept out and captured his. "*Our* lighthouse."

"Yup." Gavin escorted her to the small set of wooden steps and took out the lighthouse keys. "But that's not the whole surprise."

"You've got a key this time." She poked him playfully in the side. "Last time you broke in."

"Yeah." Gavin laughed. "Well, they got wise over the years and replaced the faulty lock. William Heffernan is the volunteer keeper; he has been for about ten years. He's done a better job than the old guy who used to do it when we were kids."

He went to unlock the door, but it was already open. Gavin frowned and made a mental note to bust Ronan's chops. Some cop, forgetting to lock the door.

"Well, it looks a lot cleaner around here than it used to be." Jordan stood behind him as he put the keys in his pocket and pushed the door open for her. "Are you sure we're allowed to be here?"

"Yup."

Gavin took Jordan by the hand and brought her inside, closing the door tightly behind him. He flipped the light switch, illuminating the cylindrical space. The brick walls and stone floor were worn by time, and the round, cavernous area was barren, except for some dust bunnies and a couple of old crates underneath the black metal staircase. The enormous spiral staircase wound up three stories high, and old wooden support beams crisscrossed below each of the three landings. The town had done a great job of taking care of the old lighthouse. Even though it no longer worked, it was still beautiful and in many ways the heart of the town.

"Uh…you might want to take off those shoes."

He and Jordan simultaneously peered down at the three-inch spike heels she was wearing before giving each other a knowing look. Gavin bent at the knees as Jordan steadied herself with one hand on his shoulder, and he helped her step out of the daring footwear. Rising to his feet, he dangled them over two fingers by their straps.

"They're sexy as hell, and later I'd love to see you in nothing but these shoes." He ran the back of his fingers down her bare arm with one long, languid stroke. "Since you're not wearing any underwear, all I have to do now is get this dress off you."

"Maybe." Jordan popped up on her toes and grabbed the shoes before planting a kiss on his lips. She tasted like champagne, which reminded him of what was waiting for them up on the gallery deck. "If you play your cards right."

"Nope." He pulled away when she tried to kiss him again and wagged a finger at her. "No funny business yet. This isn't the surprise. At least not all of it."

"Oh, fine." Jordan pouted. Gathering her long skirt in her hand, she placed her shoes by the bottom of the metal spiral staircase. Taking Gavin's fingers in hers, she leaned over the railing, looked up, and let out a whistle. "I don't remember there being so many stairs."

"Ah, it's only three stories to the gallery walk." Pulling her up the stairs, he murmured, "And the watch room."

Jordan's face reddened and she looked away, knowing full well what he was referring to. The watch room of this lighthouse was the place they'd first made love and, until recently, the last. As bittersweet as that night had been, Gavin couldn't think of a better place to propose.

The two of them ascended the towering, metal spiral staircase quickly and carefully. There were two small landings at each story, and at each landing there were three windows peering out over the ocean. When Jordan and Gavin finally reached the third landing and the door to the watch room, she was out of breath and laughing. With her hand to her chest and her long blond hair starting to spill out of her fancy hair clip, she had never looked lovelier than she did right at that moment.

"Oh boy." Jordan clutched Gavin's arm tightly and pressed herself against him as she peered down. "That is a dizzying view," she said breathlessly. "And a long way to fall."

"You know what they say, babe." Gavin opened the door and kissed her cheek. "Don't look down."

Jordan shot him a narrow-eyed gaze and looked like she was about to make a snappy retort, but when she stepped into the watch room, she seemed to be at a loss for words. Her hands flew to her mouth as a small cry of wonder mixed with disbelief escaped her lips. Gavin stood behind her and settled his hands on her bare shoulders, brushing his thumbs along the silky-soft flesh below the back of her neck.

Ronan had come through like a champ.

Ivory-colored electric candles were scattered around the window ledges in the semicircular room, giving it a soft, romantic glow. The flickering lights reflected off the windows that surrounded the space. At the center of the room, a large plaid blanket was spread out over the red-painted wooden floor, and next to it stood a tall silver bucket filled with ice water. A bottle of champagne lay nestled in the icy bath, and on the ledge by the windows were two crystal flutes and a vase holding a single red rose.

It was exactly how Gavin had pictured it, and based on Jordan's speechless reaction, he'd done it right.

"Gavin," she whispered through her fingers. "You did this?"

"Yes." He kissed the back of her head before trailing his fingertips down her arms and taking her by the hand. "Well, Ronan helped and so did the Heffernan family. They gave me the keys to the place and Ronan set this up for me tonight before the party. So that ice is probably really cold water by now."

"Those were the keys he threw to you in the kitchen," she said, looking around in awe. "But that night, the night we were here, that's when it all fell apart. I don't understand..."

Surprise and a hint of sadness filled her voice, and the combination almost sent Gavin right over the edge. She was right. That night had ended in a big, hot mess, but it sure hadn't started that way. It had begun in love, lust, and longing...and that was where Gavin wanted it to finish.

"Jordan, that night was a landmark moment for a couple of reasons." He gathered her face in his hands and tried to calm his own beating heart. "I don't regret a lot of choices in my life, but if I could go back and change that night, I would have explained myself. I would have told you how scared I was of losing you instead of barking orders at you like a macho douche." His mouth set in a tight line. "I would never have driven you away."

"We can't go back," she whispered through trembling lips. "And I don't want to, Gavin. I want to keep looking forward. For the first time in years, I'm excited about the future instead of afraid of it."

"Do you remember when I first came in the flower shop after you came home?" He kept his voice low and did his best to keep it calm and even, but his nerves were starting to get the better of him. Jordan nodded and he sucked in a deep breath through trembling lips. "You told me we couldn't magically make the past go away or change it."

"I know." A big, fat tear fell down her cheek. She inched her body closer, covering one hand with his as he cradled her face. "I'm sorry…I…"

"Stop," he whispered gruffly. Love and yearning pulling at him like the tide. "No more apologies and no more regrets."

Gavin curled his fingers around her ear, tucking that stray strand back. At the same time, he adjusted the prize he'd been hiding in the palm of his hand. Mustering his courage, Gavin dragged his hand down before holding the engagement ring up in front of her between two fingers.

"That's not a quarter," Jordan murmured, her eyes wide.

"We may not be able to change the past, but I promise that I'll do my best to give you a magical future," he rasped. Dropping to one knee, he held the diamond and sapphire ring out to her and finally asked her the question he'd wanted to ask for over fifteen years. "Jordan, will you be my wife and have me as the father of your children?" His smile grew. "Current and future."

The tears spilled freely down her cheeks as she nodded furiously and sputtered, "Yes."

Dropping to her knees with him, Jordan laughed through her tears as Gavin slipped the ring onto her finger. He gathered her in his arms and hugged her shivering body—or maybe that was him shaking? The one thing he'd wished for, secretly in the silence of dark, lonely nights, was actually happening.

Jordan was finally going to be his wife. His family.

Burying his face in her the nape of her neck, Gavin breathed in that clean, flowery scent of lilacs and Ivory soap. The one that was so uniquely hers. He pulled her hair from the confines of her hair clip and tossed it aside, dragging his fingers through the long, silky strands. He studied her as she held out her left hand, gazing at the ring he'd put there—where it belonged now and forever.

"It's beautiful," she whispered. "This was your mother's, wasn't it? I mean, I think I remember her wearing one like it when we were kids."

"It was my grandmother's originally. One of several she left my mother." Gavin popped the cork on the champagne and stopped it before it went flying. "My mom always said that when my brothers and I eventually got married, we could each pick one of the rings for our future wife. I thought you'd like this one best."

"I love it," she whispered. "So your whole family knew about this?" She sat on the blanket looking at the delicate platinum band and the round solitaire diamond framed by brilliant blue sapphires. "No wonder they were all so welcoming tonight."

"They love you, Jordan. Almost as much as I do." Gavin gathered the glasses and filled the flutes. He handed one to Jordan before sitting next to her on the blanket. "And your mother knows too."

"What?"

"Well, I had to ask her for your hand, didn't I?" He tilted his glass toward her. "I thought about asking the girls, but I was worried they wouldn't be able to keep the secret and I didn't want to overstep my bounds. I thought it would be best to let you tell them."

"Us," she corrected him. Jordan raised her glass. "Let *us* tell them, and you're right. Gracie would've blabbed."

"Yup." He gave her a smug, satisfied smile, then snapped his fingers as though he forgot something. "Whoops. And Maddy knows."

"Gavin!" Jordan feigned annoyance. "Did you tell the entire town?"

"Well, when I made the offer on the Sweeneys' house, she knew something was up."

"What?" Jordan shrieked and gaped at him with an expression of pure, unadulterated joy. Fresh tears glittered in her eyes and the words came out in a strangled cry. "You bought the house for…"

"I bought the house for us," Gavin whispered. "You, me, Gracie, and Lily." He kissed her firmly and held up his glass. "I'll admit I was a little nervous that you'd be worried about taking on too much because you're buying the business, but…is it okay?"

"Okay?" She let out a growl and rose to her knees, kissing him deeply. Sitting back on her heels, Jordan laughed. "It's way more than okay." Shaking her head, she whispered, "You really are a magician, aren't you?"

They clinked glasses, the crystal's hum filling the small space and echoing through it like music. Jordan peered at him over the rim of her glass, but before he could take another sip, she took his drink away and shook her head.

"You don't like the champagne?" he asked as she placed both glasses on the floor along the edge of the wall. "Or was there something else you wanted instead?"

"I want the future to start now," she murmured. She knelt on the blanket in front of him and gently pushed on his shoulders with both hands. "Right now. Lie down."

Gavin did as she asked, placing one hand behind his head so he could take in every gorgeous inch of his future wife. She watched him, her eyes heavy lidded, and her lips curved into a sensual grin. Jordan straddled his legs, hiking the fabric of her dress up to dangerous heights. She undid his belt and unzipped his trousers, and Gavin's entire body hardened with each passing second. He was going to ask her another question, playful and teasing, but when she released him from his trousers and stroked the full hard length of him, he momentarily lost the ability to speak.

"No fumbling tonight," Jordan murmured.

She crawled up his body and straddled his waist, holding herself above him. Jordan settled her hands on his chest and rocked her hips. He grabbed her thighs, her wet, hot sex sliding exquisitely slowly over his rigid heat. Need fired through Gavin and all he could think about was being inside her.

As though reading his mind and knowing exactly what he needed, Jordan rose to her knees, reached beneath the fluid fabric of her skirt, curled her hand around his shaft, and slipped him deep inside her. Gavin shouted as the delicious satiny heat enveloped him completely.

Hands over her head, Jordan rolled her hips and rode him with deep, swift, furious strokes. The orgasm came over Gavin with brutal force. He wanted to slow down, to give her time to get to where he was, but the woman wasn't giving up control. Gavin cried her name as pleasure tore through him in one merciless pulse. As it ripped through his body, he sat up and wrapped his arms around her, holding her there and anchoring her to him, never wanting to leave the soft warmth of her.

Jordan curled her arms and legs around him and ran her fingers through his hair, clinging to him with the same urgent desperation. Breathing heavily, her hair spilling all around his face, Gavin pressed his fingers into the smooth, perfect flesh of her shoulders and kissed the hollow of her throat.

"No…more…fumbling…" Jordan said between heavy breaths. "At all."

Tangled in the warm, soft curves of Jordan's body and with the fog of lust still heavy around him, it took a minute for Gavin to smell it.

Smoke.

Sleepy and satisfied, with his body still locked inside hers, Jordan could have stayed curled contentedly in Gavin's lap indefinitely. She really could have stayed there forever—and would have, if it wasn't for the sudden and disturbing smell of smoke. Gavin's entire body went rigid. He grabbed her by the upper arms and urged her to get up, and when Jordan scrambled to her feet, she saw the smoke. Wisps of gray streaked with black seeped under the door and started to fill the room with horrifying speed.

"We've got a problem." He was on his feet in seconds, fixing his pants as he ran to the door. He pressed his hand against it. He snapped his head around and shouted, "Get back."

Pure unadulterated terror fired through Jordan as she backed up to the window ledge. Shaking, she looked out over the ocean. It was a three-story drop to the pitch-black waters below. Gavin opened the door and looked out into the stairwell but quickly shut it. If she hadn't been scared before, the grave expression on Gavin's face would have done it.

"Take off that dress and put this on." Moving quickly, he pulled his cell phone out of his jacket pocket and tossed her the coat. When she didn't move, he came over and spoke firmly and clearly, staring her straight in the eye. "That dress has too much extra fabric that could catch fire too easily or melt onto your skin. Put on my jacket and stay calm. The fire is down at the bottom. I'm going to get you out of here."

"But I don't understand." Her voice sounded as panicked as she felt, and she couldn't keep herself from shaking while she stripped off the dress and pulled the jacket on. The oversized tux coat more than covered her, but nudity seemed like the least of their problems at the moment. "How could there be a fire? Was it one of light fixtures or something?"

"Jordan, please do as I ask. I'll explain after we get out of here."

He grabbed the blanket off the ground while holding his phone to his ear, and Jordan realized what he wasn't saying.

The firebug was back.

"Bill. It's Gavin. We've got a fire at the Old Brookfield Lighthouse. Jordan and I are up on the watch deck, but it's hot and spreading fast."

The smoke thickened in the air and stung her eyes, but the sensation of suffocation and burning in her lungs was the most horrifying part. She coughed against it as Gavin tore strips off the skirt of her discarded dress and soaked them in the water from the ice bucket. The rest of the water went to douse the blanket. The rumbling in the lighthouse grew louder... Hadn't Gavin once described fire as a beast that ate everything in its path? Between the roaring sound and the smoke, it felt like a dragon was ascending to claim them both.

"Cover your nose and mouth with this." Shouting, his voice and actions laced with urgency, Gavin gave her one of the pieces of soaked cloth, then wrapped the wet blanket around her, covering her head. "This is gonna be cold and heavy, but it will help protect you from the heat and flames. I'm gonna get you out of here, but you have to listen to me carefully."

Jordan nodded, pressing the wet cloth to her mouth and tried to keep her breathing calm.

"The smoke is even thicker out there, but we need to get down to at least the first landing. If we have to jump into the water, I'd rather not do it from here." He gripped her shoulders when her eyes widened with panic and kissed her forehead firmly before resting his against it. Gavin's voice was gruff and edged with desperation. "I swear to God, I'm going to get you out of here. You have to trust me and do exactly as I tell you. Got it?"

Trying to hold back a surge of hysteria, she nodded. Smoke curled under the door, like a deadly snake slithering closer. Her girls. What would happen to her girls if she died here? But the instant she looked back at Gavin's resolute expression...she knew everything would be okay.

She squeezed his hand and nodded.

"That's my girl." Gavin kissed her hand and pressed a wet scrap of cloth to his own mouth. "Stay close to me. Take a big breath before we go out there, and hold it as long as you can. After that, keep your breathing as steady as possible. Follow the stairs down, and don't let go of my hand or the railing."

With her hand latched firmly in his, Jordan stayed right behind Gavin and prayed they'd get out. When he opened the door, a huge plume of smoke slammed into them. Her gut instinct was to back away, but she squeezed her eyes shut and stayed with him. Her lungs burned as they hurried down the spiral staircase, and when her feet hit the second-floor landing, she almost wept with relief.

They were closer to the bottom and the way out.

Her eyes and lungs burned as the noxious smoke seemed to fill every orifice. As they moved closer to the ground floor, the heat grew almost unbearable. Dizzy from lack of air, she stumbled down a step and into Gavin. He caught her before she went to the ground in a heap.

Somewhere in the distance she heard sirens, or maybe that was her imagination. Every time she tried to open her eyes, the assault of smoke was too great and she shut them again. Weak and disoriented, she dropped the cloth. Her body started to feel heavy and cumbersome. She thought she heard Gavin calling to her, but he sounded so far away. As the world went dark, her girls were the last image in her mind.

Chapter 20

"*JORDAN!*" GAVIN SCREAMED HER NAME IN BETWEEN choking gasps for air, but she didn't respond. Panic was a dangerous self-defeating beast and it ripped through him ferociously. Her limp form slumped onto the steps behind him as they reached the first-story landing. Gavin grabbed her unconscious body and threw it over his shoulder. He pulled the damp blanket back on top of her and grabbed the railing to try to see through the smoke, but he tore his hand away when the heated metal scorched his flesh.

The heat was intense, but the fire looked like it was localized toward the back wall of the structure, opposite the door. There were flames licking at the stairs and they were creeping near the door, which was open partway.

With Jordan unconscious, he couldn't take her out through the window. That front door was their only option. The sirens wailed louder as they got closer, but if he didn't get out of there, it would be too late for both of them. The flames licked up the walls behind him and Gavin knew he had to go now. Moving swiftly down the last flight and with years of experience under his belt, he fought to stay conscious. Forcing his legs to function, he took the final few steps to the ground level as the wicked flames came at them from behind.

Dizzy and disoriented, and with Jordan's body hanging over his shoulder, Gavin ran for the door. Wait—he could swear something or someone moved past him to his right. Shaking it off as merely being delirious from smoke inhalation, Gavin forced his feet to move one in front of the other.

After seconds that felt like hours, he burst into the clean seaside air.

Gasping for breath, Gavin stumbled to the gravel parking lot and pulled Jordan off his shoulder. Cradling her against him, he shouted her name and pressed his ear to her chest. Her breath came in ragged gasps and her heart beat rapidly. Why the hell wasn't she waking up?

Just when panic threatened to drown him, those big, brown eyes fluttered open and she sucked in a gasping breath.

"That was one hell of a proposal," she said weakly.

Relief fired through him and he dropped to his knees, clutching her to him. A heavy sob of gratitude racked his weary body. The sound of the sirens grew closer, and when Gavin lifted his head, the red glow of their approaching lights lit up the night. His relief was short lived, though. Jordan's arms tightened around his neck, and she pointed past him toward the lighthouse.

"Oh my God, Gavin." Her voice was rough and raspy from the smoke. "There's someone inside."

"That's crazy. Why would anyone…" He snapped his head around and scanned the smoke-filled doorway. Squinting, not quite sure what he was seeing, Gavin set Jordan down on the ground and rose to his feet. Still feeling unsteady, he kept his sights on the open door, where smoke was spilling out. Sure enough, standing inside the burning building was a familiar silhouette.

Without thinking and working on total instinct, Gavin
ran back toward the fire.

"*Tommy!*"

"I'm doin' it right this time," Tommy screamed.

Before Gavin reached the steps, Tommy slammed the
door shut.

"*Tommy!*" Gavin banged on the door, the superheated
surface burning his hand, but he didn't care. "Open the
damn door."

"You always were the lucky one, Gavin!" Tommy's
muffled shout came through a moment before an
ungodly cracking sound ripped through the air. The
lighthouse shook and Gavin stumbled backward, shield-
ing his face from the heat as fire engulfed the structure
and Tommy went silent.

Standing in Tommy Miller's basement, Gavin found
himself at a loss for words. There was no longer
a question about who had been setting the fires
in town.

Two eight-foot-long tables were littered with various pieces of Tommy's homegrown bomb-making
equipment, and the computer, which he'd left on, was
filled with searches related to arson and bomb building. The walls were papered with articles about the
different fires and various lists and notes that Tommy
had written to himself over the years.

An old newspaper article, yellowed with age, sent a
chill down Gavin's spine. It was about the fire in the
barn all those year ago, and next to it was the faded
obituary for Tommy's little brother.

Haunted. That word rolled through Gavin's head over and over again like thunder.

That's what Tommy Miller was and what Gavin had been—until he found Jordan again. And that was what had sent old Tommy over the edge. Until Jordan came back to town, Gavin had been alone like Tommy. Seeing Gavin find happiness with Jordan had been more than Tommy could bear.

"Like I said," Rogers said around the cigarette in his lips, "firebugs are freaking nuts, and this squirrelly little bastard was no exception."

"It's sad." Gavin ran one hand over his head. "The letter he left behind said it all."

"The ironic part of the whole mess is that if you hadn't saved him at the school and he'd died the way he wanted to, he never would have set that fire at the lighthouse, almost killing you and your fiancée." Rogers dropped the cigarette butt and crushed it out on the floor. "It's not sad, McGuire, it's messed up. Hey, if a guy wants to kill himself, go for it. But taking other people out with you? Now *that* is completely screwed."

As the police finished gathering items from Tommy's basement, Gavin strode upstairs but stopped by the small brick fireplace. Sitting on top of the mantel in a tarnished silver frame was an old Polaroid picture of Tommy and Jimmy. The two brothers smiled at the camera, fresh faced and frozen in time, the image a haunting reminder of what had been lost.

Tommy had been right.

It could have been him or Ronan who perished in the barn that day. But it hadn't been—and Tommy was right about something else too. Gavin *was* lucky. Gavin

McGuire was the luckiest son of a bitch on earth, and thanks to Tommy, it was a fact he'd never forget.

———

The fog of sleep lifted and Jordan peeled her eyes open but immediately squinted against the early morning sun that streamed through the windows of their bedroom. She stretched her stiff body, a satisfied smile curving her lips as Gavin's warm legs bumped against hers. He mumbled something incoherent and draped an arm over her, immediately pulling her into his embrace. She settled her hand over his as he spooned up behind her, grazing a gentle kiss on her earlobe.

Content. Pure, unadulterated contentment. That must be what this feeling was. It was a delicious combination of happiness and safety. She was home. Safe. Loved. How many years had she dreamed of a life like this — and now here it was, a beautiful, precious reality.

Her reality.

It had been almost a month since the fire at the lighthouse and Gavin's proposal. In some ways it felt as though she'd lived an entire lifetime over that one summer. Finding Gavin again. Losing Rick. Tommy's suicide.

The tragedy of it all was overwhelming, and there were moments that Jordan thought she might be swallowed up by it. Her heart ached for Maddy, Rick, Gavin, and even Tommy.

"I can hear you thinking," Gavin mumbled, pulling her tighter against him in the warm cocoon of sheets. He pressed a kiss to her shoulder and hooked one leg over hers. "Penny for your thoughts."

"I was thinking about Tommy." She rolled onto her back and Gavin adjusted the pillows under his head, his now-alert gaze meeting hers. "And Maddy too. I wish she wasn't leaving town, but I can understand why. I can't imagine staying here and being constantly reminded of such loss... I guess that's part of what pushed Tommy over the edge."

"She'll be okay." Gavin let out a slow breath. She knew he was still struggling with a sense of responsibility for Tommy and his issues, but to his credit, he hadn't let himself get pulled back into the darkness. He cleared his throat and played with a strand of her hair. "I'm gonna give Ronan a call and have him keep an eye on her when she gets to New York. When is she moving to the city?"

"We were able to schedule the closing for the business and the house on the same day next month, so probably right after that." Jordan rolled over and curled her arms between them so she and Gavin were face-to-face. Sighing contentedly, she snuggled closer to him. "She did say she'd be back for the wedding in December, and I might even convince her to stay for Christmas and New Year's."

"Sounds good." Gavin slid his hands under the covers and ran them along her body, pushing her short nightie up and stopping on the swell of her hip. "You know what I want to do right now? Because it has nothing to do with bank closings or anything that unsexy."

"Hmm." Jordan feigned ignorance as calloused hands ran over her backside and along her thigh before hooking into the crook of her knee and tugging her leg over his. "I can't imagine..."

He waggled his eyebrows and the familiar gesture made Jordan giggle, but he swallowed her laughter with one of his bone-melting kisses. He wrapped those strong arms around her *just* as the sound of little feet came barreling down the hall.

They both stilled and broke the kiss with a mutual groan of disappointment, which quickly turned into laughter as the girls knocked on the door, not pausing before running into Jordan and Gavin's bedroom.

Lucky for everyone involved, Gavin had decided that sleeping in pajama pants would avoid unneeded awkwardness with the girls.

Lily and Gracie bounded onto the bed, immediately raining kisses over their mother's face before settling in on either side of her, Lily in the middle between Jordan and Gavin. Dressed in matching pink nightgowns and with bedhead that would rival Medusa, the two of them were absolutely adorable.

"Your bed is the comfiest," Gracie said. Settled in alongside her mother, she pointed at Gavin. "Chief, you said you'd make blueberry pancakes this morning 'cause it's Saturday and you only make them on Saturdays."

"She's right," Lily confirmed. "It's Saturday."

"Okay." Gavin gave Jordan a knowing look before giving Gracie a high five. "Deal."

The girls hooted with victory, but before they could get too comfortable, Jordan patted them both on the legs.

"Why don't you two go downstairs and watch a little television before breakfast." Jordan kissed them each on the cheek before they clambered off the bed and headed for the door. "Lily, don't let Gracie sit too close to the screen. Okay?"

"Okay, Mama," they responded in unison before running out and closing the door behind them.

As the sound of the girls' footsteps faded down the stairs, Jordan quickly hopped out of bed and went to the door. She didn't miss Gavin's groan of disappointment.

"Pancakes it is," he said with a hint of frustration.

"Hold it right there." Jordan flipped the lock on the door and spun around before peeling off her little white nightie and tossing it on the floor. "It's not quite pancake time yet. I know that marrying me comes with an instant family, and we won't exactly get that typical honeymoon phase with spontaneous sex and undisturbed mornings. So, I want to be sure that you know I'll do my best to make you happy...every way possible."

Gavin was sitting on the edge of the bed, the red plaid pajama pants doing little to cover his growing arousal. His heated green gaze drifted over her slowly from head to toe, and as he devoured her with his eyes, Jordan's own passion grew. She strode toward him slowly, completely nude, and when she stopped in front of him, she fully expected and wanted for him to put his hands on her.

He didn't.

"What's wrong?" Jordan arched one brow and ran one hand through his messy hair. "Isn't this what you want? I mean I like pancakes too...but I'd like to think this is better."

Gavin, his face stamped with need, shook his head curtly. Before Jordan could ask him anything else, he encircled her waist with both hands and pulled her closer so that she stood between his legs. He looked her up and down in one slow, lazy pass and, a moment later, dragged her onto the bed with him. Rolling her gently so her body was splayed beneath his, Gavin propped himself up on his elbows, framing her head with his arms.

She opened her legs, so that the weight of his body could settle on hers in the now familiar way, but still he didn't try to take her. Instead he gazed at her and seemed to be soaking in every line and curve as though committing them to memory or something. Behind that intent expression, she could practically see the wheels turning, and for a split second, fear glimmered.

What if all of this was too good to be true? But before the voice of doubt could take over, the hint of a smile curved Gavin's mouth, instantly melting her anxiety.

"I love you, Jordan. Tommy may have been crazy and sick, but there was one fact he was right about." His voice was gruff and strained. "I *am* lucky. I am the luckiest son of a bitch to have you back in my life." He kissed her forehead, her nose, her cheeks, and finally brushed an almost reverent kiss over her lips. "I love you. I love your daughters, and most of all, I love the way you love them…the way you love me. There's nothing else I need, Jordan. There's nothing else you could give me or do for me that would make me love you more."

Her throat thickened with a cavalcade of emotion.

Love. Gratitude. Contentment.

The full weight of his statement surrounded her and she knew, with every ounce of her soul, that what Gavin said was honest, heartfelt, and real. Love welled and Jordan took a moment to revel in the purity and beauty of it. This man would never raise a hand to her or her daughters, but more than that, he would always love them. Unconditionally.

"You know what, Chief?" she whispered. "That sounds like magic to me."

Acknowledgments

A great big shout-out to the Yonkers Fire Department arson specialist, the YFD lieutenant at Squad 11, and the guys in the Eastchester Fire Department, Engine Company 4. Thanks for taking the time to answer all of my questions and give me the info I needed to bring Gavin to life. Thanks also to Nedra and Tony for giving me extra feedback on one of the fire scenes and helping me make it more authentic. I hope I did it justice.

As always, a big *Thank You* to my editor, Deb Werksman, and the entire crew at Sourcebooks. You guys rock! Thanks to my agent for knowing exactly what to say and for being a great partner in an ever-changing business.

Most of all, thank you to my husband and four boys. You are my real-life heroes!

Read on for a sneak peek of Terri L. Austin's

HIS
KIND OF
TROUBLE

Monica Campbell eyed the refreshment table, ignoring the appetizers and zeroing in on the champagne. "Why ruin a perfectly good Saturday night with a wedding?"

Evan Landers flicked a piece of lint off his green-and-black tartan jacket. "This isn't the way I want to spend the evening either, and I'm not even related to the groom."

"Don't remind me." Monica uncrossed her arms. "Okay, I'm going in for another glass. Keep a lookout for Allie." Monica's sister had already pulled her aside once and told her to slow down. Not happening. Even Allie's disapproval couldn't keep Monica away from the booze. It was the only thing this party had going for it.

Not party. Wedding.

So her dad was getting married. Great. Monica was happy for him. Really. He was moving on, and good for him. That's what people did, right? They moved on, got remarried, started over. Totally natural. But the cloying smell of all these flowers reminded Monica of that hot, cloudless day when they'd buried her mom. Patricia Campbell had loved gardenias. Her casket had been covered with them. *You'd think he would have remembered that.*

Yeah—definitely time for another drink.

Stepping forward, Monica threw a smile at the cute waiter manning the table and trailed one hand across her bare shoulder. "How are you tonight?"

His gaze dipped to her cleavage. She showed quite a bit of it. Allie had bitched about that too. Along with the color of her dress. What was so terrible about wearing red to a wedding? It was a joyous occasion. That's why they were all here—the bride's small family, Monica's tribe—to celebrate her dad's new life.

"Good," he said. "I'm very good." He leaned forward and stage-whispered, "Technically, I'm only supposed to serve you sparkling cider."

Ugh, Allie. Monica might have been a few months shy of legal, but since when had that ever stopped her? "I hate getting technical. Don't you?"

After glancing over each shoulder, he reluctantly nodded. "Go ahead," he said. "I won't tell."

Monica plucked up two glasses. "Thank you. You're sweet." As he blushed at her words, she spun around and did a quick scan of the room. Filled with bright, delicate flowers and dripping in candlelight, the glass-walled conservatory reeked of romance. A perfect setting for a perfect couple. Yep. Happy, happy.

Monica tipped back her head and chugged the expensive champagne as if it were tap water. She ignored the burst of fizzy bubbles that tickled her tongue. Barely tasted the dry, cool flavor. She needed to get her buzz on—ASAP.

"Easy there, Slugger. This isn't a kegger," Evan said.

"God, I wish it were." Monica set down the empty flute and stood shoulder to shoulder with him. He'd come as her "acceptable date," per Allie's instructions. Evan lacked a criminal record and attended college, although *attended* might be a liberal use of the term. He deserved a best-friend award for suffering through this with her.

Monica had met most of Allie's requirements for this event. Appropriate date? *Check.* Mandatory attendance? *Check.* Stone-cold sober? *Not for long.*

Allie had commandeered Monica's day from the time she woke up this morning until now: breakfast with the bride and her family, mani-pedis, hair and makeup, pictures. Monica had reached her snapping point. She just wanted out of here.

She missed her mom all the time, but today that grief was a persistent ache. It sat in the middle of her chest—a hot, painful burn that never let up, not for one minute.

This time, Monica didn't bother to look around before she drained the champagne. If Allie didn't like it, tough shit.

"How long do we have to stay?" she asked.

Evan patted her arm. "I'm not sitting through all this without getting a piece of cake."

"I'll buy you a cake. You can eat the whole damn thing."

"Come on, Monnie. It's one day. You're tough, suck it up."

She might be tough, but she was restless and unhappy, and *oh shit*—

"Uh-oh," Evan whispered. "Incoming."

Allie Campbell Blake headed toward them, her long, white-blond hair flying outward with each step. At five months' pregnant, Monica's sister had never looked better. The bright blue dress she wore matched the color of her eyes. A fake smile she'd perfected over the years graced her lips. That smile fooled most people. Not Monica.

"Hey, Evan, do you mind if I speak to Monica for a few minutes?"

"Sure."

He turned to leave, but Monica snagged his arm and refused to let go. "He can stay."

Allie's smile grew brighter. That always spelled trouble. "I thought we talked about the champagne."

Monica raised her brows and attempted a look of innocence. "I've been drinking sparkling cider."

Evan nodded. "Yep. I can vouch."

"See?"

Allie stared at Monica until she nearly squirmed. "Okay. I won't nag you anymore." *Right.* "But this is Dad and Karen's special night, Mon. Please don't ruin it." Then she walked off to greet the officiant.

"Thanks, Ev." Monica gave his forearm a quick squeeze. "Do me one more favor? Keep her away from me."

"I'll do my best. But you could at least make an attempt at being subtle."

"I don't do subtle."

He laughed. "No kidding."

After a few minutes, Monica began to feel it—that nice little sensation starting at the base of her neck, the one that numbed her brain. She welcomed it. One more glass, and she just might make it. But before she could reach for it, Evan nudged her arm.

"And I thought you were underdressed. I think that guy stumbled into the wrong place."

Monica followed Evan's gaze. *Whoa.* Her restlessness disappeared, blown away like dust in a windstorm, and in its place stood the best diversion possible—a smoking-hot bad boy.

Monica may have been inappropriately dressed, but he took the jackpot. Long brown hair brushed his jawline. His leather jacket appeared battered, worn at the cuffs and rubbed bare at the elbows. His faded jeans fit him just right, showcasing his long legs. On his feet— black motorcycle boots. Whoever he was, he'd be right at home in a biker bar, but he looked completely out of place among the well-behaved guests.

"Who is he?" Evan asked.

What does it matter? This night had just taken a turn for the better. Her body responded to him. Attraction tugged at her, pulling her toward him. Straightening her shoulders, Monica started across the room, intent on finding out more.

Before she could take another step, the officiant walked to the front of the room, and the string quartet began the opening strains of "Pachelbel's Canon." Damn. That was her cue. Time to find a seat.

Evan grabbed her wrist and drew her back to him. "Come on," he whispered. "The wedding's going to start."

For the next thirty minutes, while her dad and Karen exchanged vows, Monica's eyes kept straying toward her mystery man. He sat across the aisle, two rows back. She tried to take Evan's advice and do subtle, angling her chin and glancing at him from the corner of her eye. Finally she gave up on subtle. Twisting her head, she openly studied him.

She tried to guess his age—late twenties maybe?

Excessively badass, that much was obvious. Who strutted into a wedding like that, completely at ease with himself, unapologetic? Monica could respect that kind of *fuck you* attitude.

Every time he moved, that leather jacket creaked, just a little bit. Her eyes slid back to him once more. He had a strong profile—straight nose, square jaw. As if he felt her staring, he turned his head and looked her right in the eye.

And then he gave her an uneven grin.

Completely charmed, she smiled back. Monica wanted to talk to him, find out his story. *Who are you kidding, Campbell? You want to fuck him.* Absolutely. But exchanging a few words first wouldn't hurt.

She tapped her fingers against her bare thigh. This ceremony couldn't end fast enough. It just dragged on and on—rings, candle lighting, pouring sand into a glass jar for some reason. All the cheesy, clichéd symbols. Was it really that easy for him to forget her mom? Commit to another woman?

Whatever. Maybe that guy would give her a ride on his bike. Then she could give him a ride back at her apartment. That seemed fair.

The next time she glanced at him, he'd slipped his jacket off. Nice arms—tanned, muscular. He threw her a broad wink, and it earned him another smile. God, he was hot. Flirty. Cocky. Just her type.

When Evan lightly slapped her arm, Monica returned her attention to the front of the room. Her dad and Karen kissed. Then, hand in hand, they gazed at each other and walked up the aisle, stopping to greet people along the way. When they reached the row where Monica sat, her dad leaned down and pecked her cheek.

"Congratulations, Daddy." It almost physically hurt to say the words.

Yet, he did look happy. Content. One chapter closed and another one opened. That was life.

The sadness that pierced Monica's chest burned a little hotter. She tried to ignore it.

Once her dad and Karen left the room, Allie took front and center. "Just a few announcements." Monica suppressed a groan. Like an airline hostess, Allie gave directions, complete with hand gestures, about the buffet dinner in the dining room.

Monica looked back once more. This time, the stranger was waiting for her. He lowered his head a notch, and his eyes traced over her face. No smile. Just heat.

Monica stood, her gaze unwavering. They simply stared at each other, ignoring everyone else. People began filing out of the conservatory. Chatter filled the air, and the quartet played a chipper tune. Hardly any of it registered.

Evan leaned down and spoke in her ear. "Are you coming?"

"You go on," Monica said, keeping her eye on the prize. "I'll catch up later."

"Okay, but whatever you do, don't get caught." He sidled past her and left the room.

Soon, everyone cleared out, even the musicians, until only the two of them remained. Monica and this stranger. He kept his eyes locked on hers as he moved forward. Every step brought him closer. Finally, he stopped in front of her, the tip of his boot resting against the toe of her stiletto. He stared down at her with the greenest eyes. They danced over her, lighting on every part of her, eating her up. Monica breathed it in, loving the attention.

"And who are you, then?" he asked. He had a British accent. A bad boy Brit. Too perfect.

"I'm the daughter of the groom. Monica Campbell." She held out her hand.

"Cal Hughes. I believe your sister married my cousin, Trevor." He took her hand and didn't let go. His skin felt hot against hers. "Felicitations on the wedding and all that." His deep voice made her nipples tighten. His gaze kept darting from her face to the tops of her breasts.

"Thanks. You have very interesting taste in wedding attire."

He glanced down at his clothes. "Sorry about that. I rode into town this afternoon. Didn't think to pack a suit."

"Rode? As in motorcycle?"

"Yeah."

Ha, she knew it.

When Cal let go of her, she missed the contact. Wetting her lips, she watched as he dropped his jacket in a chair. A hint of ink peeked from under the sleeve of his black T-shirt. Tattoos made her weak. Pretty much everything about this guy checked all of her boxes. He even smelled good. Woodsy and fresh.

"Is Cal short for something?"

He took one step closer, so her breasts brushed his chest. Now she had to lean her head all the way back to look up at him.

"It stands for Calum."

"A British name, huh?" She swung her head so that a curl bounced off her shoulder. "Do you live in Britain?"

"Some of the time. And what do you do, Monica?" The way he said her name made her skin heat up. She wanted to hear him say it again. Monica could use a good distraction tonight, and Cal Hughes was the man to give it to her. Hopefully, he'd give it to her twice.

"I'm a student." Using one finger, she lifted the edge of his right sleeve.

"Like ink, do you?"

Still feeling the effects of the champagne, she gazed up at him, a smile hovering over her lips. "I love ink." A Celtic knot. She fingered the bottom edge of the design.

"You're a student at university?"

She dropped her hand and nodded, pulling her bottom lip into her mouth. He watched it hungrily. "I haven't decided on a major yet. Have any advice?"

"No, school was never my strong suit. So what do you do when you're not studying?"

"I like to dance. Club dancing, for fun. Not pole dancing, for profit. Just so you know."

Cal threw out a surprised laugh. "You're a bit of a wild card, aren't you?"

"Sometimes." His wide shoulders blocked out the fountain. The flickering candles cast a shadow across the left side of his face, making him appear even more mysterious. He represented all of her fantasies rolled into one tasty package.

"I suppose we should join the others," he said.

Monica didn't want this moment to end. "I'm not interested in joining the others."

He lifted his hand and looped a strand of her hair around his finger. "What are you interested in?"

"Do you want a list?"

"Yes, I do. We'll fit in as many as we can."

"We could start with Trevor's garden. Have you seen it?"

"No, but it sounds as though I should." He unwound her hair and ran his finger down the side of her throat. His whisper-light touch made her tingle. "If you'd show it to me, I'd be *really* grateful." He grinned again, and that smile was her undoing.

Monica pointed to the garden door, tucked in the corner behind a potted orange tree. Cal shrugged his jacket on and followed her outside.

The night was cool. The new moon didn't offer much light, and only a few stars dotted the sky. The vast garden wasn't dark though. Tiny white lights hung from tree branches and lit the pathway.

Cal stopped walking and looked around. "This is exactly like my grandfather's garden. Except for the grotto."

"That's a Vegas thing." Monica followed the pathway past the rose bushes. From here, she could see into the dining room. Two dozen people sat at the long table. They could probably see her too, if they were paying attention.

Cal wrapped his hand around her waist. "Want to go back inside?"

"Not at all." She turned to him and splayed her hands across his chest. The knit material felt soft, like it had been washed a thousand times. Monica stood on her toes and ran her tongue along his jawline. "You know, I've never been kissed in a garden."

"Haven't you? What a terrible shame. We should fix that." Cal leaned down, but instead of kissing her, he gently bit down on the place where her neck and shoulder met.

Monica grabbed a handful of his hair. "I like that."

Cal lifted his head and nodded toward the house. "Is there somewhere a little less out in the open?"

Being out in the open made it that much more exciting, as far as Monica was concerned. But if he needed privacy, she'd go along. As she led him toward the pond, she cast one last glance at the house, glad she wasn't stuck inside. The fresh air felt good. The flowers in the garden smelled fragrant and sweet, rather than overpowering. And she could be herself out here, without everyone watching over her and disapproving.

Once the path ended, Monica walked across the thick grass to the back wall. The garden lights didn't extend this far. It was dark. Private, like he wanted.

She swung around. "What do you—"

Cal didn't let her finish. Cupping her jaw with his free hand, he bent down and kissed her.

As his mouth moved over hers, Monica felt it clear down to her toes. They curled inside her shoes. Her belly fluttered and her knees grew weak. And it wasn't the champagne. Cal Hughes took her breath away.

He let go of her hand in order to cup her breast. Monica's nipple strained against the rasp of his thumbnail. Her panties grew damp and her pussy clenched. Fuck being on her best behavior. She needed this rush of desire, this instant attraction. She felt so alive right now.

Parting his jacket, she ran her hands up his torso. Solid. Muscular, but lean.

Then his hand tugged on her bodice and palmed her bare breast. The cool air picked up a curl, and it tickled her cheek.

Monica tore her mouth away from his. "You don't have to be so gentle."

Cal's grip on her breast tightened, and his lips slipped down the column of her neck, taking little bites while he grazed her nipple with his thumb.

She reached for his dick, rubbing her fingers along the edge of his fly, getting a feel for it. "Yes," he murmured against her neck, "more of that." Then he shoved his hips against her hand. He grew under her touch. Hard and long—Monica couldn't wait to see it. Maybe taste it.

"Mon?" *Allie.* "What the hell are you doing?"

Monica peeked over Cal's shoulder. Standing at the edge of the path, Al stared at them. With a hand at her belly, she shook her head. "Oh, Monica."

"Shit," she whispered, pushing out of Cal's arms. She quickly shoved herself back into her dress.

Cal straightened. He gazed down at her, looking dazed, and ran a hand along his jaw. "Damn."

Monica stepped around him. "I...we just needed some air."

"Get in the house." Allie used a soft tone, one that spoke of disappointment rather than anger. Monica could handle anger, fight against it. But this... *Pack your bags, Campbell. There's an extended guilt trip in your future.* "Stop by the powder room and get yourself together. Your hair's a mess."

"I don't want to go back inside, Al." Cal stood next to her, silent. Waiting. She could still ride away with him, lose herself until tomorrow.

Allie dropped her hand. "Dad won't cut the cake until you're there. Please do this for him."

As upset as she was, Monica didn't want to ruin his perfect day. She took another peek up at Calum Hughes. "Maybe next time, huh?"

"Definitely." Cal bent down and gave her one last, hard kiss.

Then Monica ran toward the house without looking back.

Chapter 2

Five years later...

MONICA CAMPBELL'S CAREFULLY PLANNED SCHEDULE was shot to hell. Not just her schedule—her entire morning. She needed a do-over. If only those worked after the third grade, she'd be golden, because this day was shaping up to be a real pisser.

She'd awakened at six, bleary-eyed and in desperate need of coffee, but her machine had refused to give up the dark roast. Then her sister, Allie, had texted to switch the location of their eight o'clock meeting. Now instead of a ten-minute drive to the office, Monica had to hightail it from Vegas to Henderson. Hastening her routine, she'd sped to the nearest coffee shop and stood in line with all the other caffeine addicts in the throes of withdrawal—thirty-two minutes wasted—before heading straight into rush hour.

Allie had given no explanation for the change in locale, no apology. But since she was the boss, it was her call. And she never let Monica forget it.

One thing Monica resented above all else was having someone dick with her schedule. And today the universe had her in its crosshairs. *Roll with the punches. Go with the flow.* People uttered the trite phrases as if they were an actual philosophy. But if time didn't mean anything, why had clocks been invented? *Yeah. Argue that one, slackers.*

As the coordinator for the cancer foundation named in honor of her mother, Monica kept busy; her job was one big blur of back-to-back meetings. Allie's little hitch threw everything into chaos. So as she sat behind the wheel in bumper-to-bumper traffic, Monica sipped her sugary black coffee, called the office to reschedule three appointments, and left detailed messages for two separate committee chairs.

By the time she pulled through the gates of Allie's sprawling mansion, Monica had regained a small measure of control. She'd still have to scramble to fit in all of her appointments, but if she could keep Allie on point, Monica might finish everything on her to-do list and make it out of the office before midnight.

After parking in the circular drive, Monica walked a brisk clip to the side of the house, her mind spinning in ten different directions. But when she rounded the corner and neared the freestanding garage, her feet stopped moving altogether.

"*Bloody fucking hell.*"

Monica didn't bat an eye at the crude words. It wasn't the masculine British accent that brought her to a standstill, either. No, it had everything to do with that deep, raspy voice. It sounded very familiar, but this man's timbre was lower, much rougher than the one she remembered.

He stood bent beneath the hood of an ancient Mustang. The light gray Bondo filler spread along the car's body was as faded as his jeans—so faded they'd turned white in the well-worn creases and at the seams. The denim wasn't artificially distressed. It was the real deal.

Sounds of metal clanging against metal emanated from the engine where the stranger worked. "Fuck," he muttered.

Monica didn't know much about British accents, but she recognized a posh one when she heard it. And despite the rumbly tenor and foul words, his accent was as high-end as it got.

When he retreated one step and rose to his full height—well over six feet—Monica's heart thumped hard against her ribs. His torso was bare, without an annoying shirt to mar the smooth expanse of deeply burnished skin.

She licked her dry lips and adjusted the collar of her blouse. As she continued to gawk, he shifted his weight from one foot to the other, causing the muscles of his back to contract ever so slightly. Monica swallowed as she took in the line of his broad shoulders. When he raised a hand to brush the hair off his forehead, powerful muscles bunched and rippled in a graceful, fluid motion. Monica blinked slowly, practically hypnotized. Oh crap, he had a tattoo. Starting at the cap of his right shoulder and ending on his bicep, a set of interconnecting Celtic knots and swirls decorated his skin. Wait. She knew that tattoo.

Calum Hughes was back in town.

Fan-fucking-tastic. Monica's disastrous day just took a nosedive.

She inhaled deeply in an effort to slow her racing pulse, and reminded herself she was immune to bad boys now. Well, not immune so much as on the wagon. Four years now. Four very long years. But Monica had learned her lesson. Bad boys were off-limits. She only went for nice men now. Respectable men. Men with real jobs and life goals. Like her ex, Ryan.

That reminder helped dispel the lusty fog that clouded her mind. With firm resolve, Monica pulled herself together, straightened her spine, then averted her gaze, forcing her feet to move.

She resumed walking to the house, but he must have heard the click-clack of her heels this time, because he spun around quickly. Determined not to be diverted again, Monica kept moving. But she couldn't help giving him one last side-eyed glance.

"Good morning," he said.

Now that he'd spotted her, Monica couldn't just ignore him. Adjusting her sunglasses, she stopped and turned to face him fully.

Monica may not have immediately recognized Cal's back, but she'd know that face anywhere. With a stubbled jaw and angular features, he was more arresting than handsome. Shallow grooves formed brackets around his mouth, which tilted noticeably higher on the left side when he smiled. Deep pleated lines framed those spring-green eyes. Time had only made him more attractive.

No, not attractive. That was too benign a word. He had a strong, masculine presence, an attitude of casual self-assurance mixed with sex appeal that would entice any woman with a pulse. Monica definitely had a pulse, and hers was approaching the red zone.

She remained silent for a moment, waiting to see if he would recognize her. And as she waited, her gaze traced downward. While his biceps weren't bodybuilder huge, they were well defined. He had the look of someone who developed them in real life, not by pumping iron in a gym. His solid, carved abs stood out in relief, the tanned skin molding over them, contouring the hollows between each distinct muscle. God save the Queen, it was getting hot out here.

A trickle of sweat slid from the back of her hairline, working its way down her neck and disappearing beneath the collar of her white blouse. *Immune*, the sane part of her brain protested.

"My God, it's you." He strode forward, tight jeans riding low on his hips, pulling at his thighs with each step, and stopped just a foot away. He smelled of motor oil and sunshine. That shouldn't be such an intriguing combination. "Monica Campbell." The way he whispered her name sent a quiver shooting through her belly.

Now he stared at her, his body motionless—then without warning, he reached out and whisked off her sunglasses in a lightning-fast move. His gaze held hers, searching—for what she couldn't say—but his grin kicked up a notch. "I wondered if I'd remembered correctly. If your eyes were really that blue. They are. Your hair's different though, shorter. As I recall, it used to be curly." With his free hand, he reached out and rubbed a strand between his fingers. "Still soft," he rumbled low in his chest.

Monica forgot to inhale for a few seconds. Okay, so he still remembered her. It didn't mean anything, not really, not to a man like him—a man who probably had sex as regularly as he drank beer: each night, after a full day of hammering on a dilapidated engine. Monica was probably just a notch he couldn't add to his undoubtedly high pussy count, and that made her stand out. Still, the fact that he hadn't forgotten *that* kiss flooded her with relief. His tongue stroking hers, his hand hot on her breast, squeezing with the just the right amount of pressure…she'd never forget it. That night in the garden, the smell of roses crossed with Cal's woodsy scent—epic.

Cal's gaze flowed over her again, but slower this time, like an intimate stroke up and down her body. He took in everything, from her plain white blouse to her black jacket and slacks, all the way down to the sensible pumps on her feet. "Who died?" he asked.

"What?"

"You look as if you're in mourning." As he dropped her hair, he dipped his chin, nodding over the length of her. "Are you going to a funeral?"

Funeral? This was a perfectly acceptable pantsuit—black, classic cut. From Nordstrom. The sale rack, but so what? "No one died. I'm a professional. I wear clothes that reflect that." She jerked the sunglasses out of his hand and settled them back on her nose. She felt less exposed with the dark lenses covering half her face.

"A professional what?"

Monica wasn't going defend her life choices to Calum Hughes. She'd kissed him five years ago, and it was never going to happen again. Time to move on. She had a to-do list two miles long. Her schedule was all fucked up. Right. She'd actually forgotten about it for a moment. The sight of Cal had scrambled her brain. "I need to go, or I'm going to be late for my meeting." There. That sounded in command and unaffected. Of course, she clutched her computer bag to her stomach like it was a shield. Monica tried to subtly loosen her grip.

Cal's laugh was gruff, jagged. The sound made her nipples strain against the lace cups of her bra. She ignored them, glad her suit jacket concealed her breasts so thoroughly.

"The Monica I met a few years back wouldn't give a toss about a meeting. You *have* grown up, then."

So had he. Five years ago, he'd still retained a hint of boyishness, a softness in his face, a twinkle in his eyes. But now, his face was leaner, his cheekbones sharper. And his eyes were a bit more wary. "It happens to the best of us," she said. "I take it that's your car?"

"Yeah, just bought it." He glanced over his shoulder. "What do you think? It's not much to look at right now, I'll grant you, but it has potential."

One of the many losers Monica had dated over the years owned a Mustang. Dustin Something. According to him, Mustangs were money pits. For every one problem he'd fix, three more popped up. Since he talked endlessly about it, she recalled more about the car than the guy who drove it—air-cooled engines and drippy cowl vents and lots of rust. "If you say so."

He glanced back at her, eyes zeroing in on her lips. "I'm good at spotting a diamond in the rough."

"Well, I'll leave you to it. Good luck." She forced herself to glance away. The fine sheen of sweat coating his muscle-carved chest was starting to make Monica a little light-headed. She couldn't retreat to the house fast enough. If she didn't go now, she'd be tempted to do something stupid, like trace her fingers across Cal's tattoo, then follow it up with her tongue. "Good to see you again."

She turned on her heel and took one step before Cal's

big, callused hand snagged hers, pulling her closer to his side. She looked down, noticed how large and tanned it was in comparison to hers. His nails were super short and clean, despite the fact that he'd been toying with an engine only moments ago.

"Why don't you skip the meeting, and let's sneak off to the garden. For old times' sake?" His grip tightened just a fraction. Where he touched her, every nerve ending tingled.

Without responding, Monica jerked away and kept walking.

"Was it something I said?" he called after her.

The Good, the Bad, and the Vampire

by Sara Humphreys

—∾∾∾—

Trixie LaRoux is a pink-haired, punk rock, badass vampire with mad bartending skills. Everyone in the coven thinks she's as tough as nails, but only her maker knows the truth; underneath the sultry eye makeup and neon hair is a woman haunted by a past full of troubled relationships.

Dakota Shelton is a vampire with deadly, dangerous skills. But with a penchant for Johnny Cash, he's a good ol' Southern boy at heart. Thrown together by mutual friends in New York City, Trixie has no idea what to do with Dakota's old-fashioned chivalry. But after her tumultuous dating history, Trixie just may be ready for the one man she never expected...

—∾∾∾—

Praise for Sara Humphreys:

"Ms. Humphreys continues to possess the gift of storytelling and gathering the hearts and souls of her audience." —*Night Owl Reviews*

"Sara Humphreys writes an intelligent, inventive, and spirited series where the impossible seems possible." —*The Reading Cafe*

For more Sara Humphreys, visit:

www.sourcebooks.com

Vampires Never Cry Wolf

by Sara Humphreys

———

Vampires are nothing but trouble...

As far as beautiful vampire Sadie Pemberton is concerned, werewolves shouldn't be sticking their noses into New York's supernatural politics. They don't know jack about running a city—not even that hot-as-sin new vampire-werewolf liaison who's just arrived in town.

Werewolves are too sexy for their own good...

The last thing Killian Bane wanted was to end up in New York City playing nice with vampires. Unfortunately, he's on a mission, and when he encounters the sexiest, most stubborn female vamp he's ever met, he's going to have to turn on a little of that wolfish charm...and Sadie's going to learn a thing or two about what it means to have a wild side...

———

Praise for the Dead in the City Series:

"Humphreys is undoubtedly a rising star in the genre... The tension that unfolds between the vampires and the werewolves will have readers on the edge of their seats!" —*RT Book Reviews*

"A fascinating and complex paranormal world with captivating and intriguing characters that draw the reader deeper into the stories." —*Paranormal Haven*

For more Sara Humphreys, visit:

www.sourcebooks.com

Vampire Trouble

by Sara Humphreys

A fledgling vampire ignites a war

Maya Robertson remembers the last moments of her life as a human with haunting clarity, and every man she meets pays the price…until Shane. Finding herself in the middle of a bloody fight between vampires and werewolves, Maya has no choice but to let the devastatingly sexy vampire guard get close to her.

And that's not all that heats up

Shane Quesada, a four-century-old vampire sentry, is known for his cold, unemotional precision, but once Maya begins to invade his dreams, his world is changed forever. His job to protect her is swiftly replaced by the all-consuming need to claim her as his own.

"Humphreys is undoubtedly a rising star in the genre… The sparks that fly between the leading couple are totally irresistible!" —*RT Book Reviews*, a July Top Pick for Paranormal Romance

"A powerful love story that proves that while our past is inescapable, it is the core of our strength." —*Washington Post*

For more Sara Humphreys, visit:

www.sourcebooks.com

Unclaimed

The Amoveo Legend

by Sara Humphreys

—∿—

She brings out the beast in him...
She works hard to be normal...

Tatiana Winters loves the freedom of her life as a veterinarian in Oregon. It's only reluctantly that she agrees to help cure a mysterious illness among the horses on a Montana ranch—the ranch of the Amoveo Prince. Tatiana is no ordinary vet—she's a hybrid from the Timber Wolf Clan, but she wants nothing to do with the world of the Amoveo shifters.

But there's no escaping destiny

Dominic Trejada serves as a Guardian, one of the elite protectors of the Prince's Montana ranch. As a dedicated Amoveo warrior, he is desperate to find his mate, and time is running out. He knows Tatiana is the one—but if he can't convince her, he may not be able to protect her from the evil that's rapidly closing in...

—∿—

Praise for *Undone*:

Spellbinding...This fast-paced, jam-packed thrill ride will delight paranormal romance fans." —*Publishers Weekly*

For more Sara Humphreys, visit:

www.sourcebooks.com

Too Hard to Handle

by Julie Ann Walker

New York Times and *USA Today* Bestseller

—⁓—

"The Man" is back

Dan "The Man" Currington is back in fighting form with a mission that takes him four thousand miles south of BKI headquarters, high in the Andes Mountains of Peru. He's hot on the trail of a rogue CIA agent selling classified government secrets to the highest bidder when Penni DePaul arrives on the scene. Suddenly the stakes are sky-high, and keeping Penni safe becomes Dan's number one priority.

And this time she's ready

A lot has changed since former Secret Service Agent Penni DePaul last saw Dan. Now a civilian, she's excited about what the future might hold. But before she can grab on to that future with both hands, she has to tie up some loose ends—namely, Dan Currington, the man she just can't forget. And a secret that's going to change both their lives—if they can stay alive, that is.

—⁓—

Praise for the Black Knights Inc. Series:

"Each one is full of hot alpha men, strong witty females, blazing passionate sex, and tons of humor. Black Knights Inc. is hands down my favorite romantic suspense series." —*Guilty Pleasures Book Reviews*

For more Julie Ann Walker, visit:

www.sourcebooks.com